Michael Jecks gave up a career in the computer industry to concentrate on writing and the study of medieval history, especially that of Devon and Cornwall. He is a regular participant at literary festivals, the founder of Medieval Murderers, and a popular guest speaker – both alone and with the historian Ian Mortimer. He was Chairman of the Crime Writers' Association in 2004/2005. He lives with his wife, children and dogs in northern Dartmoor, which he walks as often as possible.

Michael can be contacted throu
www.michaeljecks.co.uk

Acclaim for Michael Jecks' my

'Captivating . . . If you care for a well-researched visit to medieval England, don't pass this series' *Historical Novels Review*

'Michael Jecks has a way of dipping into the past and giving it the immediacy of a present-day newspaper article . . . He writes . . . with such convincing charm that you expect to walk round a corner in Tavistock and meet some of the characters' *Oxford Times*

'A tortuous and exciting plot . . . The construction of the story and the sense of period are excellent' *Shots*

'Stirring intrigue and a compelling cast of characters will continue to draw accolades' *Publishers Weekly*

'Jecks' knowledge of medieval history is impressive and is used here to great effect' *Crime Time*

'This fascinating portrayal of medieval life and the corruption of the Church will not disappoint. With convincing characters whose treacherous acts perfectly combine with a devilishly masterful plot, Jecks transports readers back to this wicked world with ease' *Good Book Guide*

By Michael Jecks and available from Headline

The Last Templar
The Merchant's Partner
A Moorland Hanging
The Crediton Killings
The Abbot's Gibbet
The Leper's Return
Squire Throwleigh's Heir
Belladonna at Belstone
The Traitor of St Giles
The Boy-Bishop's Glovemaker
The Tournament of Blood
The Sticklepath Strangler
The Devil's Acolyte
The Mad Monk of Gidleigh
The Templar's Penance
The Outlaws of Ennor
The Tolls of Death
The Chapel of Bones
The Butcher of St Peter's
A Friar's Bloodfeud
The Death Ship of Dartmouth
The Malice of Unnatural Death
Dispensation of Death
The Templar, the Queen and Her Lover
The Prophecy of Death
The King of Thieves
No Law in the Land
The Bishop Must Die

MICHAEL JECKS

No Law in the Land

headline

First published in 2009
by HEADLINE PUBLISHING GROUP

First published in paperback in 2009
by HEADLINE PUBLISHING GROUP

1

Cataloguing in Publication Data is available from the British Library

ISBN 978 0 7553 4419 2 (B Format)
ISBN 978 0 7553 5790 1 (A Format)

Typeset in Times by Avon DataSet Ltd,
Bidford-on-Avon, Warwickshire

Printed and bound in Great Britain by Clays Ltd, St Ives plc

Headline's policy is to use papers that are natural, renewable and recyclable
products and made from wood grown in sustainable forests. The logging
and manufacturing processes are expected to conform to the environmental
regulations of the country of origin.

HEADLINE PUBLISHING GROUP
An Hachette UK Company
338 Euston Road
London NW1 3BH

www.headline.co.uk
www.hachette.co.uk

Glossary

amercement
the fines imposed for many offences, some of which were not the fault of the persons fined – see *deodand* and *murdrum* below.

bastide
a fortified town in France.

deodand
the sum demanded for the king, based on the value of any weapon used in a slaying. The system of claiming deodand, fixed by the coroner, was not ended until the 1800s in England, as a result of lobbying by railway companies, after some very expensive accidents in which the trains themselves were claimed as deodand.

Guyenne
those lands owned by the English on the French mainland, mainly centred around Bordeaux.

hobby
a low-grade horse, a little higher than a nag, but below a rounsey, and generally good for short distances or for use as a packhorse.

leyrwite
the fine for promiscuity among men and women – commonly for adultery in men and bearing a child outside wedlock for women.

maslin

peasant bread made from mixed wheat and rye grains.

murdrum

the fine for not being able to prove 'Englishry'. This was based on the days of conquest when, in order to quash resistance to Norman rule and halt the terrorists (or freedom fighters, depending upon your point of view) from murdering Normans, when a body was found it was assumed to be a Norman unless the local vill could prove with witnesses that the corpse was that of a local Englishman. The 'presentment of Englishry' was a requirement until 1340, when it was effectively abolished. So if a stranger was found dead, it would be likely to be a heavy financial burden on the local community.

palfrey

a good-quality riding horse – sometimes worth £4 or more.

peine fort et dure

the punishment for arrested men who refused to plead in court, this was a hideous and lengthy process whereby the victim was staked out on the ground so that he could not move, and weights were gradually added to his breast to make breathing harder and harder. Eventually it did lead to death, although the official line was that when a prisoner died from it, it was 'natural causes'.

rounsey   lower-quality horse, generally robust, but cheaper.

trail bastons   early in the 1300s, these gangs of 'club men' wandered the country, robbing all they could from the unwary. The problem grew so acute that there were special courts set up to enquire about them.

triacleur   a 'quack' doctor, known to wander the country selling potions often formed solely of treacle or some similar sweet mixture.

Cast of Characters

Baldwin de Furnshill — the Keeper of the King's Peace and an astute investigator of crimes, motivated by a hatred of any form of injustice.

Jeanne de Furnshill — wife to Sir Baldwin; widow of Sir Ralph de Liddinstone, a coarse and harsh husband who abused her.

Richalda — Baldwin and Jeanne's daughter, now three years old.

Baldwin — Baldwin and Jeanne's son, born Martinmas last year.

Simon Puttock — Baldwin's friend and once a servant to the Abbot of Tavistock; now Simon waits to hear whether he will have a post since the death of Abbot Champeaux.

Margaret (Meg) — Simon's wife, who is distraught at losing their home in Lydford due to the machinations of Sir Hugh le Despenser.

Edith — Simon and Margaret's daughter, seventeen years old, who is now married to Peter and living in Exeter.

Peter — Edith's husband.

Jane — maidservant to Edith and Peter.

Charles	Peter's father.
Jan	Peter's mother.
Edgar	Baldwin's loyal servant, once his sergeant in the Knights Templar.
Perkin	also Peterkin, Simon and Margaret's three-year-old son.
Sir Peregrine de Barnstaple	Known to hate Despenser, Sir Peregrine has become a coroner.
Sir Richard de Welles	loud and crude, he is the coroner for Lifton.
Bishop Walter	Walter Stapledon of Exeter, once the king's trusted lord high treasurer and negotiator.
Raymond, Cardinal de Fargis	the negotiator sent by the pope to adjudicate between the two contenders for the abbacy at Tavistock.
John de Courtenay	a keen monk who wants the abbacy at Tavistock.
Robert Busse	the abbot-elect, who was given the post at the election, but was not confirmed, subject to the investigation of allegations made against him by John de Courtenay.
Brother Pietro de Torrino	a monk in the cardinal's entourage.
Brother Anselm	cheerful and content, this monk lives at Tavistock.
Brother Mark	a quiet, thoughtful monk from Tavistock.
Sir Hugh le Despenser	the king's closest friend and confidant, now the richest and most powerful man in the land after the king himself.

Sir James de Cockington	the new sheriff of Exeter.
Hoppon	peasant living south of Jacobstowe.
Roger	wandering mercenary and sailor on his way to sea to escape the violence and mayhem in France.
William atte Wattere	henchman of Despenser, a violent and dangerous felon who'll do anything to support his master.
William Walle	nephew to Stapledon.
John de Padington	steward to Stapledon.
Bill Lark	bailiff of Jacobstowe.
Agnes	wife to Bill.
Sir Robert de Traci	once a knight in the king's household, now Sir Robert has fallen out of favour and has become an outlaw operating from his castle outside Bow, at Nymet Traci.
Osbert	henchman to Sir Robert, his most trusted man-at-arms.
Basil	son of Sir Robert de Traci, and heir to the castle of Nymet Traci.
Stephen of Shoreditch	a messenger for Despenser and the king.
Master Harold	Peter's master while he was an apprentice.
John Pasmere	peasant of Bow.
Art Miller	peasant from Jacobstowe guarding murder scene.
John Weaver	peasant from Jacobstowe guarding murder scene.
Jack Begbeer	farmer from near Bow.

Author's Note

This has been one of the more difficult books in the series to write. All too often an idea will come from a chance conversation, from a short passage in a reference book, or just from my imagination, and then my task is simply to elaborate on it and try to give it that feeling of logic and inevitability that is so important in works of crime fiction like mine.

However, I am getting close to that terrible period in English history when the realm was falling apart – riven by the internal disputes caused by the king and Despenser. And although I have invented much of this story, the basis of the fear that runs through the tale was genuine. The people were living through appalling times, and their suffering was not eased by the rich and powerful men whose task it was, in theory, to protect the peasants and the clergy.

Edward II had been a less than fortunate king for most of his reign. His initial attempts at pacifying the Scots led to utter disaster at Bannockburn; his reliance on one adviser, Piers Gaveston, had deeply unfortunate consequences (mainly, it should be said, for Gaveston himself) and meant that within a few years the king's authority and power was significantly curtailed. However, by the period of this tale, he had recovered much of the lost ground. He had gathered an army and defeated all the malcontents, and then embarked on an orgy of destruction. All those who had raised their flags against him were declared traitors –

he was keen on accusing people of that crime – and executed. The rank of the person involved did not matter. They were hanged, drawn and quartered, their remains put on display wherever men and women needed reminding of their sovereign's authority.

All of this caused massive ructions in the country. There were many men who had been in the wars against the king who now found themselves declared outlaw, and who thus had lost their lands, their homes, their titles – even their families. Many left the kingdom and instead went to France, where quite a lot sought out the greatest contrariant of them all, Sir Roger Mortimer – the king's Greatest Traitor. Their position grew more tolerable as the queen arrived with the young Duke of Aquitaine, the king's son. Soon they would mount an invasion to overthrow the king.

Not all Edward's enemies actually left the country. Many remained, and did indeed take on the guise of outlaws, living in the forests and on the moors. They were the reason for the sudden increase in crime in 1324–6, because they had nothing to lose. The population became increasingly alarmed by the actions of these 'rebels'.

However, not all those responsible for the very worst crimes were necessarily the men who had stood against the king. All too often, the men who appear to have been guilty of these crimes also appear to have been friends of the king or Despenser.

Nicholas de la Beche, for example, was one of the longest-standing members of the king's household in 1323 when he was arrested. He, and his brothers and father, rebelled in 1321, some nine years after he joined the household, and took over a manor owned by Aubyn de Clinton. They plundered it, and poor Aubyn was so terrified he didn't dare take the matter to the local courts. He petitioned the king to help him – and was unhelpfully advised to get a common-law writ against his tormentor.*

Others behaved in a similarly appalling manner. Roger Sapy's deputy, who was responsible for many of the contrariant castles in Wales, was attacked in July 1325. His limbs were all broken and his eyes gouged out. A half-year later it was the turn of the royal exchequer, Belers, to be murdered.

The problem would seem to have been that, for the first time in generations, the king had lost control. His household knights could not be trusted. When Sir Gilbert Middleton ravaged the north in 1317, he and his allies declared that they could not be tried in courts because they were members of the king's household – as though that meant they were above the law. They were not, as they were soon to discover.

But crime was very often organised. And all too often it was organised most efficiently by those who possessed the weapons and the training to carry it out.

To return to poor Belers, it would seem that he made enemies of the Folville family. Eustace Folville was a particularly nasty piece of work, and although he was not captured and killed for the Belers murder, largely due to the invasion of Queen Isabella and the subsequent change of rule for the kingdom, he was later to be arrested. From 1327 to 1329 or so, Eustace is supposed to have been responsible for four more murders, several robberies and a rape. It is likely that the total of his crime exceeds the total for which he was captured. However, he was pardoned (it was a good life, being a knight), and he carried on merrily with his thieving,

*See 'The Unreliability of Royal Household Knights in the Early Fourteenth Century' by Michael Prestwich, *Fourteenth Century England II*, The Boydell Press, 2002.

blackmails and murders. He even took a royal judge, while he was conducting his official duties, robbed him, and then ransomed him for a huge sum of money.

The Folvilles weren't unique. Dear heaven, if only they were. There were plenty of other families who formed their own little gangland cliques. The Cotterels were another repellent bunch. And often it was the fact that they felt immune to the normal process of the law because they were associated with the king, or with Despenser, that led to their boldness.

So when I invented the repugnant Sir Robert de Traci and his son, it was not from a malicious desire to confuse; it was because in hoping to give a realistic atmosphere for the period, I wanted to invent a family group that was believable as felons who were capable of such crimes.

I only hope that you will agree that they are all too believable.

Not that all readers have agreed. Sometimes people have written to me complaining that my books are too unrealistic, that people weren't really that nasty to each other. Some have accused me of a lack of research.

Well, in response, I can only state that I am writing about an age in which a baron of Devon plotted to kill a clergyman; in which company politics were to lead to the murder of the precentor of the cathedral at Exeter by thugs (including the vicars of Ottery St Mary and Heavitree) who had been hired by the cathedral's dean; and in which families of household knights like the Folvilles could run riot over the whole country as they wished, robbing and killing with apparent impunity.

As I have occasionally had to point out to editors: the trouble with medieval England is that I have to keep toning down true stories to make them believable.

* * *

The title for this book is fitting. It is a quote from the last lines of a court case from the period.

John Saint Mark was a fairly lowly man, but he was mercilessly harried by Sir Robert de Vere, a son of the Earl of Oxford. From the look of the matter, John was a loyal supporter of the king, while Sir Robert was a fugitive after Boroughbridge. However, John and his family lived as gypsies because Sir Robert had sworn to kill him. And although the justices were all instructed to bring the knight to book, they would do nothing when faced with his menaces against them. As Natalie Fryde said in *The Tyranny and Fall of Edward* II*, 'His plaint tails off "because there is no law in the land".'

You can read in those few words a little of the desperation a man must have felt when, threatened with death by the king's enemy, he could find no justice, no protection and no aid, even from the king's own courts. How fraught must the poor man have felt?

For those who are interested in the old roads and lanes, I should just mention one detail. The Roman road that I make use of in the later sections of the story is genuine. The line of the road may still be seen, as can the fort that protected it. For these, a proud father has to thank his daughter – and the schoolmistress who decided to give the children in her class a project about Rome!

Michael Jecks
North Dartmoor
October 2008

---

*CUP, 1979.

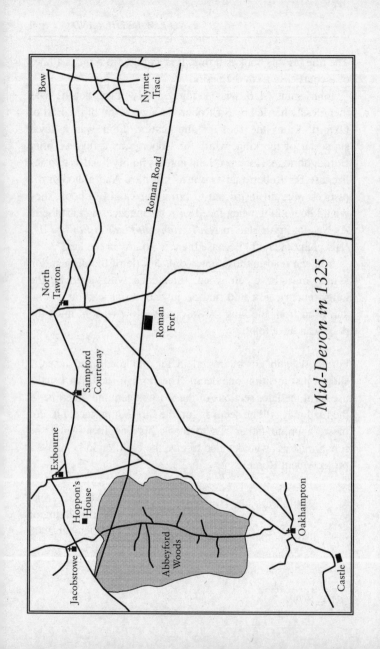

Mid-Devon in 1325

Prologue

Second Saturday following the Feast of the Archangel Michael, nineteenth year of the reign of King Edward II*

Nymet Traci, Devon, England

Sir Robert de Traci woke that morning knowing that the men would soon die, and all of them solely in order that he should reap a good reward. It left him with a sense of contented restlessness. He was keen to be up and about, but the warmth of his bed was a delicious distraction even without the benefit of a woman beside him. His wife was long dead, and it was a while since he'd enjoyed a willing wench.

It was a glorious morning. He rose and padded over to the window, staring out. The shutter was wide, and he could see from here all the way south over the tops of the trees in the little coppice a mile or so distant, to the dull greyish-blue hills that were Dartmoor. Often at this time of day he would find it impossible to see more than a foul mistiness, but today was most unseasonally clear and bright. Still, from the tang in the air, he had a suspicion that the weather would alter before long.

He dressed quickly and made his way down the steep stairs to his underchamber. There, to his mild surprise, he found his son was still snoring, alone. Sir Robert left him to it. The sot

---

*12 October 1325

had been singing and whoring the night away again with some slattern he'd acquired from his last riding, and it had been late when he returned to his own bed at last. Sir Robert had been much the same when he was a youth, and he didn't begrudge his son such pleasures. They were natural to a man.

Walking into his hall, he looked about him quickly, making sure all was normal. There was no sign of rebellion in his men, he noted. A man could not take his fellows for granted, unless he wanted to wake up one morning with a knife in his throat.

There was one whom he trusted above all of them: Osbert, the man who had served with him the longest, and with whom he had lived in virtual exile, an outcast on his own lands. Os was reliable, trustworthy and honourable. But he was off with the men who would be Sir Robert's victims – it was he who was to lead them to the trap – and their deaths.

There had been a time, only a short while ago, when Sir Robert had thought his fortune had sunk into the sea. He had once been a member of the king's household, known for his honour and largesse, proud and determined, a knight of perfect chivalry. But then he had made one error, allowing his friendship with Bartholomew Badlesmere to colour his judgement. Bartholomew had become known to be a traitor, and instantly all his friends were suspect. And one of them was Sir Robert.

Those days had been bleak. Instead of the comfort he now enjoyed, he had been cast out. He had seen this little castle of his taken over by his enemies; he had been forced to accept the shame of losing the reputation he had once considered his by birth. Shunned by all those who had once been his friends, Sir Robert had been forced to turn outlaw, robbing and stealing all he might, occasionally killing too.

And then, earlier this year, the surprise proposal.

He had never been a great ally of Despenser, but after this

year, he might reconsider his position. For it was Despenser's offer that had brought him back into the king's favour. Once he had been beneath Edward's contempt, but now he was returned to the circle of friends and allies, his lands and castle restored to him, and all was just as it had been. Although this time he was taking fewer risks. The king radiated sunshine to those upon whom he smiled – but it was only ever a short passage to the black thunderstorm that was the opposite side of his nature. Edward accepted him for now, but there was no telling for how long that would last. Soon, very soon, he might decide that the knight in that far-away county of Devon was no more to be tolerated. Some snippet of a rumour, some poison whispered in his ear, that was all it would take, and suddenly Sir Robert would wake to learn that he was again without lands or home.

Well, next time it happened, he would be vastly better prepared. Next time he would have money on his side, and he would collect all he might while he could.

Today, if he was fortunate, he might increase his wealth. Os was with the travellers who were passing near here. They were rumoured to have silver with them, silver that they were carrying to Exeter. Well, with luck, soon they would be dead and Sir Robert would be that much the wealthier.

The land was dangerous. A man had to fight to keep what was his – and take what he wanted from others. There was no other rule in the country. The King's Peace was a nonsense now. All that existed was the power of the strongest. And Sir Robert intended to prove that his steel was as sharp as any other man's.

He did not know that it would lead to his death.

Second Sunday following the feast of the Archangel Michael*

Oakhampton

Old John Pasmere had already seen his son in the town when he set off homewards.

The sight of the little market town was not impressive to him. He'd seen Oakhampton before, and he'd even been to Crediton a few times in his life. Once, he'd gone as far as Exeter, although it hadn't appealed to him. The place was too loud, too crowded and mean. The people were suspicious and made no attempt to hide the fact, and he felt all the while that he was likely to be hit over the head and robbed at any moment. No, he didn't like the place. It felt too dangerous.

Oakhampton was no better than Exeter, except it was that bit smaller, but it made a pleasant difference to go there once in a while, mainly for the market, but also for the church. He liked the priest there, who gave stirring stories about the men in the Gospels, and enduring examples of the devil and hell itself. There weren't that many as could do that, John reckoned. No, in his local chapel up at Jacobstowe, the fool kept prating on about the goodness of man and how Jesus wanted all to see the good in each other. Well, if Jesus was willing to see the best of all men, that was fine, but John Pasmere was happier keeping his own counsel and his dagger near to hand. There was much to be said for the man who was good and kindly all his life, but in John's experience, such men died young and painfully. For himself, he'd keep an eye on the dangers of life and a hand on his knife.

But a priest who could stir the blood with stories of death and glory, that was different. And in Oakhampton the lad

---

**13 October 1325

could even make John feel almost young again. There were lots of examples from the Gospels of fighting against oppressors, whether they be Egyptian, Roman or any other race, and John took from that the truth: that God was on the side of those who were downtrodden through the ages. If a man was put to great hardship by those who ruled him, then he was entitled to take back what had been stolen.

That was fine for most. But when a man lived in England today, there was little chance of justice. Be he knight, freeman or serf, he was allowed to live only at the whim of the king and his friends. If a man took against another, who had the ear of an associate of the king, he could find himself gaoled, or worse. A peasant would often be discovered dead in his home, or lying in a ditch, while the more wealthy would end up hanging in pieces on hooks at a city's gates.

John Pasmere was not willing to trust to the justice of the men who ruled this country. He had known too many of them.

Trust was a very overrated trait. Most of those who put their faith in it would die painfully. A man who trusted his lord; a woman who trusted the lord's son; any man who trusted my lord Hugh le Despenser; and most of all, any traveller who trusted guides and guards.

Those putting their confidence in such people were fools and deserved their fate.

Abbeyford Woods, near Jacobstowe

Sweet Jesus, the monk told himself, have mercy on us poor sinners!

The weight of the cart was immense. He had thought the God-poxed things were easier to push, but the wheel-hubs kept getting caught in the brambles and bushes. There were so many little saplings, too, all pushing up through the murk, some of them so thin he could hardly see them at this time of night, others thicker and substantial, so massive that several times he squeaked to himself, fearing that they were men sent to catch them and bring them back.

It had been so terrifying, when he had woken and learned that the man had done it already. So many weeks of planning, and yet now that the one-eyed man stood before him with his dagger dripping gore, Brother Anselm was struck with terror. He could only moan gently, as his entire world fell away.

This wasn't his place. He was a happy man, cheerful. All knew him to be the contented, amiable one of the abbey. It was the others who were greedy, fractious and truculent. Never Anselm. It was his part usually to calm the others. He'd been doing it for so many years that finding a new role was peculiar.

Surely it was that which had tempted him. He had been lured by the anger constantly rising in his breast as the rest of the community sparred and bickered. 'Oh, it'll be fine. Anselm can soothe them all later,' was the attitude. And until now, that was what he had done.

When poor Abbot Champeaux died, though, yes, that was when all changed. First he had begun to realise how divided the monastery was growing, with factions forming about John de Courtenay and Robert Busse, the two brothers who were seeking election to the abbacy; it was enough to blunt the loyalty he had once felt to the institution where he had lived for so long.

It was not only the abbey, though: it was the entire realm. No matter where a man was to go, there was no confidence. After the queen's departure to France to negotiate a truce, the belligerent attitude of the country towards the king had become ever more evident. People were terrified. They knew that she had been treated like a felon by her own husband, with her lands stolen and her household broken up. If the royal family itself harboured a festering dispute that could drive a wedge between king and queen, no one was safe.

No more were they. All over the realm men were living as outlaws, where once they had been loyal servants of the king. The dispossessed now formed a great mass in the land, and there was no possibility of their being reconciled to the law. The law itself was false, unequal to the struggle of controlling so many disputatious people.

'Oh, shit!' he muttered as the left hub caught a new tree trunk and the cart slewed round.

'Shhh!' hissed his companion.

There was no arguing with him. Anselm had not met him before, this old man. He looked frail and rather pathetic, but in fact he was as strong as many youths. His body might be ancient and twisted, but his muscles had the resilience of old hemp.

Besides, the old man's companion had already petrified Anselm. In the past, his worst nightmares had involved the ghosts said to occupy the moors and the abbey. Now they included the third man in their party.

This man, Osbert, was fearsome-looking, with a huge scar that ran from his temple across his face. It had put out his eye, but that only served to make the remaining orb look still more brutal and lunatic. When he stared at Anselm, the monk felt his guts turn to water.

'Shhh!'

Anselm froze as his companion held up a hand. There was no sound for a while. Nothing but the slow soughing of the wind through the trees, the creak of the cart, and the thundering roar of Anselm's heart. And then the little snuffling sound at his breast.

'Come on, then! What, you going to wait there till Christmastide? Get a move on, monk, move your arse!'

Anselm would have given him a short instruction on the merits of politeness towards a brother in Holy Orders, but he didn't like this man, and nor did he feel sure that any comments wouldn't be rewarded by more than a curt word. He held his tongue as he and the other two pushed, heaved, sweated and swore.

'You push like a woman, monk,' the man snarled as Anselm slipped in the mud.

'Damn you . . .'

'Aye, and damn your soul, little monk. Sold it for twenty pounds of silver, eh? The devil drives a hard bargain, you'll find. You won't be getting your soul back intact.'

'I am still a man of God. That confers privilege!'

'Not here it doesn't. And if you think . . .' Osbert crossed to the other side of the cart and came upon Anselm suddenly, grabbing his robes and bunching them in his fist, pulling the monk to him so that their faces were only a matter of an inch or so apart. He held him there, his one eye staring into Anselm's fixedly, while Anselm had the unappealing view of the empty socket. The man was so close, Anselm could smell the garlic on his breath, the staleness of old sweat in his clothes, the fetid odour of his unwashed body, and he curled his lip, wanting to be away from there.

The man's voice was low, sibilant and menacing as the devil's own trident. 'If you think you can keep your robes on and use them to get away, and maybe later denounce us while you try to save your neck, *monk*, you'll soon learn that my dagger has a long blade. Doesn't matter where you try to go, I'll find you, and I'll put you to so much pain, you'll wonder what's happened to you. You'll even forget who you are. You understand, you little prickle?'

Anselm nodded, but even as he did, he felt, rather than heard, the scrabble of paws at his breast.

'What the . . .?'

He was shoved away, and the man stared uncomprehendingly as Anselm opened his robe. Inside nestled the
puppy. 'I couldn't leave . . .'

The man swore, quietly but with utter venom. 'What of the
bitch?'

'I didn't bring her, I thought that—'

'You thought? Did you think that she'll soon wake and
begin to wonder where her little puppy has gone?'

'I took the pup from her last night. She slept without him!'

'Did you not think that she'll whine and howl and wake the
camp? Did you not think she'll come after us as soon as they
release her from her leash? Did you not think they would
follow her to us? Did you not think *at all*? Sweet Jesus, save
me from mother-swyving churls like this one. I'll have to take
her back.'

'You can't go and—'

'Monk, shut up! You will have to push the cart back while I
do this. You won't be able to. So put your back into it, and get
the cart back safely. You hear me?'

Osbert stepped quietly and very cautiously as he returned to
the camp. The body of the pup lay still in his hand now. He
had snapped its neck like a coney's. It would be a short while
before he reached the camp, he thought. The smell of burning
wood was in his nostrils already from the fire the evening
before. Now it had been banked, there was but a dull glow
from the mass of the embers. Nothing to give him even the
slightest of shadows.

All about there were the peaceful sounds of sleeping
people. A child up with the travellers had a sniffling whimper
– he recalled that the brat had a cold – and his mother gave a
murmured remonstration before rolling over again. The

remaining archers were snoring, while Anselm's companion was whiffing out little breaths as though he was panting in a dream. He lay in the midst of the archers, the seven about him guarding him better than they had their precious cargo.

There was no guard. Not now. Only one sentry had been set, a man who was content to wander about the camp with jealousy, eyeing the sleepers, but not one of them. When Osbert had offered to join him and keep him company until his watch was changed, he had been pathetically grateful. Then Osbert had grabbed him from behind and his dagger had made short work of him, plunging into the man's liver five times, while Osbert's hand stayed clamped over his mouth, stifling the desperate screams for help. No one heard anything, not out here at the edge of the camp where the man had gone to relieve himself. Osbert had left the body out there so that it couldn't be immediately discovered, were someone else to wake.

No one had. As he stood here, near the archers and their master, it was clear that there had been no alarm. All was as he had left it.

The dog was awake, though. She lay with her head resting on her paws, just as she had every night. It was no bad thing that Anselm had chosen to keep the pup in his robe when they had left Tavistock, Osbert reckoned. It made the bitch less distressed to sleep without him. She had grown accustomed to having her pup back during the day, but sleeping alone.

Osbert silently made his way to the bitch. He heard her stir, and then give a low growl. It was as he had expected. Quickly he threw the puppy's body to her, and he saw her move in a flash, turning to sniff at the little corpse. As she did, he stepped forward and slipped his dagger into her back, grabbing her muzzle as he did so. The surprised yelping lasted only a moment or two, and then there was nothing to worry about.

In some haste now, he retraced his steps to the bushes, and

was soon in among them, moving fast for a man of his age and size. But for all that he was over two and forty years old, he had lived here in this area for most of his childhood, and he knew the land well. The cart, he knew, had gone off northwards from here, and he would meet it later. Rather than head north, he would take the steeper, slightly more swift route east, down the valley's side to the river, and up the other side. The cart would rejoin the trail a full half-mile further on.

He made his way down the slope, slithering on the soggy grasses, almost tripping twice in thick tussocks, and then splashed his way through the river, which was quite full after the rains. On the other side, he was about to make his way up the slope when he heard the hoofs.

There were twelve of them. The man in front he knew, and the son at his side. He knew that they were noted for their ruthlessness. Across this land, these two were feared by all the peasants and farmers. No man passing near their castle could hope to be permitted to continue without paying tolls for the use of the roads. A man who refused soon found himself watching his blood pool on the ground as he died.

Aye, he knew these men. How could he not? He was their servant.

'Is that you, Osbert?' the leader called.

'Aye, Sir Robert, it's me. They're in the camp as we planned. Encircle them, and you have them all.'

Chapter One

Third Monday following the Feast of the Archangel Michael*

Farmstead near Jacobstowe, Devon

On the day the murders were discovered, old Hoppon grunted as he rose to his feet and kicked the charred sticks together, then hauled the log nearer, before bending down to blow steadily. Tab, his dog, stirred and stretched, wagging his tail hopefully as Hoppon limped to the door and peered out.

'Another shite day, feller,' he muttered, reaching down. Tab had arrived by his side already, as always, and his fingers found the slim ears, scratching at the rough, wiry coat at the base of the dog's skull. 'You think Noah's coming back? It's wet enough, I'd swear. Christ's ballocks, what I'd give for a day of sun for once.'

It had been like this for so long now, he could scarce recall a time when it hadn't been damp underfoot. Hoppon could remember the worst years when the rain fell all through the summer, the dreadful years when all starved more or less. The famine had struck ten years before, and lasted on and off for the next seven years, although it was the first two that had been the worst without doubt. Especially for him with his badly burned and damaged leg.

---

*14 October 1325

Tab wandered out and cocked a leg at the edge of the little clearing, and it was then that Hoppon saw the smoke rising through the trees.

'The poor bastards. Foreigners aren't safe,' he said, peering through the thin drizzle with a scowl.

Hoppon thought no more about it. He had enough work to be getting on with without worrying about others who had incurred the wrath of the local magnates. In any case, he had the unpleasant conviction that the smoke was not from a camp fire. Last night, late, he had heard horses. Only one kind of man travelled in darkness, and it was not the kind of man he wanted to offend.

No. He had much to do, and so he wandered outside to his chickens and began to sprinkle a few grains for them, but even as they squabbled and bickered, his eyes kept being drawn up to the column of smoke, wondering what was happening over there.

Abbeyford Woods, south of Jacobstowe

Roger, a thin-faced man in his middle twenties, was early to rise that morning. It was his way to be on the road as dawn lighted the way for him. He was happier to be busy, and in his life that meant walking. It was lonely, now, without her. Better to keep walking than think about her. It wasn't like she was his wife or anything.

There were many trees here, and that was itself a relief. As he went, he gathered up some tinder for his fire that evening. It was the usual start to any day, collecting thistledown in hand-fuls, then birchbark, thin, papery strips that curled into little cylinders. All were carefully wrapped in the remains of an old shirt, and then thrust inside his clothing, next to his belly, so that they should be dry by tonight for his fire.

When he saw the smoke, at first he was happy that he was

near people with food. After sleeping in the open, with only his ragged old cloak to cover him, the thought of sitting at a friendly fire with a bowl of hot minted water or posset was enormously attractive – especially if it meant he could hear some news or just share some conversation. He had been walking alone for a long time now. And a party of travellers would hardly look upon a single wandering sailor as a threat to them, so surely they would be hospitable.

His road here was a narrow, grassed pathway. He had walked all the way from Dartmouth, hoping to get to the north coast, where he had heard that there were jobs for skilled seamen, but the weather had slowed him. Every day seemed to bring more and more rain, and the rivers had all swollen while the roads had grown more and more clogged with mud. For Roger, it meant that his pace had been reduced to a quarter of his normal progress. What had looked like a four- or five-day march, with luck, had already taken him a week, and he was only halfway. It was no surprise that the thought of a little company and a warming fire was so attractive.

The road here led along the top of a ridge. He had come here from Oakhampton, hoping that the river would have subsided a little. He'd been waiting for two days now, and at last he had been able to cross. That was late in the day last evening, and after that he had made his way up the heavily wooded side of the hill, and built himself a shelter of sorts with fallen boughs set against a tree. It wasn't warm, nor dry, nor comfortable, but at least he could feel that there was a roof over his head, and once he had a small fire burning, he had been as content as he could be.

He passed a second roadway to the east, which fell down the side of the hill towards the river, and then he was following a pleasant, straight route with trees on either side that did not fully obstruct his view. The direction seemed to him to lie directly north, and he was happy to be able to speed his pace at last, lengthening his stride to suit the firm ground.

The smoke he had seen seemed to lie some few hundred yards ahead when he first set off, but as he marched on, he realised that it must be a half-mile distant. He passed a crossroads, then his road began to descend, although only shallowly, and the smoke remained some distance off on his right. It was as he saw the clouds break slightly, and felt the faint warming of the sun on his shoulder, that he began to smell the woodsmoke on the air.

By some miracle the rain had held off so far, but now the thin mizzle that had been blowing at him had grown into a genuine downpour, and he had to pull his hood more firmly over his head, settling his cloak about him and shifting his staff and belongings so that he could hold his hand nearer his shoulder, hunching himself against the cooler weather and trying to prevent as much of the rain as possible from running down his neck. It gave him the incentive to hurry and reach some form of shelter. Before long he saw the marks of carts in deep ruts in the mud at the side of the road, and the telltale smoke on his right, and set off to follow them, walking near the mud but not in it, and going carefully to avoid the thicker clumps of bramble that threatened to rip his hosen.

The great oaks and beech trees near the road suddenly disappeared, and instead he found himself in a little coppice. A large circular depression blackened with fire showed where a charcoal burner had been working, and all about were the little carts and belongings of about twenty travellers.

He knew there were about twenty. Their bodies littered the ground.

Wissant, French coast

After the last few days of running, Simon was for once glad to be able to set his feet on the deck of a ship, secure in the knowledge that no matter what the sea might hold for him, at least there was no risk of a sword in his back or an arrow in his chest. Compared with the land, the sea seemed, for once, to be safe.

He glanced back the way they had come, anxiously scanning the buildings at the quay for danger. In the morning's grim light, there was little to be seen, only a gentle mist washing in from the sea and giving the grey waves a deceptively calm appearance. Simon wasn't fooled by that. He knew the true dangers that lurked in the waters far from land. He had been tossed by storms, and even survived a wrecked ship in his time. It was not an experience he was keen to repeat.

'You ready to sail, eh? Ha! I could murder one of these sailors and eat his carcass, I'm so hungry!'

The thickset, bearded figure who clapped a hand as heavy as a destrier's hoof on Simon's shoulder was Sir Richard de Welles, an enormous man with appetites to match his girth. His eyes crinkled in a smile.

He was tall, at least six foot one, and had an almost entirely round face, with a thick bush of beard that overhung his chest like a heavy gorget. His eyes were dark brown and shrewd, beneath a broad and tall brow. His face was criss-crossed with wrinkles, making him appear perhaps a little older than he really was, but Simon was sure he had to be at least fifty. His flesh had the toughened look of well-cured leather that only a man who has spent much of his life in the open air would acquire.

'I am happy to be near shore,' Simon said shortly.

'Aye, but we'll both be glad to away from the French, I dare say!' the knight chuckled.

There was no denying it. In the last days they had ridden in great haste from Paris. In a short period they had managed to enrage the French king, irritate his sister, Queen Isabella of England, and ensure that they would be unwelcome forever in France. Meanwhile, the failure of their mission would reflect badly on them all when they finally had to explain their actions to the English king. And Edward II was not a man known for leniency towards those who he felt had been incompetent.

'I'll be glad to away, yes,' Simon said. 'And more glad to see my wife. I don't know what's happened to her.'

'Aye, friend, I was forgetting that you had urgent business. Still, no matter! You should be home again soon, eh?'

Simon nodded. 'I hope so. I hope so.'

Jacobstowe

Bill Lark, a short man with the dark, serious expression of one used to the harsh realities of life, was kneeling beside his fire when the knock came at his door.

'Who's that?' his wife demanded. Agnes was a tall, buxom woman of five-and-twenty, with gleaming auburn hair when she allowed it to stray, and he adored her. Now she was standing with the wooden spoon in her hand by the pot she had been stirring.

'Oh, ballocks!' he muttered, lifting his son from his lap and passing him to his wife. 'Take the Ant, eh?' He stood and walked to the door, pulling it wide.

'Hoppon? What do you want?'

The older man limped into the house, his weight all on the stick he clutched, his dog sliding in behind him, unsure of the welcome he was to receive. 'Bailiff, I needs your help. Murder.'

Bill's smile faded. 'You sure?'

'It's over top of Abbeyford, Bailiff. Sixteen dead, I counted, but there could be more. They been killed, some of their goods set afire, but most's been robbed from them.'

'Ach, shit! All right, Hoppon, you reckon you can tell me where it is, or you need to show it me?'

'You'll find it. Follow the smell,' Hoppon said. His face was twisted with disgust, but now he looked away for a moment. 'It's nasty, Bailiff. You understand me?'

'Reckon there's no misunderstanding that, Hoppon,' Bill said as he unfastened his belt and reached for his long-bladed knife. 'You have to go to the manor and tell them there. Then tell the steward to send for the coroner. Make sure he does. He's a lazy git at the best of times. Best to remind him that if he doesn't, it'll be on his neck, not ours. Meantime, tell the priest too, and ask to have someone sent to me to help guard the bodies. I'll need someone else with me.'

He pulled on a thick cloak of waxed linen, drew on a hood, and took a small bag that tied over his shoulder by two strong thongs. Grabbing a pot of cider and a hunk of bread, he stuffed them inside, before turning to his wife. He hugged Agnes and gave her a long kiss, before throwing a reluctant, longing look at the pottage that lay simmering over the fire. It was not his choice to be bailiff for the hundred, but he had been chosen and elected, and there was no escape from responsibility. This was his year.

The way was already growing dark as he left his house and took the long road that led almost like an arrow south to Oakhampton. Fortunately it was a popular route for men going to the market, and he could travel at some speed. There were other lanes that were not so well maintained, and where the way could be blocked by any number of fallen trees or thick glutinous mud in which a man could almost drown. From his perspective, any such areas were dangerous. A robber man might wait at the site of a pool of mud, hoping for a chance to waylay the unwary as they stepped around it, while a tree blocking a path might have been deliberately placed there.

These were not good times for a man who needed to travel, he told himself.

It was fortunate that there was not far to go, and before it was fully dark he was in the coppice.

He knew that many would be affected by the sight that greeted him, but he was too old to worry about the presence of the dead. He had seen enough corpses in his time. Some years ago, when he was himself scarce grown, he had buried his own parents, both dead from some disease that struck them during the famine years, when no one was strong enough to fight off even a mild chill. Aye, he had buried them, and others. The sight of death held no fears for him.

Still, there were some scenes he did not enjoy, and while he wandered about the bodies, it was the sight of so many wounds in those who were surely already dead that made him clench his jaw. It made him consider, too, and he looked about the ground with an eye tuned to the marks left by the raiders. Horses had left their prints, and the occasional boot, he saw. So this was no mere band of outlaws; it was a military force, if he was right.

He gazed about him with a stern frown fitted to his face, and as the rain began to fall again, he hurried to collect some dry timber to start a fire.

Time enough for thinking later.

Third Tuesday following the Feast of the Archangel Michael*

Hythe, Kent
Sir Baldwin de Furnshill sniffed the air as the little ship rolled and shifted on the sea.

---

*15 October 1325

A tall man in his middle fifties, he was used to travelling. In his dark eyes, as he looked at the quayside, there was only gratitude that he had once more successfully and safely crossed the Channel. The journey had become only too familiar to him in the last few months, and he was hopeful that now he might leave such wanderings and return to his wife and family, to the life of a rural knight.

'Bishop, I hope I see you well?'

'Ach!' Bishop Walter II of Exeter gave him a sharp look. His blue eyes were faded, and he must peer short-sightedly now, his eyes were so old and worn, unless he had his spectacles with him. Some ten years Baldwin's senior, at four-and-sixty, the bishop had not enjoyed a good voyage. 'I begin to sympathise with Simon.'

'He is still at the prow, I think.' Baldwin smiled. Simon had always been an atrociously poor sailor, and spent much of his time at sea bemoaning his fate as he brought up all he had eaten for a day past. This time he had attempted a popular sailor's cure, by drinking a quantity of strong ale, but that had only served to give his belly more fluid to reject, and since then he had spent the entire day and night leaning over the side of the ship, while sailors darted about to avoid tripping on him.

'Poor fellow. I shall go and offer a prayer for his speedy recovery,' the bishop said.

'Ha! Rather, pray for all our health,' Sir Richard de Welles said, joining them. 'No tellin' what chance we have of getting home.'

'Now we are all safe at England, there seems less need,' the bishop said wanly.

'Safe, eh?' Sir Richard said. 'When we have to travel to find the king and tell him that his wife has left him and taken his son and heir; that the men the king set to guard them both have all gone over to the queen's side instead of his own; and that we were powerless to do anything to support him in his endeavours? I think we might merit a little protection ourselves.'

'The king is a reasonable man,' Bishop Walter said.

From the sharp glance Sir Richard de Welles threw at him, Baldwin could see that he didn't believe the bishop's words either.

'My lord bishop,' Baldwin said, 'I am sure that you are right, but I confess to some concern that the king's favourite may deprecate our efforts.'

The bishop looked away without comment. There was no need to speak, for the three all knew the nature of Sir Hugh le Despenser.

It was left to Sir Richard to rumble, 'I would not trust that man if he told me grass grew green.'

Baldwin smiled to himself. 'I cannot deny that I would feel happier were we permitted to merely ride homewards. The thought of explaining ourselves to the king and Despenser fills me with discomfort.'

Abbeyford Woods, south of Jacobstowe

Bill Lark had woken after an unsettled sleep to find that a root had seemingly planted itself in the small of his back, while his neck felt as though it had been broken.

He stood rotating his head while grimly surveying the ground about him. Poor devils, he said to himself, not for the first time, as he began to wander about some of the trees, finding dry, dead branches low on the saplings and smaller trees about the coppice. Soon he had a couple of armfuls and could start to reset the fire.

Last night it had begun to rain almost as soon as he had lighted his fire, and then the sounds of night creatures had kept him awake too, so he had slept at best fitfully. When he *had* slept it was more a case of dozing, so now he felt on edge and fretful.

When he had his fire cheerfully ablaze, he spent a few minutes wandering about the coppice again.

First he walked around the camp itself, eyeing each of the bodies. It was curious, he noticed, that none was near the edge of the trees. It was as if they had been moved inwards, away from the thicker woodland all about. That was enough to make him scowl pensively.

Next he walked about the edge of the trees themselves. There were many tracks crossing and recrossing here, mainly horses' hoofs riding in towards the camp, and a few riding away. After making a complete circuit, he was forced to consider that there had been plenty of riders coming in, and that all had left by the entrance to the clearing, a muddied track made by the charcoal burners. So they had attacked from the woods, then departed by the roadway, either up towards Oakhampton or back towards Jacobstowe. There was even a set of boot prints leaving that way. Boots that had wandered about the camp. If he was right – and he was a moderate tracker – the boots overlapped some of the other marks on the ground, so this man had been here since the killings. Perhaps he had been here afterwards – but then again, he could have been one of the attackers.

What did worry Bill was that he could see no sign of escape from the camp. There were no prints at all that he could discern in among the trees other than those horses riding in. That itself was not surprising, for the covering of leaves would make a man's prints hard to see, but if there had been horses escaping, he would have expected to see evidence of their hoofs.

Yes. It was clear enough what had happened. The fellows had been travelling, and had stopped here for the evening. A group of felons had found them, probably dismounted nearby, and then ringed them, shooting most of them down with arrows before wandering in and stabbing the survivors. Looking about him at the bodies, he wondered who these victims might have been.

The man with the tonsure was the first to attract his attention. A clerk – perhaps someone more senior, an abbot or prior maybe. He looked too well fed to be someone lowly. Bill had to turn away from the man's ravaged features. Clearly this was a man who had made himself enemies in life, unless someone was convinced that he was carrying more goods about him than he was admitting. But that was daft. No one would kill a man in this manner when all his goods were to be taken anyway. Unless they thought he was keeping something back. Treasure, or information?

Close by was another man. This looked like a fellow who was more used to the bow than the pen. A mace or club had crushed the whole side of his face, making a foul mess of blood, bone and brains. At least his death would have been swift. Not like the monk.

The brutality of those two deaths was shocking to a man like Bill, but so was the number of the other victims. No gang of outlaws would kill so wantonly. Not in Bill's experience, anyway. He sat back on his haunches near the fire and stared around him. Just there, to the east, through the trees, he could see a long area of open pasture, and some cows munching contentedly with sheep walking round and round. There was the song of a blackbird not far away, and he could hear a cock crowing – no, it was a hen calling: 'An egg, an egg.' All seemed so normal, so sane, if he didn't look at the ground around him. This was his land. His country; his responsibility. And someone had desecrated it.

The idea of a band of murderers was alarming. Outlaws

infested many parts of the country, and there was no reason why Devon should be exempt from their predations, and yet he didn't get the impression that this was some random attack on a band of travellers. There was something too precise about it. The men who had committed this obscene act were surely not just robbers, they had not suddenly sprung in upon the camp and massacred the people in a rough melee.

He had seen that kind of attack before. Usually there were a very clear series of indications. As the first men appeared, people would bolt, some flying hither and thither through the trees, seeking some kind of safety, and then the bodies would be more spread about. Here, it would seem that the camp had been attacked from all sides simultaneously. That spoke of discipline and organisation. The men who did this had a purpose. And he would make it his job to discover that purpose, if he could.

If he could. The thought made him give a wry little grin to himself. Whether he could or not would depend on so much. And even if he did go to the effort, it would depend very much on the attitude of the coroner. So often the bastards were useless. They just lived for the money they could extort from others. Like this latest sheriff, from all he'd heard.

Still, he was nothing if not thorough, so he wandered out beyond the fringe of trees, looking all about. It was as he reached the southernmost section of the clearing that he found something that made him give a quick frown. Here there were some heavily damaged bushes and brambles, as though something – or some*one* – had hurried through. But some of them had been dragged back the other way, too, so it appeared that there had been movement in both directions. He crouched, glancing all about him, wondering what story he was witnessing here, but he could make little sense of it. Then, as he cursed the rain, he saw some speckles on the grass. Nearby there was a larger splash. When fresh, this must have formed a pool. He touched it, and although it was difficult to be certain, he felt sure that it was blood. Perhaps it was a man who had left the camp to defecate, and who had hurried back when the attack started, only to be struck down as he returned?

But looking back at the clearing, he was forced to wonder why the man's body was not here. Perhaps he wasn't wounded badly enough to collapse, but had continued on to the main camp, where he'd died with the others. Strange, though, he thought, as he peered down carefully. There was so much blood. If a man had been knocked down here, surely he would never have made it back to the main camp after losing all this blood.

He heard voices. Retreating, he set his back to a tree, listening carefully, until he recognised one of them.

'If you were trying to be quiet, you failed,' he called.

'Sweet Christ's cods! Bill, what happened here?'

'John, I wish I knew. All I can say is, whoever did this wasn't just mad. A lunatic would have been far less effective.'

'How could one man do this?' John Weaver said. He looked about him, taking in the sight. At his side, Art Miller pulled a face at the odours.

'It was a large gang. Question is, who were they?'

Chapter Two

Woods north of Jacobstowe

It had been a quiet night for Roger. The scene in the coppice last morning had shaken him more than he wanted to admit even to himself. Afterwards he had run quietly away. Before long he came to a vill, and crouched down, hiding. There was a woman in a little yard, calling and clucking to her chickens, a tall, strong woman, buxom and attractive, and he waited, watching her with something akin to longing, until she was done and went back inside, and he could hurry past and on to the north.

No one wanted to be found near a scene like that, especially if a stranger to the area. Because if any man was ever to be thought a dangerous murderer, it was always easier to think such things of foreigners. Roger had no wish to be captured by men determined to find anyone who could suit the description of a stranger and outlaw.

But it was not only the desire to put as many leagues as possible between himself and any posse that drove him on. It was also the memory of that appalling sight.

In the past he had been used to such pictures of horror. There had been plenty of bodies to see after the French invasion of the territories about Saint Sardos, those of men and women, and none of them would come back to haunt him, he knew. Not even the little tableau of the two children would affect him. He had found them under a set of rugs, as though

they had been hidden there with the heavy woollen material thrown over to conceal them, a little girl and a boy,
neither more than four years old, if he had to guess. The boy
had been cut almost entirely in half, as though someone
had swung an axe at his breast. The girl's head had been
broken by a club or mace; her death would at least have
been quick. Then the cloth had been cast over them again,
untidily. Carelessly. They had been dealt with, so their
covering could be returned.

There had been many children slaughtered in Guyenne in
the last months. Yes, he had come back to England to escape
those sights now that the French officials were tightening their
grip on the lands about Guyenne, but such things happened,
and he had seen them, and he knew he was strong enough to
survive this just as he had survived the others.

No, the deaths themselves were not enough to give him
sleepless nights or even to unsettle him. But he was disturbed
now as he thought back to the scene.

As he had entered the coppice, he had been prepared for it
all. The smell of death lay over the place in the mizzly air like
some foul miasma from a moorland bog, and he knew what he
would see as soon as he reached it.

He had stood silently a while, absorbing the images that
came to him. A cart upended, the shafts pointing at the sky; a
second collapsed where a wheel had been snapped away; two
horses dead, one on its side, the other on its back, all four legs
in the air, arrows in head and flanks, the rider nearby, with
more arrows in his back. And another man near him, his head
missing entirely. A woman . . . There were so many there, and
none of them made any impression on him. He was a fighter –
he had seen it all.

Walking among them, he had found himself casting about
carefully, for that was what a man did after a fight, but clearly

there was no profit to be had from the bodies down here. All had been killed and their property taken from them with their lives. From the number of men here, there must have been some seven or eight carts just to cope with their goods, or a number of packhorses. So many travelling together for safety, thinking that there would be strength in their numbers. He would have thought that most were moderately wealthy people, but one group in particular was different. The man near the horse, he looked like a fighter. And not only him. Roger would guess from their build that some six or eight of the men here were warriors. They didn't look like peasants, that was certain. The clothing, the boots and shoes, all pointed to people who were better off than the normal vill churl.

Roger had squatted near a man's body. The fellow had six arrows in him, and there was a wound in his eye like a stab wound, as though someone was going about the place and making sure of all the injured.

He had the appearance of a fighter: he was fairly strong in the arm, with some scars to prove that he'd been in more than the average number of fights. There was no mail or armour, but when Roger looked at his wrists and neck, there were signs of chafing. He had worn some simple armour, which had been stripped from him, if Roger had to guess. No man-at-arms would be unaware of the value of mail, and it would be taken from the fallen, either to be altered for the new owner, or for sale.

Others, when he looked, had similar marks. One was just the same, with the proof of armour and helm. When he added them up, he reckoned these two were men-at-arms, and eight others looked like bowmen. They each had the character- istically powerful muscles on their backs that were the inevitable result of regular practice as archers. From the look of them, these could well have been a force together, perhaps protecting something, he thought. And then he came across another figure.

This was no warrior. He had the belly of an abbot, and the jowls to match. A tonsure in need of renewal, and the ink on his fingers, pointed to a clerk of some form. And yet he had been utterly despoiled. His feet were bare, but the flesh was soft and unmarked. Not a man used to walking barefoot, then. He had a chemise, but no cloak or surcoat, which looked out of place, and no jewellery. However, his fingers held the marks of rings. When Roger ran his own fingers over the first joints, he could feel where the skin was raised slightly in calluses about the outer edge of the rings the man had habitually worn. To his surprise there was no wooden cross about his neck. However, it was his face that jolted Roger more than anything else he had seen there that day, more than the proofs of theft. Because this fellow had been mutilated. Although he was blond, Roger couldn't tell what colour his eyes were, because both had been taken out before he had had his throat cut. His death hadn't been good.

When he studied all the figures, there were nine who were clustered not too far from the monk, and these had two things in common: they all looked as though they were fighters of some sort, and they all had multiple arrow wounds. Only one was different – a fellow who had been stabbed five times in the back, and who was lying further away from the others, nearer to the perimeter. Surely he was killed first. Perhaps he had been the sentry?

Yes, this was the sort of picture he had grown used to in Guyenne, but not here, not in England. Still, where men lived, others would die. It was a rule of life. And while it made him sad to see children killed, it was also natural. Children followed the armies into battle, children worked, and some died. But while he was ready for that, it was the sight of the other little figures that had caused him to pause and stare with shock.

A puppy. A small black and white puppy, and its mother, she slashed and stabbed, the pup with a broken neck, both lying near a roll of torn and ruined clothing, as though they had been killed defending their master's belongings. When he saw them, he suddenly found the breath stopping in his throat. It was so unnecessary. So pointless. Men and women, even the children too, could perhaps be viewed as threats. After all, it was possible that they might later be able to recognise the perpetrators of this violent little action and bring them to justice. But the dogs? There was no need to kill them too. He bent and picked up the two bodies, tears flooding his cheeks, cradling them for a long moment, before setting them down gently at the foot of a tree some way from the carnage of the camp.

It was that, more than any of the human bodies, that made him pause and stare about him, as though seeing all the bodies for the very first time. Someone had chosen to kill this little group. No, not just kill them – wipe them out entirely.

But *why*?

Abbeyford Woods, south of Jacobstowe

It was late that evening when Art Miller returned to the camp. And now he had at least some information for Bill Lark and John Weaver. He refused to speak until he had seated himself before their fire. Once comfortable, with a pot of steaming cider before him, he began to tell all he had learned, his voice quiet and reflective.

'Seems there was a group of ten from Tavistock in one party, them and two monks. Everyone remembered them. One monk was really foreign, they said, and had such a thick accent hardly anyone could listen to 'un without they felt mazed. T'other was English, and a cheery fellow, with a pretty little dog and a puppy he held in his robe. Only the snout stuck out, they said, and he made the children laugh to see him. They arrived in Oakhampton a couple of days ago, and were asking about the best route to leave the town. They met with a party of travellers. One was a young family, mother, father, two children.' Art glanced at Bill, shaking his head. 'All told how happy and cheerful the children were. Lovely, lively little brutes, they said. There were others, though: four pedlars and tranters with their goods. One fellow from east. Apparently he said that there were dangers on the Crediton road, and the travellers were persuaded to go with him. It was him took them all northwards.'

'Did anyone know where he reckoned the problems were?' Bill asked, frowning.

'No one heard him say, but there was one merchant I spoke to, a fellow called Denfote from up Exbourne way, who said that Bow had grown hazardous for travellers. The new lord there is keen to take money from all who pass his demesne. Denfote said he would always bypass it now.'

'Did he know this man's name?'

'Yes – Sir Robert de Traci. Apparently him and his son have taken to demanding tolls on any roads about there. They're a nuisance generally, but their arrogance, he said, would lead to them killing someone soon, so Denfote thought.'

'Seems he knows how to predict the future, then,' Bill said, shaking his head. 'So how many were there in total?'

'There were the twelve from Tavistock, the little family of four, the pedlars and this guide. All told, twenty-one.'

Bill considered, sipping at his hot drink. 'That's interesting. Since we had only nineteen bodies.'

'That was what I thought you'd say,' Art said.

Nodding, Bill stood. 'I'd best take another look about this place, then. Make sure there're no more.' He hesitated, frowning. Then, 'Art, you come too, eh? Maybe my eyes have been missing something.'

'All right, Bailiff,' Art said. He drained his pot and joined Bill as the bailiff began a circumambulation of the area. 'What do you reckon?'

'I reckon this looks like a simple attack of outlaws,' Bill said.

'So why don't you think that?'

'I said—'

'Oh, I know what you *said*, Bill Lark, but I've known you longer than anyone else, and I don't think you believe it any more than I do,' Art said easily.

'No.' Bill was quiet for a little while, and then he began to tell Art about the blood, the man who surely couldn't have walked back to join the others after all that loss. 'I think that makes it look different.'

'Best way to make sure a man's quiet is to hit him hard in the kidneys or liver,' Art offered. 'Stab him there, and he soon loses his blood and dies.'

'Aye. The others didn't matter. But this one man was clobbered hard. That makes me think.'

'What?'

'Makes me think that maybe he was a guard, and the fellows knocked him down so that they could surprise the rest of the party.'

'Why do that?'

'To make their attack all the more complete? Perhaps they wanted to catch someone in the group – the man with his eyes taken out?'

Art winced. 'Poor bastard. And it's odd, too.'

'What is?'

'This man who was telling them to take the other route, he only had one eye himself.'

Third Thursday following the Feast of the Archangel Michael*

London

Sir Richard de Welles had a simple faith that whatever was going to happen would happen. It was all in the hands of God, and for that reason there was little point in worrying.

Once he had been a great deal less fatalistic. When he was a youth, he had held the belief that he could alter his life and make things better by dint of special effort. But then, when his wife had died, his attitude changed. She had been killed by a fellow he had trusted, and an event like that was bound to be enough to change his attitude.

So today, as he rode with the others under the imposing entrance to London Bridge, he did not concern himself with idle fears about the interview with the king. He had the comfort of knowing that he had done nothing in France of which he should be ashamed, and that knowledge gave him an assurance that he could see the others did not feel. If anything, his mood lightened as he jolted along on the great bridge, looking up at the flags fluttering, seeing the glorious painted buildings under which they rode. The horseshoes clattered noisily on the timbers of the drawbridge, and he could look down to see some boys playing on boats, shooting down by the massive piers of the bridge supports.

'Look at them, Master Puttock,' he said happily.

Simon only grunted in response, and Sir Richard smiled.

'Simon, whatever happens when we see the king, there is

**17 October 1325

nothing we may do about it now. Best thing to do is to enjoy the journey and leave the future to itself.'

Simon nodded, but there was no apparent ease in his manner. Not even when one of the little boats struck the point of a pier and shattered. All watching guffawed with laughter to see how the two lads inside were tipped out into the foaming waters, but not Simon or Baldwin. It left Sir Richard feeling sad that he could not lighten the mood of his friends.

There were plenty of them, after all. Although Baldwin, Simon and he had no servants with them – only Baldwin's beast, a great black, brown and white brute called Wolf – the bishop was a different matter. He had clerks, including his nephew, a squire called William Walle, three other men-at-arms to serve him, and his steward John de Padington. With these and the packhorses they led to carry the bishop's belongings, they formed quite a cavalcade.

Their way took them from the city's gates and west, down along Candelwryhttestrate, but they had to turn southwards where a wagon had shed its load, and Bishop Walter took them along narrower roads that Sir Richard didn't recognise.

'You know these lanes like I know my own manor,' he said as they rode along Athelyngstrate towards the cathedral church of St Paul's.

'I would be a sorry bishop if I didn't know this city well,' Bishop Walter replied. 'I have spent so much of my life here in London. The king saw fit to make me his lord high treasurer some years ago, and since then I have spent much of every year here – apart from those periods when he has discarded me,' he added with a thin little smile.

'Why would he do that?' Sir Richard asked.

'Because my advice was unwelcome. The last time he removed me from office it was because he split the treasury into two – one to deal with the north, one for the south. That would be a fair way to deal with the problems of the treasury, separating it into two halves in the same way as the Church is split between Canterbury and York, but only if there was a corresponding increase in staff to cope with the workload. Such administrative corrections are necessary once in a while, after all. No man could dispute that. However, the king is ever seeking greater efforts by all without considering the impact on individuals. And that is what happened here. He divided the one institution into two parts, and expected these two new courts to be able to cope with the same number of staff as the one court employed before. It could not work!'

'That is why you resigned the post?'

'Yes. I will not be a part of an effort like that.' The bishop's tone was sharp, but Sir Richard was sure that it was merely a reflection of his concern at the impending interview with the king.

That there might be another reason for the bishop's short-ness did not occur to him until they were near the cathedral itself. There Sir Richard saw Bishop Walter's eyes turn this way and that, and he didn't seem happy until they had left the cathedral behind them. It seemed to Sir Richard that there was something about that area that was distasteful to the bishop.

They rode on down the hill to the Ludgate at the bottom, and then continued on the Fletestrete. Sir Richard saw Baldwin stare down at the Temple buildings, which Sir Hugh le Despenser had taken for his own only recently, and glanced over them himself. There was not much to interest him, though, and soon he found himself studying the Straunde as they rode on towards Thorney Island and Westminster.

The buildings here were all grand. Too grand for Sir Richard's taste, if he was honest. He required only a simple dwelling. Space for himself, a few mastiffs and raches, perhaps a mews for a pair of hawks, and that was about it.

Here, though, there was an apparent need for ostentation on all sides. And when they reached the Temple Bar and passed beyond, the houses were even more extravagant.

'We shall rest here a while before continuing,' the bishop said as he turned left just before St Clement Danes.

'Where's this, then?' Sir Richard asked, eyeing the hall with some suspicion. It was even more splendid than the other places they had passed, or so he felt.

Bishop Walter was already passing under the gatehouse. It was the steward, John de Padington, who turned in his saddle and eyed the knight with an amused look. 'It's the bishop's house, Sir Richard. He built it himself so that the bishops of Exeter would always have a comfortable billet in London.'

Chapter Three

The Painted Chamber, Westminster

'It would be better that you rested, your royal highness,' Sir Hugh le Despenser said.

'I am not in a mood to rest,' King Edward II replied.

Sir Hugh ducked his head, then signalled to a waiting servant. The man nodded and fetched him a goblet of wine, bowing low as he passed it.

It was good to see men who understood their position in the world. This bottler, for example. He knew that his place was to wait for the merest signal, and then to rush to serve his betters. And Sir Hugh le Despenser was definitely his better. As the second most wealthy and powerful man in the realm, after only the king himself, Sir Hugh was the better of all. The king alone he viewed as an equal.

But even knowing his own importance, Sir Hugh could not help but stare at the bottler as he poured, wondering for how much longer he would merit such respect. It felt as though the entire realm was a tower teetering on the brink of complete failure, undermined by enemies that could not be seen, swatted away or exterminated. They were deep underground, hidden from view. And if the realm failed, Sir Hugh would die. He and all his friends must be taken and slain. The strain of his position was like a band of steel tightening around his skull. 'My lord, would you not take a seat? I can arrange for some diverting—'

'Be *still*, Sir Hugh! Do you not see when a man needs peace and silence to consider? I have much to think of, in Christ's name!'

'I do understand, your highness,' said Sir Hugh. It was harder and harder to restrain his own tongue in the face of the king's bile. 'But surely a rest would do no harm.'

The king continued as though he had not heard him speak. 'It is humiliating that my wife is not yet home. She should have returned as soon as Stapledon arrived there. What could be holding her up? There is no news, and we do not know how the French are responding. Christ Jesus! She must know how it embarrasses me. And my son is still there. I want him home again. I do not want my heir to be held there any longer than is entirely necessary. He is young, vulnerable. He is not yet thirteen years old, and already he has been forced to go and pay homage to the French like a mere knight, when he is a duke!'

'It was better that he did so than that another should go,' Despenser said. 'It was better than that you should go.'

'I couldn't!' the king snapped. He was at the farther end of the chamber now, the easternmost end, near his bed. There were three large oval windows above him, and he appeared to be staring up at them, but when Sir Hugh followed his gaze, he saw that the king was peering up at a picture of a prophet on the ceiling.

It was the most beautiful room in the kingdom. In fact Sir Hugh had heard that the French king himself was jealous of the chamber, and had ordered that a similar one be built for his own use. There were paintings over the walls and the ceilings, all with an exuberant use of colour and gilt. Even the meanest feature had decoration upon it. As Sir Hugh glanced at the window nearest him, he saw that the soffit itself had a picture of an angel staring down. Below her was a virtue, *Debonerete*, or meekness, triumphing over the vice *Ira*, wrath. As was normal, the virtue was depicted as a woman, holding a shield on which the arms of England were differenced by two bars, while the arms of St Edmund and other saints were carefully painted around her in a border. She was a stunning figure, especially since she stood some three yards tall, and gleamed with fire from the gilt and gold leaf.

Nearby there was another figure in the same vein. Here the virtue was *Largesse*, and she was triumphing over *Covoitise*, covetousness. That at least was one vice which the king never suffered from. Not in the presence of Sir Hugh.

Sir Hugh had his goblet refilled and waited. He had much patience. Sometimes he thought that it was the only virtue he required while here with the king. But he couldn't deny that he'd been well rewarded over the years for his patience. All he had ever needed to show his king was humility and deference, leavened with adoration, and Edward had repaid the effort many times over. Sir Hugh's desires became the king's desires; Sir Hugh's friends became the king's, while his enemies became Edward's most detested foes. There was nothing Sir Hugh could do that would colour the king's opinion of him. Even when the French demanded that Edward travel to France to pay homage for the territories held from the French crown, the king was happier to send his own heir, the Earl of Chester, Duke of Aquitaine, rather than make the journey himself. Some believed it was because he feared for his safety. Sir Hugh knew it was more because he was anxious for Sir Hugh.

Edward was happier to risk the life and livelihood of his own son than he was to risk the neck of his lover.

'He would have something to say about this, wouldn't he?' the king was saying.

His words brought Sir Hugh back to the present. 'Who, your highness?'

'I said, the prophet here, Jeremiah, he would have had much to say about my reign, wouldn't he?'

Sir Hugh racked his brains. 'Jeremiah – he foretold of the disaster that was about to overwhelm the Holy Land, did he not? When the Babylonians overran it?'

'Yes. He was rejected by his own people because they felt he was a doom-monger, always giving them the worst, never telling them that all would grow better. He was as popular as *I* am.'

The king had a break in his voice as he spoke, and Sir Hugh took a breath. 'Sire, you are much loved by your people. It is not your fault that—'

'I have been astonishingly unlucky. Look at me! I was feted when I was crowned, but one thing after another has set the seal on my reign. The Scottish, the French, the bastards from the borders – and there's been nothing I could do about any of it! As soon as I had the opportunity, I took my host to the lords marcher, and I defeated them, didn't I? But that wasn't good enough to recover my reign. The people detest me. No! Don't think to lie to me, Sir Hugh! I know what they are thinking. And now even my queen has deserted me. She sits there in France with her brother and entertains his friends and my enemies, and I cannot be sure what she intends. Fickle woman!'

'We shall soon know, sire.'

But the king was not to be consoled, and when Sir Hugh left him some while later, it was with a worried frown at his brow. Edward's fears were all too well known to him, but it seemed that the man's concerns were growing daily into fully developed panic. And that was enough to give Sir Hugh cause for thought. His own position in the world was dependent entirely on the king's goodwill.

Sir Hugh had thought that when the Welsh marches rose in

rebellion against him, it was a master stroke to have the king raise an army and march with him. At the time it had seemed the most ingenious response. Those who had sought to meet Sir Hugh in battle instead found themselves faced by the king's banners. Any who attempted to fight would now be branded as traitors. Their declarations of loyalty to the king were irrelevant. They had tried to impose their will on the king, and Edward had suffered from that kind of interference before. He had been forced to submit to men who enforced ordinances, restricting his freedom to rule as he wished. When he tried to reward his favourite, Piers Gaveston, the earls had captured Piers and executed him. Edward would not permit any man to stand in his way again. He had decided that he loved Sir Hugh, and any who sought Sir Hugh's destruction was an enemy of the king.

But the sheer brilliance of his scheming had concealed one possible risk. Sir Hugh had first seen to the capture of his worst enemy, the bastard grandson of the murderer Mortimer, may he rot in hell for all eternity. Roger Mortimer, the grandfather, had slaughtered Sir Hugh's own grandsire at Evesham, and the Despensers were not a family to forget a blood feud. So Sir Hugh's first ambition was to have Mortimer held for a brief period, and then executed as a traitor to the king. And he had almost succeeded. The king had agreed, after two years of careful persuasion, and Mortimer would have been dead already, except the fortunate devil had learned of the death warrant being signed, and had made a daring escape from the Tower of London. Now he was living abroad, plotting the downfall of Sir Hugh, no doubt. Rumours of his negotiations in Hainault for mercenaries and ships had come to Despenser's spies.

When the rebels were all captured or beaten, flying from the country, Sir Hugh acquired all those parts he had craved so long. He owned almost all of Wales, he possessed vast tracts of the West Country, and he was undoubtedly the second most wealthy and powerful man in the realm. No one but the king could stand against him. And while he had the king's ear, all knew that to court Sir Hugh's enmity meant to attract Edward's hatred. None dared that. They'd all seen how the king would respond to those who angered him. After the rebellion, the bodies of his enemies had decorated city gates and London's walls for over two years, until his wife's pleas for leniency had finally persuaded him to remove them and allow the tanned, leathery remains to be buried.

Which had led, in part, to the king's increasing dislike for his wife.

Sir Hugh entered the little chamber where his own clerks worked, and strode over to a chair. Sitting, he steepled his fingers and rested his lips on his forefingers, head bowed.

There was much now to cause concern.

Stories abounded that Mortimer was raising an army to invade: he was gathering shipping; he had money to pay mercenaries. And Roger Mortimer had been the king's most successful general. If he were to return to England at the head of the army, there was no telling what the outcome would be. Except Sir Hugh knew full well that if it was a simple matter of generalship, with Mortimer against the king, the king would lose. His only saving would be the fear all men had of breaking their vow of loyalty to him. That might keep some by his side. But if Mortimer proclaimed that he had no fight with the king himself, many might flock to his banner. So many hated Despenser.

But there was nothing to fear yet. He must wait until he had information. There was no point in worrying about Mortimer until he knew that the bastard was a threat. He licked his lips and looked about him. The pressure of his position was growing to be insupportable, he thought as he chewed his fingernail, running his incisor under it to nibble away a little more.

There was a sharp stabbing pain, and he withdrew his hand, looking down. The nail was separated, but had torn away some of the flesh beneath. A sickle of blood stood out at the end of his finger, and he stuck it back in his mouth, sucking.

Yes. He must wait for more information, learn exactly what Mortimer was planning, see how he could respond.

And then crush the shit without compunction.

Bishop's House, the Straunde

Simon yawned as they wandered out into the cool air again. After that short rest, he felt a little invigorated, but the halt had been too brief. Now, standing out here with their breath feathering the air, pulling on gloves or reclasping their cloaks against the chill, the men with him all looked exhausted.

It was especially apparent when he looked at Baldwin and Sir Richard. Neither was all that young, and both were fully aware of the great distance they must cover to return to their homes in the far west of the kingdom. Still, even those two did not wear such a fretful expression as Bishop Walter.

Simon wondered at that. The bishop was the oldest among them, at some four- or five-and-sixty, but his pallor was not only because of the coolness of the afternoon air. No, it was more to do with the concern he had about the king's response to their news.

They mounted, and soon afterwards they were off, through the gates and out into the roadway.

Ahead they could see the royal buildings in the distance. The massive belfry of Westminster Abbey stood slightly to the right of the other towers and walls, and between the riders and the palace there was a straggle of buildings. Some were low houses for lawyers and clerks, others taller and more prestigious properties for the merchants and traders who came here to ply their trade. Inns and shops catered for their needs, and all about there was a hubbub. Peasants and tradespeople shouting and hawking created a confusion in Simon's mind. He would be glad to be out of the city and on his way homewards once more.

'Did you see the bishop's face?' Sir Richard asked, leaning towards Simon as he spoke.

Simon nodded. 'He is very concerned just now.'

'Aye. But why should he be so outside St Paul's?'

Simon gave a thin smile. 'You're talking about that? I'd forgotten he was upset there as well, but it's no surprise. Earlier this year I was here with him, Baldwin too, and he invited us to join him to celebrate the Feast of the Purification of the Blessed Virgin Mary. We went to the cathedral itself, and just outside it a mob gathered, threatening to kill him. Apparently the Londoners hate him because he once had to investigate all the rights and customs of the city of London.'

Sir Richard turned slowly and gazed at the bishop. 'Then why, in the name of all that's holy, does the man want to come here? I'd stay down in Devon, in a pleasant land where the people all like me.'

'That, I think, is a question you could ask of any man who seeks power over others,' Simon said.

'Hmm. Fortunate then that you and I don't need any nonsense like that, eh?' said Sir Richard affably. 'No, just a good quart of strong wine, a little haunch of beef or venison, and a warm woman to snuggle up to on a winter's night. Aye, a man doesn't need much for comfort.'

They jogged on until they reached Thieving Lane, where they made their way through the gate and into the palace's yard.

Simon couldn't like this place. He looked about him carefully from the vantage point of his mount before he released his foot from the stirrup and swung himself down from the horse. Last time he had been here for meetings with the king, he had been impressed by the single-minded search for power that appeared to be the main characteristic of all those who lived and worked in the shadow of the palace. When he glanced over at Baldwin, he saw the same wariness, and the realisation that his concerns were shared made his anxiety weigh a little less heavily on his shoulders.

They followed in the wake of the bishop, and soon they were being led across the paved yard to the Green Yard, a pleasant grassed area, in through a doorway, along two corridors, and to a pair of doors that Simon remembered. These were the doors to the king's Painted Chamber. Four guards stood there, and they took all the swords, stacking them neatly on shelves to the left of the doors. Then the doors were opened, and Simon and Baldwin shot a look at each other before plunging on in the wake of the bishop and Sir Richard.

Abbeyford Woods, south of Jacobstowe

Bill was awake before dawn on the day that the coroner arrived.

The three had taken it in turns to go home and fetch more food and drink. Last night it was John who had gone, leaving his friend, Art Miller, to keep Bill company. The man seemed somewhat less conversational today than the corpse with both eyes put out, and Bill would have been happier to have the company of almost any other man, but at least Art was alive. Or so Bill assumed.

There were always tales of men wandering the lands. In the last thirty years or so there had been the trail bastons, gangs of men armed with clubs who had so devastated the countryside that the king had imposed a new series of courts to come to terms with the menace. Then, when the famine struck, still more men were displaced as they went in search of any form of sustenance. Latterly there was the danger posed by the families and friends of those who had raised their banners in opposition to Sir Hugh le Despenser in the war of three years ago. After Boroughbridge, when the king had destroyed their armies and captured many of the plotters, he had executed hundreds. The savagery of his response to their attempt to depose his adviser had shocked the whole nation, and many of those who had not been involved went in terror of their lives and had left their homes to become outlaws. Some had made their way to France or Hainault, where they knew they would not be persecuted for their opposition to the English king, but others had remained, and Bill would not be surprised if some had banded together and could have committed this crime.

John was back again before the sun had passed much over the far hills. With him he brought victuals, and the three sat around the fire to eat, chewing rhythmically. It was later in the morning that Bill heard the tramping of boots, and hurried to his feet.

A slightly scruffy-looking knight appeared through the trees with a small entourage of men-at-arms and a clerk, who walked with a screwed-up face, as though the whole of the landscape here stank.

'Who is in charge, fellow?' the knight asked, and then looked about him with a grimace. 'Sweet Mother of God! How many dead are there?'

Painted Chamber, Westminster

As soon as they entered the room, Baldwin could feel the atmosphere. Earlier in the year he had come here with Simon, and the pair had served the king by uncovering a murderer.

Then, when they entered the king's presence, although there was the awareness of the difference in their respective positions, Edward had treated them remarkably well. Now there was a very different feel to the place, and Baldwin shot a warning look at Simon as he knelt, copying the bishop and Sir Richard, as soon as they had passed through the doorway. None moved until the steward had nodded to them, then they all walked in, heads still bowed, until they were nearer the king. There they knelt again, heads bent, until there was a grunt of exasperation from Edward.

'Bishop, God speed.'

'Your royal highness, I hope you are well?'

'Me? Why should I not be?' the king said petulantly. 'My wife has been abroad, as has my son, and I am keen to see them again to learn what is happening over there in France. But still! What are you doing here alone, my lord bishop? Is my wife with you?' He made an elaborate display of peering behind the bishop. 'But wait! No! She is not here, is she? Or have I missed her?'

Bishop Walter bowed his head again at the heavy irony. 'Your highness, I am sorry to say that she is not with us, no. What is more, I fear she refused to return to you and her family. I am deeply distraught, your highness, to have to tell you this.'

'What are you saying? Do you mean to tell me that she has not received my letter?' the king said in a dangerously cold voice. 'I thought that I had given it to you for her so that it could not be mislaid.'

'She received it, your highness. More, I told the French king that you desired her to return to you at the earliest opportunity, but he replied that your queen is also his sister, and he would not banish her from his court. If she chose to leave, that was one thing; but she would not.'

'What . . .' The king spoke softly, but the words seemed

hard for him to enunciate, as though they were stuck in his throat. 'What, then, of my son? The Earl of Chester, Edward. Where is he?'

'Your royal highness, I am deeply afraid that he would not have been safe had I brought him with me.'

'What does that mean?'

'Only this, your highness. I was threatened with death were I to remain. A man waylaid me and would have killed me, I think. And your queen sought to demand money from me, suggesting that I might not live if I did not give her your letters allowing her to claim money from bankers in Paris.'

'So my wife is alienated from me, and she has taken my son to hold against his will and mine?' the king said with icy precision. 'But you all saved yourselves?'

'Your highness, it would serve you not at all if we were to die,' the bishop said with some asperity. 'I did the best I possibly could, but when it became apparent that my life was in danger, I confess I made the most urgent plans in order that I might escape the clutches of my enemies in France and return to advise you. I was forced to take on the habit of a pilgrim, merely to protect my own life.'

'Oh, you wish to *advise* me now? That is good. Very good. So, my lord bishop, why do you not? Tell me, what *exactly* would you advise me to do, now that you have lost me my queen, my heir, and . . . and . . .'

The bishop took a deep breath. 'Your royal highness. We did all we might. I had private talks with her royal highness, but she made no effort to conceal her hatred for me. I made the French court aware that she was disobeying you, her husband and master, but none would support me and your reasonable request that she return to her home. All was in vain. However, there was important intelligence that I felt sure I should bring to your attention.'

'Speak!' The king tutted to himself, then, 'And stand, all of you. You look untidy on your knees like that. I feel I should have the floors cleaned!'

Bishop Walter stood slowly, his knees aching from the unaccustomed position. When the others were also on their feet, the bishop fixed his eyes on the king. 'Your royal highness, the first news that came to me, and of which I must make you aware, is that the foul traitor Roger Mortimer has returned to the French court. I feel quite sure that he is there in order that he might negotiate with the French king, and possibly to discuss matters with your queen. I know this is sore news, but—'

The rest of his words were drowned by the king's sudden roar of anger. He stood, fists clenched, teeth showing in a fierce grimace of pure fury. 'You mean that bastard son of a diseased whore is out there with my wife, and my son too? You left them there so that the honey-tongued traitor could inveigle his way into their good natures? He will make use of their innocence to make much trouble for us, you fools. Did none of you think to try to kill him? Or at least make it clear to the French king that his presence there was an insult, a . . . a sore torment to me? Eh? Did you do nothing?'

'We had no means with which to—'

'What of the other guardians of the queen and my son, eh? I gave you a force so that you might protect Edward, my son, and the same men could be used to deal with a man who is known as a traitor and a rebel. You think the French would argue if you removed him? You should have killed the bastard, damn it, damn *him* . . . damn *you*!'

'That brings me to the second piece of intelligence, my king. The men who were with me, the men whom you set to guard the queen, and those who were told to protect your son, they have all become allies of hers. None would come back to England save these here with me.'

'You mean to tell me . . .' The king gaped, and stared at the three men behind the bishop. 'These are all?'

'My lord Cromwell, Sir Henry . . . all have allied themselves with the queen. I am truly sorry, your royal highness. If I could have, I swear, I would have enlisted the help of any of them to bring down Mortimer and destroy him.'

'Be gone! Leave me, all of you! You bring me news like this and expect reward? Just go!'

Chapter Four

Abbeyford Woods, south of Jacobstowe

'Well, fellow?'

The tone of the knight was invariably sharp, as though he had no regard for Bill or any of the others. Instead he stood about, still, surveying the damage all around, tapping his foot as though he was waiting for a porter to open a gate for him.

He watched as Bill and the others gathered up the jury and made them stand in a rough semicircle. Then they set out a board and stool ready for the clerk to scribble at, and checked who was and who wasn't present.

'All ready, Coroner.'

'Very well. Clerk, have the jury swear,' Sir Peregrine de Barnstaple said, and wandered to the nearest of the bodies.

While the jury was sworn in, he stood and surveyed the coppice again. Seeing Bill watching him, he beckoned. 'Look, Bailiff, I do happily confess that I am new to this task. I have not been a coroner for long. But I would have you tell me, do you have any idea who could have done this?'

'I have been wondering that myself. It isn't the locals about here. You can see that.'

'Why?'

'Look at us! There aren't enough to try to attack such a force as this. And why would we kill like this? This wasn't a simple waylaying, I'd wager. No, these men were attacked and killed for a definite purpose. The man with his eyes put out? Why would a robber do that?'

'That is what I thought too. So it would be a large band of outlaws, is what you believe?'

'I can only think so. But . . .'

'What?'

'A gang large enough to do this would have to have been seen or heard, Sir Peregrine.'

'True enough. So where did they come from? Do you have any idea?'

'I've searched along the roads all about here in the last day or two. There is one direction I think they could have come from. North.'

The coroner shrugged and shook his head. 'Should that mean something to me? Which castle would they be from? That's what I need to know. Who are they and where could they have come from? Are they outlaws, is that what you mean?'

Bill eyed him closely, then looked back over the dead bodies. 'There is no man within my manor who would have done this. North of here there are a number of men-at-arms in the employ of different lords, and there are men at Oakhampton, of course. But a group would have to be very sure of themselves to do such murder. Of the men in the area near here, I don't know who would dare to attack such a group.'

Sir Peregrine looked at him for a moment. 'I have the impression you are withholding something from me. Is there anything else you wish to tell me?'

Bill looked up at the coroner. Since first seeing the man, he had been impressed by Sir Peregrine's haughtiness and self-importance. The man was the perfect example of a knight: arrogant and overbearing. He was typical of all the coroners

Bill had ever met: he surely wasn't interested in justice or protecting the people about here; he was only looking at this as a means of procuring money in amercements for the king. All murders and attacks like this led to the locals being fleeced to swell the king's purse.

'I can tell nothing more than you, Sir Peregrine,' Bill said flatly.

'Very well. Let us open the inquest and see what may be learned,' the coroner said, and clapped his hands to get the attention of the men waiting. 'I call this inquest to order!'

Westminster Palace

Sir Hugh le Despenser was aware of the value of good information, and he appreciated the importance of a man who would happily bring him news. The under-bottler from the Painted Chamber was an expensive ally, but his reports were worth all the money Sir Hugh lavished on him. He paid the man now with twenty shillings, a small fortune, but one that the man's detailed account fully justified.

'I am grateful to you, my friend,' he said as he passed the money over. 'Let me know more about the king's mood when you can.'

As the under-bottler left, Sir Hugh stood and rubbed at his forehead. The pressure was unrelenting, and the sensation of having his head in a vice was growing in virulence daily. There was so much for him to do, so much to plan, if he were to be safe. One thing was certain – his new spy was only as good as Despenser's star. If his position began to wane, the under-bottler would not come to advise him. He would be seeking his next patron, rather. So when the fellow stopped responding to Despenser's requests, he might have to be taught a lesson at a dagger's point.

One thing was clear, though. If the queen and Mortimer

had become so close that even a cloth-headed fool like Bishop Stapledon could spot it, the matter was more serious than he had realised. That being so, he might have to plan differently, for that could well mean that the queen and the traitor were already so far advanced in their plots that they didn't care whether the bishop, and therefore the king, were to learn of them. Although there was the other possibility: that the queen had never expected or intended that the bishop should return safely to England. If that was so, then perhaps her devious little mind had been unsettled from its smooth road, and the result could be that the whole of her carefully laid scheme might be thrown into disarray. Although Sir Hugh had no idea how to effect that desirable outcome.

But it might not be her plan at all. Perhaps it was all conceived by Mortimer and the French king. Neither of them was a friend to Sir Hugh, of course, but if a man was being stalked by enemies, it was best to know which adversary was nearest. Was it possible that the bishop himself was also allying himself to the queen? If all the others in France had moved to support her, perhaps the bishop too had . . .

No. That was impossible. The haughty little bitch would never consider him as a friend. The bishop had seen to it that she had lost all power and influence at court, removing from her all her estates and revenues as soon as war with the French began last year. The result had been a shameful curtailing of her life and freedom, even the removal of her children so that she might not pollute their minds with nonsense about the French. She would only ever plot to see Bishop Walter destroyed, never *with* him.

Not that the others with the bishop were similarly free of suspicion. The Keeper of the King's Peace he had loathed for some time, as he had Simon Puttock, and the other knight, the sometime coroner Sir Richard de Welles, was an unknown quantity but appeared to be quite friendly with the other two.

Sir Baldwin de Furnshill, he knew, had been moderately well regarded by the queen before her embassy to France. It would be hardly a surprise if he and she had further cemented their friendship while together in Paris. And Sir Baldwin had been a thorn in Sir Hugh's side for at least a year.

Puttock was a lesser threat. He was only a peasant, when all was said and done. He was owned by Sir Hugh de Courtenay, Baron of Devon, and could easily be neutralised. In fact he might well already have been – Despenser's men had bullied him earlier this year. If he tried to do anything to harm Sir Hugh, he would find that there were other problems a wealthy man could bring to bear on him. Still, a fellow with family and no money could be turned into a useful asset.

After all, this Puttock was a known element. Perhaps Sir Hugh should have him brought here to discuss French affairs in private.

Abbeyford Woods, south of Jacobstowe

Bill Lark bent his head and rested on his staff as the verdicts were announced.

Much more of this and he'd be falling asleep while standing, he reckoned. The coroner had been as quick as he could be, admittedly, but the number of bodies to be gathered, studied, stripped naked and rolled over and over before the jury were so many that the matter had taken the best part of the day. And now that the inquest was done, there was the additional work of loading all the bodies on a cart to take them to the little graveyard, where they could be given a decent burial; seeing to the vigil while they were held before the altar; and of course collecting of the money the coroner had imposed as fines on the community for the infringement of the King's Peace.

'Bailiff, I am sorry that the vill has to suffer this,' the coroner said quietly, walking up to join Bill. 'I had no choice.'

'I understand.' And he did. The deodand was a fine imposed to the value of the murder weapon, and in a case like this, where many weapons had been used, each must be separately accounted for the injuries done to each person. Although the coroner had managed to reduce the fines a little by ignoring some of those wounds that would not have killed, he was duty bound to include all those that appeared to be more serious. The other fine, the murdrum, must be imposed where the victims were not known, and since none of these was known to any about here, the full amount must be demanded of the people of the hundred.

'We are no nearer learning who could have done this,' the coroner said.

The bailiff could not argue with that. 'We'll probably never know. Some outlaws are like that. They arrive in an area, commit a few crimes, and then move on to find better pickings elsewhere. It's likely we'll never see them.'

It was all too true. The sort of men who came and committed this type of crime were not locals. It had not been carried out by inexperienced fighters; these victims had been killed by professionals. In any case, in Bill's experience, once a coroner had pronounced on a death, that was an end to the matter. No coroner would put himself out too much – and without the support even of a coroner, there was little if anything that Bill could himself do. So he would probably never learn more about these deaths. They would be remembered by those who lived here for some years and then forgotten. Perhaps someone might pass by asking about some folks who had disappeared, but in the absence of anything to say who these victims were, no one would ever know, in all likelihood, whether their missing father or husband was lying in a grave at Jacobstowe with the rest of this party or not.

The coroner was scowling at the bodies as they were collected and slung on to the carts. 'What of the people in the area? I find it hard to imagine that no one saw or heard anyone.'

'They'd have been sleeping and—'

'*Pig shit!* You mean to tell me that a force large enough to kill these men could have ridden away from here without anyone noticing? Do you think I look that much of a fool?'

'No, Coroner, but you have to understand that we're so far apart here, many of us, that a force could have ridden between houses and gone without anyone hearing, if they were careful.'

The coroner turned away. 'They'd have had to go up that road north or south. There's no track east or west – not nearby. How far north could they have gone?'

'They didn't get to Jacobstowe, I know that much.'

'Then they turned off before that, unless they went south. But south would mean getting closer to Oakhampton,' the coroner mused.

'Why are you so troubled by them? They're someone else's problem now,' Bill said.

Sir Peregrine looked at him. 'No, man. They are *our* problem. They committed murder here, and I'll catch them if I can. I don't give a farthing for the souls of men who slaughter women and children. If I could do anything that would capture them, I'd do it.'

'We don't even know who many of them were,' Bill muttered. 'Just some monks and their guards – I suppose we can learn their names. But the others?'

There was a clattering, thundering noise from behind them, and Bill turned to see a cart approaching. In the back were five bodies. The two on the top were the children whom they had discovered under the blanket. He thought of his own little Ant as he looked at the two small figures rolling and jerking in the back of the cart. The coroner had seemed the same as all the others, but just now there had been a distinct tone of determination in his voice. It almost made Bill think that he was serious.

'We'll learn them,' Sir Peregrine said firmly. 'I will not have innocents laid to rest in graves without headstones. Damn the souls of those who did this! I want them hanging!'

'Then I'll do what I can,' Bill said. He sighed resignedly. 'Coroner, there is perhaps a little more I can tell you. But 'tis only guesswork on my part.'

Coroner Peregrine listened carefully as Bill spoke of the trampled brambles and blood which lay all about. He walked with Bill and studied the bushes before nodding. 'You know I should fine you for not mentioning all this during my inquest? No matter. I can understand why you didn't.' He stood and gazed about him. 'But I am serious, Lark. I want these bastards, and I will see them swing for this. I rely on you to find them for me. Seek them out. Seek them and let me know where your searches take you. Have your priest write to me at Rougemont Castle in Exeter, and I will come as soon as I may.'

Westminster Palace

Simon was surprised to be asked to go with the man-at-arms, but he had almost finished his meat pie, and he stuffed the remains into his mouth as he stood from the trestle table outside the tavern at the main gate to the palace grounds.

'Who wants me?' he asked through his pie.

'The under-bottler to the Painted Chamber.'

Simon shrugged. Baldwin had left him here to go and make sure that his horse was being cared for. It was typical of the ex-

Templar that he would always see to his horse's well-being before his own. He had once explained his determination to look after his horse. 'If I need to escape an enemy, Simon, I will want a horse that is fed and watered and without lameness.'

It made sense to a man who was a warrior, Simon supposed. For his part, he would always treat his horse as well as he might, because it was the second most expensive item he owned. The only thing that had ever cost him more was his house, and he believed in looking after his investment.

The bottler was one of the most important men in the king's household. He controlled many facets of the house, from the rights and privileges of the servants to the quality and quantity of the food provided, as well as seeing to the comfort of guests. It was a little alarming that his deputy had asked to see Simon, but at least Simon had a clear conscience. There was nothing he could have done in the last hours that could have caused offence, so far as he knew. It was possible that he had done something before, during an earlier visit to the palace, but he felt sure that if that was the case, he would already have learned of his error.

Entering the palace by a door he had not used before, Simon was almost instantly disorientated. The man led him along a narrow passage, up a short flight of stairs, along a corridor, and then down a tower with a tightly curved staircase, before stopping at a door. He took Simon's sword, then knocked, and motioned Simon forward.

Simon opened the door and stopped dead, his eyes freezing on the figure in the middle of the chamber.

'Please, Bailiff. Enter and close the door behind you,' Sir Hugh le Despenser said.

Simon took a step back to leave the room.

'I said to come in.'

Simon's way was barred by the grinning man-at-arms, who held his staff across his body and pushed Simon back inside.

'We wouldn't want any trouble for you at home, would we?' Despenser said. 'Your wife would be upset to know that you were prepared to make more problems for her, I expect.'

The mention of his wife was enough. 'What have you done to my Meg?' Simon demanded, turning and facing the man.

Despenser smiled at his angry response. 'Already this year you have made yourself a sore annoyance to me, and I have repaid you as I might, to remind you and your friend the knight that it is better that you respect your betters rather than make trouble for them. I only wish to ask you some questions, nothing more. Enter and sit down and we can have a sensible talk. Otherwise I shall consider involving myself in your affairs again.'

'What have you done to my wife while I was in France?' Simon said, not moving.

Despenser looked him up and down without any change of expression. He jerked his head towards a stool in front of his table, then walked around to sit behind it on a large leather-covered chair. 'I am waiting.'

Simon licked his lips. The man behind him moved away a little, and Simon turned to watch him, but when the man merely shrugged, Simon decided he might as well make the best of it. He pulled the door closed, leaving the guard outside, and walked to the table, staring down at the man on the other side.

Despenser looked worse than Simon remembered from when he had left the country. Then the strain was already showing. Sir Hugh was terrified that the king might go to France himself and leave him behind, which would without doubt lead to his death. Even were he declared regent in the king's absence, he had made enemies of so many men in the realm that his life would be worthless as soon as Edward's protection was taken away. The only thing that could be worse was that he might try to go with the king to France, for if anything the French king and his nobles were more repelled by Despenser than were the English. He had once turned pirate while exiled from the king's side, and during that time he had deliberately captured and robbed a number of French vessels. It had led to the French declaring that were he ever to set foot on French territory again, he would be executed.

The machinations by which he had attempted to protect himself had led to Sir Hugh becoming almost cadaverous. He had grown pale and haggard. But now, if anything, he was a great deal worse. He sat sucking at his forefinger, and when he took it away, Simon saw that there was a rim of blood where he had bitten too close to the quick.

'You look unwell,' Simon commented with satisfaction.

'I want to know all that happened in France. Especially with the queen.'

Simon stared at him. 'I want to know how my wife is,' he said again.

'I have done nothing to harm or alarm her since you left. The only reason I did anything to her was to keep you under control, Master Puttock. For so long as you remain civil to me, she is safe. But leave me once to think that you are being less than frank, and I shall destroy you. Understand me? I will start by making life intolerable for your wife. So hearken to my words. I want to know all, *all*, that happened in France.'

Simon considered, but he saw no reason to risk antagonising his tormentor further. In all faith, he knew that the man sitting opposite could have him killed in an instant. Likewise, Meg could be injured, or worse, on the whim of Despenser. It would be better, no doubt, to humour him.

He related the story of his journey with Baldwin in the

company of the Earl of Chester, recently created Duke of Aquitaine, as the two of them guarded the royal heir on his way to Paris. He told of the arguments between the queen and Bishop Walter, the murder of a French official, and finally of the flight homewards.

'So the queen actually attempted to threaten the bishop? That is rich!' Despenser laughed. 'I suppose the old cockerel bolted as soon as he realised she was serious? The dotard wouldn't usually recognise a threat until the dagger was pricking his skin!'

'Bishop Walter had one thought and one only,' Simon said coldly. 'To protect the king and the king's son. To do that he knew he must return alive with news of the difficulties in France.'

'And to do so he was prepared to leave the king's son in that nest of vipers? What perspicacity!'

Simon kept his mouth sealed. It was hard to justify the bishop's actions to any who was not there and had not felt the menace. He did not feel the need to remind Despenser that he himself had hidden away in England to protect himself from the same risk.

Sir Hugh set his head to one side. 'What of you, Master Bailiff? You and your friends. Did you and Sir Baldwin form an allegiance to the queen that would overrule your oaths to your king? Have you allied yourselves with her?'

'What do you mean?'

Sir Hugh slowly levered himself to his feet. He rested his hand on his sword hilt, as though to remind Simon that he was unarmed. 'Don't think me a fool, Bailiff. I want the truth from you now. Did you make a new vow to support the queen? Have you and your friends returned to England to bring messages for others and help foment rebellion?'

'I am a mere bailiff. What could I do?'

'You returned here in the company of two knights.'

'Sir Baldwin and Sir Richard acknowledge no master other than their king, and nor will they ever. They remain loyal to King Edward.'

'In truth? That is good, then. Because I would be sorely sad to have to see them killed for dishonour and treachery.'

'It is your own prerogative, you mean?' Simon said snidely.

The sword was out and the point rested on Simon's throat. 'Do not try to insult me, churl!' Despenser hissed. 'I am not of a mind to tolerate your insolence. I am a loyal subject to my king, and I seek to destroy all those who would hurt him. Remember that, if you value your life!'

Simon said nothing, and as Despenser pressed the blade forward slightly, he only stared deep into Despenser's eyes, even as he felt the skin pricked and a small trickle of blood begin to well.

'Bailiff, you have some native courage.'

'It is easy to be brave in the face of cowardice.'

'You think me a coward, then? Interesting.' Sir Hugh took his blade from Simon's throat and gradually moved away. 'I do all in my power to serve the crown, and you think me a coward?'

'Drawing a sword on an unarmed man is courage, then?'

'Living here each day does at least feel like a kind of boldness,' Despenser said more quietly.

Simon felt a fleeting frown crease his brow. The man did seem to be honest – Simon was sure he could hear a low sigh. And no matter what he thought of Sir Hugh, it was true enough that he would himself be appalled to be left here in this great canker of intrigue and politics. If it weren't for the tingling of the scratch under his chin, he could almost have felt some sympathy for the man.

Despenser stood at the window. From there he could see all

along the eastern reach of the river, with its fabulous array of ships, boats and small craft that plied their trade each day. There were some days like this when he would have been happier to be anywhere else than here in Westminster, on the stinking bog that was Thorney Island.

'There are so many places in this land that merit a visit, and here I remain,' he said softly. 'As caged as the lions in the king's menagerie.'

Simon said nothing.

'You have travelled the moors of the Dart – I have never so much as seen them. And yet I have heard so much about them.'

'They reward a visit,' Simon said after a few moments of silence.

'Tavistock is a pleasant town?'

Simon smiled again now. He had thought there must be a purpose to the questioning. Now he thought he saw it. 'Yes. And a rich abbey.'

'Which is presently vacant. There is no abbot,' Sir Hugh said, and turned to face Simon again.

'It has an abbot.'

Despenser made a dismissive gesture. 'A fool who will soon be removed, and then there will be a new one.'

'You think another would be better?'

'There is a good man there. John de Courtenay would make a thoroughly effectual abbot, I am told. This man in place presently is not competent. And he has been shown to be guilty of necromancy.'

'No. He has been shown to have visited a man who was capable in those arts,' Simon corrected him.

'You quibble. You heard that he has robbed the abbey too?'

'That is unproven, and I believe unfounded. I do not believe it.'

'John de Courtenay would be more safe at the helm of a great institution like Tavistock.'

'Clearly you haven't met the man,' Simon said with a grin.

'You are pathetic. Be gone!'

'My wife is well?'

'Why should she not be? Do you think I'd take a peasant woman for my own? I have not even told my men to use her for themselves. But you should remember this, Bailiff. My men are still in Devon, and if I hear that you have been false to your king – or to me – you will be ruined, you and your family, because my anger will know no bounds. Be careful.'

Chapter Five

Abbeyford

In his house, Hoppon grunted as he heaved on the rope. It was attached by a metal hook to the six-foot length of tree trunk he was hauling across the floor to the little area of clay where he had his fire. The old trunk was almost burned through.

There were some who laughed at him for this. Aye, they laughed, the pricks. They thought bringing in logs this size was stupid, that it took too much effort. Well, they were the fools. It took an age to slice a log into short rounds, and when he'd done it in the past, they burned through on all sides. This way, the log burned from one end only, and it lasted him longer. He'd carry on with his fires like this. It was how his old man had shown him to build a fire, and if it was good enough for him, it was good enough for Hoppon too.

He had the log in now, and kicked it slightly until it rolled into the hearth as he wanted. Then he settled down, sitting on the trunk, and watched as the sparks began to fly again.

They laughed at him. The children laughed to see his anguished gait, hobbling along in the manner that had given him his name. Aye, they laughed often enough, but some had learned to laugh from a distance. He had caught a lad once, and managed two good swings of his staff at the little bastard's backside before the bratchet had escaped his wrath. He'd think again before he made fun of Hoppon.

That leg was agony much of the time. He had been at his

master's manor, trying to rescue the animals, when a spar from the roof had fallen on him and trapped him. Christ Jesus, the pain! He still felt it. The sudden eruption of sparks, and then the baulk of timber falling, and he'd put his hands over his head, the fool, as though that could help him, and it had crashed into his back, sending him sprawling. A searing, wrenching pain at his shoulder, and then the feeling of unutterably exquisite burning as the red-hot embers from the spar scorched off his hose and began to cook his leg. That smell! That torture! Sweet Mother of Christ, but there was nothing to equal it. He had felt as though he must die just from the feel. It was as though his heart was swelling ready to burst with the torment. His mind must not be able to cope. If he had possessed a knife or axe, he would have cut his leg from his body, not from a belief that he might be able to escape, but purely because it would mean that he could leave this ruined, burned appendage behind, as well as the agony.

He had screamed so loudly that one of the men outside said they thought it was a horse whinnying in terror, but the horses were all out already. And then someone saw him in there, and three men ran in to lever the beam aside and drag him out, still screaming.

Afterwards, his master had told him he was grateful. It was as he lay on the dewy grass, knowing only the horror of what his leg had become, while he stared at the thing that had once been a part of him, that the man came out and said he was grateful. His destrier had lived. How Hoppon had hated that beast. And his master. For them he was ruined. His leg would never heal again. The flesh was burned away. The little that remained was withered for ever.

There had been enormous pleasure for him when he had heard that the destrier had reared in the river and drowned them both. That had been a day of joy for Hoppon.

Westminster Palace

Sir Hugh le Despenser lay back in his bed, his wife at his side but carefully not touching. He and Eleanor had not been intimate for some while now. Perhaps he should demand the renewal of the marriage debt, but for many weeks he hadn't felt the urge. It was as though the worries about the land, the fears about the queen and Mortimer, had conspired to kill off his natural desires.

Perhaps the cause was more because of Eleanor. It could have been the way she looked at him ever since the moment some weeks ago when he and she had fallen out. So much had gone wrong this year. First how the queen had been treated after the beginnings of the war with France, and then the way that she had been sent to France to negotiate with her brother. Nothing seemed to have gone well since those first moments of dispute. Eleanor had become cold, indifferent and argumentative, and in response Hugh had grown angry.

There was so much to occupy him. Some said that he was too unkind, that his thoughts were only ever of his own position, but that wasn't true. Not entirely. No, he would also spend much time trying to see how to serve his king.

The disastrous matters at Tavistock Abbey were just one example of the turmoil that was rending the kingdom, and on which his mind was constantly bent. Tavistock was hardly a bulwark in the defensive ring about the coast. Despenser was only too well aware of the defences at sea, having himself turned pirate for a short while five years ago. Mortimer could, indeed might, raise an army without any interference from the king or Despenser. There was nothing they could do – all their spies had been captured in recent months, and the intelligence they received tended to rely on the travellers from France who stopped at Canterbury. Prior

Henry Eastrey of Christ Church sifted their stories and sent on anything that seemed germane. But the ships in the king's navy could, and would, hopefully, block any possible invasion from the east. The Cinque Ports were full of ships that could protect the realm from attack.

But a fleet that avoided them and tried to land elsewhere, that was a genuine risk. And if it were able to make its way to the Devon coast, that would be a true disaster. For the lands there had been under the control of the queen, and many of her people were still angry at the way she had been treated – her household disbanded, her knights sent to France or arrested, her children taken away from her, her revenues and estates sequestrated, her movements restricted, and even her personal seal confiscated to prevent secret communication with anyone. Those who felt loyalty to her had been outraged that her royal person could be so demeaned.

There was another aspect, though. Tavistock had been a powerful influence in the West Country under the last abbot, Robert Champeaux. But now he was dead, and for the present, while there was a debate about who should rule the place, the sole benefit of the abbey lay in the money it was producing. While the abbacy was vacant, the abbey must pay a fine each year to the king. The payment was on its way now, Despenser knew. And the money would be useful. Because with it, he hoped to persuade Robert Busse to stand down as abbot, and allow John de Courtenay to take over unchallenged.

Politics. Politics. In the realm, politicking caused grief and hardship to many. And yet he would swear that the little, local politics of a place like Tavistock were more cruel, poignant and dangerous. National politics might affect many people, but down at Tavistock the machinations of the brother monks were threatening the kingdom, because until Sir Hugh could be sure that the fools down there were stable and settled, he must worry all the while that Mortimer's fleet could round Kent and sail all the way to Devon. With Tavistock still empty of an abbot, Hainault's mercenaries could sweep up the Tamar to Exeter, that hotbed of malcontents and rebels, and thence, gathering support as they came, ride for London. It would be simple if they were unopposed at the outset, and the easier their journey from the West Country, the quicker would be the collapse of any support for the king. And for Sir Hugh le Despenser.

Yes. All hinged upon Tavistock. Brother Robert Busse was the abbot-elect, but Brother John de Courtenay was the more malleable. With him in position, it would be easier to ensure that the abbey went on a stronger defensive footing and served to protect the coast. And that would make the rest of the kingdom so much more safe.

From bloody Puttock's words, he believed that Busse was the better man, damn his eyes! He was independent, which was why Sir Hugh distrusted him. Better to have a reliable man like de Courtenay.

And then an idea began to form in Sir Hugh's head. The initial concept was there before him, of course. It involved the money, and the attempt to subvert the abbot-elect by bribing him and then forcing him to become less independent by blackmailing him. That might still work – but if it failed, there was now this second string to his bow. Simon Puttock, the honourable, decent supporter of Busse. Perhaps he could help. Or his wife . . .

Didn't he have a daughter?

Third Saturday following the Feast of the Archangel Michael*

The road they had taken was the same they used the last time that they left Westminster to return to Devon, and Simon was fretful until he at last felt that the looming presence of the king's palace was out of sight behind him.

'You look worried, Simon,' Sir Richard said.

He was sitting back in his saddle, legs thrust forwards, rolling with his mount's gait, and with a loaf of heavy bread made from rye and wheat in one hand, while in his other he grasped the neck of his wine skin. His eyes were as shrewd as ever, but Simon knew that the main characteristic in them was the gleam of innate kindness and generosity.

'I want to be as far from the place as possible. You know, Coroner, I feel just now that I have been in danger and hunted for almost all this year. When we left here to go to France with the queen, I was anxious. When I returned with her son, I was fearful. Coming back through France was terrifying, knowing that all the while there were men who sought the destruction of my lord bishop Walter, and now, now I feel sure that Sir Hugh le Despenser has me in the sights of a crossbow.'

'You don't like that man – but that's natural enough. Not many do.' The Coroner nodded to himself, upending his skin and wiping his beard with the back of his hand.

Simon shook his head. 'He called me to his chamber two days ago.'

'What?' Baldwin asked, startled by this revelation. 'Why did you not tell us, Simon?'

'For what purpose? If I told you, it would only give you

**19 October 1325

more to be worried about. And I preferred not to explain the conversation to Bishop Walter.'

'Well, the good bishop is at his home on Straunde now,' Baldwin said. 'So tell us: what did the man want from you?'

Simon touched the nick on his throat where Despenser's sword had scratched him. 'He wanted to know what happened in France – in detail. He did not care about much else, but he was amused to hear how we all fled the French court, and then he suggested to me that we three were turncoats and supporters of the queen. That we might renounce our vows to the king!'

'Is that all?' Baldwin asked.

'No. He made more threats against me and my family,' Simon said. The man's words were still ringing in his ears. Even when he slept, he swore he could hear Despenser's voice. 'The man will not be satisfied until he sees my body dangling.'

'He is not a natural leader of men, I would think,' Sir Richard said with deliberation. He bit off a massive chunk of bread and chewed for a few moments. 'I would hope that he will soon fall from his horse and receive a buffet on the head that slows down his ability to irritate others for a while.'

Baldwin was not sure that Providence would aid the realm so swiftly. 'The man deserves to be hanged and quartered for all the harm he has done to the kingdom. It is intolerable that he continues to persecute Simon and others.'

'At least we will soon be far enough even from him to be secure,' the coroner said, satisfied with the thought.

'I wish that were true,' Simon said quietly. 'Sadly, I don't think it is. He is a fierce enemy. He has already bought my house from under me.'

'Eh?' Sir Richard looked over at him, spraying breadcrumbs.

'He bought my house's lease. I had it for a seven-year term, and missed the most recent payment because I was in France with the queen. So Despenser bought it.'

'Why? Surely he has no need of a house such as yours,' the coroner said.

Simon smiled. Sir Richard had never been to visit him at his house, but the man would be fully aware of the nature of a stolid peasant's home compared with the kind of fine property that Despenser was more used to. 'You're right. My farm is only a good-sized longhouse with a small solar. But Despenser didn't take it because he wanted to live in it himself. It was much more to do with his desire to show me that he is my superior in every way, I think. He wanted to stamp out any rebelliousness to his will that might have remained in me. He sent a man to evict my wife, and it was the purest chance that I had returned before he could succeed. With Baldwin's help, we caught the man and had him arrested for a while by the bishop.'

'So you still have the house?' Sir Richard asked.

'No. We were forced out. I delayed matters a little by having a churchman take it, but I don't know whether he's still there or not. My wife should have left and gone to our old home near Sandford.'

'Sandford?' the coroner said with a frown.

'It's also known as Rookford. A small hamlet north of Crediton,' Simon explained. 'It is a good area. Rich red soil, good pastures, and some of the best ciders in the kingdom.'

'You have some land there?'

'Oh, yes. We have enough to live on. And perhaps my wife and I can live there quietly, away from the politics in that place,' he added, jerking a thumb back over his shoulder.

Jacobstowe

Bill woke with a head that itched like a whole pack of hounds with fleas. He scratched at it with a rueful expression, but it made little difference.

'It'll be the midges,' his wife said without sympathy.

'Agnes, you have a knack for stating the blasted obvious,' he muttered.

'Well, I didn't tell you to go out there and wait with the bodies, and I didn't tell you to go out again yesterday to search for only you know what,' his wife replied tartly. 'What do you want from me? Sympathy? Faith, man, you should be so lucky. If you will go out at night when it's been raining for so many evenings, what do you expect?'

He grunted and clambered to his feet. 'I told you what the coroner said, woman. If we can only find the men who were responsible, perhaps we can visit some sort of justice on them.'

'Oh, aye. And while you're doing that, what about me and Ant?' she asked.

Her back was to him, but he could hear the softness of a sob in her voice as she spoke. She was tearing up leaves for the pottage, and now he saw that she was treating them with more violence than usual. 'Agnes, woman, stop that for a moment,' he said, pulling on a shirt and walking to her. He slipped his arms about her waist, resting his head on her shoulder.

'It's all right for you, Bill Lark. You go off and search for these murderers, and you have a purpose in life, don't you? But what of me? I am expected to wait here until you come home, but what if you don't? You can wander about the place, and if you are hurt I have to nurse you. If you die, you rest – but what of us? We will be wasted. Me, a widow, Ant an orphan. Would you see us destitute?'

'Woman, woman, woman, calm yourself,' he said

soothingly as she sobbed, open mouthed but quiet. 'Be easy. Look, I will not be getting myself into any trouble. I shall be as careful as I may be, I swear. But I want to know who it was killed those people. I cannot have travellers slaughtered as they come past here, can I? Even the coroner wants to find these men. I've never heard of a coroner so keen to do his job.'

She could not laugh with him. There had never been a murder like this before in their little parish. 'You are only to be bailiff until Michaelmas, Bill. Don't go getting yourself killed between now and then just to find justice for people you never even met!'

'I won't. Now, is there any bread? I want something to eat. I have to walk to Hoppon's.'

'Why won't you listen to me? You are to wander about the place trying to find these men, but if you do, what then? If you get them all, do you think they'll see you walking up to them and greet you politely? Bill, you're likely to be killed!'

'I will be safe, don't worry.'

'Are you really so stubborn and stupid that you believe that?' she had demanded, her eyes streaming.

It was an angry Bill Lark who left later. She had made him feel inadequate, as though he didn't care about her and Ant, and that wasn't true. He adored them both. However, he had responsibilities to the vill as well. And nineteen people had been killed here. He wasn't happy to let that rest. If there was a possibility that he could help track them down, he should. In a strange way, he felt that the coroner's dedication to the truth had sparked his own.

The distance to Hoppon's little holding was short enough. Bill walked there chewing his bread with a dry mouth.

His wife was right in one thing: for most crimes there was no need to find the actual guilty party. The most important thing was that justice was seen to be exercised. In a little hamlet like this one, it was easy to find someone. Bill had heard at the court at Oakhampton that a full third of all the men accused of crimes were strangers to the area. Some reckoned that this was mere proof of the fact that strangers were unreliable, dangerous folk, and it was better that all foreigners should be watched carefully. Others, like Bill, thought that it was more proof of the fact that when there was a harvest or the need of a sturdy fellow to help with the ploughing, only a fool would seek to determine that the man best suited to the job was sadly the one who must hang for the felony he committed a while ago. If a good worker got drunk and accidentally killed a fellow in hot blood, it was better that he remained for the good of the community than that he was arrested and slain. Better to find some other likely fellow who was not so valuable to the hundred.

There was logic to this process. Logic and hard-headed rational thinking. It was the common sense of a small community that still remembered the years of famine. Yet there was still a part of Bill's soul that rebelled at the idea.

However, in this matter, he had a calm heart and a cool head. The men who waylaid that group of travellers were not from his vill. Of that he was quite sure. There were not the people there who were capable of killing so many, and not enough who would have been prepared to see children slaughtered. No, this was no local gang.

'Hoppon! God give you a good day.'

'God speed, Bailiff.'

'The weather seems to have warmed a little.'

'Aye. Could you drink a pot of ale?'

'A cider would warm the heart more, I think.'

'Ah! I have some just inside.'

Bill sat on a log near the door. Hoppon was lame. His leg was very badly crippled, but that did not affect his strength. He tended to drag trunks whole to his door. Here he would slash the branches away, taking them indoors immediately, while the trunks were left under the eaves to dry. Bill had seen seven here in a heap before now. When they were a full year old, they would be inspected and roughly shaped, if they were needed for building, or hauled inside, where they would be set on the fire, gradually being pushed into it as they burned.

Hoppon's dog Tab came to Bill's side and thrust his nose into his hand, lifting his head to make Bill's hand fall down the dog's sleek skull and stroke him. 'You're no fool, eh, Tab?'

'So, Bailiff,' Hoppon said as he returned, a jug in his hand, cups balanced on top. He set down his crutch, hopped nearer and sat back with a grunt. 'What do you need?'

'You know that, Hoppon. We still need to find the men who did it.'

'Ach, what good will it do us? They won't be punished, not if I'm a judge. They'll not suffer, but we will. We'll have to pay for their crimes again, paying for the court to listen to the case.'

'Hoppon, you're all alone up here, aren't you?' Bill said, looking about him as though for the first time.

'You know I am.'

'And I'm on the edge of the vill too. Even men who live with their families in the middle of Jacobstowe, they still have only a few homesteads about them, eh?'

'Aye. What of it?'

'These men were happy enough to kill all those men and women. And the children, Hoppon.' Bill's eye lighted on Tab at his side. The dog's eyes showed their whites as he gazed up at the bailiff. 'They even killed a bitch and her whelp. Do you think you or I or any other could stand against such a force? No. So should we accept that, and wait until they come here and kill you and me, maybe my little Ant, rape my Agnes, and knock Tab on the head? You think we ought to do that?'

Hoppon growled deep in his throat, but his eyes wouldn't meet Bill's. 'You know that'd be wrong. I couldn't let that happen.'

'If we don't stand up to these bastards, we may as well throw them all our families and belongings, Hoppon.'

Hoppon passed him a cider cup, and drank deeply from his own, still not meeting Bill's gaze. 'You think I'm a coward?'

'No. You had your leg harmed in that fire, Hoppon. I know that well, just as do all the others here. Your courage isn't doubted by me, old friend.'

'What do you want me to do? I didn't see them. Nor did anyone.' Hoppon was truculent, but Bill was unsure why. Unless he felt guilt at not admitting to knowing something. That was something Bill felt he had to press.

'Hoppon, I've been all the way to Oakhampton, asking all whether they heard anything that night. No one did, so they say. These men didn't go north past Jacobstowe itself. I've been west from the road too, but there's no sign of people going that way. The only place they could have gone is here. Right by you.'

'You say I heard them?'

'You are a good fellow. I know you as well as I know any man in this vill. And I know you have a dog there.'

'What of him?'

'He has the ears of a bat, Hoppon. He would hear a mouse fart in the woods.'

Hoppon grinned a little at that. 'He is a good guard.'

'How many were there, Hoppon? Which way did they go?'

Now Hoppon met Bill's gaze at last. He glowered at him. 'What's the point, Bill? If we find out who they were, the most likely thing is, you and me'll be found hanging by our heels from the tallest oak in Abbeyford. That what you want? What of Agnes then?'

'And if we don't, they'll think they can kill, rob or rape any one of the folk about here. Do you want to live in fear all your life, Hoppon?'

'I've never lived in fear, Bill. Never will.' And then he shook his head. 'Ach, what's the point? You're determined to see yourself killed, are you? Well, it was Tab. He woke up and woke me too. Heard something. I didn't. Thought it was a ghost at first. Then I heard the horse neigh. It came up from Abbeyford, then east up behind my place.'

'How many?'

'I'd reckon on fifteen or so. No more. But I heard them, true enough. There were weapons rattling all the way.'

'And you know who led them?'

Hoppon nodded, but then he turned away. 'But you'll not hear the devil's name from me.'

Chapter Six

Barnstaple, north coast of Devon

Roger had made good time in his march northwards.

In part he reckoned it was due to the grim realities of life on the road. The sight of the dead travellers had been a great shock to him, and urged him on to greater efforts in order to reach his destination. The idea of being caught himself out in the open was enough to lend greater urgency to his pace. There were too many who were willing to prey on men who passed by, and Roger had no wish to be another victim.

The sights and sounds of the sea were like a triacleur's potion to him. They invigorated him. The cries of the gulls, the steady slap and wash of the waves, the odour of fish and seaweed, all hit him like a woman's touch. They soothed and eased, they caressed his very soul. Here, he thought, he could gain some sort of work to keep his body and spirit healthful.

But when he reached the town, it was soon clear that all his efforts were in vain. He had gone to the docks as soon as he arrived, keeping hold of his meagre reserves with great care; if he could find a berth on a ship, he could save the money. Any ship's master would feed his sailors, and Roger would be able to hoard his cash.

It was not going to happen, though. He could understand that now, as he walked along the narrow streets of the port, jealously eyeing the shop-boards. They all had an enticing array of goods for sale, and in the end he was forced to succumb to the urgent demands of his belly. He bought an egg, and pierced both ends before sucking it dry. After that he felt an increased hunger, though, rather than a diminution. He had to buy a small loaf of bread and a little cheese, which he ate sitting on the harbour wall, staring out to sea. All the ships that arrived he watched avidly, and as soon as a ship was docked, he wandered over to speak with the master. But each time he was eyed with suspicion, and there would be a shaking of the head and sidelong glances until he left.

He knew what it was, of course. The sailors up here might well go as far as Chatham or London, by sailing about the bottom of the land and up the Thames, but although they would travel far and wide, they were all wary of a man whose accent they couldn't recognise. Oh, a man from Ilfracombe, or one who'd been brought up by the sea at Bude, even, would be all right, but Roger's accent was from the south of the shire, and there was no one up here who would trust him. He was foreign, and no shipmaster liked a foreigner on his ship. Foreigners were alien, and might bring bad luck to a voyage.

It was possible, he considered, that he might be able to get a post on another ship – perhaps a little fishing boat, or one of the small ferries that plied their trade across the mouth of the river – but that was not what he wanted. He wished for the escape that the broad, wide seas offered a man. Escape from the memories of war and disaster.

By the end of the second day, he was half ready to give up. His resources were reducing too quickly in this expensive town, and if he kept on spending at this rate, he would soon have nothing. And then he'd have to resort to some other means of finding money. Although how was a different matter. If he wanted to sail, he wondered whether he should find a larger port, a place like Bristol, perhaps, where there was a real city and sailors travelling all around the country. Except there was no telling whether he would be any more popular there than he had been here. He could go to London. There, so he had heard, the people were used to men from all over. They had Dutchmen, Germans, French, even some Galicians and Savoyards. So long as he didn't end up on a Genoese slave galley, he should be able to find a position there. But London was hundreds of miles away.

He began to wonder whether he would be best off returning to Plymouth. Or maybe Dartmouth?

*Third Sunday following the Feast of the Archangel Michael**

Sampford Chapple

It had taken him more than a little while to find the tracks.

The idea that the men would have ridden past Hoppon's house so close showed that either they were foolish, or they were supremely confident in their power and safety. They had passed within a matter of yards of the house. It would have been a miracle if Hoppon's dog *hadn't* started barking in defence.

Bill Lark bent as he followed the trail. It was his own fault, and he blamed himself entirely. The trail must have been fine on the first days after the murders, and if he had been a little more diligent, he would have found it. There were plenty of men, after all, and a few carts, and their tracks were clear enough now he was here. What had happened seemed to be that they had ridden over a large swathe of brambles, and even where the carts had rolled, the brambles had sprung back up again by the time he had gone to seek the trail. He'd simply ridden past without seeing the signs. Many would. Many had.

*20 October 1325

But he was angry with himself. He shouldn't have done so. He prided himself on his abilities as a tracker and hunter, and now he had failed so utterly on the first occasion when it mattered. And to lose the trail of so many men . . .

It was as he was remonstrating with himself that he saw another group of tracks. Here there were only one or two pairs of boot prints and a solitary little cart, he reckoned. He could not be certain after so long. Yet although the marks joined up with the main mess, coming straight from the travellers' camp, they crossed over the main group of prints and continued up towards the ancient track in the middle of the woods. That was interesting. That old path was known only by the most local fellows. Rough now, overgrown, it was used as a private route by those who had a desire for stealth or secrecy.

No matter to him, though. The people who had gone up there were nothing to do with the raiders. Otherwise their paths would converge rather than merely cross. Whoever they were, their route took them along the lane past Shilstone, then over to Swanstone, and past it towards Sampford Courtenay.

He set off again. The trail here was easy to follow. There was more mud, and even where the grass had sprung up again, he could see the imprints of hoofs and wheels. The way took him down into the valley, and then up the other side, heading almost towards North Tawton, but then south-east to skirt around the town, and instead he found himself continuing eastwards on the old lane towards Bow.

Here the way was more difficult. The lane was much more busy than the little byways he had followed up until now, and if it weren't for a chance meeting with an old peasant who lived right beside the road, he would have found the trail dead.

'Master, God speed,' he said when he saw the peasant at his garden.

'God give you a good day,' the old man said affably, his

grizzled beard covering his face so effectively that Bill wasn't sure whether he smiled or not. He said his name was John Pasmere.

'What is this place called, friend?'

'Well, this is Itton Moor. Where do you want to go? No one comes here by choice!'

'Maybe you can aid me. I am not lost, but I'm trying to follow the marks of some men who passed by here some nights ago,' Bill said, and introduced himself.

'Aye? You want the men who rode past a week ago, eh?' Any apparent affability had fled. 'Why so, master?'

'I have good reasons, friend. Why?'

'They came from near Bow. They often do.'

'Who are they?'

The old man took his time to peer up the way Bill had come, then studied the landscape all about them before spitting into the roadway. 'Sir Robert of Traci, that's who it is. Him and his men. Friend, you be warned. There's no good will come of seeking them. No good to you, leastways.'

Jacobstowe

Agnes set the baby down again and sighed as she put her hands on her hips and rubbed. This year was proving to be more challenging than any other, and all because her husband had been made bailiff. It was infuriating.

She had always wanted him to get on, of course, and when he had won the post she'd been delighted – for him and for the family. It meant recognition, and with that there might be some potential for advancement in the future. He deserved it. They all did.

Agnes Lark was not the same as other peasants in the area. She had been born out of wedlock, and her mother flatly refused to say who her father was, even when questioned in court. That must have been a daunting experience, with the lord and his steward asking questions, and a clerk making sarcastic comments in the background all the while as he noted down the details of her incontinence, but her mother would not divulge her secret, no matter what was said or threatened. So in the end *her* father was fined the leyrwite for the birth of Agnes outside of marriage.

It was a shameful affair, of course. But the intransigence of her mother had given Agnes the greatest gift: freedom. Whereas her mother and all the rest of her family were villeins, no one could prove that Agnes was the daughter of a serf, and so the law had to assume that she was the daughter of a free man. The law was clear that if there was any doubt, a child must be assumed to be free, for there could be no greater injustice than to force a child born to a free man to a life of servility. And Agnes was thus freed.

Bill Lark had been a man she saw occasionally. When he asked her to marry him the first time, it had shocked her, and she had refused him curtly, but then he had renewed his suit, and as he asked her so often, it became easier for her to start to think of him as a potential partner. And gradually her feelings for him began to slide into affection.

They had been married now for almost three years. The Ant was the first proof of their love, and she was sure that there would be more before long. Hopefully they would be able to increase their lands and start to buy in more livestock. That was her hope, because there was money to be made from the rich pastures about here. Bill wasn't convinced yet, but Agnes was sure that she'd be able to persuade him, given time.

Where was he, though? He had left early in the morning, saying he was going to try to follow the trail of the killers, and she had no idea whether he would be home again today, or whether he was going to be missing for a day or more. It was maddening, especially since there was all the clearing to do in the little vegetable plot and the preparation of the soil for the next sowing, as well as looking after their baby.

Anthony hiccuped and she quickly picked him up, wiping his mouth and setting him over her shoulder while patting his back. He was still after a few moments, and she could set him down again in the little crib Bill had made. She pulled the scraps of material up over him, cooing softly at him and gentling him until he was asleep again.

Outside, the light was fading already. It was obvious enough that her husband was not going to return for some little while. He would avoid travelling at night, same as any would. She would have to close everything up and just hope and pray that all was well with him. She sighed, rubbed at her flanks one last time, and went outside to begin her nightly chores, putting the door against the chicken's box, seeing to the pigs in the pen, and making sure all was locked up before returning to her own door, where she stood a moment staring out at the sun as it finally sank down behind the trees on the hills north and west.

She prayed that her man would be safe.

Barnstaple

It was no good. He had done his best. Now Roger couldn't even remember the faces of all the men whom he had stopped and asked for work. One, he recalled, had had an empty eye socket and a beard that was entirely white, apart from a darker stain at the edges of his mouth. The sight was odd enough to make Roger stare at first, until he saw the old sailor pick up a rope and begin to work on it, pausing only to thrust it into his mouth. The tar was the cause of the staining, he realised.

That was the only face he remembered now, as he stood on the harbour wall staring longingly out to sea. There was a slight inshore breeze, which was throwing some spray into his face, and when he closed his eyes, he could sense it like icy darts flung at his cheeks. The way the fresh wind tore at his clothing and tugged his hair made him feel alive again, as though his feet were about to shift with the roll of the decking that should have been there.

But there was no decking. There was no ship. All the mariners he had spoken with had refused him with as much alacrity as a master rejecting the pleas of an abjurer. He was foreign, unwanted, distrusted. There was nothing else for him to do.

He threw one last glance out to sea, to the grey roiling waters with the white tops, and shivered as though someone had walked over his grave. There was an odd sensation in his belly and bowels; it felt as though God had sent him a warning that he would find no peace if he turned away and sought his fortune elsewhere.

'What else would you have me do?' he muttered. 'Starve to death up here?'

With a firm rejection of the northern seas, he set his shoulders and began the long march southwards. Plymouth had been no good to him, but perhaps he would be luckier in Dartmouth. He would try it.

Fourth Thursday after the Feast of the Archangel Michael*

Exeter, Devon

They arrived at the gate in a flurry of noise and excitement as night was falling.

At first Simon and Sir Richard had been happy enough to

---

*24 October 1325

keep at the gentle trot that had been enough to bring them over the broad plains east of the city. Wolf, too, looked as though he would appreciate a more sedate promenade, ideally with opportunities to investigate the various holes that dotted the hedges and walls about here, but Baldwin would have none of it.

'We've made excellent time to get here so quickly,' he declared, and lashed the flanks of his mount, making the beast rear. 'Come, fellows! Let us hasten to my home and rest there!'

'Baldwin!' Simon protested. 'It'll be dark before we get even remotely close to your home. It is now nearly sunset. We shall have to stay in Exeter the night.'

Baldwin looked ahead at the sun starting to sink down below the hills westwards, then up at the clouds looming overhead, before reluctantly nodding. 'I suppose we'd be unlikely to make it home tonight.'

'Not even a remote chance,' Simon said. He shifted in his saddle. 'We've made excellent time in the last four days. I don't intend to break my neck for the sake of saving a few hours tomorrow morning. Much though I'd like to see Jeanne and Richalda and little Baldwin, not to mention my own family, there's no point flogging our way over the country in the dark.'

'True enough,' Baldwin agreed. The potholes could be lethal in dim light. There was a man last year who had seen a hat floating in a puddle in a roadway, and when he lifted it, discovered the owner was still wearing it. The poor fellow had already drowned. There were so many little holes in the road, and occasionally they would grow more vast as a result of sudden rainfall, and the unwary would die. Even much shallower holes held their own risks, for they could break a horse's leg, throw a rider, and result in the deaths of both.

Sir Richard sucked at his teeth. 'There's usually a room at a little tavern I know,' he said hopefully. 'Excellent ale, better wine, and the food's acceptable too. I'd—'

Simon hastily interrupted. 'I am sure that my daughter would be happy to give us some space in her home.'

'Your daughter?' Sir Richard asked.

'Yes. Edith married on the morrow of the Feast of Gordianus and Epimachus,* and lives now with her man in Exeter,' Simon said. 'Peter is a keen merchant. Was apprenticed, but now he's working with his father, who's a merchant too. With any luck he'll be allowed to enter the Freedom of the City, and then who knows? My grandchildren may be born into the city themselves, and have all the advantages.'

Baldwin smiled at his expression. 'You would like that, wouldn't you, Simon?'

'Like it? The idea is wonderful,' Simon said, a little more sharply than he intended. He tried to cover his tone with a chuckle and an apologetic grin. 'You come from a knightly family, Baldwin. You can't quite appreciate the difference between being born a free man and being born a serf. The idea that my grandchildren will have the benefit of being born in the city is marvellous. I'd never have expected that.'

'Then let's go and see her house,' Sir Richard said. 'Any daughter of yours must be a sight to behold – especially if she has access to her own wine cellar,' he added hopefully.

St Pancras Lane, Exeter

'Are you sure you know where you're going?' Baldwin asked for the third time.

'I have only heard where the house is, I haven't been here before,' Simon said.

---

*11 May

He was rapidly growing alarmed. Edith had told him that her house was down this lane, he was sure. The place, she had said, had a limewashed front, with two large windows and a second storey that hung over the street. It had been the home to her husband Peter when he was younger, but Peter's parents had built a new house further east, nearer the Guild Hall, and had given their older house to Peter and his wife. He was their only son, after all.

'Well if you can't find it,' the coroner said happily, 'there's a very excellent-looking tavern over there. Perhaps they have a room that we could share, eh? God's blood, but a haunch of meat and a jug of good strong Guyennois wine would go down very well. There's a gap there where my belly used to be. My brain's telling me all's well, but my heart reckons some evil bastard's cut my throat.'

'It must be here,' Simon said.

The three were standing near the line of houses on the eastern side of the road, and now he looked up and down again. 'If we don't get there soon, we'll be breaking the curfew.'

'Talk of the devil,' Sir Richard said, jerking his head.

Approaching them with a scowl that would have graced a mastiff was a tall, gangly fellow. He wore a leather jerkin, his hood was over his ears, and his waxed cloak rustled noisily. Yet although he was not the most prepossessing figure, the staff in his hands was a tool to be reckoned with. 'You are out late, masters.'

'Aye,' Sir Richard said. 'We are a little confused in our ways, I think.'

'Confused, eh? Perhaps you'd like me to help unconfuse you?'

Baldwin glanced at the others. They were all cloaked against the chill, and he wondered whether the lad had realised that two of them were knights. Certainly his tone was not respectful. If anything, he sounded peevishly suspicious. Even as Baldwin turned to glance back, he saw the lad was gripping his staff more truculently. It was pointing at Sir Richard – which did, at least, demonstrate to Baldwin that the fellow knew how to spot the most dangerous of the three.

'Friend,' Baldwin said, 'please be calm. This man here is the father of a mistress who lives along this road, but we have not visited her home before. She only married earlier this year.'

'What's her name?'

Simon grunted. 'Edith. She married Peter, son of—'

'The merchant Charles? Oh, that's all right. I can show you the way there,' the lad said. Suddenly he was all affability. 'Sorry, lordings, but there are so many strangers who cause mayhem now. Some little scrotes kicked in a couple of doors two nights ago, and when my mate Phil went to talk to them, they kicked him in too. Poor bastard's up in his bed yet with a broken head. And then there's been all the other murders outside the city too. Don't blame you for coming here to stay the night. Dangerous all over the shire nowadays. There's no law in the land.'

'It was easy enough when we left,' Baldwin said.

'Aye, well, maybe that was a while ago. There are so many men wandering the roads now without any way to support themselves, if you know what I mean.'

As he spoke he took them up the road, along a short lane, and to a large limewashed front.

'This is it,' he said, rapping sharply on the door.

Baldwin and Simon thanked him, and Baldwin gave him a penny for his trouble. 'Who are you?'

'I'm called Gil. Well, my name was Gilbert, but no one calls me that. Thank you, my lord. God speed you all!' the watchman said as he left them, backing away respectfully with a happy smile on his face.

'God speed,' Baldwin said. 'Be careful, my friend. As you say, the streets can be dangerous.'

Simon was not listening. The door had opened, and as soon as it did, he beamed with pleasure to see his daughter.

Edith's face was one of utter shock at first as she registered who was waiting on her doorstep. Then, with a gasped 'Father!' she flung herself into his arms.

Chapter Seven

Ashridge, North Tawton

Sir Peregrine de Barnstaple was grateful for the peace. He sank into the chair with a grunt of contentment and closed his eyes for a moment. This was a pleasant manor, made all the more delightful by the absence of the knight who owned it. Although Sir Peregrine would usually be reluctant to enter the house of any man when the master was away, Sir John of Ashridge was rarely here, and always made it plain that he would be delighted were the coroner to visit when he had need of a roof. And rarely had Sir Peregrine had more need than tonight.

The bodies at Jacobstowe appeared to be the beginning of a small epidemic of corpses. There was the son of a merchant who'd slipped on a stone and entirely accidentally struck his head on the wall surrounding a well; a miller who'd stumbled on his way home from the alehouse, only to fall into his own mill pool and drown; a farrier who had been kicked by the destrier he was trying to shoe – that had been a messy death, with his ribs all crushed and blood everywhere. Yes, all in all there had been a flurry of unpleasant deaths and he would be glad to escape the area shortly.

He had only recently been given his duties. For many years he had been a loyal servant of Sir Hugh de Courtenay, the Baron of Devon, and his family. But Sir Peregrine had been so determined to see to the overthrow of Despenser and the other hangers-on in the king's household that he had eventually made Sir Hugh anxious for his own safety. Although the two men had not fallen out, it became clear in the aftermath of the battle at Boroughbridge that it was not safe for a man to continue to agitate for change. As the bodies of those who had opposed Despenser were tarred and hanged over the gates to all the cities of the realm, while others were quartered and hung in chains at York, London and elsewhere, Sir Peregrine had been forced to leave Sir Hugh's household.

However Sir Hugh was still his friend. He had managed to see to it that Sir Peregrine was given a number of duties that, while not compensating him for his position in Sir Hugh's entourage, would at least give him a means of sustaining himself. And he had made it clear to all the knights in his household that those who sought to continue to be viewed favourably by Sir Hugh would do well to look after Sir Peregrine's interests.

Sir Peregrine ordered food and wine and settled back as a servant boy came in and lighted the fire. Before long, sparks were flying from the tinder and the small sticks set over it, while the lad blew carefully and then began to construct the beginnings of the fire over the top.

It was one of those tasks that always made Sir Peregrine feel intensely sad. This was the sort of duty he would have enjoyed teaching a son. In his life he had met many women, but none had survived to marry him, although many had won his affection. If there was one thing that could have made his life complete, it would have been to be married with a son. A lad he could teach and educate, someone who could take his name and become heir to his little manors and farms. Without an heir, all was pointless.

Later, as the fire roared and he sat before it with a goblet of hot wine and water, feeling the warmth coursing through his veins, he had the call to the next body.

It was to become the most serious murder of his year.

East Gate of Exeter

The man arrived at the gates just in time, cantering as fast as his mount would take him. 'Urgent messages,' he called desperately as he saw the gates beginning to move.

The heavy oak timbers squeaked and groaned, but even as Stephen of Shoreditch wondered whether he would be too late, he saw the man peering around the first of the gates.

No one would want to be left out here, he told himself, riding on, casting about him. There were suburbs in all cities, of course, but few had the atmosphere of lowering danger that this one bore.

Riding up the roadway from Heavitree, he had been happy with the sight of all the well-built houses, but here . . . all was empty, all desolate. No inn or tavern, only a lowering sense of threat. He didn't like it. Nor did he like the fact of the rumours that even king's messengers had been captured and killed within the city walls. The life of a man like him was worth nothing after dark and outside a city's security.

'Let me through. Urgent messages for the castle,' he shouted, and drew back his cloak to show the king's arms on his breast.

'You're too late. Come back in the morning.'

'You want that? You want me to report you to the king? I'll be pleased, porter. Tell him how I was delayed from delivering his messages. You know what the king does to those who thwart him?'

There was a moment's silence, and he felt the dark eyes on him. 'Best get in,' the old man said at last with a bad grace. 'And I'll have you taken to the castle, since your business is *so* urgent.'

'God save you, porter.'

'He'll have to. No other bugger will,' the gatekeeper muttered, but drew the door open a little.

St Pancras Lane

Edith felt as though she was going to burst with pleasure to see her father. 'Come in, Father, come in! God keep you! And Sir Baldwin? I am so glad to see you again.'

Her father saw her hesitation. 'This is a good friend of ours, daughter. Sir Richard de Welles, the Coroner of Lifton. Sir Richard, this is my daughter Edith.'

'Mistress, I am delighted to meet you. I have heard much of you from your father. He said you were a beautiful and accomplished woman, and I see he was telling nothing less than the truth.'

'Please, my lords, come into my hall,' she said, trying to conceal her delight at his words. Clapping her hands, she summoned a young maidservant. 'Jane, fetch my husband's wine.'

She could see her father's eyes going to the hangings on the wall and the picture at the further end. She was proud of her house, naturally, but it was a delight to see how his eyes gleamed to see such wealth displayed. Not because she wanted him to be jealous, but because she knew he would be happy to see that she was as well off as he could have wished. The house was a proof of that. He need have no fears for her future.

As soon as the maid was back, Edith stood in the middle of the hall and dispensed wine to the visitors. 'You will excuse my husband. He has been out working with his father, but I am sure that he will soon return, and he will be so pleased to see you, Father.'

'Aye, well, I'll be pleased to see him too,' her father said gruffly.

His tone made her smile. 'And now, what are you doing here? I had heard from Mother that she was moving back to the old house, of course. I was sorry about that, Father.'

He nodded.

Edith had seen the effect of the man sent to bully her family from their home in Lydford. The man, William atte Wattere, had been in their hall, fighting her father, when she entered with her fiancé to ask Simon's permission to marry. The sight had terrified her. It was the first time she had witnessed her father in a fight, and although there was a fierce pride in her heart when she saw him knock the sword of his enemy away and force the fellow to submit, the scene had petrified her. Afterwards she had upbraided her husband-to-be for not leaping to the defence of her father, but as he had reasonably pointed out, he was not trained in the use of a sword, and Simon was. If he had joined in, he would have been as likely to be killed as to help Simon.

'We are just returned from France,' her father said.

As he spoke, telling her about travelling with the bishop all the way to Paris to protect the king's heir, and their dangerous adventures while over there, Edith sat and listened attentively.

It was good. She hadn't seen her father since May, when she had been married, and now, perhaps for the first time, she felt as though she was being treated as an adult, equal in maturity with him. Always before she had felt that Simon was humouring her, as any father would, but not now. With her marriage, she had crossed a great gulf, and where before she was a child, now she was a woman. Patting her belly, she knew how true that was.

Simon didn't notice, but she saw Baldwin's dark eyes flash towards her. He was always so understanding, she thought. He had a quick intuition that was almost feminine. Now she said nothing, but merely smiled. It would be wrong for her to tell Sir Baldwin before her mother.

'So you are on your way home again now?' she asked.

'Yes,' Simon said with a quiet stillness that she understood only too well.

She leaned forward and rested her hand on his. 'Father, I know it was awful the way that man behaved, but you are better at Sandford anyway. I'm happy to know that you are nearer us.'

'It was just the thought that he could evict me so easily, without any compunction,' Simon said.

Baldwin shot a look at Edith. 'It is the way of such men, Simon. You have to appreciate that there is no safety for any man in the realm while Despenser holds so much power. At least now he has done all he intends, so far as we can tell. Go home to Sandford, run your farm and enjoy life.'

'Sir Baldwin is right, Father. And the good thing for me is that I can visit you sometimes. It's only half a day's journey from here, and it will be very pleasant to see you and Mother more often.'

'Have you seen Meg?' Simon asked.

'She is fine, Father. If anything, I think she is happier now than she has been for a long time.'

'Yes. I can imagine that,' Simon said quietly.

'And I am happier,' Edith repeated. 'I know that while you are closer to us here, we can help you if you need anything.'

'I don't think you need any help anyway,' Simon said with a smile, turning the goblet over in his hand.

Edith smiled. 'My husband is a good man,' she said with quiet certainty.

Fourth Friday after the Feast of the Archangel Michael*

Sandford Barton, Sandford

Simon saw the smoke rising from the chimney as he breasted the hill and could stare down at the house.

'A goodly home,' Sir Richard said.

'But what is *that* for?' Simon said.

'It is a *house*, Simon,' the coroner said with some surprise. 'What else is it for but to help old devils like you and me to rest weary bones in front of a fire. What do you mean?'

'That thing! The chimney!' When he had last been here to his old home, it had been a simple longhouse, with the stable block at the eastern end, living accommodation on the western, and the happy sight of smoke billowing from the eaves at either end. Now it appeared to have sprouted a large red sandstone chimney. 'I don't understand it. What was she thinking of?'

'Does it matter? So long as there is some ale down there, and a bite for lunch, I don't care about the position of a chimney, old friend,' the coroner said pragmatically.

'No, of course,' Simon said, smiling, and spurred his mount down the road towards his home.

His feelings had nothing to do with the chimney, if he was honest. It was the unsettled feeling he had had since leaving Exeter. Somehow all the while on the journey here from London, his problems had seemed to be fading. All he had been aware of was the sense of relief that he would soon be reunited with his wife. And the fact that Sir Hugh le Despenser was more than a hundred miles to the east. There was no escaping the fact that Simon felt the poisonous fellow was the source of all his woes and hardship.

*25 October 1325

But now, almost home again, he was aware of a sudden increased anxiety. It was almost as though the realisation had hit him that this house was no more safe from Despenser than his last one. Could Despenser have taken over here and installed a chimney for his own comfort, leaving Simon nowhere to go?

It was terrifying to feel this panic at the mere sight of his old home. Coming here again should have been a delight. He had spent so many years here – happy years. It was where he had brought his wife when they were married; it was where his daughter had been born, and where he had been told that he was to be made a bailiff on Dartmoor to protect the Stannaries, the ancient tin mines where the king controlled all production. But as soon as he had been given that post, he had been forced to move from this happy hillside and go to Lydford, so that he could be closer to the moors where he was to earn his living.

'You all right there, Bailiff?'

Simon felt the coroner's shrewd eyes on him. He tried to clear his mind, to explain a little of his trepidation. 'She truly enjoyed living at Lydford at first, you know,' he said, his body rocking with the motion of the horse as it walked cautiously down the steep incline. His house was set on the northern side of a natural bowl, and they must ride down this, the southern side, and then up to the house on the opposite slope. 'It was only when I was moved that life grew more difficult.'

'Eh?'

'The Abbot of Tavistock wanted to elevate me, because I had done so well for him. So he gave me a new post – that of his officer in Dartmouth. But to go there would have meant uprooting the whole family. Edith was not happy to be taken away from her friends, and Meg herself was unhappy at the thought of moving so far from all that she knew – and didn't want our son to grow up surrounded by sailors. They aren't the best of companions to a well-bred lad.'

'I can imagine that. I still remember my first exposure to the folk of Dartmouth,' Sir Richard reminisced with a smile of contentment.

He had already told Simon about his affection for women of loose morals, and Simon suspected that the reason for the grin on his face was not one that should be discussed with his wife. 'Yes, well, that was why I had to move there all alone,' he said. 'Meg had to stay back at Lydford. And then we had the house taken away from us.'

'Well, Bailiff, perhaps it is all for the good. At least now you and I are free of political troubles. Hopefully Baldwin too. Wonder how he's getting on.'

'He should be home by now as well,' Simon said. 'Furnshill is about the same distance from Exeter as Sandford is.'

They had reached the bottom of the hill now, and clattered through the small stream that ran along the bottom.

'You know, it's been such a miserable year or two, and I hardly feel I know my wife any more,' Simon said.

'You know her well enough, man,' Sir Richard declared. 'It'll be easier to remember her when you're near her, though. Come on!'

He spurred his beast on, and the great horse sprang up the hill like a pony with a child on its back, rather than the prodigious weight of Sir Richard.

Simon grinned to himself. It was good to be travelling with the Coroner of Lifton. The man was loud, rumbustious, a perfect danger to a man when it came to drinking, but for all that, he was a fellow who inspired loyalty in a man. He was generous and kindly, and provided he did not feel as though he was being insulted, he was as affable as Wolf.

Simon clapped his heels to his own beast's flanks, and felt the surge of power as he was thrown forward by the first explosive movement, but already he had his balance and could lean down over his mount's neck, and he grinned as he felt the cool air wash over his face.

Road outside Bow, Devon

As he jogged along the trail, Stephen of Shoreditch looked about him with ever-increasing anxiety.

It was a standing rule that all roads should have their verges cleared for a hundred feet on either side, and it was one of the duties of the Keeper of the King's Peace in all jurisdictions to see that rule enforced, so that no one could make an ambush against another on the king's highways, but this was not one of those fast, well-maintained roadways. Here in the middle of Devon, the roads tended to be thin, winding paths with hedges that stood so high on either side that on occasion a man couldn't see over them. To Stephen, the whole idea of a track like this was anathema. He would prefer to walk by a footpath in the open, across fields and moors, than pass along a dangerous route like this, where a felon could drop a stone on his head at any moment.

Devon was one of those shires he had always tried to avoid. Down here in the wild western lands, everyone was truculent, suspicious and acquisitive, he had heard tell. It was said that civilisation ended at Exeter, and beyond that was a wilderness in which feral men squabbled and fought. Dear Christ in heaven, from all he had seen so far, it was easy to believe. This land looked about as cultivated as the Scottish marches, and the people as cultured as the poor churls living up there. Mean, ill favoured, the lot of them.

At least they appeared to be dressed. One messenger had told him that the folk about here were all so backward that they had no concept of clothing. But that was one of the hazards of asking another messenger about an area: it was impossible to tell whether the stories were true or not. Often a man would take pleasure in giving tales of strange, abnormal folk, so that all the advice must be taken with a large pinch of salt. The idea of a messenger needing to have accurate inform-ation about the places he must pass through, as well as his destination, was not new, but in the court, men had grown more and more frivolous over the years.

Not that all were persuaded to humour now. Many were looking more to their own protection and safety. The intrigues at the king's court were growing ever more hazardous to a man. There was always the risk that a joke played on another could have repercussions that couldn't be spotted. One man, so Stephen had heard, had been told that a wood was a safe passage, only to be captured and hanged in quick succession. The man who had told him of that path had been taken there and hanged alongside his companion. That was a joke that had seriously backfired.

He was fairly sure that here he would be safe, though. He had escaped from Exeter, which was itself a relief. The sheriff was out of the city, but Stephen had been able to deliver his messages and beg a space on the floor for the night, after some prevarication. No strangers were welcomed any more. There were too many rumours of the king's spies – or, rather, Despenser's.

Stephen shivered. Sir Hugh le Despenser was growing ever more wild in his behaviour – more erratic. There was a strange look in his eyes that seemed to show that he was becoming more and more divorced from reality. He was less cautious, more extravagant in every way. Not too many people would see that side of him, perhaps, but little was ever hidden from the messengers. They had contact with the king and his advisers at all times. Stephen was a messenger for Sir Hugh as often as for the king. And he was sure that Despenser was losing control.

The road was winding gently now, the hedges less tall. They appeared stunted. Stephen had seen bushes and trees like this before, especially up north, when he had travelled up to the colder lands near the Scottish. Yes, this was much like those damned, accursed marches. Just like there, the wind here seemed to scour the vegetation, often blighting one side or another, and forcing trees to bend away from the cold blast, turning them into tortured shapes. Now, looking to the south, Stephen could see over the hedges all the way to rounded hills in the distance, hills without any apparent trees. They were only moor and waste, and he thought that they must be the king's forest of Dartmoor. He hadn't expected them to be so vast, nor so deserted. Nor so repellent.

'*Hold*, rider!'

Swearing aloud, at the man and at himself, Stephen struggled to control his rounsey, which had reared up at the voice.

'I am a king's messenger,' he shouted, pulling at the reins and trying to stop the plunging motion. 'Sweet Mother of Christ, couldn't you warn a man before shouting?'

'Ah, but if we did that, you might not wait to talk to us, might you?'

Stephen brought the beast under control, and could at last pay attention to the men. 'Who are you?'

Before him stood a man with a badly scarred face. His hair was grizzled, his beard more salt than pepper, and his left eye bright with intelligence. He looked as though he had been hit in the face with a sword: his nose was slashed, the line of the blade passing through an eye that was now gone, and cutting a notch in his right eye socket. He stood in front of Stephen's horse, a sword in his own fist, smiling with a calm, easy malevolence. 'Get off the horse.'

'Be damned to you! Didn't you hear me? I'm a king's messenger!' Stephen blustered.

'A pox on you! I didn't ask what you were, I told you to get down!' the man bellowed, and spat into the road. 'Let's see if you have any money on you, king's messenger.'

Turning, Stephen saw to his dismay that there was another pair of men behind him. Glancing about, he saw two on his left and another on his right as well. Six of them. There was little chance of escaping these outlaws, because that was clearly what they were. 'You had best not assault me,' he tried. 'I have urgent messages from Sir Hugh le Despenser for Sir Robert of Traci.'

With that the man in the road gave a short bow. 'Oh, in that case, I must be more careful! Come, let us take you to him, master. Sir Robert de Traci is our lord.'

Chapter Eight

Furnshill, near Cadbury

Baldwin whistled to his dog as he reached the turn-off in the road towards his house. Wolf had been sniffing at a badger's sett, but as soon as he heard his master, he relinquished the scent and hurried to catch up.

Looking about him, Baldwin was satisfied. It was good to see that the estates had not been allowed to sink into disrepair while he had been away. But it was more than that. He had to sit on his horse and study the landscape, drinking in the picture, as though by doing so he could fix it in his mind and his life for all time.

He loved this place. It was many years ago that he had been born here, and in those days he never thought he would own it for himself. His older brother would naturally inherit. That was why he had chosen to leave the country and travel to the Holy Land to try to protect it against the onslaught of the massive armies that opposed it. He arrived in Acre just in time to be injured in the last, tragic days of the city. Also hurt was Edgar, the man who later, with Baldwin, joined the Knights Templar in order to try to repay the debt both felt for having their lives saved. Both had remained in the order until the very end. When the arrests had taken place, both happened to be out of their preceptory, and evaded capture. Later, they had made their way back to England, and Baldwin learned that only a short time earlier, his brother had died in a riding accident, and so he could return as the owner of Furnshill rather than a mere supplicant begging alms from his brother.

'Come on, fellow,' he called quietly, and trotted over the front pasture to his house.

There was a man over at the western edge of the house when Baldwin arrived. He looked at Baldwin, blinked, and then scurried off in a hurry.

Baldwin smiled to himself and dropped from his horse, relieved to think that he would not have to set his backside on a saddle for a long journey any time soon. So many days he had spent sitting on a horse in the last year, he felt as though his arse had been remoulded to fit the leatherwork.

He was just tying the horse's reins to a ring in the wall when he heard her running.

'Jeanne,' he said, and she stopped on the threshold, leaning against the door frame.

'My love,' she said, and began to weep for joy.

Sandford

The expression on Meg's face removed any doubts in Simon's mind as to her enthusiasm to see him. She pelted past Sir Richard in a most indecorous display, and threw herself bodily at her husband, arms about his neck and kissing him. 'Simon, Simon,' she murmured as she drew away, but then she was kissing him again.

Sir Richard looked at the sky. He pursed his lips and thought to whistle, but then he decided that it might be a little distracting for Simon, so he turned his back on the couple and stared out at the landscape.

There was no little vill about here, with strip fields where the peasants all laboured. Instead this was a working farm that depended upon pasturage, he saw. There was a field ahead of him, long grasses rippling in the wind. Over on the right there was a stand of trees – a mixture of all kinds of wood, with some coppiced nearer the house. In front of that there was a good-sized orchard, and a set of small pens, empty at the moment. It was a pleasant little farmstead, he felt.

'Meg, this is Sir Richard de Welles, the Coroner of Lifton,' he heard, and turned to find himself being studied with some interest by a tall woman, very fair, with browned skin and bright blue eyes. She was slim, and although she had now lost the first flush of youth, to Sir Richard she was astonishingly lovely.

'Sir Richard, God keep you,' she said with a broad smile, and ducked her head as she gave him a brief curtsy.

'My dear lady, God will keep you, I know,' he said, bowing low.

'I am honoured. Now, husband, will you come inside and I will have food and drink fetched for your guest.'

She glanced at him, her expression as serene as Simon remembered from all those years ago when he first saw her. All those years before their first son had died, before the years of anguish during the famine, the years before the misplaced kindness of the Abbot of Tavistock forced them to become separated. Before William atte Wattere had arrived and helped to steal their house from them. And then her serenity was shattered as she laughed aloud, took his hand and brought him inside.

'Sir Richard?' Simon called.

The knight was still standing outside, an expression of wonder on his face. 'Yes? Oh, yes. Of course.'

He followed Simon and Meg indoors and joined Simon in the little hall.

'You are very welcome to remain here with us for as long as you wish, Sir Richard,' Simon said. 'We have wine and cider aplenty, and some ale, which, if I say so myself, is the equal of the king's. You have travelled far in the last weeks. Will you not stay here with us a little?'

'I would dearly like to,' Sir Richard said. He shook his head as some servants entered and set out a large trestle table near the fireplace. 'But I have a need to return to my duties. A coroner has work to keep him busy no matter where he lives nor what the time of the year.'

'Yes. Well, work is something I will have to find for myself now,' Simon muttered.

'Bailiff, I am sorry. It is hard to believe that you could be without employment.'

'Oh, I have employment – I have my farm, after all,' Simon said lightly. But his face showed his continued concern.

It would be hard, he knew. The post at Lydford had been so effective for him. He was happy there, especially since it gave him the right to wander where he might over the moors he loved. Still, he told himself. This was good land, this rich red soil of Sandford. It was a good place to finish a life. And now his daughter had already left home and he had only his son to worry about. Perhaps it was better that he was here again.

'You look thoughtful, husband,' he heard his wife call from the doorway.

'I was thinking about the quiet of living here in the country again. We stayed last night in Exeter.'

'You saw Edith?' Meg asked, the eagerness making her almost drop the trenchers she was carrying.

'Yes. She and her husband seem very happy.'

'I am glad,' Meg breathed. It was hard to say God speed to a child and send her into the world. A man could be a good husband or a bad, but a daughter would always run the risk when she left her home. 'But there was never a reason to suspect that he wouldn't be a good man for her.'

'No. Not even though he's so young. God's ballocks, so is she.'

'And so are most when they marry, Simon,' Meg said a little tartly.

'Yes, I know, I am an overprotective monster. I'd prefer to have her husband dangling by his wrists for the nerve of asking for my daughter.' Simon laughed. 'But since he was so gracious last night, and poured us a goodly quantity of wine, I think I can forgive him just now, eh, Sir Richard?'

'Hmm? Yes, I think so,' Sir Richard said. He was a little confused, and he appeared embarrassed, or perhaps upset.

Simon looked over at Meg, but she had little idea what sort of a man Sir Richard was, and she merely looked back at him with confusion.

'Meg, do you think you could bring our friend some wine?' he asked, and even as he spoke, all three heard the rattle of hoofs on the stones in front of the house. Simon stood abruptly, staring at the window. There was no sign of the rider from here, for the window was high in the wall, but they could all hear the voice.

'A message for Bailiff Puttock. Is your master here? I have an urgent message from Cardinal de Fargis.'

'In Christ's name, what now?' Simon muttered as he spun on his heel and left the room.

'It will be nothing, my lady,' Sir Richard said.

Meg was standing at the table, listening intently. There was a slight puckering at her forehead that he recognised so distinctly. The frown of anxiety. He couldn't keep his eyes on her, he found. She was so like his own, dear, dead wife, it hurt to look at her.

Road between Nymet Cross and Sandford Cross
Sir Peregrine was not overly bothered by the sight of dead bodies. He never had been. Why should he be? He was a knight and the son of a knight, and for all his pride in being able to converse with the meanest villein on his lands, he was prouder still of his martial experience and skills.

A man like him who was used to the sights and sounds of battle wouldn't be concerned by the sight of wounds. He had seen friends die near him in the petty wars that plagued this disputatious land, and on occasion he had travelled as far as Guyenne in support of the king, protecting Edward's territories from the depredations of the French. But there was somehow a difference between seeing men-at-arms fighting and dying in a battle, and this.

The others were sad, of course. The clumps of bodies in the woods had been very disheartening, for such a scene was inevitably depressing, and yet the fact that Sir Peregrine knew none of them meant that he could at least maintain a professional detachment.

'Who found him?'

He didn't really care who had discovered the fellow. Sir Peregrine stared down at the body of Bill Lark with a rising sense of resentment. There were times when he felt that it was better never to grow fond of anyone, because he was invariably hurt when they died.

It was particularly true of his love life. He had almost married three women. Each had died before he could. Back in the year before King Edward took the throne from his father* he had lost his first love. He would have married her else. The next was his lovely Emily, who had died giving birth to their child four years ago when he was master of Tiverton Castle for Sir Hugh de Courtenay. And then, more recently, dear Juliana had died, leaving two children from another man, and he had taken them on himself, not reluctantly, in memory of her. But no matter how fond he was of them, he could not look upon them as his own. Which was a shame, but hardly surprising. They were not of his blood.

---

*1306

But it wasn't just the women he had loved who had died just as he had grown to think that there could be a new life beginning. His loneliness was enhanced by the deaths of men like this.

This man was scarcely known to him, of course, and yet he felt a bond already. There was something about the fellow that had inspired confidence. He looked competent, stolid and dependable. The sort of man in whom another could place his trust. And Sir Peregrine had felt quietly confident that he would do all in his power to find the men who had committed the atrocity in the woods.

'Who did this to him?' he wondered aloud.

The man had been bludgeoned to death, from the look of him. It looked as though his head had been beaten with a rock, or maybe a mace or similar weapon. Until the blood had been washed away, it would be pure guesswork to try to say what did make those wounds.

'He was found here last afternoon,' a man said helpfully.

Sir Peregrine growled at him, commanding the full jury to be brought immediately, as well as a clerk or anyone else who could hold a reed, so that they could have the inquest, and bellowed when no one seemed to want to move. Soon he was all but alone, and he squatted at the man's side, as though talking to a resting friend.

'I am sorry about this, Bailiff. Truly, I will do all I may to find the men who did this to you. And if I can, I will bring them to justice. I swear it on my soul!'

Furnshill

'You look tired,' Baldwin said as he walked inside with his wife.

It was the same as it had been. In the worst days of his travelling, when he was incarcerated in the Louvre, trying desperately to stop himself from causing offence to any French nobility, he had been prey to horrible fancies: that his farm would have suffered from drought, or perhaps from dreadful fires; that his house had suddenly succumbed, as he had seen others, and collapsed with his wife inside. All those were in many ways easy to reject as being foolish. However, he had a strange, recurring thought that when he came home there would be some appalling alteration in his family that would make his return a matter of horror, not delight. It was a terrifying thought that, when he marched through his front door, he might learn that one of his children had died; perhaps even Jeanne herself.

Now, walking through the screens passage and into his hall, he was relieved to see that his fears were baseless. It made him even more glad to be home again, and he encircled his wife's waist with his arm, drawing her nearer to kiss her.

She reciprocated, but after a shorter period than he would have liked, she drew away. In the doorway he saw his old Templar comrade, Edgar, and Baldwin inclined his head. 'I hope I see you well, Edgar?'

'Sir Baldwin,' Edgar responded, bowing low. 'I shall fetch you some wine and meats. You must be hungry.'

He was gone in an instant, and Baldwin could look down at his wife. 'As I said, you seem very tired, my love. Are you quite well?'

'Mostly, yes. The children exhaust me, I confess, but Edgar and his wife have been very kind. They both do all they can.'

'Is it the estate? I can take all the effort of that away from you now, Jeanne,' he said softly.

There was a redness about her eyes that he did not like to see. It was almost as though she had spent much of the last weeks weeping, and the idea that she should have been so saddened without his being there to calm or soothe her made him feel chilly with guilt. He was her husband, in Christ's name. It was his duty to be here for her.

'It isn't the lands or the manor,' she said after a few moments. 'There is more than that.'

She walked to her chair and seated herself, waiting for him to join her. As soon as he had taken his own seat, Edgar returned with a tray and jug. Baldwin's favourite mazer was on the tray, a beech cup with a silver band about it. Edgar filled it with wine and passed it to his master.

Jeanne waited until her husband had taken a sip before continuing. 'It is the sheriff and his men. The sheriff is a new man, one of Sir Hugh le Despenser's companions, I think, and it seems as though all are subject to Despenser's scrutiny.'

'How do you mean?' Baldwin asked.

It was Edgar who, on a signal from Jeanne, began to speak. 'I believe Despenser has grown terrified of an attack from a foreign power. Perhaps he fears that Mortimer will soon cross the sea and try to take the kingdom. Whatever the reason, he is even less trusting than before, and now he seeks to implement his control over every part of the land where there is a coast and where an invasion force could land. Clearly Devon and Cornwall are particularly dangerous, in his mind.'

Baldwin nodded. 'There are coastlines to north and south, of course.'

'And an infinite number of places where a man might bring a host to attack the king,' Edgar agreed.

It wasn't strictly true. In the north of Devon, as Baldwin knew well, there were few naturally safe harbours for a ship, let alone a fleet, but that was not the point. Devon and Cornwall were exceedingly hard to protect.

'There is more,' Edgar said. 'Of course Despenser will know that the queen was mistress of much of both shires. She controlled the mining of the tin, and she had a lot of supporters over here.'

'What of it?'

'The king – and Despenser – would hardly be natural if they didn't wonder whether she too might try to gather a force to oust Despenser. She has seen her power and authority eroded by him in the last years.'

'So you think that Despenser has planned to come here and take over the running of the West Country from the locals?'

'I think he is plotting to have his placemen set in all positions of any form of authority at the coast,' Edgar said. 'And that includes Devon, because there are so many ideal places for a bold team to land, and many potential supporters for the men who would try it. He has installed this Sir James de Cockington as sheriff, but there are others who are winning his favour as well.'

'I suppose that is natural enough,' Baldwin said thoughtfully. 'He is putting men in place to ensure that the land is safe from attack.'

'Yes, but there are other men who seem to have little regard for the law. So long as they are Despenser's friends, they feel that they can wander the land at will, taking whatever they desire,' Jeanne said. 'And that appears to include the sheriff himself. He is more corrupt than any, if what is said is true.'

'Which bodes not well for those who have shown themselves to be enemies of Despenser,' Edgar added, looking at his master with a serious expression.

Chapter Nine

Road near Bow

There were few times in Stephen of Shoreditch's life when he had been made to feel quite so fearful. In his experience, most men were more than happy to treat him with a degree of respect, because a man who insulted the king's messengers insulted the king himself. A messenger was a representative of the king.

These men hardly appeared to accord him any respect whatsoever. They didn't talk to him, nor offer him any refreshment, but insisted that he dismount and walk with them. Another man behind them had his horse now, while he walked in the midst of his captors, glancing about him on occasion, hoping against hope that they were speaking the truth and would take him to Sir Robert de Traci. Certainly he had little expectation that he would be able to escape. Although these felons had left him with his dagger and short riding sword, they were hemmed closely in on him, and the likelihood of his being able to run from them was remote in the extreme. They looked more than capable of bringing him down in a matter of yards.

It was while they were on their way that he saw the event that was to make him certain that he was in the company of dangerous souls.

They had taken a little turn, and were now walking down a hill towards what looked like a fair-sized hamlet, when

Stephen heard a squeaking and rumbling sound. It wasn't ahead of them, but over to the left, somewhere towards the south. Before long he was able to make out a little lane that appeared to interest the men with him. They wandered up to it, slinking along quietly, and crouched at the edge, where it met their own road.

Soon Stephen could see what was happening. Even as the scarred man grasped his shoulder and pulled him down, he could see that the noise was a man on an ancient cart.

'Messenger boy, if you want to live to deliver another note, you'll keep your mouth and your eyes shut!' the man said, and his dagger was already unsheathed, the point at Stephen's throat, in the dent below his windpipe.

There was nothing Stephen could say. He merely nodded his head slowly, and watched.

The man was a farmer, so far as he could see. An ordinary farmer on the way to the market at Bow, likely. He had some produce in the back of his little cart. A pathetic amount, but enough to justify the journey. The man was almost asleep as he knelt in the cart, his head nodding with the cart's jerking, his eyes all but closed.

'Old man, what have you got in there?'

Stephen looked over to see that one of the men had grabbed the horse's rein and was grinning up at the farmer.

'Who are you? I'm—'

'No, old man. What have you got in there, is what I asked.'

'Nothing. Just some beans and cheese for market. What do you want with me?'

'We are taking tolls for the market,' the man said smoothly, and nodded to one of the others.

Immediately Stephen saw this fellow slip around the cart and grab for the back of it. The farmer scowled and turned, watching as the fellow eyed the goods and reached in to take a cheese.

'I'll see you in hell before you take that or anything else of mine,' the farmer snarled.

'Pox on your threats, old man,' the man at the reins said.

'Leave my goods, you shite!'

'Who do you think you are, peasant?'

'I am Jack Begbeer, you little hog, and I won't be robbed!'

'Hey, Osbert, look at this! There's a good barrel of ale here too!' the man at the back said, and was soon clambering over the cart.

The farmer glanced at him, and then reached down to his side. He came up gripping a whip; flicking his wrist, the long end rose, curled around and lashed out. The man at the back of the cart gave a cry, and his hand went to his brow. As he stood, hands cupping his face, blood began to ooze from a slash across his forehead, and he sprang down to hide from the stinging whip.

'Old git!' the man at the reins bellowed, and ducked as the whip end came towards him.

Stephen saw it as it passed over the man's head. It had been cut and woven into a fine point, and when it touched flesh, it cut like a razor. Already the farmer was thrashing it about him with abandon, standing warily on his cart, keeping the men at bay, snarling defiance at them all. 'You think you can rob any man passing here? We all know you and your evil master. Well you won't take my things, not without some of you getting hurt, you sons of dogs! Go to hell, you soulless devils! The pox on you and your children, if you can father them!'

In front of him, Stephen saw that the scarred man had laughed at first to see the men trounced by an old peasant, but his humour was fading now. 'Old man, get down from the cart.

You've hurt one of Sir Robert of Traci's men, and that means your toll has become more expensive.'

'You? You think to steal all my goods? You think I don't know you, Osbert? Son of a whore, your father was, and you too! Think you that you can scare me? I'll be damned if I'll let you rob me like you rob so many others, damn your soul!'

As he spoke, he flung back his arm, then lashed. The whip sprang towards the scarred man like a viper. He swore, stepped aside, and let the whip fly past him, and as it rose a second time, he darted forward, under the horses, and reappeared on the other side, his dagger held by the point. He hefted it, took his aim, and hurled.

The dagger spun lazily in the air, and Stephen could see its flight as it turned over and over and then sank to the hilt in the old farmer's throat. He dropped reins and whip, clutching at the hilt, spinning as he tried to pull it free, eyes wide with horror, mouth opening and closing as he struggled to breathe. Then he fell backwards, dropping heavily on to his backside near the front of the cart even as the blood began to dribble from his lips.

'Stupid old peasant! Couldn't you restrain yourself? Eh?' Scarface shouted. 'You had to keep on, didn't you? See where that gets you, you old git! Straightway to hell. Well, give my regards to the devil!'

The farmer slumped, his body jerking and writhing as he died slowly. Gradually his efforts to keep upright became too much of a struggle, and he toppled over the cart's wall, ending up on his back beside his carthorse, his eyes fixed on the man he had called Osbert. The man with the scarred face walked to the farmer, reached for his knife and jerked it free. A fine spray of blood erupted from the dying man's throat, and Osbert laughed to see the way that the horse pulling the cart neighed and tried to jerk away from the warm blood.

'Come on, fools!' he bellowed, and kicked the farmer's body from the cart's path. He took up the reins and cracked them to get the beast moving again.

Stephen felt a hand on his elbow, and submitted to being pushed along. He couldn't help but glance back at the body in the dirt at the side of the track. The farmer's face was already mottled with death, the blood staining his clothes, while a red, oily sheen lay upon his face. Stephen was sure that he could see the man's lips working, but it was impossible to tell what he was trying to say. Perhaps it was 'Avenge me!'

If that was what the old peasant hoped, he would have to remain hopeful. Stephen wanted nothing to do with fighting those devils.

St Pancras Lane, Exeter

Edith waited at the table until her husband arrived, and then rose to greet him.

'My sweet, you shouldn't have waited,' he protested.

The maidservant was still in the room, and his greeting must remain cordial but restrained, he felt. Although he had grown up with servants in his household, it was a novel experience still to have his own maid.

Edith smiled. 'God speed, husband. Sit, please, and let me serve you.'

'I am most grateful for your attendance, my love. Send the maid away,' he added in a hiss.

At Edith's gesture, young Jane curtsied and left, walking carefully as though she might break some of the wonderful carvings on the cupboard.

'Thank you, my love,' Peter murmured, and pulled his wife towards him.

'Oho, so you want to let your food get cold?' Edith protested.

He had her by the waist already. 'Not half, my precious! Come here, and let me . . .'

Edith fell back over his lap to sit with a low chuckle. She pointed her chin to the ceiling while he nuzzled at her throat, his hands roving over her simple tunic, feeling the firmness of her body beneath, the rounded swelling of her breasts, the smooth flesh of her flanks. 'Oh, my love. I have been dreaming of this all day!'

'Well you will have to continue dreaming for a little longer. I am petrified with hunger,' she said, and was about to climb from him when there was a loud knocking on the door. She looked down at him. 'Who can that be?'

'Christ's bones, but I don't know, I swear,' Peter said with conviction, standing and walking to the door.

It was dark out, but as he threw the door wide, he could see the lanterns shining, the candles flickering in their horn boxes. 'What do you want?'

The nearest man was a stout fellow with an ancient-looking cap of steel. He had shrewd dark eyes set widely below a strong forehead, and a beard that was very dark. He was young enough not to have any frost on his head or in his moustache. He looked at Edith. 'We'd heard that Sir Richard de Welles was here. Have you seen him? Or Sir Baldwin, the Keeper?'

'Why do you want them?' Peter said, aware of Edith behind him. He felt her hand rest on his shoulder.

'There's been a murder over towards Oakhampton, and Sir Peregrine has asked for them to go to him,' the man said.

'You must send for him at Furnshill, then,' Peter said. 'They left here early this morning. They will be there by now, I'd imagine.'

'Then God speed, master,' the man said. He motioned with his hands, and the others began to filter back up the alley towards St Pancras. 'Was the bailiff with them too?'

'Who, my father?' Edith asked. 'Simon Puttock? Yes.'

The fellow nodded and set off after the other men. The last Edith saw of them was their backs as they made their way to the top of the alley and took the path left, wandering southwards. She caught a fleeting glimpse, so she thought, of another face, one that made her blood run cold for an instant, but then it was gone, and she knew that it must be her imagination. William atte Wattere, the man whom she had encountered at her father's house on the day she had gone to ask his permission to marry, was surely nowhere near here now.

Peter shut the door and rested his hand on it for a few moments, frowning. 'I do not like that fellow.'

'Why, my love? He was only a watchman, wasn't he?'

'He didn't look like any man from around here. He was one of the guard with the new sheriff at Rougemont Castle, I'd swear.'

Edith shrugged and led him back to their hall. 'What of it?'

'He didn't strike me as the kind of man who'd be sent for a simple message delivery. It was almost as though someone wanted to make sure that the coroner and your father had actually left the city.'

Road near Bow

Roger had made good time walking back down to the south coast. Embittered, chilly, sore footed and hungry, he was glad to have met a farmer just outside Winkleigh, who, after studying him a while, invited him in to sit before a fire, and fed him warmed milk sweetened with almonds, and some good thick maslin bread. Even better, he had allowed his guest to stay the night on the floor near the fire.

It was astonishing how well a man could feel when he had been rested and fed. Roger had known times in Guyenne, and in other parts of France, when he had been fighting, terrified for his life, and he and the others had found a little farmstead to take and sleep in, where the bliss of the peace was almost unbearable.

Walking here from that little farm had been much faster, and he had reached the outskirts of North Tawton the previous day. Somehow he had missed his path back to Jacobstowe. And although he knew he should have simply hurried on, down to Oakhampton, which was apparently not too many miles away, and thence to the coast and the busy port there, he had idled the day away. This morning, waking, he had been determined to get away from the area, but somehow he found himself still here. It was not until late afternoon that he decided to leave, but now, rather than seek out and walk through the woods at Abbeyford, he turned eastwards on a whim. There was no reason to go that way, other than the fact that he would have to take an easterly route at some point to get to Dartmouth, but he had an urge to take a slower path. He was enjoying the feeling of being on land too much to hazard the dangers of the sea followed by the hardship of fighting.

As he was strolling along, looking at the view from the roadway, he suddenly heard a force of men-at-arms approaching.

Most men, on hearing such a sound, would simply continue on their way. There were men on horseback all over the realm, and many of them warriors. It was a normal sight, natural in its way. So many magnates wanted to take their loyal men with them when they travelled so that any daring felons would be dissuaded from attempting a robbery. But Roger had a different attitude to such noises. In his mind there was an appreciation of the danger such men could represent. In Guyenne, the flat, treeless landscapes sometimes meant it was harder to conceal yourself, but here there were so many opportunities, it was difficult to pick the best.

The riders were approaching quickly. Gazing about him, he caught sight of a convenient tree branch at the side of the road, and used it to clamber up and over the hedge. He was just in time – as he landed, gently, on his feet and allowed his legs to fold beneath him so that he was almost flat beside the tree, he saw through the twigs and stems of the hedge the first flash of mottled armour, and heard the sound of hoofs suddenly grow louder. He saw a one-eyed warrior, and a fearful-looking man hemmed in by all the others, and reckoned that he was not a willing companion.

The damp was soaking into his tunic and his hose felt sticky and uncomfortable, but as they rode past, he allowed only his eyes to follow them. Any sudden movement could attract attention. He wasn't worried about making a noise; it was enough to let a man catch a glimpse from the corner of his eye, and if he was an experienced warrior, as these appeared to be, he would investigate.

He watched and listened until the men were fully out of sight. Only then did he realise he had been holding his breath. As he clambered back over the hedge into the grassy roadway, he felt strangely light-headed – and oddly exhilarated as well. It could have been the usual delight at escaping danger, but there was also the undoubted thrill of near action again. He was a fighter, when all was said and done.

And although in this case he had neither master nor money, he hesitated only a moment before darting off after the horses.

He would learn where they had come from.

Sandford

Simon walked up and down, while his wife watched with her blue eyes wide and anxious.

'Well, I suppose we'll continue together, then,' Sir Richard said after a while. He was looking from one to the other of them with some concern, but mainly with a scowl of incomprehension.

'Are you going to go?' Margaret asked.

Simon threw a look at her. 'Meg, I have to. I don't want to any more than you do, but I have to obey a direct command like this!' he said, and slapped the note in his hand.

They had been talking about the message all the afternoon, and Meg was no more keen to think that he was about to have to leave again than she had been before. Their son Perkin had already left to run and play in the yard after listening to the wrangling back and forth, and Sir Richard was only there because he thought it would be rude to leave the two to their discussion. Simon was glad that he had remained. The presence of the coroner forced Simon and Margaret to maintain a moderately calm demeanour.

'Isn't it enough that they have our house?' Margaret asked quietly.

'This isn't from the man Despenser sent to steal it from us,' Simon said wearily. They had been over this already. 'It's from the Cardinal de Fargis. He is living there, but not with the approval of Despenser. When we were thrown from our house, Bishop Walter had already offered it to the cardinal, and he will maintain it whether or not Despenser wants him there.'

'Simon, I don't want you to go.'

'I don't want to. But look at it sensibly, Meg. The sooner I go, the sooner I'll be back. The worst that can happen is that I'm asked to help with some matter for a few days, and then I'll be back. I will not accept another post abroad, no matter what they offer or threaten.'

'You said that in the summer. And then they sent you to France.'

'That was the king,' Simon reminded her. 'And after the way the king reacted to Baldwin, Sir Richard and me last time he saw us, there's not the remotest chance he'll want me around again. I think I'm unlikely to be sent anywhere other than Tavistock now.'

'He's right there, lady,' Sir Richard said.

'We will leave in the morning,' Simon said, more firmly.

Chapter Ten

Castle at Bow

The meal was well under way when the men turned up.

Sir Robert of Traci was not a pretentious man. He didn't have a wife, nor did he have a taste for some of the extravagance of modern courtly life in the royal household. It was fine for others to aspire to the little luxuries, as they were sometimes called. Men wanted pretty finery to show off their legs or arms. He had no need of that. His sword arm was strong enough to cut off the head of any man who offended him. Others wanted great piles of plate and pewter to show how rich they were. Sir Robert knew how rich he was. Richer than any other local magnate. In London he had seen tapestries, fabulous hangings created and set up to demonstrate the stylish elegance of their owner's way of life, to prove that the man was cultured. Sir Robert had no need of such fripperies and nonsense. He was as cultured as he wanted, and his money was put to better use in providing weapons and men. It was his job to pacify the area, not emulate some fop of a lord with more money than brains.

He had not been born rich, God knew. His journey to wealth had been long, and was by dint of effort and careful manipulation of every opportunity. In his youth he had been the impecunious son of a minor squire, little more than a peasant himself, as he had told anyone who listened. Then, he had only had dreams of money.

The famine had taken away all his father's money, rot his soul, and when his old man had died, leaving him as the inheritor of the estates, there had been next to nothing for him. His demesne was hopeless. What the famine hadn't devastated, other disasters had destroyed. Some fires, some flooding, and suddenly whole tracts of land were unviable. The vills were poor and their crops pathetic, while fields were ruined, and the likelihood of making a living as he wanted was so remote as to be next to impossible. He could only look at his future with despair.

But then his fortune changed. His uncle had a friend who was to enter the parliament, and who offered the young Robert the opportunity to join him. Robert had agreed with alacrity. That was in the thirteenth year of the king's reign*, when all was in flux. And young Robert had discovered the attractions of riches and power at the same time. He had been taken into the king's household.

Then there had been the fall. He had joined those who had sought to curb the king's power. Not because he was a fool, but because he had thought that Edward's inherent feebleness was too much of a threat to the realm. He couldn't fight the Scottish, he couldn't fight the French – in Christ's name, he could hardly control his own kingdom! So Sir Robert had joined the malcontents, men like his friend Badlesmere, who were prepared to ally themselves to Earl Thomas of Lancaster, the king's cousin, the king's enemy.

It had nearly ended his life. He had been lucky to escape the wholesale slaughter after that disaster, and still more lucky to have got away with his son. Basil had been only fourteen years old or so in the fifteenth year of the king's reign, and it had been hard for him to come to terms with the loss of everything. As it had for Sir Robert himself.

---

*1319

But those dreadful days were over now. Sir Robert had the trappings of authority once more. If the power he had once wielded was sadly declined, he still had his castle returned to him, and his son had his inheritance. And if they were to obey the commands given to them, they would be able to keep them.

Aye. If they obeyed.

'Who is this?' he bellowed as the man was pushed into the room.

'Says his name is Stephen of Shoreditch, Sir Robert,' Osbert said. He pushed Stephen further into the room, past the side benches of sitting men-at-arms, who stopped their guzzling and slurping to take a look at him.

'So, Stephen of Shoreditch, I wonder what you will have for me?' Sir Robert said musingly. He was a broad-shouldered man, if not so tall as some, and when he stood, the cloth from his tunic hung down smoothly, emphasising the strength of his frame. It was that that had first caught the eye of the king.

'Messages, Sir Robert. From your good friend Sir Hugh le Despenser,' Stephen said boldly. He held the gaze of the man in front of him with resolution.

The knight was big, handsome even, with his flashing black eyes and thick dark hair. He was clean shaven, although in need of a razor again; his chin must require a trim twice a day. His eyes, though, they were scary, Stephen remembered. He had seen the man a few times in Westminster at parliaments, and then more often when the king was holding a feast. Sir Robert was one of his loyal guests always. Sir Hugh le Despenser had a worrying habit of staring unblinkingly and unmovingly; it was one of his ways of unsettling a man, Stephen thought. As though whenever he was beginning to lose his temper, it was reflected in his powers of concentration on the poor being right in front of him.

This Sir Robert had a similar way of holding a man's attention. He would stare fixedly, without blinking, but instead of Despenser's steady bearing, the rest of his body motionless as if the whole of his being was fixed within that gaze, Sir Robert had a more feral, fearsome quality. He would slowly pace about the room, like a great cat stalking a prey, his eyes all the while on his victim, while his head sank down, his whole demeanour that of a ferocious beast. And all too often, the subject of his attention would later be discovered dead.

'Where is the message?'

Stephen said nothing, merely opened his little satchel and passed the sealed parchment to the knight. Sir Robert took it, still watching Stephen, and gradually circled around the messenger. 'Osbert, where did you find him?'

'He was on the road to Crediton. We found him up there about a mile east.'

'I see. Good. Follow me, man.'

Sir Robert turned abruptly and strode to the back of the hall. There was a heavy studded door there, and he pushed it open. It squeaked and groaned as he did so, and Stephen winced. He would have wiped some lard or goose grease over the hinges to stop that noise if it had been his own house.

Sir Robert stood in a small solar, and as soon as Stephen had followed him, he pushed the door shut and slid the oak bar across in its slots, locking it. He walked to the farther side of the little chamber, grasping a candle as he went, and used it to light a sconce. In this light, he peered down at the letters, frowning with the effort.

'Your men murdered a man on the road, Sir Robert,' Stephen said.

'Eh?'

'I said, your men murdered a man.'

Sir Robert glanced up, and there was a frown of anger on

his face as he looked the messenger over. 'Are you so young that you didn't know men are dying every day?'

'This man's death was unnecessary. He deprecated your men's demands for tolls. Did you know that they stop all travellers to take their money?'

'Messenger, you overstep your welcome here. Did I know? Yes. I knew. And what is more, I ordered them to take tolls on my roads. Because I am in the fortunate position of being responsible to my lord Hugh Despenser for maintaining the law here. In case you hadn't noticed, we have problems in the country just now, and I have been charged with keeping the peace.'

'By robbing people?'

Sir Robert's eyes seemed to film over with ice. 'By taxing those who can afford it,' he said.

There was not a sound for a moment or two.

'My apologies, Sir Robert,' Stephen said at last.

'I suggest you go and refresh yourself. You have travelled far,' Sir Robert said, and watched unblinking as the messenger left the room.

The fool. He was the sort of man who got himself into trouble over trifles. Who cared about some man killed on the roads? There was the possibility of invasion to worry about now, not peasants and other churls. Sir Robert turned back to the parchment, carefully reading the black writing. Since the disaster of robbing those travellers out near Jacobstowe, he had been wondering how to make a little more money. At least this note seemed to show how he might make a profit again.

At last, when Osbert quietly opened the creaking door, he set the parchment aside. 'Apparently good Sir Hugh wants to have a monk killed,' he said with a dry smile. 'I suppose he will pay us for this little service!'

Fourth Saturday after the Feast of the Archangel Michael*

Road between Crediton and Oakhampton

'So, Simon,' the coroner said as they jogged along in the early-morning light. 'What do you think the good cardinal will want to discuss with you?'

'I don't know,' Simon admitted with a shrug of bafflement. 'All I can hope is that it takes a short time to resolve. You saw how upset Meg was to hear I was being called away again so soon. I could take my fist and hit the man for what he's doing to me.'

'Your family has definitely been made to suffer enormously.' The coroner nodded. 'A man like me, no children, no woman, it's a damn sight easier for me. You, you have responsibilities. Something to think of.'

Simon nodded. It was a fact of life that when a liege lord demanded help, a fellow like Simon was forced to obey. No lord would have women in his household. His wife, his children, all would have their own establishment, and naturally, though the womenfolk would have maids, and ladies-in-waiting if they were of sufficient status, the bulk of their staff would still be men. And all those men must leave their wives and children behind.

'I will not agree to another long period away from my wife,' he grumbled. 'It is too much to ask of a man that he should keep discarding all those he loves the most. I missed the last months of my daughter's life before she married, all because I was dutifully serving the queen, her son and the king. I cannot do more.'

He meant it. In the last months his life had been turned upside down. First there was the problem with his position in

Dartmouth, which had soured relations with his wife; then the loss of his job when Abbot Champeaux died; and then the journeys to London and to Paris. He had done enough. Now it was time for him to rebuild his marriage.

'That is good,' the coroner said. Then he glanced over at Simon. 'Did you hear the joke about the one-eyed bishop and the courtesan?'

'Yes!'

'Are you sure?' the coroner asked, hurt. 'I didn't think I had told you that one.'

'Perhaps you told Baldwin and he told me,' Simon said dishonestly. He had no desire to be forced to listen to one of the coroner's appalling jokes yet again.

'Really? What, the one where—'

Simon was saved from hearing any more. 'What's going on there?'

They had passed far now from Crediton and Simon's home, and he looked up at the sun, assessing the time. He thought it must be well into the middle of the morning, which meant it was strange to see so many men milling. He and the coroner exchanged a glance and then put spurs to their mounts.

St Pancras Lane

Edith had enjoyed a good morning. It had been a lovely day so far. The sun was filtering in through the clouds of smoke from the morning fires, and when it kissed her face outside on the way to the baker's, she could have sworn it was summer again, it felt so welcoming, warm, invigorating. It was what a mother needed while her babe grew in her womb, she told herself, and almost laughed aloud at the thought.

It was a daunting prospect and no doubt about it. There were so many dangers in childbirth. Some of her friends were petrified of the birth, talking themselves into a fever over the possibility of death or miscarriage, but for Edith the risks seemed minor. As she reasoned, so many mothers had given birth with ease over the years, there was no reason to suspect that she would be any different. And anyway, she had good broad hips, and the old woman in the next street had said to her that she could deliver a cog for the king's navy without pain. Edith only prayed she was right.

Still, it was daunting. To think that even now there was a little child growing inside her was thrilling and terrifying at the same time. She was blessed not to feel sick in the mornings like some mothers, and with the baby, she was saved from the monthly griping and pain, which was a cause of relief and joy. She had always suffered badly when it was her time. Having the babe was not a cause for fear, but the thought that her life was about to change even more was . . . well, curious, really. She had spent so much of her time in the last two years wishing that people would recognise how mature she was, and now that she had the proof beginning to grow, she was aware only of the fear that her childhood was now over. There was no looking back once a woman had a child of her own. She was then no longer a maid.

The road here was broad as it fed into the high street, and she walked along with her maidservant behind her. No respectable woman would think of leaving home without some form of guard.

'Wife!'

She felt his voice in her breast. A thrilling, joyous sensation that overwhelmed her as much as it always had. Stopping, she closed her eyes a moment, until she could feel his presence at her side. 'Oh, my husband. I had not thought to see you here.'

'You lie appallingly, woman,' he said, and took her hand. To kiss in public would have been shameful, especially in a street so busy as this. 'I was on my way to my father's counting house. Would you walk with me some of the way?'

She would never, never be able to deny him anything, she told herself. His smile was so natural, so easy and delightful, he could ask anything of her and she would give it willingly. Even her life. It was all his.

Their time had been nothing short of perfect, she thought. Quite perfect. No one could ever have been so happy, so entirely devoted and blissful as they had been in these few months of marriage. There was surely nothing that could spoil the marvellous relationship they had discovered.

She took her leave of him at the top of the road that slipped down a little east of the cathedral close, towards the wall and his father's new home, and was making her way back homewards when she heard a strange commotion. Turning back, she saw her husband encircled by a small group of men, and she felt a quick fear that he was being set upon by a gang of cutpurses, but then she saw the breast of one of them and realised that these were no outlaws, they were merely a number of the sheriff's men.

'Husband? Are you all right?' she called.

He turned to her, and in his face she saw a clutching dread. Before he could say anything, she screamed.

She saw the iron-shod staff rise and crack down on his head, saw his knees fold, and his body slump to the road, and even as she tried to force her legs forward to go to his aid, she was aware of the hand of her servant clutching at her arm, and then the cobbles seemed to fade and rush towards her at the same time as she fainted.

Road outside Bow

'What are you all staring at?'

What the coroner lacked in subtlety, he more than made up

for in volume. As he reined in his beast, the men scattered and there was a moment's pregnant silence as they shuffled before the great horse and the rider glowering down at them all.

'Well? Who's in charge here?'

A nervous young man of maybe three-and-twenty sidled forward, his eyes fixed on the ground at his feet. He mumbled something, and Sir Richard scowled. 'Can't hear a word you're saying, man! Speak up, in God's name. He gave you a tongue so you could live to tell your tale today. What's going on here? Eh? You're all blocking the road.'

'It's a body, sire,' the man muttered.

'That's more like it!' the coroner said with satisfaction. 'Where's the stiff, then, eh? One of you lot kill him, did you?'

'No! It was no one here, Sir Knight. Must have been an unfortunate accident.'

Sir Richard threw a look at Simon, and then dropped heavily to the ground. 'Show me.'

'Here, sir. It's an old farmer called Jack from Begbeer. Jack was no coward, and if a cutpurse tried his luck, or any other outlaw, he would have tried to send them to the devil on his own.'

'Didn't do so well, did he?' Coroner Richard said without emotion. He had crouched at the side of the body and was studying the corpse where it lay. 'Who's been moving him about? Eh? Don't know? Who was the first finder?'

'Me, sir. I found him,' a lad of maybe thirteen squeaked. 'I did all I could to raise the hue and cry, but no one heard me up here, and I had to go into town to tell people there.'

Sir Richard nodded and listened as the men about started to speak of the farmer, how he had always been truculent since his house had been robbed some time ago, and how he was probably on his way to the market, or on his way back, when he had been waylaid. 'Well, this is all well and good, but I don't see I can help. Have you sent for the coroner?'

'Yes.'

It was the young fellow who had first spoken. 'What's your name, master?' Sir Richard asked, not unkindly.

'I am Gilbert, sire. From that cott over there,' he added helpfully, pointing at a small limewashed building nearby in a copse. 'I was made reeve.'

Sir Richard looked him over again. He was young and inexperienced, and if Sir Richard was any judge of character, which he knew he was, the twerp would have all manner of rings run around him daily by the sour-faced men of the vill. 'Very well, Master Reeve. When is the coroner expected to be here?'

Gilbert shrugged emphatically. 'He is based in Exeter. If he's there, it'll take a day or so for him to get here, I suppose. It'll take our man the same to get to him, so perhaps three days? Unless he's already away seeing another body, of course.'

Simon shot a look at the coroner. 'This is not Lifton, Coroner.'

Gilbert looked from one to the other. 'You're a coroner too? But then couldn't you . . .'

'I don't work here. I am king's coroner to Lifton, not this place.'

Simon could see that Sir Richard was torn; he stood some little while, chewing at his lip. 'I'll tell you, though, the coroner in Exeter will be glad of a little help, I expect. Perhaps if you could . . . Yes! Gilbert, send your fleetest rider after the fellow who's gone to Exeter, all the way to Exeter if need be, and tell the coroner that he'll have a copy of my inquest as soon as it's done. No point sending another man here when I'm already on the spot, eh, Simon?'

'No. I suppose not,' Simon said. He was fighting to hold back the frustration. Sir Richard knew how desperate Simon was to be gone to Tavistock to meet with the Cardinal de Fargis so that he could as soon as possible get home again, and here the man was, seeking to delay them both with an inquest.

'Very well. Do it now, Master Gilbert, and when you have done it, in God's good name fetch a skin or two of wine. Our throats are parched. And some meat would be good – or perhaps a couple of pies?'

Simon watched the appalled reeve listen to the demand for so much food and drink before he scampered off, calling to others to fetch the remainder of the jury, to run and ask the vill's priest to join them, and to help the coroner in any way he might require, and sending a man after the last messenger as Sir Richard suggested.

'Did you have to volunteer for this?' Simon hissed a little later as they tied their mounts to a nearby tree that had a convenient branch.

Sir Richard looked at him, and there was a serious expression in his eyes. 'Simon, look about you at this place. What sort of man would kill a farmer with a single stab to the throat? No one would think he had much money on him. But he was slain and left for dead in the ditch like a dog. I think he deserves a little time, don't you?'

Simon felt his face redden at the reproach in the coroner's voice, and he was about to apologise when the coroner leaned closer and said quietly, 'And look at the people here, Simon. They are terrified, if I'm any judge. I'd be willing to gamble that there's more to this than the simple waylaying of a single farmer.'

Chapter Eleven

Castle at Bow

Sir Robert was up late, as was usual for him, and dressed himself. He didn't like to have servants wandering about his private rooms. Only Osbert was trusted in his chambers, and no one else. There were too many knights and minor lords who had lost all – including their lives – through being too trusting about their servants. Some for being too trusting of their own sons.

There had been a time when a lord could rely on his men to be loyal. No longer. Now he was fortunate if he could find men who would serve him for money, let alone for mere loyalty. Sir Robert had no desire to be one of the fools who was killed in his bed at night just because he failed to see to his own protection. So Osbert and a couple of servants were allowed in the downstairs chamber with Basil, Sir Robert's son, while he himself slept alone upstairs.

As he entered his hall, he shot a look about him as usual, making sure where the various men were, and seeing that there was no possible threat. He was not scared of any man, but danger was no respecter of rank. The merest churl could slip a knife into his heart, whether he feared the boy or not. No one with a brain would depend on fellows like this. The only men he could rely on entirely were Osbert and one or two others; perhaps his son, on good days. Os because he was dependable: he had been with Sir Robert all through those difficult times when Sir Robert was a declared outlaw and must live off the land as best he could; his precious son, Basil, because he was utterly reliable. He was self-interested, hedonistic, licentious and dissolute, and Sir Robert would trust him always to do what he perceived as being in his own interests. That they would rarely coincide with Sir Robert's own aims would not worry him. He was seventeen years old now, and more than capable of choosing his own path.

Osbert was standing near the main door from the hall, and he levered himself away from the wall on seeing his master.

Stephen the messenger was standing in the corner farthest from Os, Sir Robert was amused to see. At least the man hadn't made life difficult by sitting before the master of the hall said he could. It would have made Sir Robert's life more troublesome if he had had to be killed before he could ride to Tavistock.

The messenger bowed. 'Sir Robert, I hope I see you well?'

'Messenger, you see me alive. There's little more to be said for any man,' Sir Robert said. He was feeling the worse for the wine of the night before, but when a man had been given good news, there was reason to celebrate. He strode to his table and peered about for the jug of wine.

'Will there be another message for me? Do you have a reply for me to take back to London?'

Sir Robert eyed him thoughtfully, although his plan was already laid. He had seen what must be done to make his life easier the last night, and now it was merely a case of persuading this fool to be a willing partner. 'Yes. There is one message I would have you deliver. It is not a reply, though. I wish you to ride to Lydford, and there to take a message to Tavistock. I will give it to you later.'

'I am a king's messenger, and I am supposed to be—'

'You are here to do Sir Hugh le Despenser's bidding,' Sir

Robert growled. 'And you will do that, by Christ, or I'll have your ballocks. You understand me?'

Stephen of Shoreditch nodded miserably. 'Sire.'

'Good. Now shut up and let me have my breakfast.'

Sir Robert glanced at the messenger and was confident that he was cowed for now. But there was no trusting a man like this. A messenger might feel that he had a duty to report to the king, anything that happened, and Sir Robert had a conviction that Sir Hugh le Despenser would be as reluctant as he himself for news of their plan to reach Edward's ears.

'Where is my wine?' he roared at the top of his voice. 'If that lazy, mother-swyving son of a whore and a churl doesn't bring my wine soon, I'll have him hanged from the tower!'

The steward was already hurrying to bring a big pewter jug and a mazer, and Sir Robert watched him unblinking until the jug and mazer were in front of him. Only then did he slam his fist into the man's belly hard enough to make him retch and collapse to the floor.

'In future, I want it here when I get up,' he said. He pushed the man away with his booted foot, looking around at the men in the hall. None appeared to take any notice as the steward crawled to the wall, sobbing silently, and Sir Robert took a long draught of wine.

The only man who looked shocked was the messenger.

Yes, Sir Robert told himself. He would have to remove that horse's arse before he could report to the king. He was a threat. 'Os? Go and find my son. I would speak with him and you. Alone.'

Road outside Bow

Simon had swallowed a hunk of bread and some dried meats while he watched the jury. There was not much that could be said, in fairness. The man was dead, killed from the stab to the throat. However, some members were talking of the fact that he had been on his way to the market, and many wanted to know what had happened to his goods. A robbery was always alarming in a small community, because if a robber dared attack one man, he would as likely attack another, and that meant no one was safe.

'I find he was murdered, a dagger used to stab him, and I estimate the value of the dagger was a shilling,' the coroner declared. He ran through the other details, and as he was finishing, glanced with an air of suspicion down at the clerk busily scribbling, for he never entirely trusted scribes to put down on paper what he had told them to.

Simon listened with half an ear while he chewed some more meat, but then he looked around at the sound of hoofs trotting. 'Dear heaven,' he muttered. Then, louder, 'Sir Richard! I think you have a visitor.'

'Eh? What do you mean?' the coroner thundered, peering past Simon at the newcomer. 'Who's that?'

'It's the coroner for the area,' Simon explained. 'Do you know Sir Peregrine de Barnstaple?'

'Hell's teeth! Sir Peregrine? Of course I know him,' the coroner roared, shouting, '*Sir Peregrine! God speed to you!*'

Sir Peregrine was soon with them. Simon thought he looked drawn and pale, but then he supposed that Sir Peregrine would think the same, looking at him.

'God speed, Sir Richard. Bailiff Puttock, I am glad to see you again,' Sir Peregrine said.

'And I am glad to see you too,' Simon replied.

'Is Sir Baldwin with you?'

'No, he is at his home, I think,' Simon said. He held out a little of the remaining bread and meat, jerking his head towards a skin of wine. 'Will you break your journey with us?'

Sir Peregrine accepted happily. Soon he was sitting at the

side of the road on an old fallen trunk, chewing. Nodding at the corpse as the men of the jury bundled it up and began to lift it to the sumpter horse brought for the purpose, he said, 'So you haven't enough murders of your own, eh, Sir Richard? You have decided to come here and look into mine as well?'

'I wouldn't, my dear Sir Peregrine, but we were passing by here, and I could hardly just leave the body lying,' Sir Richard said. 'The fellows here had sent a man to fetch you, but I sought to save you the journey.'

Sir Peregrine nodded and asked who the victim was. When he had glanced through the clerk's notes, he looked up at Simon. 'There seem to be so many murders just lately. I am returning to Exeter from Jacobstowe and another death even now. You know, I thought four years ago that the country was in a state of confusion and turmoil, but that was nothing compared to the present.'

'There are so many who were dispossessed after the battle,' Simon said.

'Boroughbridge saw the end of much that was good and stable,' Sir Peregrine agreed. 'So many families with the head of the house killed. So many arrested and executed, so many heirs who lost all . . .'

'Aye, and too many who forgot their vows,' Simon was forced to mention. He hated Sir Hugh le Despenser with a passion, but that could not blind him to the fact that the king was devoted to him. And those who opposed Despenser at Boroughbridge were forced to choose to rebel against their lawful anointed king as well.

'No excuse,' Sir Richard said uncompromisingly. 'Can't have just anyone runnin' round the place killing and taking whatever they want. That's no way to run a country. No, we have our duties – as do the sheriffs and keepers of the king's peace and so on.'

'Have you experience of our new sheriff?' Sir Peregrine enquired mildly.

'No. Who is he?'

'A repellent worm called Sir James de Cockington. Nasty little man. He came into office only a very short while ago, at the beginning of the month, and I think he's one of Despenser's men.'

Sir Richard did not know Sir Peregrine well. As a fellow knight, Sir Peregrine was familiar to him, but no more than that. The coroner was surprised to hear such a frank opinion. 'You say so, sir?'

'I do. The man would sell his mother for a farthing, and probably complain at the meanness of the sale,' Sir Peregrine said drily. 'In my years, I have known many sheriffs – some honourable men, some corrupt – and yet I find it hard to do justice to this fool and knave. The English language lacks sufficient emphasis for my contempt.'

Simon was grinning. 'What form does this man's dishonourable conduct take?'

Sir Peregrine looked over at him pensively. Simon had expected a light-hearted response, and thought that the coroner was merely thinking of a sarcastic word or two, but then Sir Peregrine looked up at the sky overhead.

'Simon, I can only think of one recent incident. It is indicative, I think, and instructive, too. A man's daughter was captured by a youth, who made play with her. You know my meaning, I am sure. The poor child was distraught at her treatment, and almost lost her mind. Now we three are all men of the law, but men of the world as well. We have all seen accusations of rape, and we all know, I am sure, that many are conceived as cheaper methods of ensnaring a fellow into wedlock. I do not dispute that sometimes there are less amiable motives behind such acts, but we all know these things happen. Once the girl has been ravished, she will have no other husband, whether she wishes it or no. Well, in this case, the sheriff listened to the pleas in his court, and decided that there was no case to answer. The boy's father had paid for his decision, and it was, if there was genuine offence given, that the girl must marry the boy.'

'It is one resolution, as you say,' Sir Richard said, lifting a wineskin and draining it. 'Usually has the desired effect. Child has a father, mother a husband. Good solution to the embarrassment.'

'Less good when the girl's family has already been told that their daughter will be given to the boy's servants to do with as they will if she demands marriage of him. Not that there was any need. The lad was at no risk. He had done too good a job of terrifying the poor child already. She dared not ask for his hand.'

'So what happened?' Simon asked, although he had a feeling he already knew the answer.

'The boy got off scot free, naturally. His father bit his thumb at the girl's father in open court. I saw him. Her father tried to leap at him, but some fellows about him held him back, and the family watched as their persecutors walked free. And then she was open to punishment for making a false accusation. She knew that she would either be punished herself, or exposed to ridicule by the man who had already raped her. She pulled out a knife, shrieked that the man was guilty, and stabbed herself in the breast.' He looked at Sir Richard. 'You've seen such things, I am sure. She died instantly.'

'The poor child,' Simon said.

'Aye,' Sir Richard agreed, shaking his head slowly. 'That is not a good tale.'

'Two days later her father too was dead,' Sir Peregrine said.

'It was said that he lost his mind and his heart when he saw his daughter die and there was nothing he could do to help her. He saw her with the dagger in her hand and guessed what she would do, but because of the men holding his arms to keep him from his tormentor, he could not reach her until too late.'

'He died from a broken heart, then?' Simon said.

'No. He was murdered in his turn. One assumes that the father or the son responsible for his daughter's death felt sure that he would seek to bring condign judgement upon their heads. The only good aspect is that so many saw her state of mind that her priest had no hesitation in declaring that her suicide was committed while she was unbalanced. She was given all the benefits of a Christian burial.' Sir Peregrine nodded with a sort of cold deliberation at the memory. 'That is the state of the law in this land, Bailiff. That is the realm we live in now.'

'Who was the man who did this?' Sir Richard growled. 'I would meet with him.'

'The son was Master Basil, the father Sir Robert, both of Nymet Traci, near Bow,' Sir Peregrine said. 'And I think that they are killing others now, as well.'

'You were talking of the sheriff, though,' Simon pointed out.

'Oh yes. You see, the sheriff is a close friend to Sir Robert and his son. He was justice in the court that found them innocent. He knew, oh, he knew what they were like. But they are all a part of the same intolerable clan – they are all associates of Despenser.'

Exeter

Pounding on the door with her fist, Edith sobbed and screamed for it to be opened, while her maid at her side tried to calm her, without success.

'Mother! Father! Please, open the door!' She was panting, and there was a pain thundering in her head at the memory of the scene she had witnessed, but there was little she could do – her entire being was concentrated on having the door opened to her so that she could demand the aid of her father-in-law in rescuing her husband.

It was an age before she finally heard the bolts shoot on the other side of the door, and at last she could stumble inside.

'Dear God, child, what has happened?'

It was her mother-in-law, and even as Edith sank down, incapable of supporting herself, so great was her relief at seeing a friendly face, she was aware of a feeling of enormous gratitude that it was Jan, rather than her more stern husband, Charles, who stood there as the servant opened the door to her.

Edith gabbled in her panic. 'Mother, Mother, they've arrested poor Peter. He was taken just now. A man hit him, hit him hard with a staff, and . . . and . . .'

'Be still, my dear,' Mistress Jan said. She was a short, dark-haired woman with a matronly figure. She knelt at Edith's side, holding her close. 'Child, you are freezing. You need a fire.'

'I am fine, it's Peter we . . .' Edith protested, anxious that Jan didn't believe her. Then, looking up, she saw the lines of fear in the older woman's face, the glittering in the dark eyes, and the compassion.

'I know. But if he's been taken to the castle, there is little we may do until we have a pleader to go and learn what he has been accused of, and why. You need to calm yourself, Edith, and I insist that you come to the fire and rest a while.' She held up a hand to stop dispute. 'Meantime I shall send a boy to my husband to acquaint him with the facts. There is nothing more we can do until he arrives.'

Edith wanted to protest. She wanted to be doing something,

anything, to help Peter, but there was a comfort in Peter's mother's voice. This woman was as worried as she was – perhaps more so. Edith couldn't imagine how hard it would be to hear that her own son had been taken, nor how difficult it would be to try to remain calm enough to soothe another woman while feeling that her own world was shattered.

'There is nothing more we can do,' the woman repeated. She helped Edith up and through to the hall. 'Sit here, and try to relax. After all, you've a duty to protect the child.'

'You knew?' Edith asked with frank astonishment.

'You thought you'd kept it hidden?' Mistress Jan chuckled tiredly.

She hurried from the room, and Edith was left before the fire, her maid beside her. Edith stared at the flames, and outwardly gave every sign of composure, but when she tried to think of her husband, her breath caught in her throat. She found herself sobbing like an old woman, with dry, hacking, choking sounds, and she discovered that all her thoughts were grim and dark as she clutched her maid's arm for support.

Road to Oakhampton

They had left Sir Peregrine when the sun was already past its zenith by a good half-hour. He had plenty of business to conduct himself, and was keen to get at least as far as Crediton before nightfall. That should not be any trouble, but Simon and Sir Richard still had many miles to go.

'What did you think of his words?' Sir Richard asked.

'I think that he is plainly alarmed by the way the law is becoming so disdained,' Simon said. He jogged along in the saddle for a few moments, thinking again about the way Sir Peregrine had commented upon the murders in the area. 'I was shocked to hear of the murder of the reeve, I confess. Most wandering bands would avoid harming a man such as he, if they can avoid it.'

'Aye. But the buggers are all over the place now. Indolent, idle and armed. It makes it all more problematic. If there's a gang that is prepared to kill twenty-odd people, that is a crime to be pursued, certainly.'

'Yes,' Simon agreed. 'Who would do that, too? A madman, surely.'

'No. Certainly not. An armed band desperate for money or food, perhaps, but certainly not a fool. They were clever enough to kill the whole lot, so there could be no witnesses, and then they took all that was worthwhile.'

'From what Sir Peregrine said, the clerical fellow had been wealthy,' Simon recalled. 'Rings and all the trappings. What kind of man would have stayed out in the wilds when there must be dozens of taverns along that road?'

'A man who feared being trapped?' Sir Richard wondered. 'I have often kept out of the smaller, less salubrious establishments while travelling, in case I may be set upon.'

Simon looked at him. Sir Richard had never, to his knowledge, avoided the meanest, foulest drinking dens. More commonly he would cheerfully declare that the better deals for wine or ale could be found in them. And then he would berate the keeper of the tavern until the very best drinks and foods were brought out for him. 'I had noticed,' he said with careful moderation.

'How far do you reckon we may travel today?' Sir Richard asked after a little while.

'I hope that by dark we should have reached Lydford,' Simon said.

He was not happy as they rode, though. For all that he had a most redoubtable companion in the figure of the coroner, this was one of the first times while passing through Devon that he had been aware of a sense of urgency and nervousness. Each great tree appeared to cast a curious shadow. At one point he was close to shouting a warning at Sir Richard when he saw a shadow suddenly shift, and it was only the quick realisation that it was in fact the movement of a branch causing it that stopped his voice. This was ridiculous! For him, a man in his middle years, to be so skittish in the face of fears was foolish in the extreme.

'I have heard of other families that live outside the law,' Sir Richard murmured.

'Sorry?' Simon asked, jolted from his reverie.

'This man Sir Robert de Traci and his appalling son. They sound dangerous to me. A man and his son who can work without the law. That makes a deadly combination.'

'The sheriff would appear to have allied himself with them,' Simon observed.

'Aye, well, there's many a sheriff – and judge – who will do that. I have heard of one sheriff who captured a fellow and kept him in gaol, torturing him until he confessed to some crimes, then forced him to name his friends as accomplices, just so he could fine them. Others will all too often take bribes to persuade a jury to go one way so that a guilty man will walk free – or to convict and hang another just so the guilty can pay him for his freedom. Cannot abide that. The thought of an innocent man being punished while the guilty is left to commit another crime is disgusting.'

'I don't know this man from Bow. Nor the sheriff,' Simon mentioned.

'Sir Robert's been there a while. Surprised you haven't met him yet.' Sir Richard explained how the knight had been a member of the king's household until he allied himself with the king's enemies, and after that had been outlawed. 'I had no idea he'd been restored to his former positions.'

'Surely the king wouldn't give him back his lands and life if he had been a traitor?'

The coroner grunted in response to that. 'Enough others have been pardoned for all their crimes.'

'I have tended to avoid these parts in recent years,' Simon said. 'Living on the moors, then down at Dartmouth; and recently I've been away so much that Bow doesn't seem a natural place to visit.'

'Aye, well, by the sound of things you should continue to avoid the place,' was Sir Richard's considered comment.

They dropped down into Oakhampton in the middle of the afternoon, much to the delight of Sir Richard, who, in the absence of a full wineskin, was growing almost morose. Then they took the Cornwall road past the castle, and on to the road south.

Simon would have liked to have left the roads, and at Prewley Moor he cast a longing glance to the moors themselves, but he was forced to agree with Sir Richard that it would have been foolhardy. There was no need to leave the roadway here. It was a good trail, with cleared verges for almost all the route to Lydford, and when they were approaching the town, they would be perfectly safe in any case. Better by far to keep to the road and make their journey more swiftly.

It was still an hour before nightfall when they trotted gently into the town where Simon had lived for such a long while. He cast about him as they went, fearing that they might even now be assailed by the men of Sir Hugh le Despenser, especially William atte Wattere, but for all his fears, there was no sign of anyone. Only some loud singing from the tavern as they passed, and the occasional barking of a dog, told them that people still lived here.

'This is my house,' Simon said as they reached the long,

low building. He stopped a moment and looked at it, feeling a distinct sense of alienation. The place had been his for such a long time, it was most curious to think that it had been taken from him so swiftly and easily. There was a shocking ruthlessness in the way that Despenser had gone about it, searching for a weakness in Simon's life, and then exploiting it without compunction. He had learned about Simon's lease while Simon was abroad on a mission for the king. A little pressure on the leaseholder was all that was needed, and Despenser owned the place. The most powerful man in the land after only the king himself was not the man to make an enemy.

So Simon had lost his home, but more importantly he had also lost his peace of mind. Any pleasure in his possessions was now marred by the realisation that they could be taken from him at any time. He had no control over his own destiny.

Of course a man always knew that the most valuable asset he owned, his life, could be snatched away in a moment. It took only a freak accident, a whim on the part of God Himself, and a man's soul was taken from him. Sometimes it was malevolent fate that men blamed, sometimes the evil in others, but Simon had been raised and educated at the Church of the Holy Cross and the Mother of Him Who Hung Thereon, the canonical church at Crediton, and the teachings of the canons there had influenced his life and thinking ever since.

His life was not something Simon had ever bothered to trouble himself over. He had a simple faith that because he was a Christian, when he died he would be taken up to heaven. There was no point troubling himself over the world and worldly things when the real life was yet to come. And yet he found more and more that the things he cared about most deeply were all too easily taken from him. Perhaps it was because of this, he thought, staring at the house. Such a solid, massive structure, so permanent, it seemed impossible to think that it could be taken from him in a matter of days, no matter what he tried to do to keep it. There was an inevitability about such things. Those things he loved most dearly, they were themselves the very things he would find being targeted by an enemy such as Sir Hugh le Despenser.

'Simon? You all right?' Sir Richard asked.

Nodding, Simon dropped from his horse and the two hitched their mounts to a ring in the wall. Then, taking a deep breath, Simon walked to his old door and beat upon it with his knuckles.

He felt sick to the pit of his stomach as he wondered who would open it.

Chapter Twelve

Exeter

Edith was walking along a screens passageway, and no matter how fast she walked, she could not reach the door at the far end, although she knew that on the other side was Peter, and she was desperate to get to him, to give him some consolation . . . And then she stumbled, and was falling, toppling over and over in the dark, and—

And then she came to with a jerk, startled from a heavy doze.

There were voices, and she sat up, still a little befuddled with sleep, rubbing her eyes as she stared towards the door.

Her maid was already there, she saw. Jane stood now at the door, and was peering out. Then she shot back into the room, staring at Edith with a perplexed expression in her eyes. It was enough to make Edith get to her feet. Whatever the horror, she wanted to hear it standing, not sitting like some invalid.

Shortly afterwards, Peter's father Charles was striding into the room, a scowl on his face, Mistress Jan hurrying in his wake.

Charles was a heavy-set man, attired in a fur-trimmed cloak and a tunic that was embroidered with gold at hem and neck. His usually calm, gentle eyes were now fretful and staring with his anger and concern.

'So, husband, what did they say?'

'They say he stands accused of crimes,' he said, looking

directly at Edith as he drew off his gloves, finger by finger. 'The sheriff said that Peter is considered a dangerous man who would seek the overthrow of the king. He is accused of plotting with others to have the king slain.'

'But . . . but that is mad, husband,' Mistress Jan said weakly.

Edith ran to her side as the older woman began to gasp, her breath coming in staccato gusts. She caught Mistress Jan as the woman started to fall. It was all she could do to support her. Jane ran to them, and she and Edith between them half carried her mother-in-law to a chair.

Her father-in-law watched as they settled Mistress Jan in the chair. There was no expression on his face as he stood gazing at them, only a kind of sad longing in his grey eyes.

Edith straightened. 'There's something else, isn't there? I can see it in your eyes. What is it?'

'He said . . . The sheriff said that this was you. If Peter hadn't married you, none of this would have happened. He said it was because of your father that Peter has been arrested.'

Lydford

Simon and Sir Richard stood in Simon's little hall, and bowed low to the Cardinal de Fargis. They waited in the doorway until they had taken off their swords and given them to a steward. The bottler arrived and stood near the cardinal as they walked to him, both falling to one knee before him, and kissing his ring.

'Please, you will stand,' the cardinal said, motioning with both hands. 'You bring honour to this little house by coming here. I am delighted to meet you both. Please, take some wine.'

He was a small, dapper man, clad in a thick woollen tunic with a heavy, fur-lined cloak against the chill he obviously felt. The fire was roaring, and Simon could see that Sir

Richard felt uncomfortably warm after the cool of the evening air. It was not only him. Simon himself felt rather like a candle left too close to a flame, as though he might at any moment melt and topple to the ground.

Cardinal de Fargis had kindly eyes, Simon thought, unlike so many other men of power and wealth. They were dark brown and intelligent, and like Abbot Champeaux, of blessed memory, he had a way of smiling with them that was entirely irresistible. It was a pleasant change to find a senior churchman who wasn't peering with short-sightedness, too, Simon felt. The cardinal seemed relaxed, calm and at his ease in their company.

'I am very glad to meet you at last, Master Puttock.'

'It is my pleasure, Cardinal.'

'And yet I understand that this house is a sad . . . um . . . the word is memory?'

'Yes, it is sad that I have lost it, but that is nothing to do with you, Cardinal. For my part, I have only good memories of this house. I was very happy here.'

'And I believe you used to be a stannary bailiff? Yes?'

'Well, yes. I was a bailiff on the moors,' he admitted. He would have liked to glance at Sir Richard, but that could have been considered rude. Any lord would expect an inferior to keep his eyes fixed on him.

'I think I have need of your assistance,' the cardinal said. He eyed Simon over the brim of his goblet, and gradually a smile warmed his face. 'There are some very sad events at the abbey.'

'I don't know that I can help with that,' Simon said. 'Both men are rather displeased with me.'

'So I have heard. You would seem to be most even handed with your enemies,' the cardinal said.

The problems at Tavistock Abbey had begun with the death

of Robert Champeaux, the last abbot. The brotherhood of monks had held an election to choose their new abbot. There were two contenders. Robert Busse was chosen by the majority, but John de Courtenay, one of the baronial family of Devon, deprecated the result, and made a series of wild allegations against Robert. Simon had been involved with Robert Busse shortly after John had begun his attacks, and had been horrified to learn that Robert had made use of a necromancer in Exeter to try to influence matters to his own benefit. Not only that; there were also allegations that plate and money had been taken from the abbey. And so, to settle the dispute, the pope had finally decided to send a negotiator to listen to the evidence of both sides and attempt to make peace between the brothers. And if that failed, to knock their heads together.

'I have much still to do,' the cardinal continued. 'And yet there is more. There are troubles on the moors and about the area. Men are taking advantage of the abbey's weakness in this period of interregnum. I need more men to control the moors.'

'I would be happy to do that,' Simon said, 'but I fear it is impossible for me now.'

'How impossible?'

'I have no house here. This was mine, but now, as soon as you leave, it will revert to Sir Hugh le Despenser, and he will take it over. He is no friend to me.'

'The abbey can provide you with a home.'

'I have a wife and children. It is better for me that I remain in my own house, where I can be with them,' Simon said firmly.

The cardinal made some more attempts to persuade him, but after their third cup of wine, he admitted defeat. 'It is a great pity, though. The land is growing ever more restless.'

'I know. Only five years ago it was quieter, even though

there had been the famine and the little wars up and down the country. I have never seen the sort of outbreaks of violence that there have been recently.'

'Yes? And what have you seen, Bailiff?'

Simon noticed that he used his old title again, but chose to ignore it. 'Only on the way here we found one poor man who had been slain at the roadside. And the coroner, Sir Peregrine, told us of another, a reeve – which is all the worse because he was investigating an attack and murders on the road near Jacobstowe.'

'Attack and murders, you say?' the cardinal asked. 'How many died?'

'He said nineteen. There was one man who may have been in Holy Orders, and a number of others. They had been robbed of a series of carts and horses, and their bodies cast to the ground and left.'

The cardinal was frowning. 'Did he say how long ago this was?'

'I think he said it was two weeks ago or so. Why, do you think you may know them? I know the coroner would be glad to hear from any man who might know who these fellows were. There was nothing on their bodies or nearby to say who they could have been.'

'It was two weeks ago that a man of mine was sent to London with a chest of money. It was the payment to the king for the period while the abbey was in a state of voidance. Abbot Champeaux was very foresighted, you understand, and purchased the right of the abbey to manage its own affairs when he died.'

'So what was the money for?'

'Your king is a skilful negotiator himself,' the cardinal said musingly. 'He sold the management during voidance for a hundred marks. That was ten years ago, on the thirtieth anniversary of Abbot Champeaux's appointment. But within the contract it was agreed that for every vacancy of forty days or fewer, the abbey must pay forty pounds to the king. And if longer, it must pay a proportionate amount, up to one hundred pounds in every year.'

Sir Richard whistled. 'A hundred pounds a year?'

'This was the first hundred pounds.' Cardinal de Fargis nodded. He looked at Simon. 'That was what my servant Pietro de Torrino was transporting. With him was Brother Anselm from Tavistock, and eight archers with two mounted men-at-arms. So you see, I would like to know if the dead man was he.'

Fourth Sunday after the Feast of the Archangel Michael*

Furnshill

Sir Baldwin and his wife had enjoyed a pleasant ride to and from the little chapel where they prayed, which was more than Baldwin could say for the sermon preached by the priest.

He was a new incumbent, this young vicar. Apparently he was the son of a moderately wealthy squire somewhere up in Somerset, and had been sent here to work for a fee when the previous man had been given some other churches and could afford to leave this little parish. It was a shame, because Baldwin had rather liked him. This fellow was an insipid little man, pale and unwholesome-looking. He had a great hooked nose set in a narrow face, which made him look rather like a hawk. But not so powerful. Rather, Baldwin thought his nostrils would be constantly dripping.

'He was only speaking as he thought right,' Jeanne said defensively.

---

*27 October 1325

'He was speaking as a fool,' Baldwin said. 'How could any man stand there and say that the Templars were evil and proof of God's enemies on earth?'

'He knew no better.'

'I could teach the fool.'

Baldwin, once a Templar, and devoted to his order, was insulted when others spoke of it in a derogatory manner, but the priest this morning had gone much further. He had said that the Templars were all so evil that they should have been destroyed utterly. The thrust of his comments was that the whole of Christendom was in turmoil because of a small number of cruel and dishonourable men, such as the Templars. If all the good men in a Christian community were to do nothing and leave the evil-doers to work unhindered, such behaviour would lead to robbery, murder and war. And then God would grow despondent and seek to punish the world. So unless people became more careful of their responsibilities, and tried to serve God, He might decide to send another famine, or a plague, or a flood.

'All because of the Templars, he said! The cretin!'

Jeanne knew that Baldwin's mood would soon pass. He was not a man who could dwell on the incompetence or stupidity of others for long. He knew how foolish men could be, and preferred to look beyond them to other men, of intelligence.

They had a short ride to their house, and on this day of rest Baldwin was looking forward to a good meal and an afternoon of utter peace. After the year he had experienced, the thought of such a day was enormously attractive. And for once there was no rain. It was not a bright sunny day, but nor was it cold or wet.

Nevertheless, he was still worried by all he had heard from his wife. The thought of the new sheriff was unpleasant, but there was nothing new about corruption in a sheriff. Baldwin was more concerned about the stories of violence in the shire generally. There were all too many outlaws now, since so many families had been dispossessed after Boroughbridge, and if their acts of violence were compounded by men who knew that they could rob or kill with impunity because of Despenser's support, it would make life intolerable. 'I wonder how Simon is faring,' he muttered.

'He'll be fine,' Jeanne said comfortingly. She slipped her hand through his arm and held on to him tightly, watching Richalda, their daughter, trotting uncertainly on ahead, stopping every so often to stare at an insect or into a puddle. Young Baldwin was being carried by Edgar's wife, Petronilla, while Edgar was immediately behind Baldwin, his smiling face moving constantly, watching hedges and fences, always alert for possible danger. He had been Baldwin's sergeant in the Knights Templar, and Baldwin knew that he could depend utterly on him.

It was a matter of pride to Baldwin that the household had grown so much now. Behind Petronilla came her own child, and then the various men and women who worked in the house or for Baldwin in the fields. It was a significant procession, he thought. Even Wat, who had been the bane of Baldwin's life four or five years ago, when he had been merely the cattle-man's son and who had got himself beastly drunk at Baldwin's wedding, had grown into a tall, good-looking soul of seventeen summers or so.

Baldwin had successfully managed to build a new life here after the horrors of the Templar persecutions. Perhaps he was extraordinarily fortunate to have been given this second chance – he only hoped and prayed that God had not given him this stability only to snatch it away again. Despenser knew that he had once been a Knight Templar, and that man was a bad enemy. It could all be taken away in an instant, Baldwin knew.

It was as they came in sight of the house that Edgar stepped forward.

'Sir Baldwin,' he said, 'do you see the horse?'

Baldwin glanced at him, and saw that Edgar was looking ahead, a slight frown on his face. Following his pointing finger, Baldwin saw that in the roadway ahead, in front of his house, there was a horse thundering over the road. Even as he watched, it turned off and pelted along his pasture, heading to his door.

'Edgar, you stay with the children and Jeanne,' he said, and set off at a trot.

Jacobstowe

Agnes knew before the knock. She knew before the face in the doorway. She knew before he began to speak, and she could do nothing.

She had been distracting herself, sometimes even – God forgive her! – swearing at poor Bill. She was trying to see to the vegetables while at the same time looking after Ant and tending all the animals on her own.

There were others there who'd be happy to help her. She knew that. But the trouble was, she had her own way of doing things, and if they were to come and try to help, she knew that it'd take her ages to get things back to the order she was used to.

Except it wasn't really that. The truth was, if she was to have another man come here to help her, she would feel as though it was admitting the fear she felt deep in the pit of her stomach: that he was dead.

He had never been away from home so long before. If he had gone to do any kind of work and been held up, he would always ensure that a message was sent to her, and if there was any doubt, he would have returned in person.

When he had gone, he said he would be no more than three days, maybe. To her that meant two days only. After that she had known something was wrong. And it wasn't only the length of time, it was the sensation in her belly. There was an unnatural queasiness there that was unsettling. She knew, *she knew*, that it meant something was wrong. But there was no one for her to tell.

The knock on her door was only the confirmation.

Furnshill

Edith almost fell from the horse at Baldwin's door as she ran to it and pounded on the timbers. 'Sir Baldwin! Sir Baldwin, help me!'

'My dear Edith, whatever is the matter?'

She turned to find Baldwin behind her, Jeanne and his household approaching up the lane. 'My husband, Sir Baldwin, he's been taken by the sheriff, and I don't know what to do!'

The door was opened, and she allowed herself to be brought inside, but she felt like one stupefied. Her hearing was less acute, her legs were unsteady, and she was all the while aware of a strange whooshing sound in her ears, which made her want to sit.

Sir Baldwin helped her to his own chair before the fire, and his wife began to issue commands. She told Edgar to fetch wine, Petronilla was ordered to bring cloths and a bowl of cool water, a maidservant was told to find some sweetmeats from the box in the pantry, and then all the other household members were ordered to leave.

'I feel sick,' Edith said. The nausea began in her belly, it was true, but it wasn't only that. There was the foul noise in her ears again, too, and now she was aware of flashing lights before her eyes. It was enough to make her heave. She had to close them just to stop the lights, to stop the urge to vomit.

'Let me!' Jeanne said to her husband, who had never been good when the children were sick, and she bellowed at the top of her voice for Petronilla again, to bring a bowl. The noise of her shouting was almost enough to make Edith throw up on the spot, but then the pandemonium eased and she was aware of a cool, damp cloth at the back of her neck, another on her brow, and even as she retched, her chest and belly tensing badly, she was aware of the effect of them. She was beginning to improve.

'Tell me what has happened,' Baldwin said.

His voice seemed to come from a great distance, as though the result of closing her eyes had made her a little deaf. It was too difficult to concentrate, too disorientating, and she forced her eyes open again. 'It's Peter! He's been arrested for treason against the king!'

Chapter Thirteen

Lydford

Simon woke with the blessed feeling that all was well with the world. He stretched languidly, aware that there were birds singing loudly outside, and smelled fresh bread baking. His head felt fine, his arms were unstrained, his shoulders worked easily, and his eyes, when he opened them, focused.

This was the best morning's wakening he had known while staying with Coroner Richard. It was almost as though the coroner had not been with him yesterday.

Simon was soon in his old hall, which felt odd. Last night it had been different. Perhaps it was because he had arrived here as a stranger, and was invited in. This morning, though, it was more peculiar. He had woken in his house, but not in his bed, and walked down to the hall which was his, and yet was filled with different people, servants and clerks who were entirely unknown to him. It made his breakfast feel rather unsettling.

'Ha! Simon, glad to see you surfaced! Can't keep a trout from snapping at the bait, eh? I said you'd be here as soon as you smelled the food. Don't suppose you slept too well, though, eh? Not enough wine,' added Sir Richard in an undertone. 'Pox on the clergy for keeping their booze to themselves.'

'So, Bailiff, I hope I see you well?' the cardinal said.

Simon nodded, bowing low. 'Very well, my lord.'

'And have you considered whether or not you would like to take on the duty I asked?'

'I would be very happy to see what I can learn about the death of your man, if it was him.'

'There is an easy way to find out. Inspect the body, and if it is poor Pietro, you will find a ragged scar as long as my hand's breadth on his right thigh. Just here,' he said, resting his hand on his upper thigh. 'He was kicked by a mule once, and the brute had a worn shoe that was as sharp as a razor. It made a most impressive scar.'

The steward hurried to his side, and the cardinal nodded as he whispered in his ear. 'Most interesting. There is a messenger from the king.'

Simon nodded, and he and Sir Richard stepped back as the dishevelled messenger appeared. He had clearly set off on his journey very early to have arrived here already.

'Where did you come from, messenger?'

'I was at Bow last night, my lord, and left there as early as I could to bring messages for you and for the abbey at Tavistock.'

'Please refresh yourself while you are here, then. I am sure a little wine and bread would be good? You should not be travelling today, though. Today should be a day of rest.'

Stephen of Shoreditch nodded, but he could not say that he was travelling because he was far from keen to remain in the castle at Bow. He was sure that he was not safe there. 'I shall take my rest when I reach Tavistock.'

'Good. Good,' the cardinal said. 'In the meantime, you can join us as we go to the church, yes?'

'I would be delighted to,' Stephen said.

Simon thought he looked worn out, but so often, he guessed, most messengers must look like that. They had to travel at least five-and-thirty miles each day, and still be bright enough to relay verbal messages or instructions, as well as being prepared to collect a reply. It wasn't the best job in the world.

There were worse, of course. And just now Simon didn't envy the cardinal. He was clearly a man who was putting on a good face as he strode along the road with his clerks behind him, their gowns flying in the wind like so many bats, while the servants struggled behind. The breeze was gusting viciously every so often, and the women were forced to hold on to their wimples, the men their hoods and hats, as they walked down the road, past the great blockhouse of Lydford Castle, the stannary prison and courthouse, to the church just beyond.

Simon had always loved this church. Once Lydford had been a great focus for the rebels against King William, so he had heard, because the townsfolk refused to accept that they must lose all their privileges and customs to the upstart king. This town, which had stood for a hundred years or more, and which was so highly regarded by the ancient kings of Wessex that they had granted the place the right to mint coins, would not listen to this new king from Normandy.

They were crushed, of course, as all the rebellious towns and cities were; as all were still. The use of force, that was the most effective power a king possessed. That was why, when Bristol refused to pay the king's tallage in 1312, King Edward II had sent the posse of the county against the city, and forced it to submit after a lengthy siege. And then his punishment of the city folk was exemplary.

But that was the way kings proved their right to rule – by regular exercise of overwhelming force. And this king was no different from his ancestors in that way. He *was* different because he used ruthlessness and vindictiveness on a scale never before seen. If a man was thought to have slighted him or his favourite, that man would be humiliated at best. Many were simply executed. But Edward took the whole concept of revenge to a new level, imprisoning wives, daughters and sons, and disinheriting boys for the infractions of their fathers. There was never a king who had used such formidable authority against his subjects before. Not in English history.

These reflections were enough to distract Simon from the sermon, which was, in any case, more lengthy than he would have liked, and the time passed moderately swiftly until the end of the service, when he found himself hemmed in by Sir Richard on one side and the messenger on the other.

The messenger looked not at all refreshed, Simon reckoned. 'You look like you could do with a rest,' he said. 'Why don't you stay with Cardinal de Fargis here for the day? You'll get no answer out of the abbey today anyway – they'll all be involved in their prayers.'

'I thank you,' the messenger said, 'but I must deliver this message, and that urgently. I would return to London as soon as I may.'

'No need to break your cods over it, though,' Sir Richard declared, earning a scandalised hiss from a cleric in the cardinal's retinue. 'What? What did I say? Did I say something amiss?'

'Do not worry about him,' Simon said, trying not to laugh. 'Do you only have one message to deliver, then?' he asked. 'I know the king's messengers will often have entire circuits to cover, but I suppose this is the end of yours?'

'Yes. And now I must be gone,' Stephen said shortly.

Simon looked over at the coroner. 'If you must, then God speed. I wish you well on your journey.'

'Thank you. And I you,' Stephen said, and strode off towards the cardinal's house and stables.

'He is lucky, that fellow,' Coroner Richard said

thoughtfully. 'If he'd spoken to me like that, I would have had his ballocks in a bucket.'

Jacobstowe

It took a little time for her to waken again. As she gradually appreciated that she was lying on the floor, she had to shake her head to clear it of the roaring sound in her ears, and then the strange conviction that there was a weight pressing down on her breast, holding her to the floor.

She tried to rise, but there was no strength in her arms, and she must strain and strain to try to get up.

'No, no, stay there, mistress! Wait, let me help you!'

'Hoppon!' she recalled. It was him. He had come to the door, two men behind him, and had drawn his cap off, twisting it between his old hands as he told her of the death of her man. Her Bill. Her Lark. Her life. Beaten to death. It was that word, 'beaten', that had made her breast start to spasm, made the sound roar in her ears, made the breath hot and raw in her throat. 'Help me up.'

One of the men had set her pot on the fire with water, and stewed some mint leaves for her. He passed a cup of it to her now, and the fragrance seemed to rise in her nostrils, clearing her mind and refreshing her. But not enough. Nothing could ever be enough, not now. 'Bill, oh my Bill!' she said, dropping the cup and gripping her stomach in a paroxysm of grief so intense she thought her heart must burst from her breast. She felt it like a clenching deep inside her, a tearing, desperate agony. Never to hold him to her, never to see his slow smile, his serious eyes turning tender and gentle when he held her, when he held the Ant. All was turned to misery and grim despair.

'Mistress, do you want him in here, or shall we carry him to the church now?' Hoppon asked.

She flung her head back. 'In here. Let me clear the table for him.'

It was something to have a reason to be busy. She stood, and for now the feebleness seemed to have left her. It took a little time to move the bowls and spoons from the table, and the pastry she had been making for a pie, and then it was clear. She took salt and a brush and scrubbed the wood until it was bleached white. The men offered to aid her, but she snapped at them. This was her grief; it was her last duty for her man.

At last, content that all was as clean as it could be, she curtly commanded Hoppon to bring in the body.

They had him on an old plank of elm. That, she thought, was suitable. There was a great elm down in the hedge at the bottom of their plot, and he had always been fond of that tree, sitting underneath it for shade on the hottest days, and taking refuge beneath it when the weather turned to rain. Once he and she had made love against the trunk, both standing, both too taken with urgent lust to walk the fifteen or twenty yards to the house. He had been such a good lover. Such a good man.

And now he was as dead as the elm plank on which he lay. The men set the plank on the table and gradually tilted it until he was lying on the table itself. Not that it was large enough to accommodate his frame. He overhung it by a good few feet, his legs dangling from the knee.

Ant sidled across the floor on his backside, gurgling, and reached out for the nearer leg. Agnes had not the heart to stop him. Instead she turned to the men. 'You have my gratitude, all of you. And now I would like to prepare him for his grave.'

'I will ask my wife to—'

'No. I will do this alone. He is my man. I will see to him,' she declared with absolute determination. 'It is not for anyone else.'

They left soon after, and she stood for a long time staring down at his face. His poor, bloody, ravaged face. She wanted to speak to him, to ask him what he had been doing, to rail at him for having the temerity to die when she hadn't expected it. But the only words that came were, 'It was only until next Michaelmas, you fool. Couldn't you have stayed alive that long?'

Ant was on the floor, looking up at her with a face that showed only utter concentration, once more as always, assessing her mood, ready to fit his own to suit hers. And as she gradually subsided into sobs, deep, womanly sobs for the life lost, the future snatched away, he began to wail too.

Furnshill

Baldwin watched, almost hopping from foot to foot, as Jeanne ministered to the girl.

Given a sword in his hand, an enemy charging towards him, a horse beneath him, Baldwin was in control. He knew his strength, he knew how to fight, he understood the points at which to aim his weapon, how to reverse his blade, how to fight in unison with others, how to deceive and slash or stab to win swiftly – but in a situation like this, with a young woman weeping and desolate, he was as useful as a wooden trivet over a fire. 'Do you want me to—'

'No,' Jeanne said curtly. 'Go and sit down. You are being a nuisance.'

'I don't understand, though,' Baldwin said, once he had taken himself away a short distance. 'How can they think that your husband is involved in some form of treason?'

'I don't know! I wish I knew – I wish I could find out! Sir Baldwin, you will help us, won't you? Peter's father is doing all he can, but he says he has no influence with this new sheriff. He said I should ask you. You are Keeper of the King's

Peace, and you have been to London to see the king himself – can't you help us?'

Baldwin looked at her. She was weeping all the time, her face red with her distress, and he felt his heart torn. 'I will do all I can,' he said, 'but you have to understand, I am not so popular with the sheriff or others. They think of me as an enemy of their master, Despenser, and would prefer to see me hurt and broken. If they thought it would offend me to keep your husband in gaol, they would do so. It is hard, I know. What of your father? Simon must be told of this too.'

'That was what they said. They said that they were holding Peter because of my father. Something about Peter being taken because of him. They said he wouldn't have been arrested if it wasn't for Father!'

Baldwin slowly walked to a stool not far from Edith and sat, studying her seriously. 'You are sure of that?'

'It is what my father-in-law said. As soon as I saw him and told him what had happened, he went straightway to see the sheriff, and the man said that it would have been better if Peter had never . . . never met me!'

Baldwin's face hardened. His sympathy for Edith knew no bounds, because he had known her since he first arrived here nine years ago, when she was only a child, and looked upon her as a man would a favourite but occasionally wayward grandchild. There had been times when he had been made angry by her rudeness to her father in recent years, but he was forced to admit to himself that most of those had been situations in which any young woman would tend to illogical humours. Even his own darling Richalda would probably display the same kind of intolerance of her father when she grew to become fourteen or more. It was the way of young girls.

No matter how often Edith had insulted Simon, she was still

Simon's daughter, and Baldwin would do all in his power to protect her.

'I will go and see this man. In the meantime, Edith, you must rest here. Jeanne, we should send Edgar to Simon's house to let him know what is happening and have him come to join me travelling to Exeter to see the sheriff.'

'Will you both be safe?' Jeanne asked quietly. She was afraid that her husband and Simon could both be arrested in their turn.

'Simon and I will visit Bishop Walter first,' Baldwin said. 'We shall be safe enough.'

'Perhaps Edith would prefer to be with her own mother when you ride to the city,' Jeanne considered.

'Quite right. What do you think, Edith? Do you want to remain here, or ride to your father's?'

'I must ride to Exeter,' Edith said without hesitation. 'My husband is there – he needs me.'

'You cannot go before us,' Baldwin said firmly. 'When we leave, you can join us, of course, but until then you will have to wait here. It would be too dangerous for you to travel alone.'

'I reached you here,' she pointed out.

'That is true, but the roads are too dangerous. The fact that you managed this far is no reason to compound your danger by riding back,' Baldwin said with a smile. 'Better by far that you wait here and rest. If not, you may of course come with me and Edgar when we go to speak with Simon.'

'I should be at my husband's side,' Edith said fretfully.

'And you will be, Edith,' Jeanne said. 'As soon as we can get you back there safely. But you know it's not safe for a pretty young woman to travel the roads here all alone.'

'And you cannot go back to Exeter now, in any case,' Baldwin said. 'You are plainly exhausted. You must rest. I am sure that would be for the best. Meanwhile, I'll have Edgar go to Simon's.'

'Could you not send me back to Exeter with one of your men? Wat is a big fellow,' Edith said. 'If you are worried about my safety, he would be a deterrent to all but the most determined of attackers.'

Baldwin had to smile at the thought. 'Wat may have the build of an ox, but he has a mind to equal it. If he was attacked, he'd have not the faintest idea what to do about it,' he chuckled. 'No, if you are to be safe—'

'Sir Baldwin, I know you mean well, but what you are asking me to do is to wait here until you have sent a man to my father's house, wait for him to return, and then go to Exeter. That means at least a whole day. And in that time, my husband lies in gaol. I will not do it, Sir Baldwin,' Edith said, and in her face Baldwin saw the resolution of her mother. Margaret, usually so gentle and calm, would every so often display the stubbornness of a mule. Edith was demonstrating a similar temperament.

'I do not think that we have any choice, child. The roads between here and Exeter are too dangerous.'

'Then let me go with Edgar to my father's house. At least then I will be doing *something*. We can all ride straight to Exeter afterwards and meet you there.'

Baldwin considered. She was clearly desperate to be kept busy, rather than sitting about. She was young and resilient, as he knew. But when he glanced at his wife, Jeanne shook her head slightly.

Jeanne touched Edith's arm. 'You need to rest. And Edgar can ride faster on his own. Do you let Edgar fetch your father, and then you can go with them to Exeter when you are rested.'

Edith's chin became more prominent. 'I will not rest. If

nothing else, I shall ride to my father's house. It is my husband who is captured, and I would tell my parents myself.'

Jeanne was about to argue, but Baldwin shook his head. 'Very well, Edith. You shall ride with Edgar and me when we go to fetch your father in the morning. However, we are not going to go anywhere today, because you are already exhausted.' As Edith began to argue again, he held up his hands. 'Enough! I believe this is best for you, and I will not have dissent. This is only because we wish to ensure your safety. Rest, and tomorrow I shall ride with you to Simon's.'

She looked away, and then gave a curt nod. Clearly she was not persuaded by all his reason, but Baldwin believed that she would at least obey.

He would have cause to regret his simple faith.

Chapter Fourteen

Tavistock Abbey

It was all over quickly, thanks to God. Stephen wanted nothing more to do with all these people. The knight and his men at Bow scared him, and he was anxious that he knew the contents of the message. The idea that he should be forced into collusion with Despenser and Sir Robert of Traci, through no fault of his own, was a dagger in his head. It felt as if a sharp blade was pressing upon his very brain.

He delivered the message while studiously avoiding the monk's eye. The man took it, read it, and nodded quietly to himself. 'Thank you. I shall tell you if there is to be a reply,' he said.

Stephen waited without showing his irritation, a silent figure standing in the doorway to the monk's chamber. It was odd to think that the man was here, in this little cell, when in theory he was to be the next abbot.

Tavistock might not be the greatest institution in the realm, but it wasn't far from the best-endowed monastery in the West Country. From it the lands extended in all directions, and it possessed estates far away. The daughter house on the Isle of Ennor was a source of fair revenues, and the fishing on the rivers and the many other ventures here in Devon ensured that in normal times the abbey would profit. However, these were not normal times. The famine had affected the abbey's stocks and herds of sheep, the rains and the river's spate had washed away several mills and damaged other investments, and finally the death of Abbot Champeaux had been a sore loss. His mild manner and calm, sensible attitude, as well as his infallible eye for a proposition that would aid the abbey, had changed the whole nature of the place. Initially, when he had been elected, the abbey had been in debt. He had changed that, so that by the time he died he could be considered in the same light as one of the abbey's founders and benefactors. Not that this happy condition could continue, from all Stephen had heard.

It was not only the massive payments the abbey was forced to pay to the king while it was in a state of voidance, nor even the sums that must be paid to the pope for the right to have the abbey's case heard and adjudicated; it was more due to the natural inclination of the monks to enjoy themselves while they might. As the abbey was technically without an abbot, there was no one to enforce strict rules about conduct, and the monks were eating and drinking far more than before.

That was itself plain even to Stephen as he walked about the grounds. Carts were arriving all the time with barrels of wine and fish, freshwater and sea, and Stephen could hear the baying of hounds. Later, as he hurried down the stairs from the monk's chamber, he knew only a relief that he would soon be away from here and back in the saddle once more.

It was a cause for enormous satisfaction that there was no message to be delivered to Bow. He would avoid that midden if he could. The casual murder of the farmer had scared him more than he would like to admit. And then Sir Robert de Traci had beaten his own servant, as though the steward's dereliction could be cause for execution – the man was only late with some wine, in God's name! So far as he was concerned, the messages had been delivered, and that was an end to it. He wanted nothing more to do with Bow, Sir Robert, nor even his son. The idea of passing through their town again was repellent.

Sadly, though, he couldn't very well avoid it entirely. He had asked a few of the grooms and some of the servants about the best way to get back to Exeter. One man had suggested taking the road south and there finding a ship to sail him along the coast, but Stephen had experienced ships before. He knew how unreliable the damned things were in the best of weather. Getting on a ship at this time of year was not to be borne. He understood that the winds were all too changeable, and that could mean either being held in port for days or weeks, or, worse, being tossed about on the open sea until every meal he had ever eaten had returned to haunt him.

There was no better suggestion, though, other than that he should head north, and pass through Oakhampton, thence to Crediton and Exeter. He had little choice, apparently. The alternative was a ride straight across the moors, but all the men he had spoken to were agreed that the roads there were still worse than the usual roads about here. Mostly there was a trail that could be followed over to the middle of the moors, but it was so boggy and treacherous that no one would offer much for his chances when he asked. The main road led from Lydford eastwards, but that was a perilous route: the mires were hideously dangerous, and too many people died on the moors each year. All agreed that it was safer by far to head north.

Stephen had his doubts, but he didn't feel justified in mentioning the fact that the moors were to him less terrifying than the thought of meeting with Sir Robert again.

As the sky began to darken, he was already on his horse and heading north. He would ride to a small inn he had seen that morning and demand a room for the night. There were not many advantages to his job, but the fact that he could demand

and expect to receive a room and food wherever he travelled within the kingdom was a great benefit on occasion.

The weather was cool, but at least for the moment it was dry, and he had on a heavy coat against the wind. This road was a foul one. It followed the line of the river at first, and then began to climb away, up one hill, and through Tavymarie, where the inn stood at the side of the road. At least here there was no need to worry about the dangers of Sir Robert, but even the mere thought of the man was enough to send a shiver down his spine.

He rode on along the valley of the Tavy, his horse's shoes sinking into the mud regularly. The river had plainly been in flood a little while ago – hardly surprising after this summer's weather, he thought. All about there was the rushing sound of the fast-moving waters, and he grew lulled by it. Not only that, perhaps. There was the natural feeling of a job done when he had delivered the last message. Now all he need concentrate on was the journey back to London, handing over his final messages, and then home for a rest. Riding so far for so long was exhausting at the best of times, but this had been the worst journey of his life, without doubt. If he never came to Devon again, he would be happy.

The patter of gravel against his leg and his palfrey's flank made him blink. He had been close to dozing, and the drowsiness was hard to lose, even when his mount jerked his head up and down in anger at such treatment.

'Messenger?' a voice said.

Stephen snapped his head around and saw Osbert on his left, a sword already in his hand, kicking his horse forward with grim determination. There was no defence against a man like him on his left, and Stephen drew his own sword as he spurred his beast into a wheel, so that he could meet the attack on his right, but even as he did so, he saw the dark, malevolent form of Basil hurtling towards him from the south. Shooting a look northwards, towards Tavymarie, he saw two more men cantering towards him. It was a most effective ambush – but they hadn't covered the east!

He hacked with his spurs, and felt the poor creature burst into action. There was a hedge lining much of the road here, but there was a small, narrow gap, which he could take. Whooping at the horse to egg him on, Stephen slapped him hard on the rump with the flat of his sword to encourage him, and bent low over his neck as they sprang through the little gap, not seeing the hempen cord stretched across it.

His horse caught the rope at the mouth, and it tore through the beast's lips, catching on his teeth and jerking his mouth down to his breast, almost breaking his neck. There was a crack like a small cannon as the rope parted, and one end whipped around, cutting through muscle and tendons on the creature's left shoulder like a razor and then ripping through Stephen's thigh.

The pain made them mistime their leap, and instead of the beast's forefeet landing square, both were angled away. There was a crack as a leg snapped, and suddenly Stephen was hurtling through the air. He had the foresight to drop his sword as he went, just before throwing his arms over his head. He landed in a pool of thick mud, which was at least soft, but winded and stunned, he remained there, panting, for a moment or two before he realised the danger.

'Oh, Christ in chains!' he muttered, and tried to stand. His head was sore, but it was the dull-wittedness from shock that slowed him. He could scarcely gather his thoughts as he forced himself to all fours. That was when he grew aware of the laughter.

Looking about him, he saw that his horse was thrashing about on his back, his foreleg flailing uselessly, whinnying in agony. The mud was flying up in all directions as he threw his hoofs about, and Stephen had to push himself away to be safe. And then, as he stared about him, he quickly fumbled in his message pouch. There were two, he knew, that should remain protected. He glanced down to check, and saw that he had the right ones. These he slipped under his shirt. These fools wouldn't think to look there, he thought. There was no bitterness in his head, only a cold, firm resolve. He would die soon, he knew. His only conviction was that he would try to mark them beforehand.

It wasn't the horse's agony that was making the men laugh. It was Basil, who was trying to pick his way through the mud without smothering himself in it. In one hand he held a sword. Fortunately their attention was all on him, and none had seen Stephen's quick extraction of the messages.

Better to die on his feet, he thought. He tried to stand, even tried to crawl to his own sword, but it was too far away, and his legs would not support him. He turned to face his opponent, pulling at his dagger as he did so, but Basil's sword was already at his throat.

'Go on then, you murdering prickle!' Stephen hissed from clenched teeth. He had to clench them to stop them chattering.

'We ain't goin' to kill you like that,' Basil said. He leaned down, and suddenly slammed the pommel of his sword into Stephen's temple. 'No, you're dying from an accident, master!'

The messenger was alive still, but his ability to resist was gone. As he was turned over and pressed face first into the mud, he could do nothing at first, and then, as the horror blazed in his mind and hideous pain started to sear his ravaged lungs, he was already too weak to fight back. He tried to kick, to punch, to pinch, anything, but the weight on his head was unrelenting, and his struggles gradually became more staccato as the life fled from him.

Fourth Monday after the Feast of the Archangel Michael*

Furnshill

Baldwin knew something was wrong even as he slept. He was aware of a looming danger, a hideous and overwhelming presence. He dreamed that there was a menacing figure over him, and that although his sword was just to the side of his bed, he couldn't reach it: he dared not. To move would be to alert the creature to his presence just as surely as calling out. The sweat was running from his body as he lay still, petrified with horror.

And then it was not him. This was not some wraith seeking *him*. It was looking for younger flesh. Baldwin realised it sought Edith, and with that the spell was broken.

He rolled from the bed, shivering with the chill as the cool morning air caught his damp flesh. The sweat had been no dream, and he was drenched, as was his bedding. At the farther extent of his hearing he could swear that there was a horse riding away, fast.

'Darling . . .' Jeanne mumbled, but he was already pulling a chemise over his head, thrusting his arms into the sleeves and hurrying to the chamber below, where Edith was supposed to be sleeping.

Jeanne was at the top of the stairs. 'Baldwin?'

'She is gone. The bed has been slept in, but the bedclothes are already cold to the touch. She must have risen long before dawn.'

'The foolish child,' Jeanne groaned. 'Will she have gone to Simon's house?'

*28 October 1325

'I don't know. I think I hope so. Better that than that she should have taken the Exeter road,' he said.

'At least the Exeter road will be quiet at this time of morning,' Jeanne said reasonably.

'Yes. But she will still need to get through the city gates. Ach! I was a cretin to trust her!'

'Don't berate yourself, Baldwin. Get yourself dressed, and I will fetch food for you to take. You will need to go to Simon's before anything else.'

'She may have gone to Exeter, though,' he said pensively. 'I shall have to send Edgar to Simon's, while I go after her to the city, just in case she is in danger. It will hasten matters if I can see Bishop Walter and petition the sheriff too. Very well!'

Turning, Baldwin went up the stairs as quickly as he could, and began to dress in a hurry.

He would never forgive himself if harm came to that young woman.

Thorverton

Edith had known the roads all about this part of the country from an early age, and she had no fears about finding her way. From the age of eight she had been riding about these lanes with her parents when they visited Sir Baldwin, and often they would continue on from his house to go to the market at Exeter or to see their friend Bishop Walter Stapledon. Just as she had been able to ride to Baldwin's the previous day, she was confident that she could get home again.

She had wanted only two things: to make sure that her father knew her plight, and to enlist the help of Baldwin too. There was no need for her to go to her old home at Sandford just now, though. She knew that Baldwin would send a man there. No, it was more crucial that she went to her own home in Exeter to begin to plan how to ensure the escape of her husband from gaol.

Peter was such a sensitive fellow, so mild of nature, so gentle and kind. She was convinced that he would find the experience of gaol absolutely horrific, and the only thought in her mind was how to get him out and free again.

There was a light mist over the ground as she dropped down towards the Exe, and she felt a chill. It had been a bitterly cold night, but then she always did feel the cold. It was so strange to experience that again now, after the last months of sleeping with her husband always at her side to warm her. In Baldwin's house she had felt dreadfully uncomfortable, but that was only because her husband was not with her. Now she was cold and tired, but that was no surprise. How could she sleep while poor Peter was in Rougemont Castle, suffering from the freezing temperatures, wet, hungry and uncomfortable? It would be unthinkable that she should remain in Baldwin's bed while Peter was there.

From somewhere there came a clatter, and she stopped to peer behind her. The mist was thicker here, and it was impossible to see anything, but she felt sure that she had heard a hoof striking stones. There shouldn't be anybody out at this time of the morning, though. The city gates wouldn't open for ages yet. She was only up this early because she was desperate to be closer to her husband. There was no reason for anyone else to be out on horseback, surely.

She felt a sudden sensation of absolute coldness and wondrous fear. It was hard even to turn back to face the road ahead, she was so nervous of whoever might be behind her, but she stiffened her resolve with the thought of Peter, and urged her horse onwards.

The road here wound about the river most of the way down to the city itself. At the bottom there was the great bridge, which gave on to the west gate. That was where she had intended to cross the river, and there was a little inn at the western edge of the bridge where she had hoped to rest a while before entering the city as the gates opened, but there was a good mile or two before she would come to the bridge, and very few people between here and there. If she was attacked, there was little likelihood that she would be able to call for help with any hope of success. No, better by far that she should hurry herself and make her way to the bridge.

She was about to whip the horse into greater efforts when she heard a voice.

'Mistress? Are you all right? No one should be about so early in the morning.'

She cast a look back, fretful, but sure that she recognised the voice.

'Don't you remember me?' he asked. He was a lawyerly-looking fellow, she thought. Hardly threatening. He wasn't a hulking, strong man with arms like tree trunks, rather he was fine boned, from the look of him. Quite slender. He wore a cloak that smothered his shoulders, and a broad-brimmed hat that obscured his features, while a cloth swaddled his throat and mouth against the early-morning chill. He looked the sort of man she could imagine her husband bringing home for wine and food. But there was something.

'I am sorry, master. You have the better of me. I do not know you.'

'Of course you do,' he said with a smile. 'I know your father. He is Simon Puttock, isn't he?'

'Yes, sire. But who are—'

'Don't you recall? You met me in his house at Lydford, just a little before I took it from him for my master, Sir Hugh le Despenser,' William atte Wattere said, grasping her wrist.

His face came into sharp focus suddenly. She remembered

entering her father's hall and seeing this man and Simon coming to blows with their swords. In the horror of the memory, she gasped, and then opened her mouth to scream.

'If you'll be a good maid, you may just live to see him again. Misbehave, and you'll die. Quickly, and without warning.'

Chapter Fifteen

Jacobstowe

Agnes had not rested. Her night had been spent alone with Bill's body, alternately weeping and praying. She was sure in her mind that she would meet him again, when she went to heaven, but the thought that she must now endure her life without his companionship and lazy grin was so hard to accept.

The idea that he had suddenly been stolen away from her . . . Her lovely man was dead. His spirit had fled. It was so difficult to understand how God could have allowed it to happen. When the priest came to try to comfort her, she had listened to his empty, foolish words, and had slowly closed the door on him. What could the man say to her, to her who had lost her darling husband? The priest had never known the love of a man for a woman. He had no concept of the bond that two people could feel, especially one that was mortared by the sharing of the creation of a child. He had no idea how love of that sort could elevate a person's *soul*. And so he had not even the faintest understanding of the utter *loss* that the death implied.

As she grew aware of the sunlight filtering through the shutters over her windows, she forced herself to her feet. There was still her work to be done. Mercifully Ant was still. He had slept all through after crying himself to sleep on her lap as she sobbed. It was natural for a child to understand the misery and devastation of such a loss. Entirely natural.

She went outside, pulling the shutters open, then scattered some grain for the chickens, letting them free from the coop, and took some scraps to the pig, before returning to the house and setting about starting the fire.

It was a miserable morning, and the day would grow worse, she knew. But she must do all she could and keep the house running. There was nothing else for it. It was what Bill would have wanted.

'Mistress?'

She was feeding Ant when the knock came, and soon Hoppon was in the room with her, his cap in his hand, while other faces she recognised peered at her from outside. Why did all these churls live, when God had taken her own precious darling?

'You'll be needing someone to take Bill up to the church, we reckoned. You want for us to help?'

She looked at him with fleeting incomprehension. There seemed no reason to take Bill anywhere, and then her mind allowed her to recall that he was dead. Anger flooded her, anger at God, at Hoppon, at the world – but most of all, anger at her husband. How could he dare to die and leave her and Ant all alone? How *dare* he!

'Yes.' She rose, shivering, and suddenly felt as though she must fall down. Her legs seemed as insubstantial as feathers. 'Yes, please help me,' she said, in a voice bereft of all but misery.

Sourton Down

Up at the edge of the moors, Simon felt more cheerful. It was always good to be here on the high ground, looking down on God's own country. West he could see Cornwall, with Bodmin gleaming in a burst of sunshine, while northwards was the lowering mass of Exmoor.

'So what'll you do, then?' Sir Richard asked as they

breasted the hill's western flank and could stare ahead towards Meldon and Oakhampton.

'I think I have little option. I'll ride on to where the bodies were all found, up near Jacobstowe, and then see if I can learn anything about the men who died. With that sort of money involved, somebody must have seen or heard something. If a small gang of felons took it all, they'll have been celebrating ever since.'

'True enough. There never was an outlaw born who had the sense of a child,' Sir Richard said. 'A man would have thought that most of them would realise that sprinkling coins about the wenches in a tavern, when all their lives they've been as wealthy as a churl on alms, would make a few people suspicious. But they never do.'

'Are you riding straight back to Lifton?' Simon asked. He felt a slight trepidation. The idea of spending too much time with the coroner was alarming, because the man was undoubtedly one of the very worst he had ever met when it came to giving him sickly hangovers. On the other hand, he was a loyal, amiable character with a shrewd mind, when it was free of thoughts of wine, women and food.

'I was thinking about that. I wouldn't want to leave you all alone. Performing an inquest on a matter such as this is hazardous, my friend. And you are all alone.'

'I am here!' protested the man behind them.

This was the clerk whom Cardinal de Fargis had commanded to join Simon in order to record all he learned. Brother Mark was a skinny little fellow, but he had the humorous face of an imp. He reminded Simon of some of the figures that adorned the church at Lydford. But he did not merit consideration as protection against a man such as the one who could beat a reeve to death, let alone a gang that could kill a band of nineteen travellers.

'Yes. I would be glad of someone to help defend me,' Simon admitted.

'What of me?' Brother Mark asked plaintively.

Sir Richard sniffed. 'I suppose it is fair to say that since this money was the king's, and was deposited with his officers, it is reasonable to suppose that I would be failing in my duties to him were I not to aid you in this inquest.'

'I can do that!' Mark stated with vigour.

Simon agreed. 'It is plainly the king's service. It would be to his advantage were you to help me in this matter.'

Sir Richard nodded, looked westwards reflectively, and then threw a glance at the clerk behind them. 'What? No comments? No arguing? No protestations of your ability to help us?'

Mark gave him a look of contemptuous disgust. 'I see no further reason to waste my breath.'

'Good. Perhaps the rest of our journey will be all the more peaceful,' Sir Richard said with a chuckle. 'In the meantime, we should hurry ourselves if we are to make our way to a house in time for dark. Simon, you know this area better than me, I am sure. Which is our best direction?'

Simon pointed. 'Straight up to Oakhampton, thence to Abbeyford. If there is anything to be learned, it will be up there.'

Their journey took them a little past the middle of the morning. Before noon they were already ambling along the roadway through the woods.

'A good old wood, this,' the coroner remarked, looking about him with an appreciative eye. 'I would like a place like this myself. A man could make a lot of money from it.'

'Yes. The people about here have good incomes,' Simon agreed. 'The charcoal burners make good use of it, and there is always enough for the coppicers to gather.'

That was obvious. No matter where they looked, little glades had been harvested. There was little that would go to waste in a wood like this. Even as they rode along, they could see wisps of smoke from some of the charcoal burners' ovens. Simon glanced about him, and then picked a broad track that led them in among the trees.

The path was straight at first, and then curved to the left and round to the right until they were almost riding back the way they had come. At the end of their path there was an area of an acre or so, in which the trees had been cut back. Coppicing was an ancient art, and Simon could see that this little clearing was well maintained. The coppicer would cut back the stems from the trees initially when they had reached seven or eight feet in height. Naturally the trees would try to grow back by thrusting up with two or even three more stems, and after six or seven years the coppicer would return to harvest these too, and so the round of harvesting would continue. Each year enough poles would be taken for making handles, for building, for cropping to make faggots for fires, or for charcoal.

At the far edge of the clearing there was a charcoal burner with his tent. When making an oven to roast the poles for charcoal, it was essential that the burner remained at the site all day and night, watching and carefully helping the fire to cook the coals without ever catching light. A week's work in cutting, and another in carefully building the fire could be wasted by a little carelessness. Simon had worked with charcoal burners in his time, and knew how difficult it was to make a good oven. The burners would build a large pyre of wood, with a chimney in the middle. About this large circular oven they would then construct a massive earthwork, first smothering all the wood with ferns, and then layering soil over the top, until the whole heap was a man's height and twice a man's height in diameter, with only a small hole in the top. At last when all was ready, and it was plain that there were no other holes from which any smoke could leak, they would drop burning coals down into the midst of the chimney, and once the fire was well caught they would block the top with more ferns and earth.

That was the fascinating time for Simon. He would watch as the smoke started to leach out from the soil. Sometimes there was a disaster, and a hole would appear in the earth, and when that happened, the burner would quickly shovel more soil over the top, sometimes sprinkling water too, to keep the soil together. Otherwise the entire crop of charcoal would merely burn like wood, and the burner would find only ash remaining when he opened the oven.

Today there was a fine smoke coming from the sides of the oven. It was a perfect-looking pile, Simon thought. Once the smoke had stopped fighting its way from the chamber inside, and the whole oven had cooled, the burners would leave it for some days before breaking into it to retrieve the cooled coals from within. That was more than a week and a half away for this one, by the look of the smoke.

'God speed, friend,' Simon said.

Charcoal burners had a reputation for being surly, but in Simon's experience it was generally the result of living so many months each year away from all other people. They tended to spend all their time in the woods, and the chance of meeting another human was remote.

This man was not like the others he had known, though. At the sight of Simon and the others, he grinned broadly and doffed his cap respectfully. 'Masters, you are welcome.'

'Master, God give you a good day,' Simon responded.

'Here he always does, master,' the burner said with a laugh. 'He gives me water to drink, food to eat, and all the wood I need for my work. What more could a man ask?'

'You are alone?' Sir Richard asked.

'Aye – but there are others in the woods within a short distance,' the burner said, and his smile became a little fixed, as though he was wondering whether these men had come to rob him.

Simon soon soothed him. 'Friend, I am sent with the good coroner here to learn more about the deaths of a number of men here some weeks ago.'

'You're a coroner? You weren't here for the inquest.'

Sir Richard shook his head. 'I am the coroner for Lifton, for the king. However, there is a religious aspect to this attack, and Cardinal de Fargis has asked us to enquire into the details.'

'Those poor travellers? Ah, that was a bad business.'

'Did you see them?' Simon asked.

'When the coroner came, I went to witness it. I thought it was right, you know? Seemed wrong for the folks there to have all been killed and no one go to tell their story for them.'

'Were there not many there at the inquest?'

'Oh, most of us went in the end. But people weren't going to at first, because of nervousness.'

'Why?' Simon asked.

'Why do you think? There was a man there, a priest, I think. He was a crophead. They'd cut his eyes out. Coroner said it might have been before he was killed. Who'd do a thing like that? A bunch of outlaws big enough to kill so many must have been a large band indeed. And any man who goes to try to help catch such people is likely himself to be killed. No one wants to take risks. But we who live here in the trees have an appreciation of how to treat people. And we have strength in our numbers.'

Sir Richard nodded. 'Yes, and the best thing is, you're all used to working with your hands and sharp tools, eh? Any felon trying his luck with coppicers would find himself down one arm! Eh?'

'Well, there is that,' the man said equably.

Sir Richard grinned and looked about them. He knew perfectly well that there were other coppicers near, and almost certainly all watching him. 'You can tell them to loosen their bowstrings, friend.'

'I expect you were asked much about the night of the attack?' Simon said.

'Yes.'

'Did you hear any attacking men that night? Passing up this road, say? Returning in a hurry?'

'No, there was nothing. The bastards must have come from north of here.' The man was very convincing in his certainty.

'Can you show us where the folks were all found?' Simon asked.

The man eyed him and the others for a moment, and then gave a nod. 'Yes, master. Follow me.'

Furnshill

The journey to Simon's house was at least a half-morning's ride, while that to Exeter was a little longer. Baldwin spent the early morning rushing about gathering necessary items ready for his journey, bellowing orders to the servants and his wife, before taking a late breakfast with Edgar.

'Do you go to Simon's house with all the speed you can muster,' he said. 'I am depending upon your speed, Edgar. You must tell Simon about his daughter's husband and her predicament. Tell him that the sheriff is an ally of bloody Despenser, and that the man is no friend to Simon. You can also tell him that Edith's father-in-law heard the sheriff say that it was her fault his son was in gaol.'

'Are you sure Simon should hear that?' Jeanne asked

quietly. 'He may not take heed of caution if he's told that.'

'I can calm him when he reaches Exeter,' Baldwin said. 'For now, I deem it essential that he understands the full danger of the situation. Tell him all that, Edgar, and then ride with him.'

Jeanne said, 'Would it not be better for you to go to Simon, Baldwin? Then you could try to dissuade him from any rashness.'

'My love, how could I stop him? This is his daughter and her husband we are talking about. I would not think even the bishop himself could persuade Simon to remain quietly at home, say, for his own security.'

Later, as he rode quickly along the faster road to Exeter, he was reminded of those words.

It was impossible to ask a man to remain safe at home when his daughter was in danger. And Baldwin was convinced that Edith was in trouble of a very serious nature. If the sheriff saw fit to take her husband, the repercussions would be extremely grave. For the man to behave in this manner, he must be certain in his own mind that he was secure. Despenser – perhaps the king himself – must have assured him that he was safe.

There was another aspect of the affair that gave Baldwin some pause for thought. The comment about poor Peter only being in danger because of Edith and Simon had been made to Edith's father-in-law, and that surely meant that the sheriff's words, and the implicit challenge in them, had been intended to be relayed to Simon. Baldwin's fear now was that there was a trap being set for Simon in Exeter. And he intended to be there for Simon when he arrived so that he could protect his friend.

He made good time. For once the weather had held, and as he clattered down the Oakhampton Road to the old inn at the foot of Cowick Street, and began to thunder at a canter over the massive bridge, past the chapel of St Edmund on his left, past the reek of the tanner's works on Exe Island, and up to the great gate itself, he was aware of an increasing fear for Simon's safety.

His luck held at the gate, too. The porter here, Jankin, was a younger man, with the cheerful disposition of a tavern keeper with a new brew to sell. His brown eyes were a light colour, with a little red in them, and he had the appearance of a man who was never far from a happy thought. He looked as though he would be more at ease before a fire with a jug of strong ale near to hand. 'Sir Baldwin, God speed!'

'God give you a good day,' Baldwin returned. 'Good Master Jankin, have you see my friend Simon Puttock's daughter this morning?'

'Mistress Edith? No. She hasn't passed by here. I know her well.'

'Are you sure? She was sleeping at my house last night. You have heard of her husband?'

'Peter, the son of Charles the Merchant? Yes. The whole city knows about his arrest. There is no sense in it, Sir Baldwin. Nobody can make sense of that. He is as rebellious as a sheepdog. He wouldn't hurt the king for anything.'

'No, I agree. But he has been accused, so must be arrested. These are hard times, my friend. Edith was so fearful, she left my house before light this morning. I assumed she came back here, but you are sure she didn't pass by?'

'I would have seen her. There's been no sign of her today,' Jankin said with certainty. 'Could she have ridden to the north gate instead of mine?'

'It is possible. I didn't consider that,' Baldwin admitted. 'It is rather out of the way, for someone riding from Furshill, unless she managed to cross the river much further north.' He frowned. That was unlikely. No, it was more probable that she had not come here, but had ridden straight to Simon's. She would want his support and her mother's sympathy.

He left the gatekeeper and rode on as fast as the streets would allow him to the carfoix, and then turned into the cathedral close. He wanted to ask for the bishop's aid. Baldwin had the strong impression that this affair could only be resolved with negotiation, no matter what the reasons behind the arrest were.

The bishop's palace stood at the south-western edge of the close. Baldwin rode straight to it, and soon he was in the bishop's hall.

Bishop Walter sat at his desk as Baldwin strode in. Baldwin crossed the floor to him, kneeled, and kissed his ring. 'My lord bishop, you have heard about Simon's daughter and her husband?'

'The city is all talking about it,' Bishop Walter said.

'Simon will be on his way here already, I expect. My lord, you must help us to have the boy Peter freed. You know what Simon's temper is like. We have to stop him from doing anything that could exacerbate matters.'

The bishop put his hand on Baldwin's sadly. 'You don't realise, Sir Baldwin. The sheriff has the full support of Despenser. I am afraid I don't think there is anything you or I can do. The boy will have to remain in gaol until the sheriff decides to put him on trial. And we just have to pray that when he is put to trial, the sheriff and his friends don't present false evidence or have others to lie in court. But,' he added heavily, 'for my part, I believe that such a hope is forlorn.'

Abbeyford Woods
Mark stopped his mount and looked about him as they approached the clearing where the bodies had been found. He

had a faint superstitious wariness about the place. It felt . . . *foul*. There was some repellent atmosphere that lingered, he was sure. It was the sort of feeling that would make any monk recoil, and he held back, aware of a curious and deeply unpleasant feeling in his belly, as though he was preparing himself for the sudden appearance of a series of demons and ghosts, all ready to assault him. It was, for a moment, supremely terrifying.

And then the moment passed. A single beam of light from the sun burst through the clouds and trees above, shining down into the clearing, and Mark smiled, because he knew God had chosen to ease his mind.

The knight was not happy with him. Well, he wasn't happy to be here at the beck and call of such an arrogant pig of a man. He had the eating habits and drinking capacity of a hog. Mark had seen him at their short breakfast, guzzling ale until it ran down his chest, mingling with his beard and staining his tunic, chewing while drinking. Utterly revolting. Clearly one of those lower-level rural knights with little in the head and less in the heart.

Mark blew out a long breath and cast about him. The most important thing was the money. That chest with the coin inside was a large casket, fettered with iron and padlocked. It was too much for one man to carry, much too much. It was on a cart, with the archers set about it and two men-at-arms on horseback to give added protection. Not that they had succeeded, of course, he thought sadly, thinking of Pietro and Brother Anselm. He didn't know Pietro de Torrino well, of course. The portly old fellow had only arrived here in Devon with the cardinal. Brother Anselm was different. He had been at Tavistock for an age. A quick-witted, humorous fellow, Anselm was always playing practical jokes. If it was true that he was dead he really was going to be sorely missed. He was one of those characters who made the misery of cold nights in the church in mid-winter almost bearable.

There was a flash from the sun glinting on metal, and Mark wondered what it might be. Probably an arrow lying on the ground, its energy spent. The men who attacked here must have expended a number of missiles to be able to wipe out so many speedily enough to ensure that none escaped, he thought.

It was a most distressing thought. The idea that a group of men could willingly set themselves to attack a band of wanderers, slaying men, women and children. The charcoal burner had spoken of the nineteen people found here, but he denied that he had heard anything. Almost certainly he was lying – but who could blame a man for being silent on such a matter? As he had said, few would want to expose themselves to the risk of being attacked from men of this sort. And yet no one appeared to know who was responsible, nor where they came from.

He caught another glimpse of the sparkle from the sun. On a whim, he kicked his little beast on, and rode over towards it.

The thing, whatever it was, lay in the midst of a thorny bramble, and he was most reluctant to do anything about it. In truth, he was just thinking about leaving it, when he noticed that a large stick had fallen from a tree nearby. It appeared so fortuitous, that he wondered whether God had been leaving him a most virile clue, and he groaned to himself, dropped from the saddle, and picked up the stick. With it, he was able to push aside the worst of the brambles and see what it was that had glinted so fascinatingly.

There was a thong of leather set in it, and he hooked this with his stick and tried to lift it free, but naturally the thong was untied. It had been removed from a man's throat, after all. Mark had to push down the worst of the brambles, and then risk reaching in to grab his prize. It was a marvellously wrought crucifix, a most rare item, made from silver, with tiny enamelled decorations up and down each part. Truly, it was a beautiful piece of workmanship.

'Mark? Mark, where are you?' he heard Simon call, and he poked about a little more in the brambles, hoping to find something else, but there was nothing.

'Look. I found this over there in the bushes,' Mark said. 'I know this piece of work. It was Pietro de Torrino's. It's not English-made. I think he brought it with him from his homeland.'

Simon picked it up and sighed. 'Yes. I suppose they took it from him and dropped it as they left.'

Mark nodded. The coroner, however, was less convinced. 'What do you mean? Over there? That's far from the way in or out, ain't it?'

It was Mark who frowned and said, 'So what? Perhaps he took it off himself and flung it away so that no one would take that which he most prized?'

Simon said, 'Sir Richard, do not forget – we were told that the monk had been tortured. His eyes were put out before he died, so they thought. If that was so, perhaps they were questioning him about where he had thrown his cross?'

'If they saw it fly through the air, they'd have known. Oh, I suppose the bastards could have just been trying to make him suffer for throwing the thing away. They wouldn't have found it in the middle of the night, though, would they? No one with a brain would think they could in a wood like this, eh?'

Simon weighed the crucifix in his hand. 'You're sure this was Pietro's? Well, if so, you'd best keep hold of it and take it to the cardinal. But it is curious that it was thrown away. A man like Pietro, surely, would value something like this so highly that he wouldn't fling it into the woods? He would hold on to it, hoping that he might escape death from his captors. Not many would willingly slay a priest or a monk.'

'You have a point,' Sir Richard said. 'But slay him they did, and the cross was in the bush, so read me the riddle, Simon.'

'If I could do that, I would be a coroner or keeper!' Simon chuckled. 'But I'm a mere seeker of the truth in my own little way. Come! Let's see what else may be found.'

Chapter Sixteen

Tavistock Abbey

Abbot-elect Robert Busse was a genial man in appearance. He had the good fortune to have been a brother within the abbey for many years already, and he was known and loved by most of his brothers here in the abbey.

It had been a dreadful shock when Abbot Robert Champeaux suddenly died. But the working of the abbey must continue, no matter what tragedy was sent to test the brothers.

After all, monks were one of the most important of the three classes of man. They were the religious arm, whose duty was to save souls. They worked ceaselessly, praying and honouring God for the protection of those who were dead, and those who would die.

The *bellatores* were the second. These, the warriors, the knights, squires and men-at-arms, existed to protect all others. They had a duty to uphold the laws, to serve the religious, and to keep the third class in their place. These, the peasants, had the task of providing their labour such that the other two classes, and their own, would have enough to eat and drink.

These were the three legs of the world, the tripod that supported all mankind. And like any tripod, the three had to balance. If one was enormously more powerful than another, the leg too long, then the tripod would be unbalanced. As soon as a weight was hung from it, the lack of symmetry would become obvious. If one leg was too weak, the same rule applied. Ideally, like a tripod, all the legs should be exactly the same. Strong enough to support each other, strong enough to carry a heavy load.

But today in the kingdom, so much was out of balance. If the king was taken as the head of the *bellatores*, then the warrior class was vastly overpowerful. The men who were supposed to serve and protect were instead like wolves running down a hill to attack a flock of sheep. Meanwhile the other two arms were weaker, relatively. The Church had suffered so much in recent years. There were the obvious stories of Pope Celestine V being murdered by Boniface VIII, and the tales of corruption that were so hard to deny – no man who had travelled to Avignon to see the papal palace could have any doubt about that. And no man who had read the life of St Francis could fail to be moved by the appalling waste, the profligacy, and the shameful misuse of so many funds.

Certainly Robert Busse was not going to make excuses for the men who lived so well. He and his brethren in Tavistock were far more humble. Their own meagre rations were perhaps a little more generous than those of the average peasant living in one of the nearby vills, but no one could have accused the brothers of living a life of ease and extravagance. The only one who truly deserved such a reputation was Brother John de Courtenay. The man was a dreadful spend-thrift, and his habit of hunting with his hounds was a local disgrace. Added to that was his atrocious dress sense, for the man would keep trying to follow all the new fashions, and he was rapidly becoming a laughing stock among the lay brothers and other servants.

The abbey needed certainty. Especially now, with money being paid to the king for the period of voidance. There had been stories that Hugh le Despenser was trying to take the cash for himself. Robert Busse found that all too easy to believe. From all he had heard and seen, the man had an insatiable appetite for money. Still, the fact was that the money must be paid. And the sooner the abbacy was settled, the sooner they could stop paying out vast sums.

He crossed from the cloister out to the abbot's private little garden, and sat on a turf bench. A curious innovation, which would have been more in keeping in a lady's garden, he wondered whether it would give him piles, it was often so damp. But today, in the sun, it felt very comfortable.

And he needed comfort so that he could consider the note the messenger had brought to him. Opening it again, he scanned the contents of the little parchment roll once more. It told him that the king desired to see the matter of the abbot's election completed, and would like to have Robert installed. If Robert were able to arrange for a sum of money to be deposited with Sir Robert de Traci, the king would use all his good offices to see to it that the abbacy was once and for all settled upon Robert Busse. After all, he had won the election. There was no sense whatever in leaving matters dragging on.

Robert Busse tapped his lips with the roll of parchment. It made sense. The appalling greed of Sir Hugh le Despenser was known to everyone in the land. From all he had heard, the king would always enthusiastically reward his favourite with money when he was given it, and perhaps the idea was that he would take any funds from Tavistock and settle the abbacy, while giving the money to his friend. And all Robert Busse need do was take the money to Sir Robert de Traci.

One of the series of accusations levelled against Abbot-elect Robert was that he had stolen £1,200 from the abbey earlier this year. Oh, and that he had taken gold and silver plate worth another £800 – and a silver casket. Clearly the stories of his greed had become widespread, he noted sadly. A man who began his reign as abbot with all these tales against him was bound to the handicapped from the start. There was little he could do about the malicious lies being told about him by the de Courtenay faction in the abbey, though. It would seem that the stories had spread so widely that they had come to the attention of the king and his friend in London already. And knowing his reputation, they had come to consider him open to this proposal.

It did not matter whether it was the king or Despenser who had had the idea. Probably it was Despenser, he thought. That man would leave no purse unopened in his ambition to be as rich as Croesus. And thinking that the abbot could have been himself guilty of similar greedy manipulation of events, they thought that they could take advantage of his desires.

So in order to become abbot, he need only collect the sum demanded, and in return the king would confirm his favoured position. If he were to pay, he could guarantee Edward's approval. That would be a strong inducement for a man of limited honour and much greed.

'Father Abbot! Father Abbot, you should come at once.'

'What is it, my son?'

The novice was a boy called Peter, and he stood before Robert now, panting, his round face ruddy, eyes staring. 'It's the messenger. The king's messenger? He's died, Father Abbot. He was found over at the roadside near Tavymarie. Looks like he fell from his poor horse and died, Father Abbot, drowned in a pool of mud at the river's side!'

Robert Busse nodded and stood. He looked about him with a little smile, the roll of parchment still in his hand, and then glanced down at it. He carefully stowed it in his scrip, before following the lad to view the body. The messenger would have to be laid out in the parish church of St Rumon, and the abbey would have to find money to provide mourners and pay for the body's wrappings. And for another man to take the pouch with all the replies and messages to the king.

He smiled again now, a broad smile of understanding that did not touch his eyes.

If he was cynical, he might think that someone could have wanted to catch a messenger with an incriminating message. Perhaps a message from an abbot-elect agreeing to pay for the post to be confirmed. Even a message that gave details of the precise amount to be paid, signed by the abbot himself. Such a piece of parchment would be worth much to a man who was ruthless enough to consider taking it. Such a scrap could be rewarded by an abbacy.

It was fortunate, he considered, that he was neither cynical nor a fool. And that he had no intention of stealing money from the abbey to fund his elevation.

The abbacy was entirely in the hands of God. Robert Busse would not demean the position by stealing to gain it.

Abbeyford Woods

Simon and Sir Richard gazed about them as they returned to the wide space in the middle of the trees. It was a glorious place for a camp, and Simon could easily understand why it would have been chosen, although there was one detail that confused him. It had been in his mind already, but Mark's discovery of the crucifix had somehow solidified it. 'What were they doing so far north of the road from Oakhampton?'

Sir Richard looked at him questioningly. 'Eh?'

'Just look at this place. The Exeter road is due east from Oakhampton. If they'd been going to the king, they'd have carried on to Exeter and London, so they'd have left Oakhampton by the Crediton Road. Why turn north?'

The coroner shrugged. 'That is something to consider,' he agreed. 'Perhaps they were lost? It happens. I once left a town near London and started off towards home, as I thought, but when the clouds cleared I learned I was heading off to Scotland. When it's cloudy, it is easy to become confused.'

Brother Mark sniffed haughtily. 'It was a clear day.'

'What was?'

'The day that these fellows left. It was just over two weeks ago, and we have had excellent weather from then until a week ago. Do you try to tell me that they would have had the immense stupidity to think that north was east? If this was the group, there were two good brothers with them, and although Pietro didn't know the area, Brother Anselm would never have made so elementary an error.'

'Oh, really?' the coroner said, and would have continued, but then he frowned, and nodded. 'Even a monk with a butcher's crop must know where the sun rises and sets.'

'Well, Anselm did. I know he was good at directions. It makes no sense for him to have come up here.'

Simon left them and began searching about the area.

The charcoal burner was standing watching the three, arms akimbo, an expression of amusement on his face. 'What are you looking for?'

'Anything that could tell us what happened here,' Simon said shortly. 'Sometimes the men who commit acts of this nature can leave signs behind to show who they were.'

'There's no doubt who they were,' the charcoal burner said.

'You know?' Simon asked.

'I reckon anyone east of here would be able to guess. They don't often come here, but just recently there's been a number of folks killed on the roads.'

'Not here, you say?' Sir Richard demanded. 'Where, then? Who do you think could be responsible?'

'Sirs, I come from Coleford. I only wander over here a few times each year. Round my home, there are always stories of men being knocked on the head and their goods stolen. And I'm told that there is a large force in Bow. A force of men that would be able to fight even a large party of travellers.'

The coroner's face took on a scowl. 'Bow? That's where Sir Robert lives, isn't it? He's a knight.'

Brother Mark gave a short harrumph.

'What is that supposed to mean, Brother Mark?' Sir Richard said sharply.

'Only that there are enough knights who have failed to live up to their chivalric ideals. Would you be so shocked to learn that this Sir Robert was another in the same mould?'

'Monk, you overstep your position,' Sir Richard said. 'But in this case you may be right.'

Brother Mark sniffed disdainfully.

'Do you know many who live about this area?' Simon said to the charcoal burner.

'A few. Most are up at Jacobstowe.'

'How far's that?' the coroner said, still eyeing Brother Mark suspiciously.

Simon could answer him. 'It's only a matter of a mile or so. I assume that's where they took the bodies?'

'I reckon,' the charcoal burner agreed.

'Did you tell the coroner about your suspicions?' Simon said.

'No. He didn't see me. The others around here, they all wanted to keep it quiet.'

'That's stupid,' the coroner declared. 'Keep it quiet and they'll be fined all the more.'

'Aye, perhaps that's true,' the burner said easily. 'But at least they won't have Sir Robert of Traci coming to visit and ask 'em why they have been telling stories about him.'

Crediton

William atte Wattere had kept a tight grip on her all the way from the Exe to here, and Edith dared not make a sound as they rode up the high street, only praying that none of her father's friends might see her and ask where she was going.

There were enough people whom she knew here. This was the town where she had gone all the time when she was a child, the only large market town near her home. And her father had regularly brought her here with her mother when he came to have discussions with the priests, especially Dean Peter at the church. It had sometimes seemed to her that more of her life was spent here in Crediton with her mother in the shops than was spent at their farm.

Surely someone must see her and comment? She hoped not. The thought of the man's reaction were that to happen was too dreadful to contemplate. It made her shiver, and she could feel the hot bile in her throat at the thought. If anyone challenged them, he had made it clear what he would do.

The road was a great broad swathe through the centre of the town, and the rich red mud was stirred by travellers, splashing liberally over horses and men alike. People at the side of the road would dart back away from any approaching horse and rider: all were reluctant to stand too near and have their finest clothing stained and ruined. Few even turned to look as she was led up the slight incline that gave on to the town proper from the flat pastures east of the town. There was one woman whom Edith was sure she recognised, a woman called Beatrice, who was the wife of a silversmith, but the woman only frowned at the fast pace of the horses, and turned with a scowl of contempt at people who threatened other folk's tunics with their urgency.

There were monks and canons, traders, hawkers and merchants all over the town. They were most of them known to Edith personally, and if she were to call to them, some might recognise her, perhaps even run to her aid.

'Oh Holy Mother, please don't let them know me,' she whispered.

Because by the time anyone managed to reach her, she would be dead. Wattere had slipped a rope about her neck, and even now it lay there, a heavy, prickly mass that felt like death itself. If she was to try to ride away, if she was to merely stop, or turn her horse aside, he had threatened that he would immediately spur his own beast, and drag her from hers by the throat. She would be throttled within a few yards, if she didn't break her neck.

Not that anyone would see it. He had carefully bound it about her throat and then hidden it beneath her cloak so that prying eyes wouldn't notice. All anybody could see, if they were close enough, was a cord joining her horse to a loop over his wrist.

But it did mean she daren't call out. Any opportunity for doing so had flown as she cowered from him and he tightened the hemp about her like an executioner on the gallows. No, she dared not call for help, even though the thought of what he might do to her was enough to leave her petrified with terror. Although if he was going to rape her, surely he would already have done so, wouldn't he? And he must know that there was no point trying to rob her. She had nothing of any value on her person. No, it was more likely that he wanted her for some other reason.

But if it wasn't rape, and it wasn't to steal from her, she had no idea what that reason could be. All she knew was that worry about her fate was sending her half mad with fear.

Chapter Seventeen

Exeter's West Gate

Baldwin stood at the gateway with a deepening frown on his face. It was past the middle hour now, and the sun was beginning the long, slow journey to the west, and there was still no sign of Edgar.

That was unfair, he told himself for the hundredth time. The distance from his house to Simon's, followed by the journey from Simon's to Exeter, meant that there was little likelihood that Edgar could have reached here yet. And every moment that passed meant it was more likely that he had found Edith there with Simon. So Edith and Simon would have to mount their own horses to make the journey here, which would hold up matters a little longer – all of which meant that it was good news that he had seen no one yet. If there was bad news, Edgar would arrive all the sooner.

He forced himself to sit on a nearby bench and lean against the wall. Every so often in the last week the sun had broken through the clouds, and when it did, the flash of warmth would make a man feel as though he was a king. But not today. Today Baldwin felt more like a pauper who craved any form of succour. It was strange how the disappearance of Edith had shocked him. It was only to be expected, of course, because she was in his care from the moment she arrived at his house, but it was hardly his fault if the wayward woman had decided to leave without telling him.

Ach, in God's name he prayed that she was safe. It would break Simon's heart were she to be hurt. She could have fallen prey to thieves or outlaws; she might simply have fallen from her horse, and even now be lying in a ditch, for all he knew. The idea of the poor child sobbing in the dirt made his scalp tighten. He could feel the anxiety as a tightening band over the top of his skull.

It was *intolerable*! He stood, striding to the gate again. At this time of day, the flow of people in and out was not at its peak – that would be when the gates first opened and all the farmers from around would wait patiently to enter the city to sell their produce – but it was busy for all that, and Baldwin had to curb his tongue as he was jostled and shoved by the peasants who were fighting to get inside.

And then, thank the Lord for His mercy, Baldwin saw a familiar face in among the people pushing their way up the steep hill: Edgar.

Instant relief flooded his soul. At last the others were here. And without a doubt, Simon would be just behind, concealed by the throng. Hopefully Edith would be with them both, he thought, peering around the faces approaching him. He could see Edgar clearly enough, but there was no one else with him, so far as he could tell. No sign of the father or daughter.

The tension in his head grew steadily until Edgar was with him. 'She was not there?'

'No, nor Simon either. He's over at Tavistock, Sir Baldwin. He went there with Sir Richard of Welles.'

Baldwin stared out to the west. 'Sweet Jesus, Edgar. She could be anywhere, couldn't she?'

'I saw no sign on the road. There are not that many roads she could have taken,' Edgar said reasonably. 'If you did not see her on your path, then surely she will be either already in the city, or—'

'She is not. I have hunted for her already,' Baldwin said.

'Then perhaps she has halted for some food?'

Baldwin looked at him. 'What did you tell Margaret?' he said, not bothering to dignify the comment with a response.

Edgar was patting his mount's neck as he spoke. 'Nothing. I only asked whether Simon was there, but when she said he was not, I did not tell her that Edith came to see you. I thought that without Simon there, it would not be kind to tell her.'

'Good. The last thing we need to do is leave her in a state of fear as well,' Baldwin said. 'Dear God, where can she be?'

He walked away from the crowds, away from his servant. There was nothing to be gained by any further remonstration or mental self-flagellation. It would not help Edith. This was a time when action was required. He paced up and down, head down, deep in thought, while he considered options. At last he took a deep breath and returned to Edgar.

'Very well, we have to raise the posse to search the roads if we can. I shall have to ask the sheriff if he could support the hue and cry being sent along all the paths from here to Furnshill. It is possible that she lies somewhere between Furnshill and Sandford, but we shall have to take that risk.'

'After all we've heard about the sheriff, is he likely to help?' Edgar said without emotion.

'We shall have to see,' Baldwin said.

Jacobstowe

The church had been filled to overflowing as the vicar stood at the altar and went through the formal ceremony that acknowledged Bill's death, but Agnes knew nothing about that. Her eyes remained fixed upon the funeral hearse and the form of her husband beneath.

Her eyes were gritty from tears and from lack of sleep, and whenever she blinked, it felt as though she was rubbing dirt into the lids, but the pain didn't concern her. It was almost welcome, as though this was her penance for still living when her darling Bill was gone. How could he do that to her! Just die, without a passing word to say how much he loved her, without saying all those things she'd wanted to hear. There had been no leave-taking, other than the perfunctory form, as though he would only be gone for a few hours. Now he was dead, and she must cope with all the aftermath.

But perhaps it was a justified punishment, for so crassly trying to put all the blame on him for her feelings now, when after all, his poor beautiful face was evidence enough that her man was the one who had suffered and paid for his mortal sins in those last moments of life.

Oh, if only she had been there to take vengeance on the men who did this!

The vicar was motioning to her to turn, and she realised that the hearse was being lifted, to be carried out to the cemetery. In a daze, she followed it, behind the vicar, as he mumbled his incomprehensible words in that weird language.

The graveyard was behind the church, and from here she could see the sweep of the land about. The cemetery was high up, as though the souls would need a tall springboard to make their way to heaven. Not that her man would.

It was a cool day, the sun smothered by grey clouds, and she could feel a shiver run through her body as she looked down. The grave looked so desolate. She would have liked to sprinkle flowers in there. Forget-me-nots, cowslips, poppies, all the flowers he had adored. But this time of year there was nothing. Nothing at all. Even the last roses had given up their petals. All poor Bill could have was his hood. She had brought it with her, tucked into her bosom like a talisman against this hideous ending.

Ant sniffled, and the vicar hesitated, glaring at him as

though it was the boy's fault that he had been interrupted. He should have understood that a child's despair could not be willed away or thrashed from him. He had to have his cry. It was the natural way.

Anyway, what was the use of the vicar's words, when no one could understand them? Some said they liked to hear them because they were comforting, like the little rag dolls children would take with them to bed. Well, she had no need of such toys. She would have been happier if he would only talk to her in English, in the good tongue of the land here, the language her husband had spoken, but this gobbledegook was meaningless. It was the language of the priests and vicars who tried to protect souls, and who couldn't protect her man from those who wanted to kill him. The religious folk were no good to her. She needed a man who could find her husband's murderers and kill them for her. But there were none about who could do that. The coroner himself had said as much.

At the grave, the body was lifted clumsily and three men helped the sexton to lower it to the edge. The hole looked enormous to her, compared with the frail bundle of linen that had been her husband. Her Bill.

The corpse had been stiff as a plank when they brought him to her. Overnight she had thought it was as if he was gripping hold of his body still, determined not to give up his life, desperate to retain his hold on it. But not now. She could see that his limbs were flaccid and loose. There was no form of life in that wrapping. It was just an accumulation of bones and meat, like the animals killed and butchered each year. It wasn't her man any more. He had gone. Truly, he had gone.

She wept again now, silent tears that flowed down her cheeks, while Ant began to wail. She had to pick him up and cradle him as he bawled for his incomprehension, for his father, whom he could never know. For the world that had suddenly become so threatening to him.

It was in the midst of her tears that she saw the three men standing and watching. And then, as the people began to depart, she saw them walk towards the vicar: one knight, one monk and another man, with a grim face.

She saw them, but didn't take notice. Instead she walked to the graveside and peered down with Ant. In her hands she had the hood now, and she took it out, holding it to her face, inhaling his scent as though that would keep him here with her just a little longer. A shred of linen moved aside, and she found herself staring at a small patch of his flesh, just about his cheek. It was the last sight she would have of him.

'Madam? May we speak with you about your husband?' she heard, and turned to find the three men nearby. The man who spoke was the grim-faced one. But now, as she looked at him, she saw that there was something else in his eyes, and it made her spark to rage in an instant.

She didn't want his *pity*.

Road near Oakhampton

'You worried about passing through the town again?'

Basil was sitting with one thigh flung over his horse's withers, picking at a scrap of meat that was wedged between two teeth as he cast a grin at the other men.

Osbert didn't look at him. There was no need to. He knew all about Basil. He was the sort of weakly creature who'd make fun of those stronger than him when he had men at his back, just to show that he had the greater force with him. Arrogant, foolish, he had grown to manhood with violence all around him. Living rough, as they all had, Basil had never known the gentle comforts of life in a great hall, had never seen the subtle interplay of characters as those with authority negotiated their way around the customs and little delicacies that were so essential to life in a large household. Instead he believed in simple, raw power. And because he was his father's son, he believed in exercising that power at every possible opportunity.

'Not scared, no.'

There was plenty to think about. Osbert had been through the messenger's pouch, looking for the message that should have been there, but there was nothing. It was possible, he knew, that the man had been given a verbal message, but if that was the case, it was so much the better that he was dead. No one would want him to go straight to the king and blurt out something about the offer made to Busse at Tavistock. No, it was probably better this way. And since the monk hadn't accepted, they'd have to think up some alternative. Sir Robert had more or less hinted that he reckoned that would be the way of things. He expected that they would have to take some other approach to forcing Busse to drop out of the running for the abbacy. He didn't believe Busse was as corruptible as Despenser felt; perhaps it was merely that Despenser assumed everyone had a price.

'Oh, I didn't ask if you were scared, Os. I wouldn't suggest that. No, I thought you might be a little concerned, though. Anxious, right? After all, that was the town where you showed your ability to lead strangers, eh?'

Osbert groaned to himself. The lad would keep on needling at a man. 'It's easy. Told them the road past your father was too dangerous.'

'And it is, isn't it? But the way you took them, that was perfect. Just far enough to make them secure for us to catch them. The only problem—'

'I'm not worried about Oakhampton. It's not for me we avoid it.'

'Oh, it's for my good, then?' Basil laughed.

There were times like this when Osbert could still see the little boy that this lad had once been.

Before their fall from the king's household, branded traitors and forced to wander the roads and forests, Basil had been a happy-go-lucky boy. There hadn't been a great problem with him. He'd been the same as all boys: using slings and bows, practising his swordplay, and most of all enjoying a joke and some fun. But somehow something had loosened in his head or his heart. Osbert reckoned he had needed the calming influence of a woman while he was younger. Too late now. Now he was a man, and he wouldn't listen to anyone. That had been shown by his capture of the miller's daughter. They'd had to have the sheriff agree his innocence in court for that, and later see to the death of the miller himself, just to ensure that Basil was safe.

Osbert was sure that Basil would be the last of his line. He would be sure to die before long, once his father's restraining influence was gone. If he kept up this behaviour for much longer, it would be Osbert himself who killed him. While he kept on making snide little comments about the others all the time, winding a rope about their souls tighter and tighter, until at last a man had to explode, that was one thing; if he tried it with Osbert, he would soon learn his error.

'Yes. We avoid the town for your good, Basil.'

'Tell me, how could it be in my interests? There are taverns in that town, aren't there? Places where the whores go, places where I could catch a smile and a kiss.'

'That's why 'tisn't in your interests,' Osbert said. 'If you go in the town, you'll find a bint and hold us up for hours. We don't have time.'

Basil nodded and straightened his leg, settling it in the stirrup again. 'Well, many thanks for your protection of me, but I think I can cope. You hurry on homewards. I'll probably catch you up anyway.'

'Your father wouldn't want you to go and stop in town,' Osbert said.

'Well he's not here, is he?' Basil said, gathering up his reins.

'No. But I am.'

'I don't give a turd for you, though. You're only a servant, Os.'

Osbert nodded. Then suddenly his hand whipped out and slapped Basil's cheeks, first the left, then the right, then the left again. Basil's hand fell and gripped his sword, and it was half out when he realised that Osbert already had his dagger in his hand, held by the tip in that gentle, relaxed manner Basil had seen so often before.

'Os, you shouldn't tease me.'

'I didn't. I slapped you, hard. Because I'm older than you, boy, and I've the experience you're lacking. You know what that means? It means I'm faster than you. Faster and more dangerous. You start testing me, and you'll learn that you'd best respect me, because if you don't, I'll see you hurt.'

'Hurt? What, like those children? Or their mother?'

Osbert shrugged. 'They were in the way. If we hadn't killed them, they could have got away and told all about us.'

'All about *you*, you mean. None of us would have been seen in the dark,' Basil pointed out, but already his anger had left him. Now he contemplated the road ahead, a small smile on his lips. 'It was a grand attack, though, wasn't it?'

'Was it?' Osbert said.

In all honesty, he wouldn't know whether an attack like that was good or bad. It was only successful or not.

'That man I spitted on my sword!' Basil said exultantly. 'I

stuck it in his gut, and it just opened him from cods to collar, all his bowels spilling on the grass!'

Osbert remembered that. The man had been holding his hands over his head, as though that could be any protection! Basil's sword had almost completely eviscerated him, and then some woman – his wife or sister – had run to his side, and Basil had paused, then ridden back to thrust his sword into her back, a short way below her neck, a cruel blow that had pinned her for a moment to the man. Then Basil had laughed, that high, keening laugh that showed always that his blood was up and his spirits flying, before tugging his blade free and hunting another.

The surprise had been complete, after all. Osbert had led them to the points where they could attack, and the little force had thundered in at the same time, hacking and stabbing all as they rose, befuddled, wiping the sleep from their eyes, before any could grab more than a dagger to protect themselves. Soon there was only the monk remaining alive. And he had endured a bad death, cursing them all in his strange foreign accent as they beat him, cut small incisions in painful locations, and finally, at Basil's suggestion, took his eyes as well, just to make sure he really didn't know where the money had gone.

'Well perhaps you're right,' Basil said at last.

Osbert grunted his gratitude. Basil set off again, lolling indolently in his saddle, while Osbert followed a short distance behind. But Osbert wasn't fooled, and he kept his dagger loose in its sheath.

Chapter Eighteen

Exeter

The castle was ever a bustling place, but today it was still more busy than usual, and Baldwin gazed about him with surprise as he entered the gates. Grabbing the arm of a clerk hurrying past with an immense pile of rolls in his arms, he asked what the reason was for all the activity.

'There is to be a court of gaol delivery,' the clerk snapped, snatching his arm away and hurrying on, clutching at his records as though fearing that they might be prised from his arms before he could deliver them.

Baldwin shook his head. The court might well delay matters. If he was to try to interrupt its decisions while it was sitting, the sheriff might feel it inconvenient at least. Many sheriffs could take umbrage at such interruptions, and Baldwin had no desire to set off on the wrong foot with the man.

'Come,' he snapped, and hurried over the courtyard.

Rougemont Castle was a sadly dilapidated fortress. The towers were in a poor state of repair, and parts of the curtain wall had been rebuilt recently after a collapse. Until thirty years ago, many of the towers had been without their roofs, and three had fallen twenty years before. The rubble from two still formed piles near the wall where they had stood. It was not a picture of martial or judicial intimidation.

However, it was the centre of justice for the whole of

Devon, and the hall at the far end of the yard was the site of the courts held in the king's name and in the presence of the sheriff, his deputy for the area.

Baldwin passed into the great chamber, and was relieved to see that the sheriff and his advisers were not yet in their seats. Some men mingled, indulging in self-important posturing behind the tables, while clerks set out their inks and reeds, knives and quills, ready to begin to record the great decisions that would soon be taken. Meanwhile there was a steady clanking and rattling of chains from the chambers nearby, where the prisoners stood in abject terror, waiting to learn whether they were to live or die today.

'Where is the sheriff?' Baldwin asked a guard, and the man looked as though he might tell Baldwin to leave the chamber and take up an affair with his own mother, before he saw the urgency and resentment in Baldwin's eyes.

Soon Baldwin and Edgar were waiting in a chamber that was considerably smaller. They had been asked for their weapons, and Baldwin felt oddly undressed here without his sword. For some reason, it felt very peculiar to be preparing to meet another knight without it.

It was perfectly normal for a man to be asked to relinquish his weapons at another man's hall. After all, assassination was an unpleasant reality, and one means of defending against such an attack was to ensure that visitors were unarmed. But it was more than that – it was also a sign of respect to the master of the house – and in this case, it was a mark of respect to the king himself, for this was his castle, and it was his sheriff holding court in his name.

There was a door at the far end of the room. The latch rattled, and the door slammed wide as a man strode in, tugging at gloves as he came. 'These gloves are shite! Tell that prick of a glover that if he can't adjust them to my hands, he can take 'em back and burn 'em, because I'll not pay for 'em. Sod the bastard! Right, you, what do you want?'

He had reached a large throne-like chair, and now he flung himself into it with an expression of bitterness on his face. 'Well?' he demanded.

Sir James de Cockington was an arrogant man, fairly young for a sheriff, perhaps six-and-twenty, fair haired, with rather too much authority for Baldwin's taste. He wore a thick blue tunic with plenty of golden embroidery at the neck and hem, and there was a lot of gold on his fingers. An emerald and a large ruby, among others, but Baldwin couldn't see the rest as the man sat and waved his hands. His eyes were cold, his demeanour uncaring, rather as though he was a great lord and a retainer had come to plead with him for alms. He was undoubtedly good looking, but Baldwin felt that there was little generosity of spirit, for all his fine clothes and decoration.

'I am Sir Baldwin de Furnshill, not some mere petitioner,' Baldwin said with restraint. 'I am a King's Keeper of the Peace. I believe that a respected woman of the city has either been hurt in an accident, or may have been taken by outlaws.'

'Why?'

Baldwin felt Edgar's pique at the sharp tone. 'Because she left my house this morning and has not arrived here. She was not on the road I passed along, and—'

'And you feel guilty at having let her travel alone, no doubt. Well, your guilt is your affair, Sir Knight, not the king's. There are thirty men here to be hanged today, and I have to get through them all. So if you want this little chit, I suggest you hurry back home and check the roads yourself.'

'This woman is a respectable—'

'Respectable enough to visit you at night, eh?' the sheriff said with a slow grin.

'Your meaning?' Baldwin asked quietly.

'What did you do to her? Come, we're all men here. Did you scare her when you pulled her clothes from her?'

'She is the daughter of a good friend of mine,' Baldwin said. 'She suffered no indignity at my hands, nor would she ever.'

'A good friend?' the sheriff repeated, his head tilted slightly. 'You don't mean that wench married to the fellow in my gaol?'

'You have her husband in the gaol, yes,' Baldwin said coolly. 'Perhaps this would be a good moment to enquire what his offence might be?'

'He may be guilty of treason,' the sheriff stated airily.

'With whom; when; what was the nature of his offence—'

'Do you mean to interrogate me, Sir Baldwin?' the sheriff asked, slowly leaning forward to peer at Baldwin as a man might study a curious insect.

'I mean to learn under what pretext an innocent man has been beaten, arrested and held.'

'Then you should stay to listen in my court. Perhaps you will learn about justice and the exercise of it,' the sheriff said, leaning back in his chair again. But all pretence was gone now. His eyes gleamed as he spoke. 'In the meantime, the man will remain in gaol. Perhaps, if I can get through a heavy workload, we may listen to the case against this Peter. But then again, I may find that the court is slow today. Business can so often be lengthy, can it not?'

'Why? Just tell me why?' Baldwin said, eyes narrowed. 'You have nothing against this man, nor his wife, do you? So why do you persecute them?'

'The king is alarmed, and so is my lord Sir Hugh le Despenser. Men are plotting against them, they believe. So plotters must be found. I have found one.'

'You hold an innocent man.'

'I hold a man who has been declared to be guilty of plotting against the king,' the sheriff said flatly. He leaned back casually. 'If he's found guilty, he'll be executed, just like any other traitor.'

Baldwin rocked on the balls of his feet. The man's rudeness was justification for assaulting him now, offering him a duel, or simply beating him with Edgar, but that would serve no purpose, other than to ensure that he and Edgar would themselves be outlawed for attacking a king's sheriff. He could not attack, but he could not allow the man to hold Edith's husband – nor could he allow himself to be held while Edith was in danger.

'So, Sir Baldwin,' the man said with some disdain. 'If there is no more business, perhaps you should leave me to continue with mine? It was most pleasant to discuss these things with you; however, I am a busy man in the king's service. I am sure you will understand.'

'I wish to have the aid of the hue and cry to seek the girl.'

'Bring me the body, and you can have a posse, Sir Baldwin. But as matters stand, I fear I see no reason to assist you in seeking this child who appears to have fled your . . . um . . . hospitality.'

Baldwin had to move this time. Edgar was about to leap. Baldwin knew his man too well, and he also knew that the sheriff could die swiftly at Edgar's hands. Edgar might look amused and lazily laconic, but that was when he was at his most deadly – and a man trained by the Templars to be a committed killer was always a deadly opponent.

'Edgar, no,' Baldwin said softly. He could see that the tension remained in Edgar's stance, but he knew his man would not disobey. They had been together too long as warriors.

'I wish you a good day, Sheriff,' he said. 'I shall take your advice and seek her myself. However, I recommend you do nothing to upset me or my friends.'

'You threaten me?' the sheriff said. He sat straighter in his chair, sneering at the thought of this rural knight trying to menace him.

'I make no threat. No. But the man you hold is son-in-law to my friend, who is also friend to the king. Insult the lad, and you will pay for it.'

'You think so? If he's found guilty of treason, old man, his family and in-laws, as well as his *friends*, will all be studied in a new light. I should go home and enjoy your peace while you still may.'

Jacobstowe

'Good lady, we were sad to hear of your loss,' Simon said.

'It was a terrible thing. And I can think of nothing but revenge. But how may I win justice for my man?'

'If we may, we shall aid you,' Simon said. 'Can you tell us anything about his death?'

Agnes shook her head, confused. 'What do you want me to say? He was beaten to death in the road. No one saw anything, no one wanted to know anything. It was just one of those things. A man died, and no one cares.'

'Many do care, but we need to learn who could be responsible. Did he have any enemies?'

'Not in the vill here ... But the men who killed the travellers, he hated them. He was trying to find out who they were, so he could capture them.'

'Did he find out?' Sir Richard rumbled.

'No. I don't think so, anyway,' she admitted. 'He was trying to learn all he could, but then he died.'

'That may well mean he learned all he needed,' Sir Richard said. 'Where was he when he died?'

She looked at him with a new hope. 'Hoppon would know.'

'Who is this Hoppon?'

'He is the man who lives nearest, I think. He's at the edge of the woods, near the boundary of our parish. I know he was trying to help Bill to find the men who killed the folks in the woods.'

She took them down from the church to a little house where a woman sat shelling the last of the summer's peas at the doorway, and left her son there before striding on purposefully southwards.

The land here fell away a little from Jacobstowe itself, and soon they were walking a path that ran along a broad ridge down towards Oakhampton. The woods themselves were very clear, sitting like a saddle over the ridge and both flanks, but before they reached the trees, Agnes took a turn to the left, and followed a trail between hedges that took them down towards a river.

Here, halfway to the water, there was a little hovel. It was nothing more than a single-bay building, with sticks and twigs gleaned from the woods to fill the gaps, and cob daubed over. Once it might have been a clean, pleasant little home, limewashed and well thatched to keep the cold at bay, but now it was sadly dilapidated. The walls had lost all their colour, and were a mixed grey and pale brown with little whiteness remaining; the thatch was faded to the colour of slate, with moss lying heavily on top, and there were holes all over where squirrels and birds had made their homes in it. A large area near the door had been eaten away, and Simon could see the ribs of the roofing poles beneath.

Outside, it was like any other peasant's house. There was a small vegetable patch with six plots set out, containing kale and other leaves, all of which looked tough and unappetising so late in the season. A rough stockade of hurdles had been built to the side probably for lambs or kids earlier in the year, and was now falling down, but in one asset at least the place was rich. Under the eaves was a good-sized woodpile, with a number of large boughs. Behind were smaller branches and bundles of faggots. At least the house would remain warm in the winter months, Simon thought.

The man who hobbled along from the rear at the sound of their voices was a stooped fellow of some fifty years or so. His name probably came from his gait. One leg was partly crippled, so he must hop on the other to walk, and he used a long pole as a staff to aid his passage, but there was nothing to suggest that he was disabled in any other way. His face was quite handsome, with a strong jawline, heavy brows, and dark, serious eyes, which stood out in his pale face. His hair was almost white, and there was a thick stubble of beard and moustache to show that he had used the last barber to visit the vill, but the colour looked almost out of place. His features did not appear old enough to justify the leaching away of all colour from his hair.

'Hoppon, these men are here to try to learn all they can about my husband's death,' Agnes said as he approached.

Hoppon studied the men seriously for a moment, and then nodded and gave them a bow, while gripping his staff with both hands clasped about it at chest height. 'My lords, I'm honoured. God give you all success in your searches.'

'We are interested in all to do with the death of the travellers, as well as this woman's husband's murder,' Sir Richard boomed. 'Can ye tell us aught about them?'

'The coroner has been already – he heard all the evidence,' Hoppon said, glancing at Agnes as he spoke.

'We know. We've seen Sir Peregrine,' Sir Richard said. 'But he doesn't live here, and we want to find out what we can from someone who knows the area.'

'I'll tell what I can, but I doubt me it'll be of much use to you,' Hoppon said. 'The travellers were over there. I saw their smoke in the morning, but I didn't think anything of it. Why should I? There are woodsmen all over the place, what with the winter coming on. People are there all the time to gather their faggots for the fire, and the charcoal burners make enough smoke to hide a city.'

'When did you realise that there had been an ambush and slaughter?' Simon asked.

'Not until later that day. I had to wander up there anyway,' Hoppon said reluctantly.

'Why?' Simon asked.

'Fetch some wood.'

Simon's gaze went from Hoppon's face to the wood store by the house. That was plainly a lie. The man had no need of any wood.

Hoppon's face coloured slightly. 'When I got there, it was obvious that there'd been an attack. Bodies lay everywhere.'

'Was there any sign of money? Jewels? Anything to indicate that they'd had valuables to transport?' Simon said. 'Was there any sign that there were churchmen among them?'

'Oh, I didn't want to stay and study them all. One or two looked soft enough to be priests, and one was tonsured, I remember. The poor man with his eyes plucked out. Him and one or two others hadn't done much work in their lives, not with their hands, that was for sure,' Hoppon said. 'But the others were all younger, stronger lads. I'd say that most were fighters of one sort or another. There were about ten of them. And there were some folk who looked different again. A woman, some children . . . They even killed a bitch and her pup.'

Simon offered a short but heartfelt thank-you to God for

keeping Baldwin away from this. He was invariably on the side of hounds and other beasts.

'The man who could have been a priest – did he have any distinguishing features that the coroner noted?'

'Only one – he had a scar on his right thigh. Looked like a slash from a knife.'

'I think it was a kick from a donkey,' Simon said. 'That shows that he was the priest Pietro from Tavistock, then, with his force of men-at-arms. With so many fighters about him who looked strong, it'd be no surprise if others decided to join them for safety. There is more security when in a band than alone. That will be why so many were there.'

'True enough.'

'The killers would have to have made noise when they rode off,' Simon said. 'Did you hear nothing?'

Hoppon took a breath, glanced at Agnes, and hesitated for a long moment before finally giving a short nod of his head. 'I didn't want to admit it at first, because I didn't want to put myself in danger's way, but yes. There were some carts and horses rode past here that night. I heard them because Tab here barked at them. He's a good guard.'

'Where would they have gone?' Sir Richard asked, taking a couple of steps past Hoppon's house to stare down the path.

'That leads to a ford. I think they went along the back of my house on another path, and from there to the ford. Once there was a manor behind us, down there,' he added, pointing. 'The place burned down, though, and now there's little left behind. But the path to it remains. And from there the old trail takes a man down to the ford.'

'Whose manor was it?' Simon asked.

'Sir Edmund's. But he died years ago. He was the last of his family. I served him until his death.'

'How did he die?' Sir Richard asked.

'An accident. He fell from his horse into the river and drowned.'

Sir Richard and Simon nodded. It was one of the most common accidental deaths for anyone who lived near a river.

'So,' Simon said, 'how much of all this did you tell Bill Lark?'

'All. He knew it seemingly before he asked me,' Hoppon said with a slow grin. 'Agnes knows what her old man was like. He'd only ever ask something when he'd already worked out the answer, usually. That day, he came down here, and he sat there, on that log, and told me he'd worked out that the men must have come up here. He told me he'd asked all over the place, from Oakhampton to up past Jacobstowe, and east and west too, and there was no sign of carts or horses on any of the paths he'd looked at. Well, I realised when he asked me that he knew where they'd gone already. If all the other paths were blocked to them, he said, they must have come near here.'

'You weren't going to tell him, then?' Sir Richard growled.

'Sir, no, sir. It's dangerous to get in the way of men like them.'

'Like who?'

'Like men who can form a large enough group to attack a party of nineteen and slaughter the lot,' Hoppon said reasonably. 'Perhaps I'd feel safer if I lived in a smart city like Exeter, but I live here, between the parish and the woods. There's no one within calling, no one who'd notice if I was missing. What would you have me do? Report a rich lord and hope he'd be arrested before he could hurt me? Perhaps he wouldn't wait until the court opened before he killed me.'

'The courts are here to protect you as well, man,' Sir Richard said.

Hoppon looked up at him. 'You think so? When the stories all say that the sheriff will take money to release the guilty, just because they can afford it? When it's said that he will arrest the innocent on purpose, just so he can take a bribe to let them go? Oh, the courts may seem fair and reasonable to you, Sir Richard, but to an ordinary man like me, it looks much safer to keep away.'

'We wouldn't let anyone hurt you, fellow,' Sir Richard said with an angry shake of his head.

'So you'll protect me?' And now there was a sarcastic tone in Hoppon's voice. 'You would see to it that I didn't end up like her husband, eh? You'd make sure I wasn't buried six feet under like Bill Lark, would you?'

Chapter Nineteen

Exeter

Baldwin hurried from the castle and the suave sheriff with his unsubtle threats. He was shivering with rage, and he had to force himself to stop and calm his breathing before he reached the high street.

There was no time to be angry with that fool, he said to himself. Not now. Much more important was doing everything he could to find Edith. 'Edgar, if we are to cover all the roads between here and Furshill, it will take us days,' he said bitterly. 'But we must try to do so, and check all those places where she might have been thrown. God *damn* that smug fool!'

'We have no proof that she did in truth come this way,' Edgar said gently. 'Sir, she may have travelled to her father's and there been attacked or come to some mishap.'

'Yes,' Baldwin said. 'But—'

'Sir Baldwin, her mare was a strong little beast.'

Baldwin shot his servant a look. 'Eh?'

'I have seen many accidents. Sometimes the mount will be scared by something, and will run away until the fear dissipates. If the rider is unfortunate and falls, she may not be easy to find, but that kind of event is rare. Then there are some accidents in which the rider is hurt, but quietly; when she has been so involved in her thoughts she has been silently knocked from the mount. In most such cases the horse will remain at the rider's side.'

'What are you trying to say?' Baldwin snapped, but he already knew.

'Sir Baldwin, if she had fallen, it is more than likely that someone would already have found her. None of the roads between Furnshill and here are so quiet that on a day like today she would not have been seen. To imagine so is not sensible. So perhaps she has already been found and even now is resting on a bier in a peasant's house.'

'Or?'

'Or she had no accident, but a mishap. Someone decided to capture her. If that is the case, our task of finding her will be that much more difficult.'

Baldwin nodded, staring out over the city towards the west. 'She is there somewhere, Edgar. What if she has been captured by some felon . . . ?'

'If she has, then we shall have to do all in our power to rescue her,' Edgar said imperturbably. 'However, we can do little until we learn what could have happened.'

'Yes,' Baldwin said. Now that the cold rage had left him, he found his mind was functioning more efficiently again. He continued staring westwards, but now with narrowed eyes, as though he was searching through the fog of distance to see the slim form of the girl as she lay at the side of the road, her mare standing protectively over her, or perhaps struggling with a gang of felons as they dragged her away, hands bound, their knives at her throat.

Neither was to be suffered without making an effort to rescue her.

'Come with me,' he said, and turned back towards the castle.

Near Abbeyford Woods

When Hoppon had finished speaking, Simon nodded. 'Very well. You have explained your situation clearly. It's not our place to comment on your behaviour. If the good coroner Sir Peregrine was content, so are we.'

Sir Richard was about to comment, but Simon walked over to him, and he subsided, shaking his head reluctantly.

Simon continued. 'No, Hoppon, that is nothing to us. However, we do need to try to learn who killed all those people. Two of them were religious men, and they were carrying money for the king. Whoever killed them stole from the king, so whether you feel uncomfortable about talking or not, the fact is, the king himself wishes to see these men in gaol – and that is where they will be going, very soon. So any help you can give us will be to your advantage, because it will entail their being taken away that bit sooner.'

Hoppon shifted uncomfortably on his bad leg, still leaning on his staff. At last he nodded. 'I'll tell you all I know, or guess at. And I only pray that you'll be sensible about it and catch the men. Very well then. It was Tab who heard them first, as I said, but as soon as he started barking, I heard them too. Horses, carts, men talking loudly, laughing. As they always do.'

'Did you hear anything of note?' Sir Richard demanded.

'No, only that they were to go back to their base. They didn't say who they were or where exactly they were going.'

'Who is there who lives over east of here, then?' Simon asked.

'Oh, I know nothing about the lands over that way,' Hoppon said, and Simon was quite convinced he was lying. However, the man was being forced to tell two officers of the law about the illegal affairs of men who had shown themselves willing to kill nineteen folk and rob the king. It was hardly surprising that he was reluctant.

'Very well,' Simon said. 'What can you tell us about the death of this widow's husband?'

'Oh, poor old Bill,' Hoppon said. 'I found him over towards Swanstone Moor.'

'Where is that?' Sir Richard asked.

'It's that little patch of moor over yonder,' Hoppon said, pointing.

Following the direction of his finger, Simon could see a small area of moorland over to the east, slightly south of a hillock on the other side of the river. 'Where was he in there?'

'There is a large beech tree at the edge of the moor,' Hoppon said, squinting as he peered. 'See it there? Just to the left of the line of that hedge.'

Sir Richard glanced down at Hoppon's leg. 'Can you ride a horse? Doubt you could walk so far as that, could you?'

'I think I could, so long as you don't have a great hurry. I've walked further than that in my time,' Hoppon said.

'Hoppon used to be an archer,' Agnes said.

'Really?' Sir Richard said, letting his eyes pass over Hoppon's frame. 'A while ago, then.'

'Why do you say that?' Hoppon asked.

'You've lost the muscles in your shoulders,' the knight said. 'Archers have bigger shoulders and upper arms than most men.'

'You're right,' Hoppon said. 'I was bigger when I was younger. Before this,' he added, tapping his thigh.

'What happened?' Simon asked as they walked, matching their speed to Hoppon's slow gait. 'Was it in a battle?'

Hoppon glanced at him, then at Agnes just beyond him before anwering. 'No. It was my own stupid fault. When I was younger, I thought I was invincible. There was a fire in a barn on the old manor, and I ran inside to rescue what I could, but a spar from the roof fell on me and burned my leg badly. I'm lucky I can walk at all. Still, I brought out a few items of value, and my lord rewarded me well enough.'

'That's the old manor where the knight died?' Simon asked.

'Yes. My lord Edward. Right, here we go!' Hoppon said. They had reached the edge of the river, and now he plunged in, hobbling as fast as he could, before the waters soaked his boots entirely.

Simon and Sir Richard exchanged a look, and then glanced at the monk and Agnes. The monk curled his lip, but hitched up his robes, looped them over his forearms, and trotted through.

Agnes returned Simon's look coolly enough. 'I want to see where my husband died,' she said, and with that, she drew up her skirts to display her knees without any outward sign of shame, and waded in.

Sir Richard shrugged. 'If they're all going . . .' he muttered, lifting his sword's sheath high. He stalked forward rather like a warrior marching into battle, head low on his shoulders, glowering ferociously as he went, as though daring the river to seep in through the leather of his old boots.

Simon crossed immediately after him, and soon the five were making their way up an ancient stone pathway that had become wildly overgrown. Looking about him, Simon couldn't help but think that if Baldwin were here, he would be able to make much more of the trail than he himself could.

Suddenly he slowed a little, frowning. At the edge of the roadway brambles had encroached. Here, as he looked down, he could see, clear on the stems, the marks of crushing. 'Sir Richard, look at this.'

'Eh?' The knight squatted at his side, studying the marks Simon had pointed out. 'Aye, Bailiff. I reckon you're right. Definitely the signs of carts passing by here.'

'I told you,' Hoppon said. He was leaning on his staff again, his hands clasped in that curious manner. 'Think they came up here.'

'And you told Bill as much?' Simon asked.

'He guessed as much. But he came up here, yes. And then he was found here, a few days later. Head all bashed in till his skull was broken. A terrible sight.'

'Where was he?' Sir Richard asked.

In answer, Hoppon merely shifted his grip on his staff and began to make his way up the hill, hobbling painfully. He could only move with care, especially now it was more stony. His staff with its unshod foot could grip quite well, and he hopped and skittered over the ground with a fluid gait that was quite surprising to Simon.

'It was here,' he said at last, just at the foot of the beech tree he had indicated from outside his house. 'He was lying here.'

He was pointing at the base of the tree, but his eyes weren't there. His eyes were fixed upon Agnes.

Bow

Edith knew only abject, blinding terror.

She had been raised in the house of a man who was a regular traveller and fighter. Simon had never been one to rest when there was work to be done, and he had been relentless in pursuit of those who had committed crimes. At times, Edith had known that his life could have been in danger. Her mother had even spoken once of a time when she herself had been captured by a man and Baldwin had rescued her, but this was different. It was terrifying to be so completely at the mercy of someone she scarcely knew. All she recalled about Wattere, after all, was a brief, shocking glimpse as he fought her father earlier in the year, trying to kill him in their house. Later Simon had managed to have him arrested, but that was months ago. So long, indeed, that she had almost forgotten his face.

She was so *stupid* not to have recognised him. He had approached through the mist, it was true, but that was no excuse. She should have recognised him. Oh, she could sob now for the foolishness of her behaviour, she could wail and beat her breast, but the truth was that it was entirely her fault. She should not have left Exeter alone, nor should she have tried to make her way back again today when Baldwin had already said to her that he would do his best. It would have been safer for all were she to have been escorted to her father's house. She could have remained there while the men went to free her husband. Then at least she would have been secure in the knowledge that Peter would have had the very best opportunity of gaining his freedom again.

'Not far, my little dove,' William atte Wattere called to her.

She made no comment. Her hands were growing more and more numb by the minute, and when she looked down, she could see that they were turning blue below the rope. At least the rope had been taken from about her throat. It had chafed and worn at her flesh until she was sure that she must be bleeding, and she had been surprised when she found that there was no stain on the rope or her tunic, though she was sore from the shoulder upwards, as though she had been scorched in a fire. Still, when he took the rope away, she was aware of an odd sense of gratitude, as though he was being kind by removing it, rather than intensely cruel in placing it about her in the first place. It shamed her to be grateful.

There was a possibility that she might be able to escape, she felt. Looking up, she could see the sun as a brighter glow behind the clouds. She had been raised on Dartmoor; she was used to navigating by a half-concealed sun, and she thought that this was probably a good sign. Surely the man didn't realise that she was so familiar with this area. She was sure that the moors were over there to her left, and this road must be the one that wandered from Crediton to Copplestone, and then on up to Bow, before curling around to Oakhampton. That was good, because if he was taking her that far, there might be a possibility of escaping him. She had already tried to loosen the ropes at her wrists, but the problem was, her captor had tied them too tightly. Not only could she not release them at first; also, now that she had lost all feeling in her fingers, there wasn't even a possibility of working at the knots.

'Will we rest soon? My hands are hurting so much.'

'Soon we'll rest,' he said, his eyes fixed on the road ahead. Then something caught his attention. He threw her a look. 'You all right?'

'My hands,' she said again, holding them up for inspection.

He sucked at his teeth as he looked at them. Then he muttered a short curse, stared ahead for a moment, and quickly beckoned her. He tried to prise the knots apart for a moment, and then spat an oath. Pulling his dagger from his sheath, he set the blade to the rope. Looking up, he gave her a wolfish grin. 'Don't move, or this'll hurt more than it need.'

With a careful sawing motion, he cut through the knot, and the cords fell away. At first there was no feeling, no pain, just a strange tingling that seemed to begin at her fingertips, but soon that changed. The tingle became a stinging agony that reached all the way to her wrists, which now hurt like the torment of demons. She knew only screaming pain, so intense that she could not even consider holding her reins. It was impossible, and she wept as she tried to shake the pain away. She warmed her hands under her armpits, then rubbed them on her thighs, all to no avail.

Wattere looked on as her weeping began again and

intensified. 'Woman, what is it? Are you making mock of my good intentions in releasing you? I'll not have that, I swear.'

'My hands are on fire! Oh, oh, the pain! Oh, oh!'

Eventually he took her hands in his and studied them carefully. He could see the rawness where the rope had bound her, but the hands themselves showed no injury. 'I am sorry I tied you so tight,' he said. 'But I can't help that. I don't want you to escape. If you swear to me that you'll not try to run, I'll allow you to ride on without a rope. What do you say?'

'I swear it!' she hissed.

'Very well,' he said. He slipped the rope about her waist, but even as he did it, he was gentle, and he didn't make any attempt to touch her breasts, waist or thighs. It made her realise that he was according her as much respect as he might, under the circumstances. Once it was round her, he tied it off, and then took the loop in his hand again.

'Where are you taking me?'

'You'll know very soon. Sir Robert of Traci's manor. You'll be safe there.'

'Why, though, sir? Why do you take me there? My family will be alarmed when I am missed. What have I ever done to you?'

'You haven't, mistress, but your father has. He has cut me with steel, and humiliated me before my lord. I won't let that happen again. No, I'll see him in hell first,' he spat.

'But you don't need me. Let me go!'

'After so much effort? No, I don't think so, mistress. Better that you come with me and we finish what's been started.'

Edith wailed at him. 'But *why*? You've already stolen our house, you've taken away our family's peace and comfort, and now you've caused me to be terrified! What is it all for?'

William atte Wattere eyed her. 'Because, mistress, your father is an important man in the area. That's why. He can settle the dispute in Tavistock. And he will have to.'

'Why?'

'Because if he doesn't, you'll . . .'

But he couldn't finish his sentence. Instead he spurred his horse into a trot again, and they rode on. Not for much further, Edith prayed.

Her head was already nodding. There had been no possibility of escape, even though the feeling had started to return to her fingers quickly, once the ropes were taken from her wrists and the blood began to flow once more.

There had been some roads that had looked possible. The way down to Coleford was one lane she knew very well, and with the low, overhanging branches, she might well have been able to lose her captor if she had been able to evade him at the outset, but he had ridden past the lane between it and her, almost as though he knew she would make an attempt, his attention fixed upon her the whole time.

She didn't have the courage. If she'd spurred her beast, it was possible that she might have been able to escape by surprising him and yanking the rope from his hands, but the likelihood was that he'd have caught her instantly, and then all she'd have won would have been the rope about her wrists again. No, if she was going to bolt, she was going to have to do so at a moment when there was the best chance of making good her escape. The next lanes were little help. All small, uniformly straggly, difficult for him to chase after her, but also very tough for her to ride away at speed. And looking at him, she was filled with an unpleasant assurance that the fellow would ride like the devil if he saw her making good her escape. She was as likely to break her mare's leg as he was his palfrey's, and then no doubt she'd be forced to walk with her hands bound. No, she couldn't risk it, not on roads she didn't know.

Before they could reach Bow, he took her along a back lane

that curled round to the south, and thence up to a road that led towards Nymet Traci. She knew this area. There was a strong house down here, she recalled. An old knight had lived there. A good, kind fellow, she remembered – she had met him a few times when there was a market at Lydford. Her father had always liked him too. Perhaps she could shout for help there as they passed. There was no rope about her neck now. She felt safer than she had all day, and surely there would be someone who would think nothing of riding to the aid of a woman in distress.

Soon they were in full view of it. A large stone-built house surrounded by a good castellated wall. 'There you are, mistress. The castle of Sir Robert de Traci.'

Chapter Twenty

Rougemont Castle, Exeter

The gaol in the castle was a dark, foul chamber built beneath the walls on the eastern side of the grounds.

It was not often used. There were other little chambers that were more suited to the storage of felons and other criminals, but those prisoners who held a particular importance – or, as Baldwin ruefully admitted to himself, perhaps value to the sheriff – were kept here, near to hand, within the castle itself.

There was one advantage to being held in the castle grounds. At least the sheriff had shown that the prisoners here were of significance to him. That meant that Peter was less likely to die from neglect or beatings. There were always a number of deaths of prisoners in the city gaol: starvation, disease, dehydration and peine fort et dure were common causes, but less likely for prisoners as important as those held here.

It was rare that action would be taken against prison guards who allowed their charges to die, unless they were astonishingly harsh. For prisoners, death was normal and expected. The coroner would hold an inquest over any death, of course, and if the warders were found to have been guilty of deliberately causing it, they could be arrested as homicides and potentially put on trial – but they were unlikely to be convicted. After all, any juror accusing them could at some point in the future end up in the gaol. There might well be some form of retribution for a juror who had tried to convict a warder. So prisoners would die, and their deaths were invariably pronounced as being the result of natural causes.

Peter might have been treated better than most, but it did not mean that he enjoyed a luxurious existence. When Baldwin and Edgar found him, he was sitting forlornly on the floor. There was no chair, not even a simple log on which to rest. The light was poor, from a window high in the wall, and the atmosphere was cold and dank.

'Master Peter?' Baldwin said. 'Are you well?'

The boy looked as though he was in his thirties. He had aged so much in such a short time that Baldwin almost didn't recognise him. In the last days, Peter had lost the fine, gentle appearance of privilege, and instead had taken on the mantle of poverty. There was a haunted look in his eyes, and a line of what looked like dried spittle had trailed down his cheek from his mouth, as though he had been screaming or dribbling with terror.

It was all too easy to imagine him utterly horrorstruck in here. As Baldwin looked about him briefly, he was struck by the bleak foulness of the hideous little chamber. As he knew, it was in similar little chambers in France that his comrades and friends had been tortured. The bestial level to which mankind could sink was a source of wonder to him – the more so the older he grew. As a youngster, he had accepted man's cruelties and injustices as natural, but no longer. The Temple had given him a new life, the chance to witness how other societies lived, and how men could order themselves to exist alongside other races and religions, without resorting to the madness of attempting to kill each other.

There was something entirely repugnant about torture, he thought. It served no useful purpose, for a man would confess to anything in order to stop pain. He would lie about his faith, his family, his friends. The three great betrayals. Nothing that was given by a torture victim could be trusted. It was worthless.

But the cruel enjoyed inflicting terror on their victims.

'Peter, are you well?' he asked again, more softly.

'What do you want?' Peter asked weakly. He was wincing, peering up at them with eyes that were mere slits, while trying to push himself back against the wall.

'Master Peter, it is me, Sir Baldwin de Furnshill, and my good servant, Edgar. We are here to try to help you.'

'Oh God! My Christ, thank you!' Peter sobbed as he recognised Baldwin's voice. 'Can you get me out of here? Please, *please*, save me from this!'

As he spoke, he crawled forward on his hands and knees, and held his hands up to Baldwin.

'Peter, stand. You are no creature that deserves to go about like this.'

'You don't know what they've . . . The sheriff says I'll hang. Why? Why does he wish to kill me, Sir Baldwin? I haven't *done* anything!'

Baldwin looked down at Peter's filthy, tear-streaked face and knew he couldn't tell the lad about Edith. 'Tell me, Peter, is there any reason you can think of that could make the sheriff wish to hurt you? Have you met him? Spoken to him? Have you ever spoken about him, or has your wife, for example?'

'No! No, nothing at all, I swear it! I know nothing about the man. How could I? I was apprenticed to Master Harold in Tavistock until just before I married, and since then I've been too busy here in Exeter.'

'Do you have any family who could have had a dispute with him?'

'No, I swear! He is neighbour to my father's lands in Heavitree, but beyond that, I don't think I have ever known him.'

'Neighbour to your father's lands, you say?'

'He owns the little manor next to my father's, yes, but that's all. They've never had a dispute, so far as I know. It would be hard: the sheriff has hardly been there in years. He's proud of his connections in the king's court.'

'Does your father support the king?' Baldwin asked softly. It was not a question that he wished to have overheard.

'Of course he does! As do I!'

'Is there any reason you can think of why the sheriff might wish to do you harm?'

Peter's face was full of desperate enthusiasm. 'No, not at all.'

'Peter, *think*! Someone has caused you to be arrested. I do not believe that the sheriff has acted purely for reasons of suspicion against you. There must be a reason why he would have done this.'

'I know no reason! None! Why would he want to do this to me? I don't know him! He's only a neighbour of my father's, neither friend nor enemy to me!'

As they left the chamber, paying a penny to the guard outside for allowing them to visit, Baldwin stood frowning. 'Edgar, if the boy had done something, *anything*, to anger the sheriff, the man would not have let him make such a mistake. He's too arrogant to do that. There must surely be something . . .'

Edgar was about to comment when they heard a voice hailing them.

'Sir Baldwin! I hope I see you well, old friend!'

Baldwin reluctantly fitted a smile to his face. 'Sir Peregrine de Barnstaple! How very good to see you again.'

Jacobstowe

Agnes watched the men as they studied the land carefully.

The younger one, the bailiff, was methodical in the way that he searched all about the land, his face grim and frowning as he walked up and down the area, looking for any clue, be it ever so small.

'You were here, then?' he asked Hoppon.

'I found him, poor devil. I walked up here because I had a fancy I could see something from my house, a little huddle of something. When I got here, it was him, poor fellow. He'll be missed, will Bill.'

'But he was here. You went all the way up there,' the bailiff said, pointing to the brow of the hill.

Hoppon's face clouded with suspicion. 'How do you know that?'

'Your staff's easy to see on this soft turf. It penetrated the grasses and stabbed down an inch or so when you used it going up the hill there. You put more weight on it as you use it to help you uphill, I guess. And then coming back, you used it less forcefully.'

'Oh! Oh well, aye, I suppose so. I think I came here, saw him lying on the ground, and went up the hill at once to see if anyone was still there. I was looking to make sure I wouldn't be knocked on the head as soon as I crouched at his side. I made sure that he was dead, and said a prayer over him, the Pater Noster, before going to Jacobstowe to fetch help.'

'Yes, I see,' Simon said.

Agnes could see that he was making sense of this senseless murder so far as it was possible. The bailiff asked a few more questions, and the coroner demanded to know the details of how the body lay, and what the injuries were.

'He was lying on his side, with his arms outstretched,' Hoppon said. 'He had a great bloody mess on the side of his head just here,' and he indicated the right side of his head above and in front of his ear. 'His eye was almost hanging out, he'd been hit so hard.'

There was a great deal more in the same vein, but Agnes was incapable of absorbing it. It was hard enough to come to terms with the fact that her lovely Bill was dead, let alone the reality of how he had been killed, his head crushed like a beetle. It made her sick in the pit of her stomach just to think of it. 'He was away for so long. To think that he should have died so close here.'

'Mistress, I am sorry,' the coroner said. He was a great hulking bear of a man, Agnes thought. The sort a woman would go to for sympathy. From the twinkle in his eye, he might welcome approaches of a different sort as well. But there was nothing in her that would reciprocate any advances. Her womb felt shrivelled. Her soul was dry and unloving. All had gone when her man was killed. She longed for the sight of his killer dangling from a rope, the hemp cutting slowly into his throat as he swung, legs flailing. She could know no pleasure until he was dead, whoever he was.

But she was a mere peasant woman. A widow. She had no means of learning who could have done this.

'Did you see a weapon?' Simon was asking.

'No.'

Agnes saw the bailiff nod and glance about him. It was plain enough that he didn't expect a man like Hoppon to have seen much in the way of evidence. The hill sloped away from this spot towards the river, and the bailiff wandered down that way, whistling tunelessly, casting about him.

Hoppon scowled, but said nothing as the fellow kicked about some nettles at the bottom. They were old nettles, their leaves brown, their stems withered and very tall, sheltered under a sprawling oak. Agnes watched as he walked around in them for a few minutes, and then began to flatten the stems in a circle, stamping them down with vigour.

'Here it is,' he called. 'Sorry, Coroner! A free weapon.'

'Hah! So it is too,' the knight called down. He peered at the clerk, who was standing a short distance away and wearing a look of long-suffering tolerance sorely strained. 'Hey, Mark, ye see that? The blasted deodand is worth nothing, eh? Oh, sorry, mistress.'

Agnes scarcely noticed his words. As the bailiff clambered up the hill, a heavy, smooth river pebble in his hand, she could not take her eyes from it. It was black and crusted with something in places.

'This is the weapon,' the bailiff said, tossing it lightly to the coroner. 'Someone, I would think, was here behind him, and clubbed him to death with that. It's good and heavy – it would do the job in no time. Afterwards he just hurled the stone back towards the river, where he probably found it in the first place. Lucky – if he'd dropped it here, in the open, nearer the body, the blood would have been washed away, I expect. Down there, it was partly sheltered by the grasses and overhanging branches.'

The coroner was turning the stone over and over, feeling its weight in his hand. 'Plenty to break a man's head there, yes. Odd, though, eh?'

Bailiff Puttock nodded shortly. 'I think so.'

Agnes asked, 'What is odd?'

'The weapon,' Coroner Richard said, still studying the rock. 'All the men in the party at Abbeyford were slaughtered with blades – knives, daggers, swords or axes. All of them. And your old man . . . my apologies, your *husband* was killed with a rock, such as any man could pick up.'

'We will need to discuss this, and what we do next,' the bailiff said. He glanced at Agnes and smiled. 'Mistress, this is a sore, sad way to spend your afternoon. You will want to be home with your son, I am sure. Let's take you home, and if there's a small inn or tavern in the vill, we can sit there and make our plans without troubling you further.'

'You are good to me,' she said. 'But I only want to learn that my husband's murderer is caught. Do not trouble about me.'

'Well, mistress, it is like this,' the coroner said. 'We could carry on right now, searching all over this hillside and beyond, but if we do, we'll only make a mess of things because we're tired and hungry. There's no point doing that. Soon it'll be dark, and in truth, we haven't eaten in half a day. My belly's almost on fire with hunger, and I need a large flagon of wine to recover my spirits. I know that you're in a hurry to find the murdering bastard who did for your old— sorry, I mean, your husband, but we need to keep our own bodies and souls together. So we're going to return to Jacobstowe for now, and tomorrow look at the way to carry on our investigation.'

'I see,' she said, and for the first time in the afternoon, she was aware of a heaviness in her throat, as though there was a plum's stone stuck there. It was a thick, sore sensation, horrible, and suddenly she felt only a hideous lassitude. A realisation of the pointlessness of this attempt to find the killer. He was probably long gone by now. Drinking and carousing in some far-off town like Launceston, or Exeter itself. There was no justice in the world. She would struggle on for some years, while all about her tried to help, tried to aid her and her child, and perhaps some husband of a friend would turn up at her door, offering her the sympathy of the bed in return for a cabbage or a bowl of broth.

She had no life now; she was an empty, futile figure. Perhaps a source of lust in the eyes of a few men, but mainly a pathetic, lonely widow-woman who lived in her memories of what had been, and what might have been. A focus of shame, and perhaps of pity. Nothing more.

Her thoughts were of misery and grim reality all the walk home. She could not switch her mind to any happy subjects. It would be better if *she* had died, she thought. At least then Ant would have a father to protect him. There was precious little that a mother could do. He would be better as an orphan, for then at least the vicar would see to it that someone in the vill would take him in, and he might have a surrogate family to replace her and Bill. Poor Bill! Poor, darling Bill!

They had left Hoppon at his house, and were almost at the vill already when Agnes suddenly caught at her breast, gasping for breath, desperately moaning in her distress. She was suddenly lost. Hopelessly confused, she could not help herself. She didn't recognise the road, didn't know the scene of the vill in front of her, could not discern a single building that she knew. Overwhelmed by the feeling of dislocation, she struggled to get her lungs to work.

It was a shock to the men. None knew what to do. The monk was hopeless. He stood, panicking, flapping his hands, literally. The sight was almost enough to make her mood lighten, for he looked exactly like a young bird experimenting with flight, a stupid, wide-eyed expression on his face; and the coroner wasn't much better, standing and harrumphing like an old stallion but uneasy about comforting her. No, it was the bailiff who came to her aid. While she thrust out a hand to break her fall, feeling her legs begin to wobble, a loud roaring in her ears, and a most peculiar flashing in front of her eyes, she found herself caught up. Her legs rose before her, and her shoulders were gently borne, and as the world darkened before her, she was aware of floating, carried by the bailiff.

Chapter Twenty-One

Exeter

Baldwin had persuaded the coroner to leave the castle for a while, and now the three men were at a quiet table in a tavern beside the east gate to the city. Edgar stood, his eyes flitting about all the others in the room, watching carefully for any sign of danger to his master – and keeping all those who might have wished to listen at bay. His was not a demeanour that would brook any argument about whether or not he had the right to prevent others from coming to a table.

Sir Peregrine was not a man whom Baldwin had ever liked. He felt sympathy for him, for he knew well that Sir Peregrine had loved three women, and all had died. Their deaths had marked him in some way. He had apparently grown more patient and sympathetic. But he was still the devoted ally of the men who had set their hearts against the king, and although Baldwin himself was growing impatient with Edward's excesses, and his irrational devotion to the hideous, avaricious adviser Despenser, yet he was still the king and Baldwin owed him allegiance.

Despenser was the one point of mutual understanding, Baldwin now learned. Both detested him.

'You are coroner still, then?' he asked.

'I fear that there is an ever-increasing need for such as me. The shire is growing yet more fractious,' Sir Peregrine said.

'In what way? At my home there are few signs.'

'The first proof is the number of felons wandering in gangs. There was a time ten to twenty years ago when the trail bastons wandered with impunity. Now they have been superseded by this latest menace. There are as many wandering bands as there are malcontents with the king, or so it would seem now.'

Baldwin grunted noncommitally. 'I do not wish to—'

Sir Peregrine interrupted him with a faint smile. 'Sir Baldwin, I do not plot or scheme against the king. I have but one desire: to see the kingdom ruled more effectively and in the interests of the crown. I am no malcontent who would see Edward removed from his office. I have changed somewhat since our last discussion. However, it is plainly true that there are numbers of men who were once opposed to the king's adviser, and who through him have been dispossessed of all their lands and titles. Many have seen their relations thrown into prisons, or have learned that their children have been deprived of their inheritances, their wives removed from their houses, or their lords accused of treason, executed barbarically, and their limbs hung on city walls up and down the land to feed the crows. There is a great deal of bitterness.'

'I do not care about those who have been shown to be disloyal to the king,' said Baldwin. He leaned forward, elbows on the table. 'Troubles in other parts of the realm are for others to worry about.'

'This is not far from you, Sir Baldwin,' Sir Peregrine countered. 'In only the last few days I've had a group of nineteen slaughtered, and a matter of days later the local reeve slain while he tried to discover who was responsible.'

'Where was this?' Baldwin asked.

'Over near Oakhampton. The men were slain in the woods a little north of the town, while the reeve was from Jacobstowe, and his body was discovered a short way east.

That is what I mean, Sir Baldwin, when I say that the country is unsafe no matter where you travel.'

'It is worse than only a short while ago.'

'Yes. And now there are men of rank who are stealing and killing, men with influence, men with castles.'

Baldwin was silent as he considered. 'This is sorely troubling,' he said at last. 'Simon's daughter has disappeared, and the sheriff has arrested her husband, alleging that the fellow is guilty of some form of treason.'

'Simon Puttock? I saw him with the king's coroner from Lifton only two days ago.'

Baldwin looked up. 'Where was he then?'

'Just a little past Bow, on his way to Tavistock, I think. Why?'

'I would like to have news taken to him about his daughter. Someone will have to go and seek him.'

'Perhaps I can help with that,' Sir Peregrine said. 'I would be happy to send a man to find him and tell him.'

'That would indeed be helpful. And then I have to try to ensure that the girl's husband is released as well,' Baldwin said.

'I should speak with the lad's father and tell him to keep an eye on his son to make sure he stays safe, then leave him to sort it out,' Sir Peregrine said. 'The girl is the one who must take up your efforts. Whether she is fallen from her horse or has been captured doesn't matter. Either way, she must be found urgently. There are too many felons and outlaws who could seek to take her. I regret that I cannot assist you personally. I have some matters to work on in court. However, when I am free, I swear that I will do all in my power to see the boy released.'

'I thank you for that. You are right, of course,' Baldwin said. He felt as though it was a weight being lifted from his shoulders, hearing the clear-sighted Sir Peregrine voice his own feelings. 'Edith must be found first.'

'Good! God speed, then, Sir Baldwin.'

Baldwin nodded and gave Sir Peregrine his hand, both rising. Sir Peregrine promised to send one of his own servants to find Simon, and to send any other men he could find to aid Baldwin in the hunt for Edith, and then the two parted, Baldwin striding purposefully into the gathering dusk with Edgar along the high street.

'Where are we going?' Edgar asked.

'We must speak with the husband's father. This man has some authority in the city. Surely he must be able to do something for his son. He may not be able to get the lad released, but he can at least see to it that he gets some food.'

Jacobstowe

At the vill there were a couple of women chatting on a doorstep, and the coroner bellowed at them to fetch help.

One of the women looked at him with some alarm. The other looked as though she was about ready to run immediately for help in the form of men with billhooks, but the coroner stood and glared at them. 'What is it, gossips? You more keen to discuss the doings of your husbands and daughters than help a neighbour? Come here, the pair of you, and tell us where we may install this poor woman. She's your neighbour, in Christ's name!'

'What have you done with her?' This was the woman in the doorway. She appeared reluctant to leave it while the coroner stood before her, and her sharp, weasely face moved from Coroner Richard to Simon with deep suspicion.

Sir Richard stared at her. He was not yet over his initial shock at seeing this woman collapse before him, and the fact that it had been Simon who had realised what was happening, and not him, lent additional force to his voice. He took an immense breath, and then bellowed, *'In the name of Christ, you stupid, malodorous bitch, since you haven't the wits God gave you at birth, run and find a woman who has some! Fetch someone who knows what to do with a poor widow who's fainted, and if you don't do that in less time than it takes me to draw breath, I, Coroner Richard de Welles, will have you attached and amerced for your astonishing stupidity!'*

She was already fleeing along the road towards the middle of the vill as he roared his last words, and as she ran there was a satisfying sound of doors being wrenched open, and even the clatter of a bowl being dropped and smashing.

Before long, Simon and the coroner were inside a small hovel, setting the widow on a low palliasse, and hurriedly pushing past the women who thronged the doorway to see what was happening to their neighbour.

The coroner took a deep breath of the cool early-evening air. 'Right, Bailiff, Brother Monk, we have been working and travelling all the weary day. It is time for me to have at least a gallon of wine and mead before I take responsibility for a large joint of meat of some sort.'

'I think we shall be fortunate to find a decent meal here,' Simon said with a tired smile. It had been harder than he would have expected to carry the poor woman the relatively short distance to her own house. For such a small-bodied woman, it was a surprise how much she seemed to weigh after a few feet.

Coroner Richard hesitated, fixing Simon with a look of puzzlement. 'You think so? I've never yet found a place that couldn't provide a perfectly good meal if you know who to speak to. Mind you, this is a strange-looking vill. Not the sort of place I'd think to stop in usually. But there must be an inn or something nearby.'

He saw a man staring at the door to Agnes's house. The fellow was surely on his way home from a day in the fields, and had seen or heard the noise of their return. Noticing the coroner bearing down on him, he squeaked and would have fled, but Sir Richard's voice was pleasantly modulated for him. 'Friend, I am in need of wine and vittles. Do ye know a good tavern about this place?'

Even with the coroner's most gentle smile, the man looked ready to bolt, but Mark was already behind him. 'My son, you need only point out the way to the tavern if that large fellow intimidates you too much. Personally, I think his bark is worse than his bite. But then, having heard him, you wouldn't want to get too close, would you? I don't anyway. So please, put us all out of our misery and just tell him where to get some wine.'

It was a rough little building, but Sir Richard declared himself delighted with it and its rustic charm. Simon looked about him and thought it looked marginally worse than some of the brawling drinking chambers in Dartmouth where the sailors would go to forget their woes. There were no stools, only a few large round tree trunk logs to rest on, and one bench that appeared to have been made by a man who had heard of such things but had never actually seen or used one. Simon stood eyeing it for some little while before resorting to leaning against a wall.

Sir Richard was less particular. He stood at the hearth in the middle of the room and warmed his hands on the rising heat. There was a tripod set over the fire, and a pot held a thickening pottage with some lumps of indeterminate meat bobbing about occasionally. A young girl of perhaps nine summers clad in a simple shift stood and stirred the pot seriously, spending more time warily keeping her eyes on these three strangers. Mark had walked straight in, sighed, and made his way to the bench, on which he rested his backside with a show of caution – a display that appeared unnecessary, for there was not even a squeak of protest from the wood as it took his weight.

'Child, where is your father?' Simon asked.

She said nothing, but nodded towards a door at the opposite end of the room. Simon walked to it, and soon there was a man with them. He was as old as Simon, but his face wore the years with less ease. He was also a deal slimmer than the bailiff, and his hair was almost all grey, while his brows were black as a Celt's beard. In a short time they had ordered ales – there was no wine – and bread, pottage and a steamed suet pudding of apples and pears.

For some little while there was an appreciative silence as the three finished their meal and sat back contented. The coroner gave a belch, and then a trumpet blast from his arse. 'Hah! I needed that. There's nothing so disorders a man's humours as having no ballast in his belly. And a pot or two of ale helps the digestion, I always reckon.'

'I will be happier when I've had a sleep,' Simon said. He stretched his arms over his head and felt the tension in his shoulders with a grimace. 'So much still to learn and do in the morning.'

'Aye. Well, we will be up early, I dare say,' the coroner said with a rueful glance at the floor. They had agreed with the host that they could sleep in a room at the back, but it looked a verminous, unpleasant bedchamber. Sir Richard's only hope was that the promised straw for bedding was not too smothered in fleas or lice. He had slept rough before and had no wish to do so again.

'I find your attitudes astonishing,' Mark hissed. 'Today you have wasted so many hours in merely wandering about the land, asking all kinds of questions about a dead reeve, and learned nothing at all about the murder of two priests and their guards. These are the men the good cardinal requested you to ask after, but you've done precious little to learn *anything* so far as I can see.'

'Aye?' Sir Richard said, fixing a genial look on the monk. 'Why is that?'

'I assume you are still new to this kind of inquest,' Brother Mark said. 'In God's name, I wish we had found another to do the job.'

'Do ye now? Hmm. How many deaths have you investigated, Master Monk?'

'Do not be ridiculous! I have never—'

'None? Ah. And how many dead bodies, then, have you buried?'

'I have been to a number of funerals.'

'Not what I asked. No, you see, I was wondering whether you had buried many of your own family?'

'I was present at my mother's funeral not long ago.'

'Oh? Your mother's? Was she murdered?'

'No, she was old, though.'

'Oh, I see. Well then, Master Monk, you should remember that Simon and I have actually investigated more than a few deaths. Me, I've held more than a hundred inquests on corpses in my time; and I've seen enough felons hanged to fill my days. I have what you could call *experience*, if you were to be so crass.'

'Then why did you ask nothing about the men today, and instead spent so much time on the reeve?'

'That is why I asked whether you had lost a close relative. When you have, when you've had to find someone who's close to you, when you've had to help bring that loved one home again, so that you can bury her, and when you have suffered all the misery and recrimination, all the self-loathing and hatred, for being so stupid as to let her die while you were off enjoying yourself, master, then, and only then, can you criticise us. I left my wife alone one day, and she was killed. I know what it feels like to lose a loved one. For now, let me remind you that you are here in the vill where an honourable, decent reeve lived and worked, with all his friends and companions from the area. He was a man of this vill. He did what he could for the folk here. They have had a loss that cannot be mended. And his wife, you will remember, was with us. How would she have felt were we to have ignored her old man and instead spent all our time in asking about a group of foreigners she'd never known? Eh? There is such a thing as compassion, Master Monk. Perhaps you have heard of the term?'

Mark was appalled. He could not meet their eyes, but shortly afterwards he silently walked from the room while Sir Richard squatted at the edge of the fire, poking at it with a long twig. 'Has he gone?'

Simon nodded. 'So, do I take it that you forgot about the travellers, then?'

Before answering, Coroner Richard cast a quick look over his shoulder to make sure that Mark wasn't in earshot. Then he gave a sly grin. 'Aye. I was thinking more of the reeve. Takes a damned monk to remind us of our jobs, eh?'

'We will learn more tomorrow,' Simon said. 'And I am sure that the murderer of the reeve is somehow connected with those of the travellers.'

'How so? Same men did them all, you mean? Looks unlikely to me – the weapons were all wrong, like we said.'

'True. But perhaps there was one man left behind who realised the reeve was growing close to them, and decided to kill him. He may have picked up a stone purely because drawing steel would have betrayed his intent.'

'Perhaps. I don't deny it's possible. If that is right, though, it would imply a well-organised force.'

'How do you mean?'

'Just this: a rearguard left behind to cover their trail or to guard against attack shows military thinking. But if someone was left behind they would have gone within hours of the force passing by. No, it cannot have been a guard. More likely it was a fresh person out for personal gain.'

'So you consider it likely that the killing of the reeve was entirely unconnected? Or it was a man on a freelance mission? Riding out, he sought any suitable target for his attack, and picked upon a lone wandering reeve with no money?' Simon said with a grin.

'You may chuckle, Bailiff. I would wager a few pennies that the reeve was more unfortunate than you'd think. He could have been at home, curled up around that wife of his, but instead he went out and was met by a man on his way. The fellow realised he had money—'

'Scarcely likely.'

'Well, perhaps he thought the reeve was on the trail of his companions, so he chose to remove him before he could learn where they all came from.'

'And where did they?' Simon wondered aloud. 'They cannot fade into the undergrowth. A force large enough to kill so many in so efficient a manner must have a goodly number of men.'

He turned. The host was in the rear of the room, and when Simon beckoned, the man hurried over. 'Masters? How may I serve you?'

'About here are there any large manors with a knight or squire living in them?' Simon asked.

'Not near here, no, lording. There are no great lords about here. Not even a squire for miles.'

'Where is the nearest man-at-arms, then?' Sir Richard demanded. 'A man with a small force who're trained to the saddle and to arms. There must be someone not too far away.'

'There is Sir John de Sully. He lives up at Ashreigny.'

'I know him,' Simon said.

'I too,' Coroner Richard agreed. 'He's an honourable man. Who else?'

The landlord scratched his head. 'There's the castle at Oakhampton. The Courtenay family maintains a small force there.'

Simon considered. 'That would make more sense, certainly. The men there could have seen these travellers as they passed along the Cornwall road, for they would have journeyed up there once they were off the Tavistock road, just as we did this morning. But the coppicers and charcoal burners were very sure that no one came up from their direction, nor returned that way.'

'Yes. And the Courtenays are not so foolish as to try to rob and kill so many,' the coroner responded.

'No,' Simon agreed thoughtfully. 'Although the baron himself lives mostly in Tiverton, he may have a castellan at Oakhampton who is less level headed.'

'True enough. There are men all over the country who are less reliable than they should be,' the coroner said sadly. 'My own wife was killed by a servant I trusted. No man can entirely trust even his own men.'

'There is nobody else,' the host said helpfully.

'What of the east?' asked Simon. 'The reeve's footprints were heading in that direction, Sir Richard.' And the charcoal burners had mentioned the men from Bow, which was east.

'Aye. True enough,' the coroner said, cheering up. 'What of that way?'

'There's no force at Tawton, nor at Sampford,' the host said, scratching at his head with a frown. 'Think there's a small fortified manor east of it, though. What's that place called?' he added to himself in a mutter. 'Bow! Sir Robert of Traci, he's over there.'

Chapter Twenty-Two

Nymet Traci

Sir Robert de Traci stalked along his hall and out into the yard, one hand on the pommel of his sword. 'Osbert? How was it?'

His henchman shook his head. 'As you'd expect.'

The knight shrugged. 'Well, no matter. I didn't expect more. So the abbot-elect didn't send a note with the messenger?'

'There was nothing there, no,' Osbert said.

'The messenger's dead? I don't want any risk that he could get back to the king. Good, good. The main thing is, the message was delivered. Now we'll have to use a little guile to bring in the big fish. You don't catch a salmon by beckoning, do you? The idea was all right, but there was never much likelihood that it would work for a man like the aspiring abbot. He's too wily for that. No, what we need is a more realistic temptation for him to come to us.'

'What will you do to tempt him, then?' Osbert said. His good eye was fixed on his master.

'We'll have to think of something. After all, there cannot be too much in the life of a man like him. All we need to do is figure out what little latch will open his heart. What key will fit it, and how to turn it. Money failed, which means perhaps avarice is not the way. He's a man, though, and a monk, so perhaps a suitable woman?'

Osbert shrugged. 'I never understood the sort of men who would want to hide away in an abbey.'

'No. You and I are two of a kind, Os. We prefer the reality of this world to dreaming of the next, eh?'

Osbert snorted as he busied himself about his mount. 'What of the next world? So long as there's time to say a Pater Noster, we'll be allowed in anyway. Why live like a monk with no cods, when you can live like a king down here?'

'Quite right. One thing, Os – the messenger had no other messages in his little pouch?'

'Nothing I saw. I reckoned he had some verbal messages. Nothing much I could do about them, though. Basil killed him as soon as he could.'

'Ah yes. My son,' Sir Robert said. 'And where is he?'

'In Bow. There's a girl there—'

'I see. Which?'

'The little black-haired one with the long legs. You know the one? Lives at the farm in the middle of the high street on the north side.'

'I think I do, yes.'

The knight was plainly worried about his son's tardiness. Osbert nodded as his master took his leave, and then set about removing saddle and bridle. There were plenty of ostlers and grooms, but this was no simple palfrey he had used; it was his own horse, and one thing he had learned in eighteen months of wandering the roads was that his own horse merited his own efforts. A horse was like any other tool: if a man valued it, he would be rewarded by it.

While he brushed the sweat and dirt from his beast, Osbert was thinking again of the messages in the messenger's pouch.

It was true that there was nothing directly relevant to him or to Sir Robert, but there had been the one little note in there. The cylinder had opened easily enough, and Osbert had been able to read it with ease, even with the mud all about. The message had said that a shipment of over one hundred pounds had been stolen from the abbey on its way to the king.

Osbert had stared at it expressionlessly while the other men stamped their feet and muttered about the God-damned cold, before he dropped the cylinder back into the leather pouch.

After all, there was no point hiding the robbery. All would know about it soon enough.

He was still there when there was a banging at the door, and some ribald shouts. Looking up, he saw a pair of horses appear in the gateway. One of the riders was a scrawny-looking fellow who might have been a lawyer from his appearance, but the other was very different: a slim, rather beautiful young woman with the haughtiness of a countess, who stuck her chin in the air and ignored the comments that washed about her.

Before long she had been helped from her mount, and willing hands guided her to the hall, where a maidservant came to meet her and took her inside.

It was nothing to Osbert. He continued with the long, regular strokes of his brush that he knew his horse most appreciated, until Sir Robert appeared beside him a while later, laughing and rubbing his hands in glee.

'You seem happy, Sir Robert,' Osbert noted.

'And why not, Osbert? After all, we were discussing how to unlock the abbot's heart, weren't we? I would think we have the key now. After all, what could be better to aid us than the daughter of one of his friends?'

Tavistock Abbey

Robert Busse walked the short distance from the choir to the chapter house, and had seated himself at the stone bench that was fitted into the wall when the knock came.

It was an irritation. There was so much for him to consider, especially with the sudden death of the messenger. 'Yes?'

'Brother, the men have discovered something.'

Busse sighed. If the whole community was going to behave like this overenthusiastic puppy, he would resign his post and run away to become a hermit somewhere far from here, he told himself. Oh, the boy meant well, but he was so keen to see Robert installed as abbot that he was always about his ankles like a devoted mastiff. Robert found he was forever tripping over the lad. Perhaps it was planned, he wondered. Perhaps in fact the boy was the devoted servant of de Courtenay, and spent his time about Robert so that the abbot-elect would grow completely enraged by his solicitous attention and give up all hope of the position.

The idea was enough to wipe away the final vestige of grumpiness, and in its place he fitted a smile. 'How may I serve you, Peter?'

'This!'

The lad dramatically opened his hand. In it was a pair of small cylinders. Robert recognised them instantly. 'Where did you find them?' he asked.

'They were in the messenger's shirt, Abbot.'

'Nay, I am not abbot,' Robert chided him gently.

'But you will be, Abbot!'

Robert shook his head. 'What are they?'

'You must see them. The others, they were in his pouch or scattered about, but these two were inside his shirt and hidden. I suppose he thought that they were too important to be left behind!'

Taking them, the abbot-elect felt a tingle in his fingers, as though the small scrolls were themselves trying to tell him that they were to be most significant for him.

'The seals are broken on them?'

'I fear, Abbot, that the men who found the body didn't think.'

He nodded, not believing a word of it. The men who would have found the body and brought it to the road would have been unlettered. These had been opened by Peter or another monk. Still, they had been already read, so he might as well do so as well.

The writing was tiny, to be able to fit in such a small scroll, but perfectly legible, and as soon as he took in the words, Robert Busse felt his mouth open in disbelief.

'You see?' Peter said, his voice hushed.

'I will take these,' Robert said. 'You did right to bring them to me, Peter. And now, please leave me.'

He had never before held anything quite so shocking in his hands. For this was written proof that a companion of his in the abbey sought his murder.

Bow

The light was almost gone now and Edith realised that they were close to the end of their journey. As they clattered down the stony path towards the stone house she remembered as Sir Harold's, she could see that it was a strong fortress. Where Sir Harold had lived in modest comfort and without exacting too much in the way of taxes from his serfs, the new owner of the house was more determined to impose his rule on the landscape.

It was clear enough in so many little ways. When she had last been past here, she had seen a pleasant home. It was a good-sized hall for a small household, set inside a circling wall of grey stone, but the wall was only some five to six feet high, so not a deliberately defensive enclosure. Rather, it was enough to keep the sheep and cattle from wandering, and to prevent foxes or wild dogs from attacking the chickens. Trees had grown up close to the walls to the north-east, making an attractive area for sitting on hot summer days. To Edith's eye it had looked like a pleasant little homestead.

Not now. The wall had been expanded to encompass a broader area. The little barns and stables had grown, and there was a cleared swathe of land for a good bowshot in all directions. Where the original wall had been more use as a stockade, now it was a distinct fortress. There was more height to it, and added thickness, as well as battlements. It was made to withstand attack, and money had been spent to ensure that it would serve its purpose.

'What has happened to Sir Harold?' she asked nervously as they rode towards the little gatehouse.

'He's dead. This is the property of my lord Sir Hugh le Despenser now,' William replied with a quick look at her. 'He took it when Sir Harold died and his son, Sir Robert, was found to have committed treason. The de Tràci family was disinherited immediately. It's only by my master's good favour that Sir Robert has been reinstated and pardoned. But my lord Despenser keeps ownership.'

Everyone in the kingdom knew Sir Hugh would take what he wanted and to hell with the owners. He had a reputation for cruelty that was unequalled.

'Master, what do you want with me?'

'I want nothing, mistress. It's not me, it's what Sir Robert and my lord Despenser want that should trouble you.'

He said no more, but led her to the gates, her mare's reins in his hands. She had no means of escape – even sliding from the mare and running was no option. There was nowhere to run to from here. All the land about this northern wall of the house was clear of bushes. She would not make even a hundred yards before recapture. A man on horseback, even a knackered hobby like his, would surely run her down in moments.

The gates loomed up, grim grey moorstone with solid oaken doors that looked as though they could withstand the massed artillery of the king's forces. Edith felt like a mouse in the claws of an owl. Utterly helpless. There was no escape from here. In her mind, she saw herself making off in a dozen ingenious ways: turning her mare at Wattere, spurring her so that she ran into him and knocked him from his beast, snatching her reins and riding like the wind until she was safe; getting close to him, close enough to pull his sword and strike, and then riding off; talking to him, persuading him that she was worth saving from whatever might happen in there, thankfully taking his protection as he fought off the whole of the guard . . . And then they were under the gates and inside the castle.

Behind her, she heard the slow grinding and graunching of the gates as they were pushed shut. And then there was a rumble as the massive baulks of timber were dropped into their slots to keep the gates closed.

It sounded like the gates of hell being closed behind her.

Jacobstowe

Sir Richard paused dramatically, and then gave a flourish with his hand. 'This maid, then, was captured and bound by her captor, and was rescued by a saviour who wanted to assure himself of her condition, to make sure that she was unharmed, if you know what I mean, eh, fellows? He needed to know no one had been sheathing his pork sword where it shouldn't have been sheathed, eh?'

His crudeness won a round of happy chuckles from his audience, and he was content as he refilled his quart pot. 'So, she was happy to answer his questions. "Did he bind you?" She replied with a shake of her head and much discontent. "I am afraid he did, my lord." Her saviour continued, "Did he bind your mouth to stay your protestations, child?" And she was able to reply with a sob, "Why yes, my lord. He did." Her saviour was grim faced by now. "Did he tie you up so you couldn't escape?" "Yes, yes, he did, my lord. To my disgrace, I could not save myself." "Did he bind your legs?" But here she could smile. Eh? "Nay, my lord, for by God's good grace, I made sure I kept my legs so wide apart he couldn't bind them together!" Eh? Eh? Good joke, eh?'

Simon couldn't help laughing. It was an old joke, but the coroner had a childlike delight in retelling it, and a number of other ones equally as bad. Often he was so incoherent by the time he reached the end of the joke, laughing so much at the approaching *coup de grâce*, that the enthusiastic audience could make out nothing of his words, but they would all laugh in any case. It was easy to see that the coroner, while in his cups and not working in his usual position of authority, was a good-humoured soul who enjoyed amusing people.

'There is another one, too,' he said, before launching into the next little tale.

Simon watched him with a faint grin. It was very hard not to like the man, even though he generally caused Simon to panic whenever they were near to a tavern. It wasn't his jokes; it was his ability to drink everyone else into a stupor that really concerned Simon. It tended to leave him feeling as lousy as a youth after his first serious bout of drinking. That sense of the room swimming about his head as soon as he lay down, the repellent bubbling in his gut, the morning-after feeling of acid in the throat and the knowledge that his head had swollen to many times its usual size, with the concomitant fluffiness in his brain that was only ever relieved by the pain – as of four daggers being thrust in slowly from the temples and his eye sockets. No, he did not like drinking with Sir Richard. The resultant anguish was too horrible.

As the coroner continued, Simon fell to thinking about the dead bodies. It was curious that there had been no reports of the money being stolen until he had spoken to Cardinal de Fargis. He would have thought that others should have heard of such a large theft. But the trouble was, it was the very knowledge of such transfers of cash that led to the ease of their robbery. It was normal for even huge sums of money to be transported about the country with only four or five archers involved as guards. In this case, it would seem that eight archers and a couple of men-at-arms should have been perfectly adequate, and yet the size of the force that attacked them must have been greatly superior.

His eyes narrowed as he considered some aspects that had not occurred to him before. First, the men had not travelled very far. It was a distance that Simon and Sir Richard had covered in a half-day. That was odd, although it could have been explained by the weight of the money they were carrying. A hundred pounds of money in coin was a heavy cargo. And then there was the fact of the location. The men should not have been north of Oakhampton.

There was another detail: most commonly, when a robbery of this kind was perpetrated, Simon was sure that it was no accident. Men did not happen to fall over a bullion transfer. No, the attacks were made by those who had heard of the money being transported and wanted to grab it for themselves. It was not a matter of luck; it was a military ambush based on good intelligence. Someone who was close to people who knew about the money must have managed to release news of its movement to colleagues, who then took it.

So someone within the abbey, possibly, had told the attackers of the presence of the money.

Simon considered this with a frown as the noise about him rose, Sir Richard laughing aloud, the men all around roaring too, as he hit another punchline with the precision of a master story-teller.

The idea that someone in the cardinal's household could have betrayed him was not entirely surprising. Men would always think with their two brains: one for skirts, one for purses. It was scarcely a shock to learn that a man had heard of money being moved and bethought himself of the profit he could make. However, the result of his actions must have come as a shock. To learn that nineteen had died would surely make even the most avaricious thief pause for thought.

Then again, perhaps not. Simon knew that Sir Hugh le Despenser had happily caused the torture and ruin of many men and women, and none ever appeared to give him a moment's trouble. He was happy only so long as he was increasing his wealth and power. It was hard to imagine him being plagued by concerns for his victims. He would happily sell his wife into bondage, Simon reckoned, if it meant he would win a good property or profit by the arrangement.

And then he had another thought. If a man in the abbey or the cardinal's household had seen fit to tell thieves about the money, they might also think it sensible to warn of the king's officers being sent to hunt down the outlaws involved and find the money again. And they might think it expedient to locate any such officers and kill them.

Simon took a long pull at his ale. Even without a hangover, he was starting to feel deeply uncomfortable.

Chapter Twenty-Three

Agnes's house, Jacobstowe

She began to come around only a short time after the bailiff and his companions had left, but in the midst of the noise in her chamber she didn't open her eyes.

Agnes knew what was happening about her. It was the same as when a woman went into labour. The rest of the women of the vill, friends and others alike, would congregate in the woman's home and drink and gossip, offering some useful advice amid the general hubbub, enjoying the opportunity to have time with their own sex and no men about to cause trouble or arguments.

But Agnes wanted only peace. She could recall the sick headache beginning, and she remembered vaguely being picked up and carried here, but the reason for her sudden collapse was still a mystery. Men always said that women were weaker because of the womb. It was a strange organ that would move about the body in a predatory manner, giving rise to the odd emotions that assailed even the most intelligent of women.

This was nothing to do with organs, though. She knew that this was the result of her rage at the world and her husband. He should not have left her in that way. He had deserted her. His death had left her desolate. Her life now was barren.

Except it wasn't his choice, was it? He wouldn't have voluntarily killed himself. The poor man had loved her, and loved Ant too. He was a good man, a good, kind, gentle husband and father.

She *would* avenge him.

Exeter

Baldwin beat upon the door with his fist, paused, and then pounded again. 'Open the door!'

There was a shout from further up the lane, and Edgar touched Baldwin's shoulder. 'Sir.'

Turning, Baldwin saw that there were two watchmen striding down the lane towards them. 'Oh, in Christ's name,' he muttered, and slammed his open hand against the door once more. There was still no answer.

'You are late to be banging on doors, masters,' said the first watchman.

Baldwin stared at him. 'Do I not know you? Did you not help me and my friends find our way to his daughter's house?'

The watchman peered at him. His friend had a filthy cloth wrapped about his head, and Baldwin had a sudden flash of memory. 'Your name is Gil, and this must be your friend Phil, who was hurt while walking at night.'

'You were with the men who wanted the son of Charles the Merchant.' Gil nodded. 'But this isn't their house.'

'It is his parents' house. I need to speak with them about their son – he's been arrested. And his wife is missing too. But they will not open the door.'

'Maybe they're not there,' Gil said.

Phil shook his head. 'There's someone behind that shutter up there,' he said, pointing. 'I can see a face.'

Gil looked up. 'Well, they don't have to open their door to you, sir. Not if they don't want to.'

'Perhaps so, but I am Keeper of the King's Peace, and I do

not want to gain a reputation by breaking it myself,' Baldwin said suavely.

'No. Can't have that,' Gil said. He hesitated, reluctant to annoy a senior member of the city's hierarchy, but also unhappy at the thought of upsetting a King's Keeper.

Phil grunted. 'Oh, in Christ's name, Gil. Just kick at the door. They'll open it.'

'You bleeding kick it. That thing'll break your foot, you fool.'

'Then use your staff. If you want, I can try your head instead. It's thick enough, your skull should open the sodding thing.'

'Oh, ha, ha,' Gil said humourlessly. But he held his staff up and beat upon the door's timbers heavily, three times. 'If you don't mind, sir, I'll tell him you said you needed to speak with him,' he added quietly, before bellowing, 'Open the door in the name of the king!'

There was a muted rattling of bolts, then the lengthy rasp of the door's lock being turned, and the door opened to show a furious-looking Charles, his steward just behind him with a face that looked sickly with anxiety.

Baldwin made a point of giving the curtest of nods to the two watchmen. 'You may wait here,' he said before marching inside, his shoulder clipping the merchant's.

Charles began to bluster. 'Who do you think you are to beat upon my door and walk into my house without . . .'

As he spoke, he became aware of Edgar, who was standing extremely close, right behind him. Charles drew back from Edgar's smiling features, and Edgar gave an appreciative nod, reaching for the door and pushing it quietly closed.

Baldwin was already in the hall. 'I would speak with you, Master Charles.'

'Well, I wouldn't want to speak to you! State your business, and be gone.'

Baldwin's face did not alter, but Charles grew ever more conscious of how close Edgar was to him.

'Master,' Baldwin said, 'I am aware that you must be concerned about affairs here, but I am trying to help. I am keen to help your son, and his wife too.'

'Then go! In Christ's name, just leave us! Don't you think you've done enough damage? You and Edith's father.'

'What do you mean?' Baldwin demanded.

'The fact that you are here ruins all!' Charles said despairingly. He walked to his chair and dropped into it. 'To think that yesterday I woke and the sun still rose in the east. All was normal and without trouble; and now all is turned to ruin and disaster! My son lies in gaol. My only son!'

'What have you done to try to have him released?' Baldwin asked.

'I have done everything I can, of course! What do you think I've done?' Charles spat. 'I've begged that horse's arse the sheriff to release him, I've spoken to the city's mayor, I've even gone to the receiver of the city to see if he can help, but no! All of them say that if it's a matter of treason, they can do nothing. Poor Peter lies in that foul place while all the men in the city tell me that he cannot be freed. Why? What else could I have done?'

'Nothing, my friend,' Baldwin said, attempting to soothe the man. 'I have been to the sheriff myself, and I will be speaking with Bishop Walter too. To hold the fellow is plainly wrong. He is innocent of this charge. I will ensure that he is released as soon as may be, but have you had a thought to easing the wheels of justice?'

He was reluctant to mention bribes, but there was no escaping the fact that many sheriffs were particularly venal, no matter what county they hailed from.

'It was the first thing we thought of,' said Jan as she walked into the room. Her eyes were glittering with misery, and Baldwin bowed to her in deference to her fears. 'We offered him money, gold, even shares in my husband's ventures, but the man would listen to no reason. He refused all we could give, and then he laughed at us.'

'Have you given him cause to persecute your family?' Baldwin asked the merchant. 'I can see no reason why he would behave in this manner.'

'No. I have had no dealings with him at all,' Charles said.

'He owns land near to you?'

'Yes, but he's never visited that I know of. I doubt this has anything to do with that.'

'Your son said he had contacts in the king's court?'

Charles's face was in his hands now, and he left it there as he spoke. 'All I know of him is that he is a close ally of Sir Hugh le Despenser.'

Baldwin felt the blood freeze in his veins.

'That is all we know,' Mistress Jan said. She took a shuddering breath, then gave a grimace. 'If only I thought that there was some reason behind it.'

Her husband slowly withdrew his hands. 'There is a reason. There is some cause for Despenser to detest Edith's father. It is all his fault. The sheriff is acting on Despenser's orders, you mark my words! The fool has brought all this upon our heads.'

'It is not Simon's fault if Despenser has grown bitter towards him,' Baldwin said shortly. 'Simon cannot be blamed for attempting to uphold the rule of the law.'

'I can blame him!' Charles spat. 'I can blame him and anyone else for bringing this disaster upon our house. The bastard should have kept quiet and not threatened the livelihood of his own daughter and son-in-law like this!'

'It is his daughter I am most concerned about,' Baldwin said. 'She is missing now. Have you seen her since last afternoon?'

'No. She left here in the morning yesterday, and we haven't seen her since,' Jan said. She had an earnest expression, as though to confirm that she was indeed keen to help.

'She stayed at my house, but tried to ride back here first thing in the morning,' Baldwin admitted. 'We had no idea she would try such a thing, but I saw she was gone as soon as I rose.'

'Good!' Charles said. 'Perhaps if she is gone, the sheriff will release my boy and let us return to normal!'

'Husband, good husband,' Jan murmured. She walked across the floor to his side. 'Don't be cruel to her. She is our family now, and this is not her making.'

'She sprang from the cods of that fool her father,' Charles said. 'I rue the day I first saw her.'

Baldwin grunted impatiently. 'Well, if you will take that attitude, there is little more to be said. I will wish you God speed. However, if you have a brain left in your head, you will try to bring food and wine to your son. He will be in sore need of good food and drink. Also, bribe the guards to look after him and tell you when anything untoward is threatened to him. In that way, you may do him good.'

He turned to leave, but suddenly there was a scraping on the floor and he realised that Charles was flying towards him. Baldwin made no move, but suddenly Edgar was at his side, and with a swift rasp of steel his sword flashed out. The point came to rest on Charles's throat.

'Call your dog off me!' Charles snarled.

Baldwin stepped back, pulling on his gloves. He lifted the sword up and away, but continued walking towards Charles, who took a pace or two backwards at the sight of Baldwin's face.

'First, Master Charles, you are lucky to be alive. Most men who try to hurt me while my servant is at my side only ever have the opportunity to make one attempt. Second, my friend Simon is a good, honourable, upright man who would walk over fire to help you and your son. You would do well to attempt similar loyalty in return. Third, his daughter is one of the kindest, most delightful young women in the city. You forget yourself when you do nothing to find her now when she could be lying in a ditch at the side of the road. It is one thing to think only of yourself, but when that means deserting your own daughter-in-law, your behaviour sinks below the level of the meanest felon in the city.'

'I seek to protect my son.'

'You should also seek to protect the others who are now in your care,' Baldwin said. 'Reflect on that.'

He strode from the room, unable to trust himself to say more. The behaviour of the man struck him as so dishonourable, so demeaning, he would have expected to see it in the actions of a mere tanner or scavenger, not in a man of position and importance.

But perhaps he was being unreasonable. The man was a merchant, not a knight. He was no warrior, but a man of numbers and money. He had no experience of coping with threats and the power of a man with money and men behind him.

Baldwin was still musing on Charles and his problems when he found himself confronted by the watchman again. Gil was frowning and chewing his inner lips.

'You wanted me?' Baldwin asked mildly.

'Sir Baldwin, I don't know whether it matters or anything, but there's a man saw Mistress Edith earlier today.'

Baldwin was listening, but after a day of travelling, of being browbeaten by the sheriff, and now with his mind full of thoughts of the man he had just left, it took a moment before he comprehended what Gil had said.

'What? Are you sure he said *today*?'

'Yes. It was old Arthur. I met him at the gate earlier. He said he was sure that he saw the mistress heading back west on the Crediton road. She didn't look happy, he said, but the man with her was enough to make anyone look unhappy.'

Baldwin felt at last as though he was getting somewhere, and there was a wash of relief that flooded his body as he smiled at Gil, but then he realised what he had said. 'Edgar, quick! Someone has taken Edith and has forced her to ride west from here. We must hurry and follow.'

'We will not be able to leave the city now,' Edgar said. 'The gates will be shut.'

Baldwin nodded, but he looked at Gil. 'This lady has been captured, you understand me? She has been taken against her will, and even now she may be lying injured at the side of a road – or suffering much worse at the hands of her captors. Will you aid us?'

'Any way I can, Sir Baldwin,' Gil said.

'I need to leave the city. *Now!*'

Fourth Tuesday after the Feast of the Archangel Michael*

Nymet Traci

Edith woke with a sore head and the feeling that all was not well. As soon as she opened her eyes, her mouth fell open in a silent scream as the events of the last days came flooding back. She scrabbled away from the bed, falling to the floor and pushing herself backwards to the corner of the wall, where she sat, back jammed hard against it, panting hard like a trapped mouse.

Her hands were sore, but not so bad as she had feared the night before. Her neck was rough too, where the rope had

---

*29 October 1325

abraded the skin, but generally she did not feel as though she had been too severely treated. In large part, she knew, that was due to the caution of her captor.

Looking about her, the room was a comfortable enough little chamber. She recalled last night seeing that it was in the solar of the hall. Where the knight Sir Robert had one end of the roof space for himself, this room at the opposite end of the hall had been allocated for her. It was warm up here in the eaves, but that was no cause for pleasure on her part. She was aware of an overwhelming rage at her treatment. Stolen away from the road, when she was trying to return to her home and her husband.

Her husband! In her fit of anger at being taken, she had forgotten all about poor Peter, and yet he was still there in the gaol in Exeter, no doubt. He would be terrified, sitting there in the gloom, without companionship or comfort of any sort. Just the thought of his suffering was enough to make the tears well up in her eyes again.

There was a window in the far wall, and she crossed to it, letting the shutter fall down and peering out. The view was to the west, but if she craned her neck she could see the huge rounded mass of Cawsand Beacon over to the south and west. It was enough to make her feel just a little soothed. There were few enough sights that could help her, but the knowledge that Dartmoor was close was itself balm to her soul. She had been so happy there with her parents at Lydford, at their old house.

While she stared, she heard the door open behind her. Instantly she whirled about, keeping to the wall. 'What do you want?'

The man who had entered was only a little older than her. He had a beard already, which was thick and black, and his eyes were a strange pale grey colour. His body was slim, but powerful. He gave the impression of whipcord instead of muscles. 'Awake? Good.'

'Who are you?'

'You can call me Basil of Nymet Traci, wench.'

She was suddenly aware of his power as he allowed his eyes to slip down her figure. He made her feel as though she was naked, as though he could see through her thin shift, and his gaze passed lingeringly over her breasts and her rounding stomach, down her legs, and back to her face again. 'It is good to see that the daughter of the troublemaker is so handsome,' he said. 'It'll make the whole process more interesting.'

'Who are you? What do you want with me?'

'What I would like with you would be a good roll in the hay, mistress. You look as though you'd be a bawdy wench. Do you know how to waggle your tail? But what you mean to ask is, why are you here, isn't it? And that is easier to answer. You are being held here to make sure that your father behaves himself.'

'What does that mean?' Edith demanded. 'He will behave honourably at all times.'

'Oh, you'd best hope not,' the man chuckled. He stood aside, and a small, frightened woman entered with a trencher holding some pottage and a wooden spoon, with a jug of ale in the other hand. She set them on the floor near Edith, and hurried from the room again. The man looked her over once more, with a smile of appreciation, and then closed the door quietly behind him.

She heard the bolt slide across, and then sat on her mattress, staring down at the food and drink.

It made her feel like throwing up.

Chapter Twenty-Four

Jacobstowe

'Wake up, Simon, it's time to get moving!'

Simon came to only slowly. The past day, with the travelling and the investigation when they had arrived here, had made him groggy. At least this time it was not a result of the coroner's carousing for the night, he told himself wearily as he rolled himself off the palliasse. He shivered in the cool morning air as he pulled on a tunic.

'Ye know, Simon, that drink last night was not all bad. I was quite taken by his strong ale. It was well flavoured, and it's given me not the faintest after-effect whatever. Sometimes, you know, I can feel a vague lassitude in the morning after a few quarts, but today – no! I feel absolutely wonderful.'

They were in a small room at the rear of the tavern, a lean-to chamber that had all the comforts of a pigsty, but did at least appear to have clean straw in the palliasses, and although Simon was aware of an itch, he didn't think it was the result of flea bites but of a straw that had stabbed him during the night.

There was a leather pail of water, and Simon went to it and cupped a handful over his head and neck. It was freezing cold, but enormously refreshing, and he closed his eyes and thrust his head into the bucket. 'Ah, that's better!' he gasped.

'You're mad. Ye know that, don't you?' Sir Richard said with affable amusement. 'Food'll be ready in a few moments, so if you want some, ye'd best hurry.'

'I will take it with me,' Simon said as he pulled on hosen and boots. 'I never eat this early in the morning.'

'You will fade to naught if you're not careful,' the coroner said disapprovingly.

The door opened behind him, and Mark entered. He looked dishevelled and pasty, and entirely unamused.

'Good morrow, monk,' the coroner said. 'Been praying?'

'If my prayers held any force, Sir Richard, you would be dead even now,' Brother Mark said with cold loathing.

'Eh? What have I done?'

Simon grinned as he slipped his linen chemise over his head. 'Mark, do not worry. After the third or fourth night, either you are so tired that you sleep immediately anyway, or you grow accustomed to the snoring.'

'Me? Snore?' the coroner demanded with shock. 'Never snored in me life!'

'We shall go as soon as the horses are ready?' Mark asked Simon, studiously ignoring the coroner.

'Yes. I want to head down past Hoppon's place and see where the reeve Bill could have been going when he was murdered.'

He wasn't keen to mention that the only place that appeared to make sense, after talking to the host of the tavern last night, was the castle over towards Bow. It would be better to follow any trail they might and see where it took them, and it was in that frame of mind that he mounted his old rounsey and began to ride off towards Hoppon's house.

It was a cool morning, but the clouds were very high and the sky was a perfect blue. Looking at it, Simon was convinced that the weather would remain dry and probably would grow quite warm. With that in mind, he didn't pull on his heavier jerkin, but merely tugged his cloak around him. Later he would be able to loosen it as he became hotter with the ride.

Their road was fine all along to the place where they had been told the reeve's body had been found. From there Simon eyed the ground carefully, looking for cart tracks and horses' hoofprints. There were many of them all over the ground here. However, there was no road south that he could see being taken by any of the prints, only a steady movement east.

He continued along after them, his eyes for the most part fixed on the mess of mud and churned grass, but in reality there was no need for him to keep on staring down. The truth was, the men who had come here had been remarkably lax in concealing their way. Others might take a route of stonier paths, or ride up along a stream bed, but these had the arrogance of knights who knew that they were safe from arrest. Their position afforded them total assurance. Well, Simon intended to prove that they were wrong in that conviction.

It was as they rode up a hill that Simon realised how far they had already come. He could see on the side of another hill not far away a town that seemed familiar. He quickly ran through their route. They had already passed Sampford Courtenay and North Tawton, and now they were at the foot of the hill to Bow, he realised. A good distance already. But the trail was not leading them direct to Bow; it was heading more southerly.

There was a little hamlet, and as they trotted towards it, Simon saw an older man in his doorway shelling peas.

After giving the customary greetings, Simon indicated the path he was following. 'Where do all these go, master?'

The peasant was a kindly old man with a ready smile. His hair was almost pure white, but his eyebrows were grizzled with black to show his original colour. His skin was the same dark, ruddy colour as Simon's own, and his eyes were as brown as well-cured leather and as sharp as any lawyer's. His name, he said, was John Pasmere.

'Why do you want to know, sirs?' he enquired.

'Because they could be the prints of murderers,' Sir Richard said.

The peasant kept his eyes on Simon. 'I'm sorry to hear that. Someone died?'

'You don't want to help king's officers?' Simon asked.

'There are people whom it is not a good idea to upset, sir.'

Simon nodded. 'And some will threaten much to a man who betrays them. Especially when the fellow is dependent upon them for his home.'

'Aye.'

'On the other hand, the men here may have set upon a large party travelling through, and robbed the king,' Simon said. 'Any who aid outlaws and felons who've robbed the king could be viewed as enemies of the king.'

The old man glanced behind Simon at the coroner. 'Oh, aye? And what would a man do then, I wonder?' he said sarcastically. 'Have himself arrested and forced to tell under peine fort et dure?'

'Very likely,' Sir Richard grated. 'Since a man concealing such information is aiding the king's enemies, I'd personally recommend that it be pursued to the extreme limits of his endurance.'

'Which would take hardly any time for you, old man,' Mark said.

John Pasmere peered at the monk. 'Aren't you a little young to be warning older men about their life expectancies?'

Simon threw his reins to Mark, in large part to stop the young monk from making any further intervention. 'Friend, let us enter your home for a moment.' He dropped from his horse and walked to the house.

Inside it was a sparse little dwelling, but the man had obviously enjoyed the better weather of the summer. He had a filled wood store, his chimney had a whole ham slung over the fire, and there were herbs hanging from the rafters. 'This is a goodly home.'

'Meaning, I suppose, that it'll be a shame to lose it? Look, sir, I know what you are about. You want me to tell you all, and you will threaten me with losing my home and limbs and life if I don't. You see, the problem I have is, they threaten the same. And to be honest, I think that they will be the more savage about it. You understand my dilemma? I think my choice is made.'

'That is interesting,' Simon said. 'Because I was going to do nothing but ask you. I have no threats to offer. Only the good of the vill and the shire. Whoever killed that party will continue to kill others. A man who thinks he has nothing to fear from the law is a danger to all.'

'But he has no fear. Don't you realise?'

'Realise what?'

'The man you seek has been given the right by the king and his friend.'

'I don't understand you.'

'The king has a close friend and adviser,' John Pasmere said with the attitude of a man tested beyond patience. 'Despenser. And the man who did all this is a friend of the king's friend. He has recently come here to take over the manor. With Despenser's support.'

'That is no reason to murder travellers. Nor a local reeve merely trying to learn what really happened,' Simon said.

'What reeve?'

'The fellow elected to serve the vill of Jacobstowe. All I've heard says he was a good man.'

'About this tall? Strong fellow?'

'I don't know. I never met him. But I heard much. And he

didn't deserve to die, certainly not without having his death avenged.'

'I saw a man,' John Pasmere said slowly. 'He appeared here, just like you, and he was keen to learn who'd killed the travellers. This would be the same man, I think. Bill?'

'Bill Lark. Yes,' Simon said.

'Shite! Those bastards! They think they can just slaughter any, don't they?' John Pasmere said, and he slumped down on to his stool.

Simon studied him closely. There was little to show his thoughts, but he had suddenly blanched, and all his strength, which Simon had seen out in the open air, appeared to have fled. He was now just an old man, aged before his time.

'If you will tell naught, I will leave you, friend,' Simon said quietly. 'There's no threats. But Lark had a wife and child. She's widowed – the babe's lost his father. How many others have to die?'

'Poor bugger,' John Pasmere said, shaking his head. 'You say you are a bailiff. Is that true?'

'Yes. I am,' Simon said. He was about to explain that this was only a temporary position with the Cardinal de Fargis, that he had lost his old post on Dartmoor, but something made him hold his tongue. There were times, as his friend Baldwin often said, when it was better by far to be silent than to chatter on. Occasionally a witness wanted to talk, and then it was best to wait and listen.

There was a kind of suppressed urgency about John Pasmere as Simon watched him. The fellow looked up at Simon, then out through the door towards the irritable coroner and the monk, and then to his fire. His mouth moved, although for some while no noise came, and then suddenly the dam broke, and he began to mutter.

'There's no one safe from those evil bloodsucking bastards.

Who'd trust them to their word anyway? There's no rule here except theirs, and then they make it up and change it whenever they want. The bastards! They live here, taking all they want, all *we* need, and threaten any man if he so much as raises a complaint, but when a decent man—'

'Pasmere, calm yourself. I don't understand . . .'

'Oh yes, they can promise death and ruin, but what does that mean to us? Eh? We live in the shadow of the great lords all the while, and then they deign to notice us if they want something, but more often they ignore us. Unless we have something they want.'

Simon waited and watched. The man was working himself into a fine froth. He reminded Simon of a small dog he had once seen, tied up, barking at a cat that lay basking in the sun a short distance away. It was clear to all that the cat was there to taunt the dog, as cats will, and yet the only creature there who did not understand was the dog, working itself into a maddened fury and testing the strength of the thong binding it. In the end it was stilled when a man sent the cat flying with an accurately aimed stone.

John Pasmere was rather like the dog. Barking ineffectually, raging incoherently, he could no more harm his cat than could the dog. It was tempting to strike the man, but Simon could not do so. Instead he made as though to leave.

'No, sir. I will be calm.'

Simon said, 'I have no time to listen to a madman's ravings. I have much to do if I am to seek to avenge the reeve and the others.'

'It was the men – *his* men – Sir Robert of Nymet Traci. They're the ones killed your man the reeve.'

'How do you know?'

'Because it's my fault,' John Pasmere snapped, his face as hard as stone.

Nymet Traci

William atte Wattere sat on the stool with a grunt of satisfaction. The previous day had been painful. Sleeping rough was not novel to him, but to rise so early as he heard her horse pass him, and then the need to catch her making him hurry over packing, grabbing his horse, saddling and bridling the brute while he tossed his head and jerked against the cinch, did not improve his temper. And then he had to ride all the way almost to Exeter before he managed to get close enough, just so he could bind the bitch and bring her all the way back here again.

It hadn't been easy, trailing after her. He had wanted to catch her the day before, when she was riding to Sir Baldwin's house, but it hadn't been possible. She had ridden like a woman possessed, and the roads, while not full, were less empty than the next morning. The next morning, however, while she was still a little fuddled so early, it had been much easier.

But that all meant a long day in the saddle. Perhaps he could have shortened the way, but at the time it seemed sensible to take a little more time and not scare her. A woman in more fear might have had a fainting fit, or panicked and tried to ride off, meaning he'd have to kill her, and she was no good to him dead.

My lord Despenser had told him to catch her and bring her here safely, after all. That was the purport of the message. Bring her here to Nymet Traci and make sure that she was protected. And then, later, when her father knew where she was, and had complied with Sir Hugh le Despenser's demands, and the matter at Tavistock was resolved, then she could be released. Quietly.

Meanwhile, William intended getting outside a quart or two of wine and snoozing the day away.

He was in the buttery when a slim figure appeared in the

doorway, a dark-skinned man in his early twenties. 'Ale, you ballock-faced hog,' the newcomer called to the bottler.

William looked at the bottler with interest to see how the fellow would respond. When he had first entered this little chamber, the bottler had immediately struck him as a man who would be enthusiastic about laying about him with a cudgel if any man was rude. He was about five feet six inches tall, but his barrel chest was enormous, and his biceps were each the size of a small oak. Still, even with the provocation offered by the man in the doorway, he made no comment. Instead he ambled slowly back to his bar and filled a large jug from the barrel. He stood for a moment with the jug in his hands, and William thought he would throw it over the new fellow, but instead he appeared to steel himself, and took the ale to the man.

'Master Basil,' he said, proffering the jug.

William watched as the man drank the ale, then lightly tossed the jug in the bottler's direction, striding off before the man had managed to catch it.

'Who's he?' William asked.

'Sir Robert's son,' the man said gruffly. 'You'd do well to avoid him.'

Wattere couldn't agree more. He finished his drink and walked out into the sunshine, but here he almost tripped over a cat.

'Hoi, you cretin! Be careful.'

Wattere was angry, having almost fallen, but there was something about the voice that seemed familiar, and when he turned, he saw the same man.

Basil was standing in the shadows, pulling on a piece of string that the cat was toying with as he dragged it away. He glanced at Wattere with contempt, then returned his full attention to the young cat.

It was a lively little thing. Golden, with white patches; almost a kitten. It reared up as the string was flicked upwards and then crouched to spring forward as it was drawn away. Gradually, pouncing and leaping, it was brought closer and closer to Basil, who grinned to himself. 'You brought the girl here, eh?'

'Yes. She is called Edith.'

'I don't give a shit what her name is. She is a fresh little chauntle, isn't she? Ripe as a berry,' Basil said with a smack of his lips.

'She is a fair little maid, certainly.'

'I'd bet she could squirm like a snake. Thighs like little pillows, and her lips as lucious as a fig.'

'She's only here to be kept safely,' Wattere said pointedly.

'Are you telling me what I can and can't do in my own castle?' Basil said, looking up. There was an expression of genuine surprise on his face, Wattere saw.

It gave him the confidence to speak out. 'This castle is still owned by Sir Hugh le Despenser. Sir Hugh is my master.'

'Oh.'

'She is here because he asked me to bring her, and your father holds her for Sir Hugh. She is not to be molested, Master Basil.'

'Really?'

Wattere felt his senses heighten. It was the way of a man when he was preparing to do battle, for every aspect of perception to increase. His hearing was never stronger, his nostrils could detect the faintest odours, his eyes appeared to be able to focus more intently, and as he stood there, the picture of apparent ease, he was aware of each and every muscle in his arms, in his shoulders, in his thighs, even in the fingers of his hands. All were singing to him the song of war, of killing and of death. 'You don't think my lord Despenser should see his orders honoured?'

'Of course he should,' Basil said. He flicked the string and smiled as the cat approached a little, then sprang back out of his reach, sitting and waiting for the next game. 'His every whim should be honoured. In any castle he owns.'

'You realise you are talking about the most powerful man in the kingdom,' Wattere said.

'Yes. Not in this castle, though.'

'What?'

'In this castle, here in my father's hall, my father is most powerful. And I am second, man. And if I want something, I *take* it!' he added. He had withdrawn the string, and now he tied a small lead weight to the end. 'I can take anything I want – from here in the castle, from the roads outside, anywhere I want within reach of the castle. And no man will stop me. And if there is a young, fresh filly waiting to be ridden, I will take her for a ride. I don't give a shit who her father is, who her friends are, not even who her supposed guardians are in here. You understand me?'

He had the weight fitted now, and he tossed it lightly to the cat. She leapt up, forelegs straight, back arched, and fell upon the weight. He drew it away at the last minute, and she crouched, legs beneath her body, purring with ecstasy.

'Sir Hugh will crush any who tries to damage his property,' Wattere said.

'He will crush them, eh?'

Basil flicked the string again. The cat flew forward, a clawed paw striking at it, snagging it, pulling it to her mouth, and then the string was away again.

'He will crush *me*, I suppose you mean,' Basil said, and flicked the string again. As the cat sprang into the air, he twisted his wrist. The string flew up, the weight whirled, and the string wound itself about the cat's neck. Another flick of the wrist and there was a snap like a small twig underfoot. The cat was dead before it hit the ground.

Basil gave the string a jerk, and then whirled the cat's body around his head a few times before letting it fall to the ground. In a moment it was free, and he tied the string into a loop, which he dangled about his own neck.

'Because you are my father's guest, I will let you live for a while, old man. But don't forget: here, in my castle, no man threatens me. Not if he wants to live.'

Chapter Twenty-Five

Copplestone

They had ridden as far as they dared in the dark, but by the time they reached the outskirts of Crediton, even Baldwin was persuaded to halt for the rest of the night. The moon had shone brightly at the beginning of their journey, but as they rode into the town, it was only a smudge in the sky behind ever-thicker clouds, and the risk of falling into a hole in the road was too great. It was not a risk worth taking, and eventually Baldwin had to admit that they would be better off resting.

Their night had passed quietly enough. It was pointless even to hope that they might find a room in an inn or tavern at so late an hour. If they were to knock on a door in the middle of the night, they would be more likely to earn themselves a stab from a terrified host, rather than a welcome. They were forced to make the best they could of their situation. Baldwin knew an old farm not too far from the river, out on the road to Tedburn, and he took Edgar to it. It was out of their way, but they had made good distance already, and he felt it was justified for a warm and safe rest.

The tenant here was a kindly soul, but Baldwin was reluctant to wake him. No man was happy to be disturbed during the night watches, and just now, with the ever-present risk of outlaws and murderers, a man some miles from the nearest town was going to be yet more afraid. Still, Baldwin was sure that he would not mind if they made use of a roof for shelter. The stables were too close to the house, but there was an old byre he knew of, and he made for it. The cattle weren't inside – they must be kept nearer the house, he realised – but the hayloft was filled with the results of the harvest. He and Edgar spent some while settling their beasts for the night, removing their belongings and the saddles and accoutrements, then rubbing the beasts down with handfuls of straw and leaving them loose in the stable, while the two men settled themselves up in the hayloft. It was not the warmest rest Baldwin had enjoyed, but then he was a man used to travel all over Europe, and chilly nights were all too common in much of the world. With a bed of hay, his bag under his head for a pillow, and his heavy riding cloak over him, he was as snug as he could hope to be.

In the morning they had risen early and paid their respects to the farmer.

'Sir Baldwin, I'm honoured. But why did you stay out there?'

There was little need for explanation, but the old farmer shook his head. 'A bad business, this. So a man must sleep in a byre rather than wake a friend? You'd have been welcome in here by my fire, sir.'

'Your wife, perhaps, would not have been grateful for being woken,' Baldwin pointed out gently.

'We'd soon have been used to it,' she answered. She was a slim woman in her forties, bent with labour, but her smile was as fresh as a girl's. 'And you'll have to eat with us before setting off again.'

'Mistress, we would like to—' Baldwin began, but she clucked her tongue.

'You are not leaving my house without food, sir. Sit yourselves down, please. I won't be long.'

By the time they had finished their meal, drunk to the health of their host and hostess, and set off again, the morning was already well advanced. They took the road back to Crediton, but now at a slower pace. It would be better to warm the horses gradually in this weather. And when Baldwin saw how badly rutted and potholed their road was, he was glad that they had stopped for the night. After all, as he reasoned, it would not aid Edith to kill one or both horses and give them the need to acquire another.

In Crediton, Baldwin made his way to see the dean at the church. As soon as he explained their urgent mission, the dean sent men to speak to the officers in the town itself, and they were soon returned, one with a large, sandy-haired man. He looked at Baldwin as he was introduced.

'Master Thomas, you saw the woman?' the dean asked.

'Yes. Reckon so. She was riding through the town with a man at her side.'

'What did he look like?' Baldwin asked.

'A quiet, cheery, amiable man. A narrow face, but friendly. Looked like the sort who'd be fun to spend an evening with in a tavern. Bright eyes, ready smile.'

Baldwin frowned. 'Did he have a slight squint?'

Thomas screwed up his face with the effort of recollection. 'Yes, reckon he did.'

'Where were they riding?'

'Out on the Copplestone road, to the west.'

'Dean, you must excuse us. I think I know who this man is.'

'Who?'

Baldwin looked at Edgar, who nodded, unsmiling. 'I think it sounds like Wattere, the man Despenser sent to take Simon's house in Lydford.'

Exeter

The sheriff's court opened with the usual bustle and chaos, with pleaders shouting and demanding space, bawling for ink and reeds, while their servants and clients milled helplessly and haplessly, taking their places before the clerks and recorders, shouting to have themselves heard over the general hubbub.

Rougemont Castle was a disorganised place at the best of times, and seeing it in the middle of a court session was not the best of times. Sir Peregrine crossed the floor, trying to contain his anger at being jostled by so many churls who should not have dared to cross his path in the streets. But they were here to have their cases heard by the sheriff. It was no surprise that they were anxious. Some of them might be dead before the week was out.

The guards at the sheriff's door were standing attentively, but the coroner was a known man, and he was soon in the sheriff's office.

'Well?' the sheriff demanded as he marched in. He had a large goblet of wine in his hand, and he sipped from it as he looked at Sir Peregrine. According to the normal conventions, Sir Peregrine did not sit in his presence, for that would be rude. And from past experience, he knew that Sir James de Cockington would deprecate any such presumption. It was the place of the more senior man to sit and then, perhaps, to invite his guest to be seated.

There was no such invitation.

'Sir James, I am alarmed to hear that you have a young man in your gaol. A fellow called Peter?'

'You mean the lad I've held for treason?'

'Yes. I am sure you know exactly what you are doing, of course.'

'Preventing a serious case of treason? Yes, I think I know perfectly well what I am doing, sir.'

'Oh, that is good, then,' Sir Peregrine said, and bowed preparatory to making good his exit.

The sheriff slammed his goblet down on the table before him. 'You mean to say you called me in here and delayed my blasted goat-ballocked court to ask one damned question? What is the meaning of this, Coroner?'

'I was just worried you weren't aware. After all, it could be damaging to your reputation, but if you know—'

'What could be damaging to me?'

'You know who the boy is, don't you?'

'Yes, yes, yes. Of course I do. His wife is the daughter of that petty little bailiff from Lydford and his father is a merchant and freeman. But even freemen don't have all the power in the city, you know, and—'

'No, I meant his circle of friends.'

The sheriff leaned forward eagerly. 'You mean that he's got powerful friends, eh?'

Sir Peregrine looked at him and with an effort managed to conceal his contempt. The sheriff was as transparent as the glass in his window. He was hoping that Peter's friends were rich so that they could be arrested, and then ransomed. This sheriff was said to be one of the richest Exeter had ever seen already, and his wealth was based on the bribes and blackmails he charged.

'He has very powerful friends, yes. Including the nephew of the bishop here. And the nephew has his uncle's ear.'

'That is all good. But I have the ear of Despenser,' the sheriff said smugly.

'Then it probably doesn't matter.'

'What doesn't?'

Sir Peregrine essayed a look of mild surprise. 'The nephew – he is a close confidant of the Cardinal de Fargis. You know, the man who is deciding the case of Tavistock Abbey? The pope's own special representative here? I just didn't want you to be in trouble. After all, the cardinal will report to the king and the pope about the area. About how his own monk was murdered on his way here, and how the money for the king was stolen by outlaws, and now there's the tale of Peter too. I mean, it would sound to some as though all law and order had broken down. That the King's Peace was no more in Devon.'

The sheriff's face had blanched. 'But holding a treasonous fellow shows how I am working to bring order back to this godforsaken land,' he tried.

Sir Peregrine laughed aloud at that. 'Oh, yes. But of course the rumours are that you are merely taking bribes for such arrests as you have made. And the allegations are ... But I should say no more.'

'Allegations?'

Sir Peregrine departed the room a short while later, leaving behind him a reflective sheriff.

Later, when the court closed, it was said that the new sheriff appeared to demonstrate more common sense and deliberated more than at any court remembered in the city for these twenty years past. Some wondered whether at last there was a good, honourable sheriff in the castle.

Sir Peregrine was content to go to the gaol and order Peter's release. It was only hard to see what could happen to a lad in so short a space of time. The boy brought from the gaol was thin, with sunken eyes and a nervous, fretful manner.

'Who are you?' he asked.

'I am no one, my friend. Come, let us take you home.'

Jacobstowe

Agnes was glad to wake and find that old Emily was still in her room. Someone would be needed to look after the Ant, and Emily had two grandchildren of nearly Ant's age. When pressed, she declared herself happy to tend to Ant as well for the day, and so soon, once the chickens were fed and the chores completed, Agnes closed the door behind her.

There was no sign of the coroner and Simon, and when she asked, she was told that they had left early that morning, heading down to Hoppon's. Agnes decided that they must have a good idea what they were about, and she was assured that they were still trying to find out what they might about the dead men, so she followed after them.

Hoppon had not seen them, he said, but the hoofprints were clear enough on the road's surface, and she was determined to carry on after them, but he persuaded her to pause a while and take an ale with him.

'Why would they have gone on down that way?' he asked.

'They want to know who killed my Bill,' she said. 'It was the same men who killed all the travellers, I suppose.'

'Do you think they'll find them?'

She looked at him. 'Bill had worked out who it was, I think. That's why they killed him.'

'What a world,' Hoppon said, shaking his head and staring at the ground. He took a long draught of ale. 'Maid, there's no good can come of all this. You realise that? If they do learn who's done it, it can't help you. It won't bring Bill back, will it?'

Agnes looked away, over towards the woods in the distance. 'I can see him avenged, though. That would be enough. The thing I dread is knowing that the men who killed my Bill could still walk about the land as free as any other. That thought fills me with horror. One of them could have a daughter, and she could meet my Ant and marry him. Without knowing. That would bring shame to us all. And then there's the fines imposed on us for the murders. The coroner had no choice but to inflict them, but if we could at least find the culprits, there would be some kind of justice for all the hardship and suffering they have caused.'

Hoppon nodded with a grunt. 'Is there any news in the vill about these men? Did they say aught last night about what they meant to do?'

'No. Not that I heard. I think they seek to find the killers, and when they do, they will report to their master.'

'Who? The king?' Hoppon looked genuinely alarmed at the thought.

'No! I think it's Tavistock, the abbey, that told them to come here. There was a huge sum of money with those travellers. They want to find it.'

'Oh, yes. They said that there was money there,' Hoppon agreed. But then he glanced up again. 'Look, Agnes, you shouldn't be here, though. It's not your place as a woman to be hunting down men. You should be at home, looking after your child.'

She looked at him, very straight. 'And if they hadn't killed my man, Hoppon, that's what I would be doing.'

There was no further discussion after that. She was grateful for his concern, because it obviously sprang from his desire to help and protect her, but he didn't understand that she was dedicated to helping find the men who had taken her man away from her. It was essential that she did so. There was a flame of hatred burning in her that would engulf her eventually if she didn't use it to sear them.

It was very easy to follow the tracks. The path led her along the narrower grassed routes, but on all, the surface had been heavily churned. That itself was strange. Men who wanted to travel generally wanted to hurry. They would eschew these lanes in favour of the broader ways, like the Crediton road. A little way like this was too narrow, making it straightforward for a man to be waylaid. For so many to have passed this way seemed to her to show that their reasons were clandestine, and that itself made them suspicious. She had no doubts already that these tracks were those of the men who had killed the travellers and who had then silenced her husband for ever.

She continued for several miles, until she reached the top of a level area and found herself alone. Suddenly she was assailed by doubts. It was the first time since she had made her commitment to find her husband's murderers that she had been prey to such a heavy emotion, but suddenly she realised she had no idea what to do. What was she chasing after Simon and the coroner for? They had a duty to hunt down killers; they had the duty of seeking the king's stolen property. But she? She had nothing. She didn't have a reason to be here, not a reason that was justified in law. And if she did find the killers, if she learned who was responsible for Bill's death, it would help no one. Least of all her. For what could she do against a gang sufficient to attack and slaughter to the last man a force of nineteen?

Slumping to the ground, she was overwhelmed with the futility of her quest. She had been fooling herself if she thought that she could help to bring justice to her man. There was no justice for someone like Bill. He wasn't important enough. Not compared with clerics and a box of gold. The tears welled in her eyes, and she began to sob with the desperate unfairness of it all. It was so dreadful, so miserable, so unfortunate. She was all alone, and poor Bill would be forgotten soon, by all around except for her. There would be no one who would recall his smile, no one to remember his gentle humour. Ant would never be able to recall anything about his own father. And the men responsible would still be about.

That was the truth. Those who committed the most heinous crimes were secure in the knowledge that none dared attack them.

And then a spark of resentment flared, caught, and engulfed her again. She would not surrender to the strains of such pathetic feelings. Bill deserved better. She would find his murderers and bring vengeance upon them! 'I will, I will find you all. All who joined to kill my husband, all will pay!' she vowed aloud.

She rose and set off again, filled with determination once more. As she walked, she felt sure that she could sense something. It could have been a horse, but when she looked about her, there was none to be seen. The hedge on her left was thick and stock-proof, so there might have been cattle or a horse in there, she thought, but it was impossible to see. No matter, she thought, and carried on.

But now she grew aware of something else. A steady, rhythmical drumming on the ground. Not too fast, and not too slow, and then, even as she listened to it, it changed, and became a ragged, discordant percussion, and she knew it was cantering horses. There was a shout, a gleeful shriek, and the noise grew quickly louder.

She was aware of her heart thundering in her breast as though it was beating in time to the hoofbeats. Panic was rising as she thought that these might well be the very same men who had brought her here today. If they were, she would not be able to escape them. There was no escape from a band such as this. There was no running away from men on horseback, and no hope that standing still and looking chaste would save her.

There was a small tree that was not cut down, though. She might be able to clamber up it and into the field beyond.

It was better than staying here to be caught or raped and killed. She darted to it, and began to scramble up the sapling, but it was too weak to support her. Instead she flung her hands into the hedge itself, hoping to haul herself up, away from the approaching menace, but her hand caught a blackthorn bush, and the long spikes stabbed her fingers, making her sob with the pain.

There was no hope, she thought, and she was about to let go and fall back into the road when a face appeared above her.

'In God's name, woman, take my hand!' Roger hissed urgently.

Chapter Twenty-Six

Nymet Traci

'What about the maid, Father?'

'Oh, the wandering son returns, eh?' Sir Robert said. He was standing with Osbert near the stables.

Basil was clad in parti-coloured tunic and hose, the tunic tight over a linen chemise. He swaggered to the horses and patted a neck. 'You've been riding them hard, Father.'

'We were in a hurry. You know I like a good gallop of a morning.'

'Oh, aye. This wench, anyway?'

Sir Robert clapped his son on the back. 'You were gone a long time, boy.'

'I was busy.'

'Where, my son?'

Osbert watched impassively as Sir Robert took hold of his son's neck.

'Father, that is painful.'

'I am glad. I meant it to be.'

'I want you to let me go, Father.'

'Where were you?'

'With a maid in Bow.'

'The whore in the tavern?'

'No, a maid from a farm. She pleases me.'

'She doesn't please me,' Sir Robert said.

'What of that? I do not offer her to share with you.'

'I would have you leave her alone. I expected you to be here last evening with Osbert.'

'He is boring company, Father. Whereas my friend is more amusing.'

'You will return when I order in future, son,' Sir Robert said.

'That hurts!'

'It is meant to.'

'Let go, Father!'

'This is my castle, boy, and I give the orders here.'

'Very well!'

'One of my men said that you'd gone to our guest and offered to sheath yourself in her. Is that right?'

'She's only a little slut . . .'

'You cretin!'

Osbert saw the dagger suddenly drawn, and as soon as it was clear of the sheath, his hand snapped out sharply and grabbed Basil's wrist. He twisted and pressed with his thumb into the hollow of Basil's wrist, and the dagger fell to the floor. Osbert placed his foot on top to keep it safe.

'So you were plaguing the girl?' Sir Robert asked.

'I went to see that she was well, that's all.'

'I do not want you there, boy.'

'Yes. And I want to see her.'

'I wasn't clear enough, obviously. When I said I didn't want you annoying her, what I meant was, I want you to leave her alone. And I still want you to leave her alone. Yes?'

'Yes.'

'Oh, and one other thing, boy. If I ever see you draw a knife on me again, I will personally break your arm. Don't try it again. Is that all right?'

Basil said nothing, but watched with a baleful eye as his father walked away.

Osbert said nothing, but remained with his foot on Basil's knife.

'Get your foot off it. It's mine.'

'Of course. Your father won't want it to remain in the dirt, will he?' Osbert said, stepping away as he released it. He eyed Basil as the boy bent and took it up, and the two men stood for a few moments, Basil with the dagger in his hand, balanced, while Osbert remained seemingly relaxed. But neither was. Both knew that at any moment there could be a sudden flare of death.

It was Basil who broke the spell of the moment. He gave a short laugh, tossed the knife up and caught it, then thrust it into its sheath again. 'It'd be unkind to kill someone as old as you. Where's the honour in slaying an old man?'

Osbert smiled at the thought. 'I feel honoured you can think in such terms. You are too kind to me.'

Basil saw his grin, and his own smile faded in an instant. He slapped the hilt of his sword, spun on his heel and marched away.

Road near Copplestone

They had passed through Crediton and were approaching Copplestone when Edgar cleared his throat.

'Sir Baldwin, I am concerned as to why that man would take Mistress Edith.'

'A young woman like her? There is likely only the one reason, Edgar. You appreciate that well enough.'

Edgar ignored the reminder of his womanising past. 'But we are both aware of this man Wattere. We know what sort of person he is. He is Despenser's man in Devon, is he not? The sheriff himself told us that he arrested Peter because the king and Despenser were seeking traitors in the realm. But surely he has some ulterior motive for capturing the boy.'

'I do not follow your thinking,' Baldwin said.

'We know that Edith's husband has been captured. The charges against him are such that he will not easily be released. He has nothing of value, but his father has lands. That seems to mean that there could be pressure being brought to bear. But I do not understand why someone would also capture Edith, unless they are seeking to influence Simon directly.'

'Perhaps her capture was a random matter? Nothing to do with her husband's arrest?'

'Sir, do you believe that?' Edgar said with a pitying smile. 'The man Wattere happened to be riding past and found her on her own. He is the most committed enemy of her father in the land since their fight. Simon scarred him, do not forget.'

'So? What do you mean by this?'

'Sir Baldwin, the son and the father both told you that the sheriff is close to Despenser and the king's court. Wattere is Despenser's man. Surely this is all a scheme by Despenser? He has his own men in Devon. That is no surprise, for he and the king will have their men placed in all positions of authority now because their authority is itself being undermined. However, it seems like a great scheme to deprive Simon of his daughter.'

Baldwin winced at the thought. 'Despenser has already deprived Simon of his home. Why would he want to do this too?'

'Because he is thoroughly foul,' Edgar said. 'He seeks power over others, and when he is thwarted he seeks to destroy them.'

Baldwin need say nothing to that. It was the simple truth. 'So what will he do now?'

'I think we have to hope and pray that it is him,' Edgar said. 'Because if it were Wattere who took her, and Wattere was not under Despenser's control, it is likely she could have been taken just for her looks. A man who seeks to rape her and discard her later would be more dangerous. He may already have achieved his aim. And that could mean she has already been killed.'

'So you say that the best we can hope for is that she has been taken by the most powerful felon in the land?' Baldwin said. 'It is a curious hope you dispense, Edgar!'

'Aye. But at least,' Edgar said more quietly, 'it is some kind of hope. Some is better than none, Sir Baldwin.'

Near Bow

The man who had hauled her up into the tree was swarthy and powerful. He had the wild dark hair of a Cornishman, and blue eyes that seemed to look through her without any feeling. Most men on looking at her would give her the impression that they liked her buxom breasts, or would touch her arse with mild enquiry until she slapped invasive hands away, but she had the feeling that this man, if not immune to her charms, was at least without the desire to take her against her will.

He yanked her up from the roadway with such a jerk that she could hook her legs and feet under her, and swing straight over the hedge with ease. Almost immediately he sprang down to the ground at her side, a hand on her back, pushing her down to the grass, while he stayed rigid as a cat staring at a prey, all tension and controlled energy, so focused on the road he might almost have turned to stone.

There was a large thorn still in her hand. She tried to move to look at it, but the pressure on her back increased, subtly, and she heard the sound of the horses increase.

They were there! A group of scruffy, noisy men who would not look out of place in the pictures of demons she had seen on the church walls. Their horses were small, hardy creatures, stocky little fellows with stamina to cover huge distances. The riders were armed and easy in the saddle, like men who were accustomed to long rides with their beasts, and they rode along without chatter or laughter, only a set look of determination. The leader was a large man with a belly and a single eye. The other he had lost. He looked so powerful and full of bile that Agnes had to glance away as a cart rattled past in their wake.

Her sense of inadequacy returned. She was sure that these were the same men who had killed her husband, and the sight of them was enough to prove to her that she could never hope to attack them and win.

The sound of hoofs gradually faded, and as it did, she felt the man's hand lift away, and then he was moving swiftly back to the hedge. He swarmed up the tree again, and she saw his head lower as he kept his eyes on the party until they were out of sight. 'It is safe,' he breathed, and jumped down again, agile as a monkey.

'Where did you learn to do that?' she asked.

He looked at her closely, studying her face. 'You were in Jacobstowe. I saw you there two weeks ago.'

She withdrew, just slightly, from his serious blue eyes. 'What do you want with me?'

'Nothing, maid, if by that you mean what do I intend to do to you. I'm not that kind of man. But those men there. Did you see them? Did you recognise them?'

'No. I've never seen them before.'

He nodded, his attention apparently fixed on the hills in the far distance, but the faraway look in his eye seemed to imply that he was thinking of something else.

She felt curiously slighted, as though his lack of concentration on her was an insult. She was unused to such lack of interest. 'Do you know them? You look like a man who has seen a ghost.'

'Yes. I feel as though I have,' he said quietly. Then he looked at her, at the hedge, and up at the tree again. 'Do you wish me to help you back to the road, maid?'

Nymet Traci

It was hard to see how she could escape. The castle itself was scarcely impregnable, but for Edith to make her way out, she would have to pass between all the guards and servants, and then somehow find a means of climbing the walls, without falling the other side and harming herself. The only real means of escape was by the doors, but she had already seen that the gates tended to remain closed through the day. The only time they were opened was when a rider approached.

She could hear the gates opening now. A low rumbling as the baulks of timber were slid sideways into the recesses in the walls, and then the creaking and squeaking of reluctant metal as they were pushed wide. It was like a Dartmoor gate, she saw: any force pushing at the gates would be pushing them against the rock of the walls, and the great timber locks would prevent them being hauled open from outside. Simple, but most effective.

A party of riders entered, a small cart behind them, and as she watched there was ribald laughter. Four, no, five men were there, and then a big ugly brute with one eye sprang lightly into the bed of the cart and looked about him with satisfaction at the contents. He jumped down with every appearance of happiness, bellowing about him, and she heard the rumble and thump of barrels being rolled and set down from the cart, then moved off towards the buttery and storerooms.

It was a sight to set her heart fluttering. Such joy in the faces of the repellent guards about the place could only mean that the barrels were full of ale or wine. There was no protection for her in here. The men could drink themselves into lust, as all men could, she knew, and if they did, there was little if anything she could do to defend herself here in her little chamber.

As the sounds of revelry rose from the yard, she shivered, feeling a fresh sense of panic. There was no one in all this household upon whom she could place any trust. The idea that the men were steadily drinking themselves to foolishness was appalling. All the more so because she was filled with the empty despair of knowing that she was entirely alone. And she dreaded the reappearance of the man called Basil.

Even Wattere was preferable to him.

Bow

Simon stared at the man. 'Why do you blame yourself?

'He came here. A few days ago. The man Lark. He was here, and he asked the same sort of questions you have, and I was as reluctant to talk to him. But he was a pleasant fellow. Plainly came from around here, too, which made me trust him that much more. There aren't all that many men who speak your own language. He was from Jacobstowe, and I came originally from Exbourne, so we weren't too far adrift.'

'What did you tell him?'

'All about them in the castle. Sir Robert and his son Basil. They rule this country like demons. Everyone has to pay them for anything. If a man doesn't, he finds his lands on fire, his stables afire, his cattle dead, his sheep stolen. No one may stand against them.'

'There is the law!' Simon growled.

'Not for us there isn't. The law is for those who can afford to pay lawyers. What, do you think I could plead against them? They have the ears of the justices, of Despenser – of power.'

'I have heard of these men before,' Simon said,

remembering his conversation with Sir Peregrine. 'Was it not this man whose son raped a woman? Sir Robert and his son Basil?'

'That is the pair. Yes. But they do not travel lightly or alone. The two men have a large host.'

'What did you do to cost the reeve his life?'

'I defended my own. When the man had left, two riders came a little later. Basil, and his father's henchman, Osbert. They threatened me.'

'With what?'

'They said that they had heard of a man asking about them. Did I know anything, because they would burn my house with me inside if they heard I'd talked. So I did tell them. But they laughed when I said it was a reeve. They swore they had nothing to fear from a shit-arsed tatterdemalion from Jacobstowe, and rode off still laughing.'

'But you'd told them already?'

'Yes. God save me! I told them he'd been here. But they did promise that they'd do nothing about him, Bailiff. You have to believe me! I thought they'd been amused to learn about him because he was so lowly there was nothing for them to fear from him. And . . . even now . . .'

'Yes?'

'There was no need. He was so far below their station, he could do nothing to harm them.'

'That is hard to imagine, surely,' Simon said.

'Sir Robert was for a long while in the king's own household. He is a close confidant of Sir Hugh le Despenser. That is a name even I know of, Bailiff. Any man who is a friend of Despenser's is safe anywhere in the land.'

Simon nodded. He was still musing over the tale he had heard as he left the cottage and mounted his horse. He snapped the reins and kicked with his heels, and the horse trotted off.

'Well?' the coroner said, almost unable to contain his frustration. He was not used to being left outside while others spoke.

'Sir Richard, do you recall Sir Peregrine telling us about that appalling court case? The man whose daughter was raped by the son of a knight?'

'I lost my wife to a dishonourable cur who should have been slain at birth,' the coroner said heavily.

'Yes. I'm sorry, Sir Richard. Of course the matter will still be fresh in your mind. Well, I think that the men who were said to be responsible for that are the same who are responsible for the death of the fellows on their way to the king.'

It was Mark who responded to that. 'You mean to say that the man who had all those people killed was also a rapist? Why was he not captured and punished?'

'Because the fellow was a friend to Despenser. And to the sheriff, too, according to Sir Peregrine,' Sir Richard growled. He glanced over at Simon. 'That's what he said?'

'He was reluctant to talk – he had been told that they wouldn't hurt the reeve, though.'

'Hah! And he believed them?'

'Yes,' Simon said slowly. He was still thinking about the expression in John Pasmere's eyes as he spoke of Bill Lark's death. There was an infinity of self-loathing there, as though the man had himself committed the murder. 'But the truly fascinating point is that they might have killed the reeve – but why not kill that peasant too? If they were going to silence the man who'd learned about their crime, why would they not kill the informer?'

'Aye, why?' the coroner said.

'Perhaps because they did neither?' Simon wondered. But that was ridiculous, he knew. There was no point in thinking such thoughts. It was idle. Surely the men who had such notoriety were the same who were responsible for the murders at Abbeyford.

He stopped his mount and stared ahead. Without thinking, he had let his horse have its own head, and he had gradually gone further on the road away from Pasmere's house, wandering south and slightly east. Now he saw that there was a broad plain in front of them, with trees over to the east, leading along the line of a ridge up to a long, tall, castellated wall. It was solid-looking, and grey like moorstone, and Simon looked it over with an appreciation of the construction.

This, he thought, would be a place that would be very difficult to take by force.

'Whose place is that?' Mark asked.

'That, I think,' Simon told him, 'is the house of the men who killed your priests and their party.'

There was little more to be said at that. They could see a path that led up north and slightly east, and taking the chance for a good scout about the walled house, Simon led them up and along it. There was a fine view all over the house's grounds, and he could see that the place had a goodly stock of fish in a nearby pond. The surface of the water leaped and bubbled as flies approached. Outside the walls there was a huge flock of sheep, and Simon had no doubt that in the summer the woods nearby would echo to the snort and snuffle of pigs. This was no small estate, but a huge working manor, from the size of the space all about.

'What now?' Mark said.

'Now, my boy, we leave before we're considered as spies,' the coroner said firmly. 'Best thing to do is head for the town up there. Bow, isn't it; Simon? If we go there, we may just learn something to help us. It's the little towns where you can get the best help, I always say.'

Simon agreed, and they all clapped spurs to their mounts and continued on their way, up past the woods, along the top of a ridge, and then down into the town itself.

They were sitting outside the tavern in the main street, enjoying a few moments away from their saddles, drinking strong ale, when they heard horses approaching.

'Dear heaven! Baldwin!' Simon shouted when he recognised his old friend. With a thrill of pure delight, he put down his drinking horn and hurried into the street, stopping at Baldwin's horse. 'Baldwin, it's so good to see you again. I could not hope for better fortune!'

His joy was not reciprocated, he saw, and gradually he grew aware that his friend wore a grim, sad face.

'Simon, I doubt you will still think that in a moment. I am so sorry. I have dreadful news,' Baldwin said.

Tavistock Abbey

Robert Busse was happy to hear that the Cardinal de Fargis had arrived at the abbey for further discussions and to hear more evidence. It could hardly be a better time, he thought.

The whole of the previous evening and night, he had been almost unable to sleep. It had not been helped that whenever he looked in the direction of John de Courtenay, he saw a man who seemed to have a little smile fixed to his lips. The man was insufferably proud, of course, and he had always had a hatred for Robert, but that was no excuse for his seeking Robert's murder. It was astonishing that a man who professed love for all others, and who wanted such an important leadership position in the abbey, could at the same time have been so avaricious that he would pay to have a rival removed.

'You wished to see me?' the cardinal said as Robert entered the abbot's hall and bent to kiss the episcopal ring.

He remained on the floor kneeling, his head bowed. 'Cardinal, I fear that I have some rather terrible news.'

'There appears to be little shortage of bad news about here,' the cardinal commented drily and took his hand away.

'The king had a messenger here. He came to bring messages.'

'That is somewhat less than news,' the cardinal said sharply.

'Some were for John de Courtenay. And he took messages back from Brother John, too.'

'Well?'

'He fell from his horse and died a little way from here. In his shirt were two of the messages. Here they are.'

The cardinal took them, warily eyeing Brother Robert. 'What do they say?'

'One is from Brother John, and he thanks Sir Hugh le Despenser for his offer to aid his campaign to become the next abbot. He states that he will be willing to pay Sir Hugh from the income of the abbey.'

'The second?'

'That is another message from Brother John to Despenser, saying that he has a friend in Tavistock, Master John Fromund, who is prepared to put into action my assassination as soon as Despenser approves his action. Apparently Master Fromund has many companions who would be happy to assist Brother John and Sir Hugh le Despenser.'

'I see,' the cardinal said. He stood and walked over to the table. 'And tell me, you know a man called Langatre?'

'Oh, well, yes, but he—'

'And I understand that in February this year you removed one thousand and two hundred pounds from the abbey's treasury?'

Busse was quiet.

'And later that month you returned with a small force of

men-at-arms and took another eight hundred pounds in money, gold and silver plate? Is that correct?'

Robert closed his eyes. 'It is. But I had to remove it to a place of safe-keeping, to protect it from Brother John.'

'And he sought to remove you for the good of the abbey because he says that you are a danger to the community. Too divisive, he says, and too keen to promote those who are your friends, rather than those of quality or merit.'

'That is entirely unjustified. I seek only to serve the abbey.'

'I wonder,' the cardinal said, 'whether any man here actually seeks the best for the abbey.'

'You may be assured that—'

'No. I may not be assured of anything.' The cardinal opened the first of the small scrolls and gazed at the contents. 'It is his writing, I believe. Very well, Brother Robert. You may leave this with me.'

'Am I safe?'

The cardinal looked at him. 'I shall speak with Brother John, if that is what you mean. However, this is a matter that will require the pope's intervention, I believe. You had best remain here at Tavistock.'

'Thank you, Cardinal.'

Brother Robert was almost at the door when the cardinal's quiet voice halted him. 'One more thing, my friend. There will be no more money removed from the treasury. Nor plate nor gold. I hope that is understood. Because if any money goes missing, I shall not pursue your case with the pope or anyone else.'

'I understand, Cardinal.'

'Good,' Cardinal de Fargis said. As the door quietly closed, he closed his eyes and offered a quick prayer for patience. 'In Christ's name, Father, if these men cannot live without each of them seeking the death of the other, what hope is there for peace within this community?'

But that was not the point. That a baron should seek to work for one man and could consider the murder of the other to aid his case was atrocious. There had not been a similar plot since the death of Becket. The pope must be told, and that quickly.

He sat and wrote his note carefully, the reed scratching on the parchment, but then, as he signed it with care, a thought struck him. It would take an age for the message to reach Rome.

Without hesitation, he began to write a new message, this time addressed to Sir Hugh le Despenser.

Chapter Twenty-Seven

Bow

Simon sat back as Baldwin spoke. He felt as though his veins had been opened. It was as though the blood from his body was draining into a pool at his feet as Baldwin described the sudden arrest of Peter, the boy's incarceration, and Edith's disappearance.

'But surely she could have gone to—'

'She would only have gone to your home or back to Exeter,' Baldwin said. 'Unless you can think of somewhere else? But that does not explain how it was that a man saw her, and another in Crediton thought he saw her in the company of a man who looked like William atte Wattere.'

'Sweet Jesus! This is all the work of that prick-eared cur. Christ's ballocks, if I learn that Despenser's had anything to do with this, I'll have his cods on my knife in a week. Dear Christ, if she's hurt . . .'

Baldwin put his hand out, only to have Simon knock it away as he bellowed, enraged. 'That mother-swyving churl, the illegitimate son of a diseased sow, the god forsaken dunghill swine, the—'

This time Baldwin set his hand on his friend's shoulder and gripped it hard. 'Ranting will not help anyone. And at present we do not know that the man has anything to do with her capture. No! Rather than swearing and making oaths that must only raise the humours in your heart, use your head, man.

What we need is a means of finding her, first, and then we must betake ourselves to think of a way of rescuing her.'

'Baldwin, if there is even a hair of her head that is hurt by this prick, I'll have his heart! I knew she shouldn't have married that milksop youth, in Christ's name. He was always too feeble.'

'Simon, he is a boy. He was taken on the sheriff's orders. What would you expect him to do against that kind of force? And once in gaol, he had no choice, no means to help his wife. Do not blame a victim for the actions of his persecutor.'

'Perhaps you are right,' Simon said, and then he bent his head and let his face fall into his open hands. 'Poor Edith! Oh God, if someone's raped her . . .'

'If that was to happen, I would personally help you to take vengeance,' Baldwin said.

Simon nodded, but suddenly he couldn't trust his voice. The thought that his little girl could be held by some churl who might even now be defiling her was so hideously terrifying that he could not fully comprehend it. Instead his mind seemed to slow, and his breathing grew shallow, while his heart raced. It felt as though his body was packed with ice, and he shivered, even as his breath started to sob in his throat. It was not right! Surely his little Edith hadn't been hurt. Wouldn't he have felt it, wouldn't he have known, if she had been molested? But he hadn't known that she had been captured. Surely he should have done, if he were a good father? Shouldn't a father's relationship with his daughter mean that he would know as soon as she was alarmed, scared or in danger? It was the least a man should feel. And yet he was a failure in that as in so many things. Here he was, a useless bailiff without a bailiwick, searching for the killers of people he didn't know, while his own daughter was the subject of capture and possibly molestation. He should have been there, at home, for her.

'Don't blame yourself, Bailiff,' Coroner Richard said. He was at Simon's side, his head lowered, glowering about them with a truculence that seemed entirely out of place for him. 'It ain't your fault some bastard's done this.'

'It is my fault,' Simon said, sniffing hard. 'If I'd—'

'Nothing, my friend. If you had been there, all that might have happened was that you'd got yourself killed. That wouldn't help anyone. And if someone else decides to break your peace by attacking your little girl, it ain't your fault, it's theirs. Don't blame yourself.'

'How did you know how I feel?' Simon asked, looking at the coroner from the corner of his eye.

'My wife was killed, remember? I told you. A miserable, lying cur of a felon whom I'd had working for me as steward and bottler took a liking to her, and when I was away, raped and killed her, before killing my dog too. Poor brute tried to protect her, but the bastard cut his throat. And I know exactly what you're thinkin'. It's what I was thinkin' too. I blamed meself, and I didn't think about anyone else. It was just my guilt I swam in. And it was stupid. Because I didn't kill the hound, I didn't kill my wife. It was him. All him. Hope he's rotting in hell now, learning how hot it can be. But that's not the point. Point is, life's here to get on with. And to be fair, I waited until I'd killed him before I set about wallowin'. You, Bailiff, have a job to do. You have to find her, save her, and then kill the bastards who've done this.'

'How do we do that?' Simon asked. He stood up and stared about him. 'Where would they have brought her?'

Baldwin chewed his inner lip. 'They passed through Crediton. We do know that. We hope that they passed this way after Copplestone, but I have no means of confirming that.'

It was Edgar who sniffed and looked up at the sky. Clouds were forming south-west over the moors.

'What is it, man?' the coroner demanded.

'We know that the sheriff is allied to Despenser. We know that Wattere is Despenser's man. And we know that he was heading this way with her. Unless he acted on his own, I would think Wattere took his orders the same as always. That means Despenser took Edith, and would want her to be held somewhere safe, I'd imagine. Perhaps he seeks to blackmail the bailiff into some action that would not usually occur to him? While holding the bailiff's daughter, he would have a powerful incentive for the bailiff's compliance.'

'You think so?'

'If he was – excuse my bluntness, Bailiff – if he was intending merely to rape and slay the maid, he would do so without the risk of parading her through the county. We'd have found her yesterday in a ditch near Exeter. Instead he brought her all the way to Crediton and beyond. Surely that means he has some other objective for her than merely seeing her slain.'

Simon gaped suddenly and stared at the coroner. 'Dear God, and we were told by Pasmere that Sir Robert of Nymet Traci was an ally of Despenser! She could be here.'

Nymet Traci

In her room, Edith huddled by her bed, shivering, her arms wrapped about her. It was less the cold that troubled her, more the continuing fear of what would happen. She *should* have made her escape on the way here. At the time, though, terror had controlled her, and the idea of trying to gallop away had been just too daunting. However, the result was that she was stuck here with all these men and now she was petrified that she might not escape. She had heard of plenty of women who had been kidnapped, and none had escaped rape – and some women had been forced to endure much worse.

It was so terrifying that she felt she had no energy. If she had been told that she could be so enervated by such a situation, she would have laughed. The idea that being taken by a man like Wattere could lead to a maid being so petrified with terror that she might be incapable even of rational thought would have struck her as the merest nonsense. She was an intelligent woman. She knew how to defend herself. If there was a knife at hand, she would have used it to protect herself and her maidenhead from ravishment. But it was one thing to laugh during a conversation in front of her fire, perhaps with her father or her husband near to hand, and friends who were enjoying themselves with her. Here, in a chilly room, with her soul frozen in her heart, where every sound made her think that the foul man who had leered at her this morning was approaching again, it was different. And there was no weapon in the room. Not even a knife for eating.

The thought made her rise. There must be *something* here she could use. If the man returned and tried to force himself on her, she could lie back as though compliant, perhaps, and then strike him. A shard of metal or glass . . . A long pin. Her brooch would do service, she thought, pulling it from her shoulder. It had a long bronze pin that was weak generally, but she could use it for stabbing at a man's eye. The floor was of wood, but the walls were stone. She could sharpen the pin on that.

But as she was about to rush to the wall, she heard steps. The hurried steps of a man who was eager to take advantage of a woman who was entirely at his mercy. She looked at the wall, but there was no time. Instead she gripped the brooch in her fist, so that the long pin protruded. If he came too close, she would stab him with all her might, she told herself. She had never fought with anybody, and the thought was almost more alarming than resigning herself to being raped. The idea of stabbing a man's eye as he approached her with puckered lips was enough to make her stomach spasm. She saw in her mind's eye the spurt of the humours as the pin punctured it, she felt the splatter of it on her face, and she had to avert her face from the vision, but not with any diminution of resolve. If he intended to rape her, she would sell her body as dearly as she might.

There was a rattle of bolts on the door, and she felt the bile rise into her throat. The acid made her want to choke. But then there was a knock, a gentle, apologetic little tap of a knuckle.

'Who is it?' she asked.

'William atte Wattere,' he answered. 'Mistress, do you object if I enter?'

She felt the solid, reassuring weight of the brooch in her hand. In God's hands. She was in His hands. Although she was reluctant to let Wattere in, she knew she couldn't stop him if he insisted. At least he didn't sound drunk.

'What authority have I in me to prevent you?' she said bitterly. 'And what strength?' she added sadly.

The door opened quietly and in the doorway stood Wattere. His anxiety was obvious from the first moment she saw him. 'Well?' she demanded.

He did not enter for a moment or two. Then he whipped off his hood and licked his lips before stepping over the threshold. 'Mistress, I am come to apologise.'

His words made her heart leap in her breast. 'There's been a mistake?' but as soon as she spoke, she knew that it was unimportant. Whether there had been a mistake in capturing her or not at the outset, the men here at this castle were not likely to release her – not until they had received a payment at least. In Basil's case there would be a different type of reckoning, too.

He curled his lip. 'Truth is, you were to be held here safely. There wasn't to be any nonsense. You were only a toy to be bargained with, I swear. You weren't to be harmed.'

'You took me against my will, held me here, and I wasn't to be harmed?' she spat.

'No. You were only to be kept here until . . . well, until my lord Despenser achieved what he needed. And then you could be released.'

'And what, pray, was his object with me?' she demanded sourly.

'You were to help force the abbey of Tavistock to his will. With you here, he felt sure that Robert Busse would surrender his claim to the abbacy, and then John de Courtenay would win it for himself.'

'What have they to do with me?'

'Little. But Busse is a friend of your father's. Sir Hugh considered that if you were held, your father would move heaven and earth to seek your release, and he'd persuade Busse to give up his claim. If not, he thought your father could even slay the abbot to give the seat to John de Courtenay.'

'He was in his cups when he thought of this. Why would Busse listen to my father on a matter such as this? And my father wouldn't kill a man for that. For me.'

But she knew it was a lie. Simon would commit any crime to protect her. He would kill a man, he would rob, steal, or even commit suicide for her. He was as entirely devoted to her as a father could be.

Then another thought struck her. 'Why are you apologising to me now?'

'Because it's going wrong, maid. I am sorry. I am really sorry. But you have to protect yourself against Basil. He's no better than a common cowman. I think he means you . . . means you harm.'

She was still suddenly as she felt ice enter her heart. 'You mean he will rape me?'

'I think he intends to. And there's nothing I can do to save you.'

'You say so? You brought me here, churl! If you wanted, you could at least stay at my door and stop anyone from entering.'

'Fight a man like him? If I was whole, I could do that. But I have wounds still from your father,' he said with a slight sneer. He felt sorry for this woman, but her father would only ever know his enmity. He detested Simon Puttock and would do nothing to help him. And yet this woman was not her father. It was leaving him feeling torn. 'I am sorry.'

'Then you could take me away from here, man! Don't leave me here to be raped and slain by a fool in a drunken fit! What can I do to protect myself?'

Wattere winced and looked away as she stood. 'Mistress . . .' Suddenly a vision appeared before him: a picture of a dead cat, gold and white, with scarlet blood dribbling from its mouth, the head hanging at an impossible angle like a man swinging from a gibbet. It was enough to make his resolve waver as he looked back at this lovely fair-haired . . . *child*. 'What can I do?'

'Work out a way to take me from here,' she pleaded. 'I am only weak, I've no weapons, nothing! You brought me to this – surely you can think of a way to help me escape?'

He stared down at her, and thought of the cat. The idea of this maid lying on the bed, blood at her thighs, was enough to make him feel a surge of guilt. The other idea, that the next time he saw her she might be lying on the bed with her neck broken, a trickle of blood lying at her mouth's corner, was enough to reinforce the guilt and urge him to action.

'I will see what may be done,' he said. He hesitated, and then reached behind his back. Withdrawing a small dagger, he gave it to her, and then stood with his breath stilled, half expecting her to stab him.

But no. Instead she gave him a thin smile and took the knife, which she secreted inside her tunic. 'For that I thank you, Master William. But please, please try to think of a means of escape for me? Please?'

He felt a strange twisting in his breast – an impossible urge to grab the knife back and return to normalcy; but then a pull at his soul made him stop himself. He could not force this woman, this girl, to submit to Basil. That man was no better than a felon waylaying a maid in the street. The difference was, he had her at his power because Wattere had brought her here. It would be better for her to kill herself than submit.

No, Simon Puttock was no friend to him, but his daughter was no more Wattere's enemy than was the Archbishop of Canterbury. She did not deserve this fate.

'I will do what I can,' he said with a firm nod of his head. Then he turned and fled before her tears of gratitude could melt his heart any more.

Road near Nymet Traci

Agnes was not sure about this hard-handed stranger. He looked too worn and battered. Of course, many travellers looked worse, but that was little consolation. This one looked like a man who would have little compunction in taking a woman for his own, and she would not allow that. No man would have her, she resolved.

He had swung her out into the road, and now he followed her, as nimble as before.

'So you are a sailor, then,' she said as he dropped lightly at her feet.

'You know many sailors up here?' he asked with some surprise.

'We see them. Often they come past here as they walk from coast to coast.'

'I can believe it,' he said wryly. 'But there are no jobs at either coast.'

'Not even for you?'

'Plainly you see more in me than the shipmasters of Devon,' he said mildly. But already he was staring along the road in the direction the men had taken, back east. 'Did you know any of those men?'

'No. I'm not from near here. I live in—'

'Jacobstowe. Yes – I know.'

'You sound as though you know them, though.'

'I saw them a few days ago. That one-eyed bastard in front? He was up the road from here, and I saw him kill a man.'

'Who?'

'Just some farmer,' Roger said.

Agnes felt her face blanch. Her legs began to fail her, and she felt herself waver. 'Who?'

'Don't know. Just some fellow on his way to market, I think.'

He realised her weakness, and quickly took her elbow, holding on to her until the spasm had passed.

'Are you well, mistress? Do you want to sit?'

'No, I am fine. But I want to see that one-eyed devil hanging.'

He nodded, as though this was the most natural desire of any woman. 'Let's see if we can tell where they were going. I think they must live not far away from here, for it was close by where I saw them kill the farmer.'

Chapter Twenty-Eight

Nymet Traci

The yard was clear enough for now. All the castle's men had repaired to the buttery with the ale they'd confiscated from the alewife transporting it to Bow, and already half the men were singing a series of bawdy songs. Their rough singing could be heard all about the courtyard, and the fact that they seemed already to be drunk was reassuring, but he couldn't just jump on top of them all. That was impossible.

He stood indecisively for a while, outside the hall, listening to the raucous babble from inside. Up on the walls, he could see more men walking about. They weren't drunk. And from a quick glance, it was clear that there were at least four of them up there, two at the front, and two chatting in the farther corner. Security today was not a major concern.

There had been times before when Wattere had felt incompetent. Most recently was earlier in the year when he had been told to evict a man, and shortly thereafter had found that the tables had been turned on him. And here he was, seriously contemplating making a lunatic bid to save that same man's daughter. His wounds stung him with renewed vigour at the mere thought – and yet he was not persuaded to turn from the decision he had taken up there in Edith's room.

'You all right, old man?'

A youth of not yet twenty, he was. He had a face erupting with spots that gave him a humorous appearance, but any suggestion that he was prone to such an easy temperament was discounted by the unfeeling expression in his cold grey eyes. He was a little taller than Wattere, but although Wattere felt fairly sure that he could best the lad in a fight, he was not here to pick quarrels. Instead, he made a muttered response, ducked his head and walked over to the stables, where he went to his mount and checked the beast over. There was cause for bitterness there. The horse had not been brushed and cleaned from their last journey, and there was still dried mud clinging to his forelegs.

There was no excuse for not looking after a horse. It made him angry to see his own animal being ignored. But here he was in a strange castle. It would not be sensible to cause a fuss. Especially when he was trying to conceive a plan to help Edith escape. So he merely gritted his teeth, walked to the corner where the brushes were all stored, and grabbed a couple. While making long, regular sweeps over the horse's back and flanks, he watched the activities in the yard.

He had no idea how to save the child. Perhaps she could simply hide from the guards, and later, when they had gone to find her, she could make her way . . . But there was nowhere to hide in that little chamber. Nowhere at all. It was impossible. There was nothing he could do here all alone to try to rescue her. It was just ridiculous to think that he could.

Rubbing down the mount, he allowed his thoughts to turn to the more sombre reflection that it was entirely due to his obedience to his master that she was here. Sir Hugh le Despenser had always been a good master to him, though. Reliable, in all ways. If a man betrayed him, he knew what he could expect, just as a man who provided good service for him knew that he would be rewarded. He had himself enjoyed Despenser's favours over the years. And now he was here in a castle in the wildlands of western Devonshire with a beautiful young woman, having delivered her, so it would seem, to be toyed with by the son of a friend of Despenser. She would soon be raped or dead, if he was any judge.

He had performed similar tasks in the past, capturing women and men so that they could be held hostage, but never before had he known this kind of despair. In the past, they had been treated moderately well, and released when they had served their purpose. He wouldn't have procured them had he known that they would be treated in the way that Edith would soon be.

A wave of nausea washed through his body like a cramp. He almost fell to the ground, and had to grab hold of the stall's bars and breathe in deeply, cheeks hollowed and loose, his belly complaining, as he felt the threat of all the men about the place. This was lunacy! He couldn't think to help her. If he did, and he was discovered, as he must be, he would be ruined. Despenser would never forgive him, even if he managed to escape, and he couldn't. If he was to try to fight all the men here, he would die. But he couldn't escape without silencing at least a number of them. It was impossible.

He had just come to this conclusion when he looked up to see Basil striding towards the hall's door. As he reached it, he glanced up to the right, towards the part of the hall where Wattere knew Edith was being held.

It was enough to steel his resolve. 'You bastard,' he muttered. 'You sodding bastard!'

He gripped his sword hilt and would have marched across the yard right there and then, perhaps to die, trying to protect her from her assailant, but then he saw two men up on the battlements and thought again.

If he ran in on Basil raping Edith, the only result would be his death. That wouldn't help Edith at all. Better to persuade Basil to leave the hall.

Suddenly Wattere's eyes narrowed as he cast about, looking around the stables. At one end was a heap of straw. It was enough to make him march purposefully along the stalls.

He would give Basil a diversion he would *never* forget.

When the door was thrown wide, Edith had not expected it.

She was sitting on the stool by the window, gazing out at the hills to the west, filled with longing for the broad open moors and freedom. Anything would be so much better than sitting here in the chamber with nothing to do but brood on her misery, filled with dread for her future. With a start of guilt, she had just realised that she had hardly thought about Peter at all for the last day, and now she was half sobbing at the thought of him languishing in the foul gaol at Exeter. She had been there before, and she knew how disgusting such a cell would be to her fastidious husband. She only hoped that Wattere could help her somehow.

Jerked to the present by the sudden eruption of noise, she almost fell from her stool. Then, seeing Basil enter, she sprang to her feet, stepping behind the stool, reaching for the dagger. But before she could grip it, Basil had slammed the door shut, and now he advanced to her, a smile fitted to his face as he set his head to one side, surveying her as a knight might study a newly won town. 'Oh, but you're a pretty one. Will you give me a kiss?'

'I will do nothing.'

'Oho, you will, lady. You'll bed me tonight, I think. Hold! You think that your husband will come to rescue you?'

Her expression was so bleak at that sally that he laughed again. 'You know about him, then, do you? Ah, it is a shame that he's so busy just now. Answering questions, no doubt. They say the new sheriff has some inventive ways of getting the answers he needs, you know. Probably aided by men of Sir

Hugh le Despenser, I'd imagine. He was always creative, so they say. Still, you'll probably be able to recognise your old man when you see him again. So long as they don't treat him like a traitor, anyway. You wouldn't want to see him hanged, eh?'

She could hardly keep the vomit at bay. There had not been any capital trials for traitors since she had moved to Exeter, but she knew what they entailed as well as any. She had been told that the sound of the headsman's axe striking the body into quarters was the same as that of the butcher's cleaver as it divided a hog's carcass.

'Of course, if you were to be nice to me, I could get you released. I might even help you to get to the sheriff and persuade him to release your husband.'

'You would—' She realised her error and closed her mouth sharply.

'If you were to be nice to me, yes. I might just do that. Would you like a pact? You swear to comfort me, and I'll swear to see you released and ride with you to Exeter. How would that be?'

Edith stared at him. 'I cannot. I am married. How can you ask me to betray him with you?'

'Oh, it's easy, lady. You see, if you do, then you will go to see him – but if you don't, I may have to take you anyway. Because there's not much you can do to stop me, is there? If I want to, I can take you. I just prefer to have you willing. And I think a little strumpet like you will enjoy it anyway. So that's an end to it. Will you submit?'

'I won't.'

'You'll have to give yourself unwillingly, then,' he declared lazily. He began to step into the room towards her, but as he did, there was a clamour from the yard area, with loud shouting from the gates. He stopped, hesitated a moment, and then muttered a curse and hurried out, bolting the door after him.

Edith slowly and shakily made her way to the stool. Feeling around for it, she felt as sickly and ancient as an old crone. Soon she had her rump on it, but she could only sit and stare at the door as though he might spring in through it again at any moment.

The torture of not knowing what to do for the best made her mind feel as though it must shred into tiny fragments of hope and despair.

It took them little time to mount their horses and make their way to the castle. Simon rode in front, with Baldwin and Sir Richard a short way behind him. Edgar had for once forgone his accustomed post a little behind Baldwin and rode to one side to protect his flank, and Mark trailed behind them, demanding to know what made them think that the girl was in the castle anyway.

'Tell that man to be silent,' Sir Richard muttered to Edgar as they rode, but before long Mark had realised that his comments were not going to win him any friends and was content to mutter to himself.

The road was well used, Simon saw, and as he came around the bend and could see the castle again from this direction, he was struck by the careful positioning of the place.

With trees cut down in all directions, it would be very hard to assault. That was certain. It was not a true fortress, in that there were no towers at each corner of the wall, but the place was strong nonetheless, and the battlements would mean that any attacking force would have its work cut out. Simon had not been in a siege, but he had heard Baldwin talk about such affairs, and the idea that he could bring a force here to hold the castle and make it surrender filled him with horror. For Edith would be inside, and at the least she would suffer with the garrison. It was even possible – if not likely – that they would make a show of her. Perhaps raping her to shame her and Simon, threatening to kill her, or torture her ... The possibilities were appalling.

He found his speed slowing as the thoughts whirled through his mind. 'Sweet Jesus, Baldwin, what can we do to get her out if she is in there? It is a fortress. And they must have plenty of men inside, too. What could we few do?'

'Let us first find out whether she is truly inside,' Baldwin said reassuringly. 'Then we can decide what to do.'

'Yes.'

They rode up to the gates, and waited for a challenge. 'I am Keeper of the King's Peace. Open the gates in the name of the king!' Baldwin bellowed when a face appeared over the parapet.

There was some while before another man arrived to peer down at them. This was a swarthy-looking man with the face of a surly felon, Simon reckoned. 'Who are you?'

'I am Sir Baldwin de Furnshill, churl, and I am Keeper of the King's Peace. I demand that you open the gates immediately.'

'Well, I am son to the knight who owns this manor. You have no right to demand anything of us, sir. We have business to which we attend. If you wish, you may return tomorrow and we shall consider your request.'

'We believe you are holding a woman hostage here. We would speak with the castle's owner.'

At this there was a loud step on a wooden walkway, and soon another man was staring down at them. 'I am Sir Robert de Traci. You say you are Sir Baldwin de Furnshill?'

'Aye. And this is the King's Coroner, Sir Richard de Welles. We are here—'

'I heard,' Sir Robert said drily. 'You think to come here to my home and accuse me of such behaviour? I am surprised.'

'If the woman is not here, could you not let us inside so that we can verify the fact? We can then continue in our search for her. She was brought this way. She was seen along this very road, in the company of a wandering felon by the name of William atte Wattere,' Baldwin lied. 'Do you know of him?'

'Wattere? You say he is a convicted felon? How would I know him?'

'Where else would this road lead?' Baldwin asked, pointedly staring at the track that continued after the road had petered out just behind the castle.

'It leads nowhere. But since the woman is not here, surely your witness was mistaken,' Sir Robert said. 'In any case, I do not have time to investigate the matter further.'

'Wait! Sir Robert!' Baldwin cried, but the other knight had already left the walkway beneath the battlements.

Only his son remained, and now he laughed at the men before his gates. 'What, would you storm our walls, masters? Eh? We have a force in here that is plentiful enough to defend them, I assure you. But feel free to try, if you must!'

'Your name, fellow?' Baldwin said. It was hard to keep his horse under control. The beast was spirited, and he could tell that his rider was trying to control a rising anger.

'I am Basil of Traci, *fellow*,' Basil sneered.

'Then know this: we shall leave here now, but if I learn you have lied to me, I will return with the king's posse. And when I do, I shall raze this castle to the ground, with you inside it if necessary. If one hair of that maid's head is harmed, I will visit every indignity and pain upon you personally. I will see you crawling to plead for mercy, boy! If she is here, beware!'

'Old man, you need your meal. I've heard that aged fools

can be driven mad if their food is late. You are raving,' Basil said. 'Go home and eat, and ease your poor old head.'

Baldwin's jaw set, and he whirled his mount about before he could listen to any more taunts. In a fury, he set the horse's head to Bow, and rode off along the road.

Simon could see his inner rage, but he could hardly restrain his own fury. Baldwin had failed him, and had failed Edith. All Simon knew now was inner turmoil and a clammy fear that his little Edith, his daughter, was in dreadful danger.

And he could do nothing about it.

Chapter Twenty-Nine

Nymet Traci

The stables were well afire already when Wattere pushed through the press of men and entered the hall.

He felt a fool. Over to the straw he had gone, collecting a little pile in his hand, and then taking some charcloth and striking his flint until it had begun to glow gently, a mottled series of little red blooms on the black surface. Then he began to blow on it, encompassing the cloth with some straws, and adding a little fine tinder on the glowing dots, until the tinder caught, and then the straws as well.

He was just finished and had risen when he heard the voices at the gate. Walking out slowly, his hands in his belt, the picture of ease and innocence, he had realised that Basil and his father were both up on the wall above the gates. It was galling to think that all his efforts had been pointless, but then he heard the sudden moaning of the fire as more straw caught light, and he began to sidle away.

It was shortly after he had reached the door that he saw other men begin to look about them. Before, most of them were up on the walls, staring out at the strangers. Others were down in the yard, and as the blaze began, they were all occupied. It was one man up on the wall who first noticed. Wattere saw him sniff the air, puzzled. The odour was not the same as clean woodsmoke. No, the sharp, greasy tang on the wind was that of hay and straw, rich and grassy, and for a moment he was confused. Turning, he stared hard at the house and the little kitchen beside it, but the smoke was not emanating from either chimney. Next his eyes were drawn to the thatch on either building, but a short while later the wind gave a low soughing, and then it was that the first sparks began to soar and he caught sight of the flames erupting from the stable blocks.

That first guard gave the warning shout, and soon others had joined in, men rushing to the fire from all directions, grabbing buckets, barrels and even helmets, anything with which to carry water and try to help put out the fire. In a short space of time, only a few men were left up on the walls. Even Sir Robert himself was in the thick of it with the men on the ground, bellowing himself hoarse as his servants and fighters all exerted themselves before the fire could reach the main hall. The noise of crackling mingled with the creak of tormented wood and the shrill, horrified shrieks of the horses remaining inside. Two men took axes, wrapped wet cloth about their heads, and darted inside, hacking at all the tethers holding the beasts, and in a short while the maddened creatures had bolted from the stalls and escaped, all bar one piebald rounsey, who was so deranged that she galloped at full speed into the farther wall, instead of towards the door. They found her later, burned badly, her neck broken.

Wattere eyed the men rushing witlessly in the yard and nodded grimly to himself. He would have liked to have pushed Basil into the fire if he could, but the arrogant prickle was there at the back of the press. Instead Wattere pushed on through the door and ran over the floor to the solar where Edith was being held.

Her chamber was up a short flight of wooden stairs, and he was soon at the door. There was a latch, and a bolt to lock it. Basil and his father had not thought anything stronger would be necessary to hold a dull-witted wench, and in any case, with the gates shut and barred, what was the need? She was as caged whether she was in the room or wandering the yard. She could attempt to leap the walls, but that would likely break her legs, and not many would be prepared to run that risk.

He pulled the bolt open and shoved the door wide. 'Maid, come quickly. I think I can save you.'

She had risen, and he saw her hopeful expression, but as he beckoned urgently, her face changed, and he saw the blank terror return. He tried to duck and move out of the way, but Osbert's blade sank into his shoulder before he could, and Wattere clenched his teeth against the horror of that slick, sharp steel wedged deep in his shoulder and collar bone.

It was the shouting that attracted Edgar's attention at first. As they rode away, his sharp ears caught the sound of barked commands, of shrieks, and then the whinnying of animals in dread. The flames were clearly visible when he glanced over his shoulder, and he halted his mount to stare for a moment before calling to the others. 'Sirs! Master Puttock! Something most odd is happening.'

'What in Christ's name!' Sir Richard muttered. Then a gust of wind blew, and the angry orange flames were fanned. There was a loud crunching and rending sound, and the flames rose still higher. 'Sweet Mary's tits! The place is on fire!'

He was already the last. The others were all riding pell-mell for the castle, Simon and Baldwin racing almost neck and neck, while Edgar galloped behind. Even Mark was reluctantly clinging to his own seat, his mount having decided that this was a good day for a race.

'Oh,' Sir Richard said to himself, and then yelled, 'Ya hoi!' and clapped spurs to his weary beast's flanks.

The gates were still shut and barred as they rode, but then

Simon saw a chink between them. He scarcely dared hope that they were actually opening, and for a moment tried to convince himself that all he had seen was the gleam of light through a natural gap in the wood, but then the little flash of light broadened, and he saw the gates open wide. A trio of horses appeared, led by a stable boy, then four more, two rearing wildly, while an older lad tried to calm them. After them came more, all driven mad by the nearness of the fire, all desperate to get as far from there as possible.

Baldwin looked about him, over either shoulder, and then smiled with a gleam of his teeth as he whipped his mount on at the gallop, in through the smoke and sparks, under the gates and into the yard.

Sir Robert coughed, a hand held up to protect his eyes as smoke gushed through the doors of the stables and blew at him, a foul, reeking gust of the devil's own wind. It felt as though his face's flesh was being seared away, and he could hear his own hair brittlely smouldering. He must close his eyes against the bright glare. All about him the men were carrying buckets filled with water, hurling their contents at the fires and retreating.

At least it would be safer with the horses out of here. Already three men had been injured trying to release the terrified beasts. Old Hamo wouldn't get up again. A flailing hoof from a terrified palfrey had sheared away the whole of the side of his head, exposing the brain. Two others nursed dangerous injuries, one a badly broken arm, the other a crushed hand. All in all, this was a hideously expensive disaster. 'What the shite is happening here?' he muttered, staring about him. There was a clattering of hooves, and he saw that the last of the horses was being taken out at the run by a little tow-haired youth. The lad was one of the guards' sons, he remembered. That was good – at least all the mounts would be safe then. The boys were taking them away from the castle to calm them down.

He had turned back to the fire, but as he did so he heard a rough bellow from the house. Shooting a look at the hall, he saw Osbert in the doorway, grinning with pleasure. In his fist he held Wattere by his jacket, which was thickly clotted with blood.

'Thought you'd like this piece of turd, Sir Robert. He was up there trying to get his fists on the wench.'

Wattere could not answer. He was close to collapse, and the agony that was his shoulder was enough to make him want to vomit. He could only stagger as Osbert hauled him out, and then he was suddenly thrust forward, and his legs could not carry him. His right folded under him, and he fell stiffly, his torso twisting to keep his ruined shoulder from the ground, but the jolt of falling was enough to make him scream shrilly with anguish. It was like a dozen swords slashing at him simultaneously. The sort of hideous torment that a soul in hell would expect. He could feel the hot, bubbling vomit hit the back of his throat, and then he puked a fine, thin acid.

'Trying it on, were you, Wattere? Despenser will be disappointed,' Sir Robert said. He rested his booted foot on Wattere's shoulder. 'Let me see. We have a fire, and in the middle of it,' he pressed down hard, 'you rush to the maid.' He listened as the scream faded, bubbling. 'If I was less than intelligent, I might think that there was no coincidence. Do you think I should?'

'It was not to rape her . . .'

'Hmm? You wanted to say something?'

'I didn't bring her here to see her raped by your son. That little prickle was going to force himself on her and—'

'And it's none of your business. But what *is* my business is that you committed arson on my stables. And even now, all I can hear in the yard is the block burning.'

'Don't let your son—'

'You still talking, then?' Sir Robert said. He kicked once, hard, and then again. 'I don't like arsonists, Wattere. You know what? I think they ought to be shown why what they do is so dangerous. So I'm going to let you find out. Osbert, show him to the fire.'

Osbert looked at Wattere, then over at the fire. He snapped an order at one of the other men, and picked up Wattere by his bad shoulder. The two men hefted him between them as Wattere shrieked with the pain, and then began to walk him to the burning building.

Chapter Thirty

Nymet Traci

His feet dragged, and the pain in his shoulder was a continuing stream of fire that scorched his soul as Osbert pulled him on. Wattere had to open his mouth to scream in a constant, hoarse howl of anger, horror and mind-destroying terror. He set his feet to stop the onward progress, but that meant that the hand at his bad shoulder started to tear his muscles, and he could feel the grating of the sheared bones scraping against each other. This time the pain was so exquisite and intense, he could not make a sound. His mouth drooped wide, but nothing came. He was aware only of the sensation of floating a little over the ground. A loud drumming came to him, a drumming as of the blood pounding in his head, and he felt sure with relief that soon he would feel no more. He would have the sensation of fainting, but then his suffering would be ended. 'Swyve your mother,' he gasped.

Osbert turned to look at him, and his free fist clenched as though to swing at Wattere's face. It was enough to make Wattere want to flinch, but the effort was too great. Then, to his astonishment, he was dropped on the ground. All the feeling returned. He was no longer floating; now he was forced back to reality. He felt soil in his mouth, and rolled over, whimpering with the pain, as he prepared himself for the boot that would slam into his body.

He heard a bellow of rage, and as he tried to look towards

Osbert, he saw the other guard's head lift from the man's torso on a fountain of blood. Osbert had his sword clenched in his hand, and a look of maniacal joy on his face as he withdrew, carefully stepping back out of the light and into the smoke and fury of the fire.

It was enough for Wattere. He allowed his head to fall back and slipped away from consciousness.

Simon urged his horse on with spurs and reins, aiming straight for the smoke-filled gap that was the gateway, aware of Baldwin at his side, knowing that Edgar was a short way behind. As he slammed into the roiling smoke, he tried to catch a breath to scream a war cry, but the thick fumes burned down his throat and into his lungs, and he was forced to hack and cough until he reached a patch of daylight. He saw Sir Robert, and put his hand to his sword hilt even as he set his beast for the man.

Sir Robert was no coward, but nor was he a fool. A man on horseback had an advantage over a man on foot. He shoved past the other men to reach the front door of his hall, and would have slammed it closed, but Simon threw himself from his mount and hit the door as it was closing. It lurched open, and Simon was inside with Sir Robert. The knight pulled out his own sword, a longer one than Simon's, and instantly tried a stab, the steel coming wickedly close to Simon's flank. He slashed at the blade with his own, knocking it away, and it seemed to waver as though the man's arm was numbed. Simon saw Sir Robert's eyes register pain and disbelief, but he didn't trust him not to be acting to try to tempt Simon in more closely.

He decided to test Sir Robert, and made a feint, stabbing in and withdrawing. The reaction was so swift, it would have sliced through Simon's throat, a sweep around that then continued perhaps a little too far. It was beginning to move back already as Simon made his choice, and committed himself, hurling himself forward bodily, his right fist clenched about the hilt, clubbing at Sir Robert's wrist. His left hand shot out and gripped the knight's tunic at the neck, while he hammered again at the man's hand with the steel pommel of his sword. Once, twice, and on the third vicious blow, Simon allowed his sword to continue a little further in its motion, so that the point was now under Sir Robert's chin. He lifted it higher, so that it was close to penetrating his flesh, and at last Sir Robert swore and Simon heard the clatter of steel as the other man's sword fell to the ground.

'Shit, I yield!'

'I should finish you now!' Simon said from clenched teeth. 'Where is she? Where is my daughter?'

'Right here, master. Why, did you think we'd lost her?' Basil said, and Simon turned to see Edith gripped by the neck, his sword resting on her perfect white throat, her eyes wide with utter terror.

If there had been more men here, Baldwin would have been more alarmed, but as it was, the majority of the guards and servants had been outside and defending the yard from the flames. None had a bow or gonne with them, and not many had so much as a sword. There were three or four who bore axes, but they had been so completely surprised that two had already been struck down, and the two remaining had hurriedly dropped their weapons.

Baldwin had seen Simon rush for the door to the hall, but before he followed, he went to the figure lying on the ground near the burning barn. 'Well, this is a pretty sight,' he murmured, looking at the gaping wound where Osbert's sword had made its mark.

He peered around to look at the man's face and was surprised to recognise him. 'William atte Wattere,' he breathed.

Standing, he saw the monk nearby, gazing about him with a pitiable expression of shock on his face. 'Mark, brother, will you look after this fellow for me, please? He may be of some use to us.'

'Will he live?'

'Long enough, I hope, to feel the hangman's rope about his neck. This is the evil character who kidnapped Simon's daughter. Where he is, she will probably be near,' Baldwin said. He wiped a little of the sweat from his brow. It was almost unbearably hot in the yard. The enclosing walls concentrated the heat, and turned the space into an oven.

About him he saw that Edgar and Sir Richard had herded all the men from the yard into one corner, and although there were some seventeen of them, the two men were nonchalant in the way they held their weapons. It was obvious that none of the men they had captured relished the prospect of throwing themselves at them.

Baldwin was content that the two could easily cope with the cowed guards, and hurried after Simon. He was about to rush in through the door when Simon appeared, walking backwards, his sword in the hands of Sir Robert de Traci. Baldwin swore under his breath, and would have run to conceal himself, but Sir Robert saw him and jerked his chin. 'You too, Sir Keeper. Your sword on the ground now.'

'No.'

Baldwin saw Simon's agonised expression, but it would not affect him. He kept a firm hold on his weapon as two more figures appeared in the doorway: one was the one-eyed man, the other the knight's son, who held in his hand Simon's daughter.

'Edith,' Baldwin called. 'Are you quite well? Have these men hurt you in any way?'

Basil taunted him with his response. 'You think we'd have tainted the little wench? Nay, Sir Knight. She's still unsullied, so far as we can tell. Who knows what she has been getting up to in Exeter while her husband's away, though, eh? Good little rump on her, this filly. Have you seen the way she can jiggle it? Like two rats in a sack when she walks, by my faith! And those lovely titties. So entrancing. You want to try her? We haven't damaged her yet, so if you want her, you may be able to—'

'Basil, shut up,' his father growled. 'Sir Baldwin, I think I said you should put down your sword?'

Baldwin eyed him. He was too close to Simon for safety. Edith was close by the knight's son, too, and she was in great danger. Basil's sword lay across her throat, the sharpened blade touching her neck. She had a cloak on, loosely thrown over her shoulders, he saw, but the blade was above that. 'Sir Richard, Edgar, do not drop your swords. Clear?'

'Sir,' Edgar responded.

Sir Richard grunted and kept tight hold of his own weapon.

'There, Sir Robert,' Baldwin said. 'I feel we are at an impasse. I will not drop my sword, and you will not pass me to escape while I hold it.'

'You will drop it, Keeper, because if you don't, I shall tell my son to start removing pieces of that woman. Perhaps first we should see her shamed? Shall we strip her of all her clothing, Basil?'

Simon gave a tortured roar: '*No!*'

'Oh? You prefer that we should gradually remove every finger?'

Simon turned to Baldwin. 'They'll kill her! You must throw

down the sword, Baldwin. If you love me, old friend, please. I beg.'

'Simon, I cannot. If we all give up our swords, they will kill us all. That will not aid Edith.'

'What, you enter *my* castle, you have your accomplice burn *my* damned barns and stables, you rush *my* hall, and you say that I am the villain? Dear Christ in chains, you have a bold mouth on you, Sir Baldwin,' Sir Robert expostulated. The spittle flew from his mouth as he spoke. 'I am here without harming any, and yet you do so much damage.'

'We had no accomplice in your midst,' Baldwin said.

'No? That man who tried to destroy my castle wasn't yours?' he sneered.

'No. He brought Simon's daughter here to you, did he not? And you held her here. Perhaps you have seen her raped, treated shamefully, to satisfy your greed.'

'My greed? You fool! Dear heaven, I call on you to witness this imbecile! The girl was to be kept here safely, just so that pressure could be brought to bear on her father. That was all. There was a need.'

'What need?' Baldwin demanded.

'To protect the realm. It was only to guard Devon against Mortimer in case he tried to invade from here. Who else causes so much trouble and fear?'

'How would your holding Edith help guard Devon?'

'Tavistock. If this girl's father was anxious enough, it was thought that he would persuade the monks there to support the man who would be the stronger, more suitable abbot.'

'So for that, to effectually play with the election of an abbot, you were prepared to hold a young woman indefinitely?' Baldwin said. His contempt dripped from his voice. 'And you killed all the men at the woods just in order to reap the profit?'

'What men in the woods?'

Baldwin stared at him hard. 'The men whose money was taken. Women and children, monks and guards. You killed them all.'

'I don't know what you are talking about. I didn't kill anyone and take their money. What, do you think I am a common felon?'

'Not very common, no,' Baldwin said.

Sir Robert gave a slanted smile. 'Very well, I admit that we did tickle them up a little. But there was no money to steal. We spent long enough looking for the goddamned coin, but it wasn't there.'

'Then where is it?'

'If I knew that,' Sir Robert said with chilly certainty, 'I would have brought it here. I didn't, so I couldn't. Now, enough of this bickering. Will you let me pass?'

'No,' Baldwin said. 'Not with hostages. Either you give them up, or I will prevent you from leaving.'

'Basil, you can remove her shift and tunic. Let us see what she is made of, eh?' Sir Robert said.

But just then there was a howl from behind him, and Sir Robert spun, recognising the sound of his son's voice.

'*No!*' Simon roared, and lunged. His left hand slapped at the blade, knocking it away, and he was at Sir Robert's throat.

The knight had not expected so simple a manoeuvre, and he was forced to stagger backwards even as he saw his son lift his hands to his face, saw the blood gushing from his eye, heard the sword rattling on the ground, and saw the girl stoop, pick up the blade and thrust it into Basil's body, just under his ribs, a loose, inaccurate stab that wouldn't kill, but might hurt like blazes ... and then he felt an odd, uncomfortable, dragging sensation in his breast, and found that there was a peculiar tingling in his knees and a hollowness in his belly. He slipped to the ground, staring dumbly at the oily sheen on his sword blade. There was something wrong about it, he was sure, and as he gazed down, he realised that the blade was protruding from his own chest.

He felt his head as an insupportable weight, bringing him forward, the mass of his body dragging him to the floor, but even as he felt his life leaching away into the stones, his face was turned to his son. His last thoughts were for Basil.

Roger was close to the walls when he saw a figure on a horse, and he swiftly thrust Agnes down behind him.

This was so much like the scenes he had witnessed in France. Smoke pouring from a homestead as men and women milled about, terrified in case they would be captured. Today, he had the idea that there would be more killing, from the look of the men who had ridden in so wildly.

The smoke was clearing a little now as most of the thatch and straw was gradually consumed, and soon there was only the reek of old wood and tar and leather burning. At least with that there was less thick smoke, though, and now Roger could peer through the wavy air to see the men beyond. Not that the view was very clear – he was sure he could see the men who had ridden into the place, all standing about with their weapons drawn, but now he could see the men from the house, arguing; he saw the girl turn, the flash of a weapon, and the man behind her screamed hoarsely and fell, even as the knight dropped his sword and another man snatched it up and stabbed once, with all his strength.

'What is it?' Agnes demanded.

'I think this place is less of a threat now,' Roger said. He stood and began to walk towards the castle, aware that Agnes was hurrying to keep up. In the gateway, he saw the men gathered over in the corner of the wall. As he entered, there was a flash of steel, and he found himself looking into the face of a man who could kill in an instant. It was the kind of face he had seen all too often in France.

'Who are you?'

Roger said, 'I am a sailor, on my way to Dartmouth. Nothing to do with these men, except a few days ago I saw them slay a farmer.'

'I am Sir Baldwin de Furnshill, the Keeper of the King's Peace. What are you doing here now? A man who witnessed a murder would not normally follow the murderer. He would run to the nearest bailiff or reeve to declare the crime.'

'It occurred to me that finding a body in an area where I was unknown might not be conducive to a long life. I preferred to think that I could escape attention. But I thought it would repay me to follow some of these fellows and learn where they lived. Then I started to wonder where they were going, to see if they were attacking anyone else.'

'You waited about here, by your admission, for some days, when you could have been hurrying to your ship? When, as you say, you feared that by remaining here you would be throwing yourself in increased danger?'

'I am very public-spirited.'

Baldwin looked at him. 'I don't have time for this right now, but, friend, I will be speaking to you later. Who is this?'

Mark was still crouched at the side of Wattere in the midst of the ruin and savagery, and he looked up to see the woman at the gate. 'She is the wife of the reeve who was murdered, Sir Baldwin,' he said. He had dipped the hem of his robe in a horse trough, and was wiping Wattere's face with it. 'She is no threat to you,' he added sarcastically.

'Mistress, I am sorry about your loss,' Baldwin said.

Agnes was walking like a woman in a dream. 'Where is he?' she asked.

It was a strange dreamlike experience, being here in the courtyard with bodies lying nearby. She found her toe striking something that rolled, and looking down saw a man's head, the eyes wide in surprise as they contemplated her, but there was no body beneath it. She carried on walking to where the young woman was sobbing, cradled in the arms of a much older man. At their feet was a young fellow, who rocked back and forth on his knees, wailing quietly, while blood trickled from between the fingers covering his face. Nearby there lay another man, who had a massive wound in his breast that was still slowly oozing blood on to the floor. There was no rage in his face, though, only surprise and a kind of wistfulness.

'Is he the one?' she asked.

Simon saw her, and although he could not relinquish his daughter, he nodded. 'It's Sir Robert, the man who owned this castle. I think he was the man who ruled those who killed your husband, Agnes. I am sorry.'

'I am avenged,' she said quietly, and then spat on the dead man's face. 'That is for my husband, a good man, a good father, and a good reeve.'

She turned on her heel, and was about to walk away from that hideous area, but the other woman's misery called her back, and she went to her and put her own arms about her, looking at Simon as she did so. 'Let me take her out of here,' she said, and led Edith out of the courtyard, Simon following.

'Simon,' Baldwin said as Simon drew level with him. 'I couldn't let my sword go. You do understand that, don't you? If I'd dropped my sword, they could have overwhelmed us in a moment, and it'd be us who were lying in the dirt instead of them. You understand that, don't you?'

Simon looked at him, and Baldwin was shocked to see the resentment that burned in his eyes. 'Tell me, Baldwin. If that had been your little Richalda, and I had refused to drop my sword, what would you have done then?'

Baldwin was silent for only a moment, but then he shook his head. 'I would have agreed with you, Simon. It is impossible to surrender your weapons to men such as these.'

'You think so? Or would your friendship have turned to hatred and loathing, Baldwin?'

Chapter Thirty-One

Tavistock Abbey

In the cloisters, Brother Robert Busse was strolling thought-fully when he heard his voice called.

Behind him, angrily stalking towards him, his black robes flying so great was his speed, came Brother John de Courtenay.

'I suppose you think you are mighty clever!' Brother John hissed.

'Brother, I think nothing of the sort. However, I have done all I think I need to do to protect myself.'

'Pah! Protect my arse! You think you'll be safe from my fellows? You forget who you're talking to, churl!'

'Brother John, please, let us be calm.'

'Calm? I've just spent an hour or more in the company of the precious cretin from the pope. You know what he said to me?'

'He accused you of plotting my murder, I suppose.'

'Yes . . . You gave him my notes?'

'They were found on the messenger, and opened before it was realised quite what they were.'

'I will not tolerate this, Robert. My family is the most important in the shire, and I swear, I'll have the post here whether you'll accept me or not, you understand? If you stand in my way, I'll—'

'Kill me? Oh, Brother John,' Robert said. 'If you do that

now, you will never have this abbey. You don't understand? We are both in the same position, my friend. If I take any more money or try to do anything else to win the seat, I will be barred from it.'

'Good!'

'And conversely, if I die, for whatever reason, whether it be a sudden apoplexy or an accidental fall down the night stairs to the choir, my friend, you will also never win the seat. We are both blocked.'

'Ballocks!'

'Quite. Yes, I think I can agree with that sentiment. For now, Brother, I think that we must resort to the expedient of merely accepting whatever fate throws at us.'

Brother Robert watched as the furious Brother John kicked at a stone on the ground, and then made off towards the calefactory.

It was a pleasant thought that the other monk was as bitter and resentful as he himself, he reflected.

Bow

As soon as they arrived in the town, Baldwin sent Mark to seek out the reeve.

'But I don't know where he will be!'

'Nor do I – but you can be sure that he will either be in the tavern or over in the market somewhere. Go and find him. Tell him we have these men and needs must have them held securely somewhere. Do you go! Now!'

It took the monk little time to find the reeve, and in a short while the men were all held in the gaol, which was by no means large enough to accommodate them all, but there being nowhere else for them to be placed, Baldwin advised them to make the best of their situation. He was more concerned about his old friend Simon.

Simon would not look at him, but instead spent his time with his arm about Edith's shoulder, his whole attention fixed upon her. Even when Baldwin quietly called his name, Simon did not respond.

There were several men who had been wounded, not only Basil. Most of the others were suffering from the fire or from the terrified horses, rather than from the weapons of Simon or Sir Richard.

The boys sent to look after the horses, whom they had seen as they rode hell-for-leather to the castle, had all clearly taken the view that they would be better served by making themselves scarce than by waiting, and Baldwin had a shrewd idea that the animals would be discovered in one of the many horse-trading markets about Exeter before long. The boys would be long gone, though, and he was not overly worried about them. With luck, some of them might discover a talent for avoiding crime in future. But when he mentioned them to Sir Richard, he had another interest.

'Not bothered about those little scrotes. It was the other bastard with the face like an axe had gone through it that worried me. Where did he get to?'

Baldwin suddenly recalled the one-eyed man who had been holding on to Wattere as they arrived. 'I didn't see him.'

'No, nor I, but I had me hands a little full with those other arses. Still, it'd be a shame if the knight's sergeant escaped us.'

Baldwin agreed. He bellowed to a lone watchman, who stood looking confused at the door, and told him to see if he could organise a posse to go and track down the one-eyed man.

They were sitting now in an inn that lay at the southern side of the road, a strange little building on top of steps that had been carved from the hillside, which was here steep. For all that the accommodation was peculiar, it was a comfortable chamber, with a cheery fire roaring in the hearth in the middle of the floor, and an amiable young wench to serve them, while her father, the host, held a wary eye on them to ensure that his little strumpet was not harmed by this sudden infusion of strangers. For Baldwin's part, he was alarmed to see that his own servant was demonstrating his old amorous skills with the girl. He resolved to speak with Edgar later and remind him of his wife back home at Furnshill.

For now, though, as trenchers were brought to them filled with slices of good bacon and some thickened pease pudding, Baldwin was happy to eat and not remonstrate. He noticed the wandering sailor as he ate, though, and soon beckoned the man across.

Looking Roger all over, he nodded. 'So you assuredly are a sailor. I've only ever seen such rough hands on men who spend their lives hauling ropes.'

'I am. Although I confess I haven't always been one. In the past I was a fighter. But the French put an end to all that.'

'You were there when they invaded?'

'Yes. I was in a little town there.'

'Which?'

'Have you heard of a place called Montpezat?'

Baldwin considered. 'It was the town held against the French last year, was it not?'

'Yes. And when they took it, they razed it to the ground. It was all over that little bastide at Saint-Sardos.'

Brother Mark frowned. 'What happened there? I never understood.'

Baldwin explained. 'The Abbot of Sarlat in France wanted to build his new little town, because he knew it would make him money, but also because he knew it would embarrass our king. Although Sarlat was in France, Saint-Sardos is in English territory. But the abbot claimed that any territory owned by his abbey, because his abbey was in France, could be viewed as privileged. In other words, if he had a daughter house of his abbey or some manors within English jurisdiction, he thought he should be able to build fortress towns there. So he decided with Saint-Sardos, even though the seneschal of Guyenne had said already that such construction was illegal. When the abbot went ahead and began building, Raymond Bernard of Montpezat and Ralph Basset the seneschal went to stop the works. Tempers grew heated, and the French official in charge at the site was hanged from his own flagpole where he'd been flying the French flag. That is why we went to war with France.'

'And it's why all the French lands have been taken,' Roger finished. 'The French overran the duchy when Raymond and Ralph refused to surrender to French justice, and utterly destroyed Montpezat. I was lucky to escape with my life.'

'And you came back to England,' Baldwin said.

'Where else would I go? I thought that the best thing to do was to return here and find employment. But that failed, so I thought to find work on ships, and I've been working on them for some little while. I was raised near Brixham, and much of my childhood was spent on the water, so it was no hardship to turn to sailing again. But there are few places on ships for a man like me. And although I've been up to Barnstaple and all over the north and south, I've found no work. It is hard.'

'Why are you still about here?' Sir Richard said.

'I told you. I saw a man killed. It was the one-eyed man and that young cub you captured up there when your friend's daughter stabbed his eye.'

Simon was at a nearby bench with Edith, and he shot a look at them as Roger spoke. Baldwin saw his look, but did not allow Simon's anger to distract him. 'So you say you saw one murder, but did not report it or go to escape – instead you remained up here and discovered for yourself where the men came from. Why?'

'Because if I could show who the men were who'd killed, I thought they might be captured.'

'There is much here, my friend, that you aren't tellin' us,' the coroner grunted. He rested his elbows on the table and studied Roger fixedly.

'Sir, I do not know how I might convince you,' Roger said.

'Begin by telling the truth,' Baldwin said flatly.

Roger sucked his teeth. The man before him had dark, intense eyes, with the look of someone who had seen enough of the world, perhaps, to understand the strange gusts and currents that could drive a man on to the shoals of ruin. That was how he viewed his own life, certainly. He had known fabulous wealth for some months, but they had been followed by disaster and the anguish of ignominy and humiliation. He had drunk the bitter dregs of existence, and although he had returned here to England, yet there seemed little respite. Every opportunity he had attempted, he had failed. No seaman would allow him on his vessel, no peasant would accept his assistance, no lord his service. His life was already at its lowest ebb.

He took a deep breath. 'While in France, after Montpezat, I became a wanderer. It was dangerous to be English and alone.'

'Yes, I can imagine that,' Sir Richard said. 'What of it?'

Baldwin put a restraining hand on his arm as Roger continued.

'I joined a gang of men who had been with Raymond. We escaped before the castle was surrounded, and made off, living from the land as we might.'

Sir Richard and Baldwin said nothing. They had both been involved in warfare. Both knew to what he alluded: the inevitable concomitant of warfare was living off the land, which meant killing and robbing the local peasantry. Some wandering bands of mercenaries made a lot of money, occasionally winning small castles for themselves.

'I did not enjoy that life.'

Roger was silent for a short while. It was not easy to explain his feelings. 'Sirs, I was used to ships, as I said. The life of the sea is hard, but at least a man can feel free. While I was in France, I found a little dog that was being played with by some lads. They were tying sticks to her tail and beating her to make her run, dragging these sticks behind her. And . . .'

Unaccountably, his eyes began to well with the memory of that little bitch. A white mutt, with only a short tail, but when she was happy, a man could look into her eyes and see only love and joy. How anyone could hurt such a lovely little beast, he didn't understand.

'I saved her, and when I came back here to England, I brought her with me.'

Coroner Richard grunted and shifted on his seat. 'When you get to the point, let me know,' he muttered.

'Sir, I will be brief. I made friends with that little dog in France. She came home here with me, and I gave her to a man for a good home. Or so I thought. He was a priest who was going to be leaving the area shortly, he said. I gave her to him because I thought, when all was said and done, that a life on ship was no life for a dog unused to it. Especially a little dog who had just had puppies. She stopped when I was at Tavistock and had a small litter. Only one survived. He and his mother I gave to Brother Anselm, from Tavistock Abbey.'

His tale had attracted even Simon's attention. He was still with Edith, but Baldwin was glad to see that he was now listening. 'That was the man travelling with the abbey's money for the king,' Simon called. 'Cardinal de Fargis had the two men: his servant, Peter . . . no, Pietro de Torrino, and Brother Anselm. They were in the group that was slaughtered.'

'Yes. That is the man. I heard that Pietro de Torrino and Brother Anselm were to be with the group that was going to London. But Brother Anselm was not with the men when they were killed,' Roger said, and now his voice had subtly altered.

Baldwin, looking at him, was struck by the way he had changed. His eyes were more fixed, his gaze unwavering. Even his breathing seemed to have slowed. It was like watching a man who was suddenly calmed after a long exertion. 'What are you saying? You saw the men in the woods that day?'

'I found them early in the morning,' Roger admitted.

'Do you say that you found all those dead fellows and did not report them?' Coroner Richard demanded, aghast. He gaped, forgetting even to bellow for more wine. The idea that a man would not perform this most simple of duties when such a mass killing had been committed was utterly beyond his understanding.

To Baldwin, Sir Richard's shock was endearing. At a time when most coroners knew full well that almost every murder went intentionally undiscovered, because to report one would immediately incur a fine to ensure that the first finder would attend court to give evidence, it was pleasing to find one man who could still be appalled by someone who confessed to such an action.

Roger was unrepentant. 'Yes. I came across those poor devils early that morning. I didn't see the attack, but I found the bodies shortly afterwards. And I found the poor monk, Pietro. They made him suffer before they killed him. Why? They killed all the people with him too, even the children. Well – I suppose that was necessary, because they wanted no witnesses. But they killed my little bitch, and her pup. And there was no need for that.'

He snorted, shook his head, and then leaned back. 'So no,

Coroner, I didn't wait. I left. Because I thought that if any stranger to the area was found within ten leagues of the murders, he'd be considered the obvious suspect, and if anyone heard that I knew Brother Anselm, it might be thought that I was an accomplice to the killers.'

'Why would anyone think you an accomplice?' Baldwin asked.

'Sir Baldwin, in Tavistock everyone was talking about the great sum being sent to the king, the paucity of the guards, the huge prize for the man who was prepared to risk his life, and the marvellous riches a man could expect after winning it. As soon as I was discovered there, and a representative of the abbey arrived to investigate the theft, they would learn that I had been to Tavistock. What hope for me then? It would mean gaol immediately, and as a foreigner to the area, I would be sure to be found guilty.'

'You said that Anselm was not there?' Simon asked. His interest had been sparked now, and he had left Edith and was standing behind Roger. 'Are you sure? Could his body have been concealed? There were so many there . . .'

'What makes you think that his body was concealed?' Roger said. 'If I knew that the men were transporting all that money, don't you think others would too?'

Simon nodded. 'It was my own first thought: that someone would have had to have told the thieves that the money was being moved. And someone within the household of the Cardinal de Fargis would have news of that before anyone else.'

'But how would this Anselm have got to learn of Sir Robert de Traci?' Baldwin wondered.

'The same way that a man would have heard of any dangerous felon in the shire,' Sir Richard said. 'The stories about these devils are rife. And a man like this one, who can apparently claim the friendship of the highest in the land, is plainly a man who had a reputation of some sort.'

Simon nodded slowly. 'And Sir Robert had contacts with the abbey at Tavistock, didn't he? He said so; he said that Edith was taken in order that Despenser could try to force Busse to surrender to John de Courtenay's bid to take the abbacy.'

'So he was in contact somehow with de Courtenay's companions,' Baldwin said. 'I wonder if this Anselm was the go-between.'

'It is certainly possible,' Sir Richard considered. 'Although how he would have got messages to Sir Robert is anyone's guess. Anyhow, why'd the other one get his eyes popped?'

Baldwin looked up at Simon. 'Sir Robert said that there was no money, didn't he? He denied stealing. But if it had been there, he would have had it as soon as blink. So perhaps he was trying to torture the poor monk to learn where it might be.'

'But the monk would have told him,' Simon pointed out. 'No one would be able to suffer both eyes being put out without telling where it was.'

Baldwin nodded. 'But if it was already taken, so Sir Robert couldn't find it, and the poor monk didn't know where it was, the torture would achieve nothing. He could not tell them anything.'

'You mean some fellow had already stolen it?' Sir Richard said. 'And then they put the blame on the poor monk and let him take the medicine intended for them, eh?'

'That is how I would read it,' Baldwin agreed. He nodded to Roger and stood. 'I think we should return to Jacobstowe and take another look at the woods.'

'There is one other thing,' Simon said quietly, throwing a look over his shoulder at Agnes. 'If this is all correct, and someone else stole the money, that still doesn't explain the reeve being murdered over towards Hoppon's house.'

'No. Not unless this Hoppon was himself involved,' Baldwin agreed tersely.

Near Nymet Traci

Osbert lay on his belly and shook his head at the sight of the smoke rising from the castle.

There was no point in returning to the place, not now that the main house had been destroyed by fire. He could see how the blaze from the stable blocks had reached over to the roof of the hall, and now that was almost entirely gone. It was enough to make a man weep, to think of the sweet profits this place had brought in in the past. So much money they had made, in only a few months. And now the whole lot was gone. Up in smoke.

He couldn't have planned it better himself.

As he stood and dusted the dirt from his tunic and hose, he was already plotting. He had enough money now to go to London if he wanted. He could buy a house and live in style. But that wasn't his desire. A man who was content to take a bit of money and rest was ready for his grave, in Osbert's opinion. No, he wanted more. More excitement, more pleasure, more money, more fun. Perhaps he ought to see whether he could go to the king's French territories. There were big profits to be made there, so they said, so long as the English recovered all their lands. Here in England there was too much interference all the time. Over there, a man with muscle and a sword might just make some money. All those French peasants were so weakly that a bold man should be able to live well.

It was a thought.

He pulled his cloak about him and set off homewards. It would take him some little while to get there, but at least he knew all these roads. And then tomorrow he would be able to start to plan.

After all, now that his old life at Nymet Traci was gone, it left him with some decisions to make. And although these would have had to have been taken before long, he hadn't expected them to be forced upon him so soon. He had expected a few more months at the castle.

No matter. He would hurry home, and make up his mind about the rest of his life.

Chapter Thirty-Two

Fourth Wednesday after the Feast of the Archangel Michael*

Jacobstowe

They rode into the vill from Bow in the middle of the morning.

Their departure had been delayed while they waited for news of Osbert, but there was other business to be taken in hand too. Wattere was still clinging on to life, with a determination that even Simon found grudgingly impressive. Baldwin made provision for him. There was little point in keeping him in gaol, for there was no possibility of his escaping, and the local priest said he would be happy to have the dreadfully injured man in his home, where he could be watched and nursed. It was unlikely to be for long.

As they rode, Baldwin was thoughtful. Simon had been civil to him, but there was a strong undercurrent in all that he said and did, and Baldwin was aware of the lingering resentment whenever he looked into Simon's eyes, but he couldn't apologise. There was nothing wrong in what he had done. If he had passed over his own weapon, just as Simon had, it was certain that Sir Robert would be alive, and they would not. It was clear to Baldwin that the worst way in which a man could deal with a threat was to instantly surrender.

---

*30 October 1325

Better by far to have an opponent who could carry out a threat and then suffer for it than an enemy who could threaten without compunction or fear of consequences.

'Do you wish to know what he said?' Baldwin asked Simon. His old friend looked away, towards Edith, but did give a curt nod of the head.

Before leaving, Baldwin had visited the men in the town's little gaol. In truth, he would have preferred not to have gone to the noisome little chamber. It was filled with the odour of faeces, of damp rocks and earth, and the chill was relentless. One man, when Baldwin looked about him, was very still, and wore the grey sheen of death. He was one of those who had been struck down by the horses, Baldwin recalled. He nodded to Basil, and the watchman with him grabbed the fellow by the shoulder, yanking him to his feet and half dragging him out through the door, while the others glared and snivelled.

'What do you want with me now?'

Basil had spirit, Baldwin saw. The fellow might be a most unappealing sight, with his right eye ruined, and blood and pus dribbling down his cheek, but for all that, and although he must have been in pain, he stared at Baldwin without apology.

'Your father is dead. You know that?'

'Yes. And as soon as I may, I will have the whole matter laid before the king and my lord Despenser,' Basil spat. 'And when your own part is explained in these affairs, in the murder of my father, in the ravaging of my manor, the destruction of the stables and sheds, the wanton—'

'Be silent, viper! I am not here to listen to your feeble threats. Do you think you can intimidate me as you did those poor devils on the roads about here?'

'You tell me to be silent? You old cretin! You will not be so proud when you are before Sir Hugh le Despenser and trying to explain yourself. You rode into our manor, you—'

'Released a woman whom you had captured, illegally, and against all the rules of chivalry, fellow. And proved that you had been attacking all who passed near and robbing them of their goods. I think there is not a court in the land that would protect you. No matter how many jurors the good Sir Hugh were to place at the court's disposal.'

'He would be able to provide many, you piece of shit,' Basil blustered, leaning forward. 'He will buy up all the jurors, and the judge, too, in order to break you.'

'Even when we show that you robbed the party on its way to the king? You stole the king's silver when you robbed those men.'

'We didn't,' Basil sneered. 'Show we did it!'

'I shall,' Baldwin said. 'You killed not only a group of archers, boy; you slaughtered two monks. You will not be set before a court that Sir Hugh can buy up. You will stand accused before a court in Exeter, in the presence of Bishop Walter. And he will have the pleasure of convicting you to die on his own gallows.'

Basil was shocked by that. 'We didn't kill two monks! We only found the one. The other one must have made off before we got there, rot his bowels!'

'Hardly likely,' Baldwin said.

'It's the truth!'

Gradually Basil had told the whole story: how the man Osbert had insinuated himself into the group of travellers, how he had persuaded them to turn north from Oakhampton, to avoid the known danger of Sir Robert's men, while in reality leading them all into Sir Robert's trap.

Baldwin repeated the story now as they jogged down a hill near the tiny vill of Sampford Courtenay, and even as they rode, Simon's attention was taken by the tale. 'You mean they'd been planning this for some days, then?'

'They must have been,' Baldwin agreed. 'Simon, just consider the effort involved. They had to make sure that this man Osbert was ready to join the group at the earliest moment, probably not long after they left Tavistock. He had to have time to get to know them, after all. And probably to start to spread concern about the depredations of his own master. He wanted them to be so fearful of Sir Robert that they would willingly and swiftly agree to his suggestion of an alternative road to Exeter, bypassing Bow completely. They could hardly go south, not with the paucity of roads in that direction; their only path must take them north. And that meant Abbeyford Woods. The rest of Sir Robert's men knew where he would lead them.'

Mark was frowning. 'But Anselm, he would know that was a daft idea.'

'That was, I think, the point,' Baldwin said caustically. 'One stranger would be unlikely to swing all behind him. But if there was another there, a man who was viewed as knowledgeable, who was wearing the cloth, that would inevitably help.'

'You mean he colluded in this? No!' Mark was emphatic. 'I will not allow that! To suggest such a slander is a disgrace, Sir Baldwin. You shame yourself more than his cloth and our order when you say such things. Where is your evidence? What proof do you have, eh?'

It was Simon who shook his head sadly. 'Mark, Baldwin's right. Look at it sensibly. Sir Robert needed details of the men in the guard. And if Anselm had nothing to do with it, where is he now? What happened to him after the robbery? Why wasn't he there with all the other bodies?'

Sir Richard rumbled as he considered. 'So this one-eyed arsehole was there to lead them all astray and he colluded with the renegade monk to get them all up into the woods?'

'That's how I read the tale,' Baldwin agreed. 'Except the money wasn't there. So someone had taken it already.'

'Perhaps Anselm himself?' Sir Richard said.

'No!' Mark protested. 'He wouldn't take the money and see all those people murdered.'

'Perhaps,' Baldwin mused, 'he aided Osbert in doing that.'

Simon shot a look at Sir Richard. 'It was a large sum of silver, wasn't it? More than one man could carry, I'd bet.'

'Sirs, there is one thing,' Roger said. He was walking briskly at their side. 'I saw the camp on the morning after. I am sure that all the people there were deliberately murdered. One man I found had six arrows, and yet someone had stabbed him through the eye to make sure. All were like that, bar the monk himself and one other – a man who was lying further away from the middle of the camp. He was another fighter, I think, and yet he hadn't been taken down by the attack – he had been stabbed in the back some four or five times.'

Baldwin was nodding. 'And you think . . .'

'That he was a sentry, the first to be killed. If this Osbert was in the camp as you believe then this man was killed so that the money could be removed.'

Simon shook his head. 'It wasn't there. I looked most carefully, and there was no sign of it near the camp. I even looked about the woods to see if anything could be learned. So did Mark here. He found a lovely cross, all enamelled. It was Pietro's, apparently.'

'I remembered it,' Mark said. 'It had been thrown into a bush.' He drew it from beneath his robes now and displayed it.

Baldwin pursed his lips. 'I would that I had been able to see the site after the attack. Perhaps I would have noticed something . . .'

'We all did our best,' Simon said coldly. 'As did Sir Peregrine.'

'I was not criticising,' Baldwin said.

Sir Richard had his mind fixed on the money and seemingly did not notice Simon's petulance. 'So we think that this Osbert had a heavy hand in the robbery and killings. But the money was already gone? Did the cardinal send it by some other route, and this was a mere distraction to tempt robbers?'

'No. The money was with this party,' Simon said. 'The cardinal would have told us if it had already been safely sent, surely.'

'How would Sir Robert's men have known that the party were there already?' Mark said. 'Is it possible that some other man than this Osbert killed the sentry and took the money?'

'He could hardly carry all that money himself,' Baldwin said. 'I doubt one man on his own could.'

Simon frowned. 'The man Hoppon was nearby. He could have helped take it.'

Mark nodded. 'And when poor Anselm realised that the money was stolen, he trailed after in order to tell the camp who had taken it, and to where.'

Simon looked ahead. 'Or Anselm saw Osbert kill the guard and decided to take the money himself. He picked up the chest and made away with it.'

'A money chest full of silver?' Baldwin questioned.

He was right. It would be too heavy. 'There was Hoppon nearby. He is crippled, though. His leg is all but useless. Still, perhaps he could help a man take a chest and hide it?'

'I have often noticed that men who have been injured will have increased abilities in other ways,' Baldwin said. 'A man with one weak leg will have the other much stronger, a man with poor hearing may have better eyesight than most, or a fellow who's lost an arm will have a more powerful remaining arm to compensate. Perhaps this Hoppon is the same?'

Sir Richard gave a loud 'Ha!' that made Edith jump almost

from her pony, while Mark blanched and threw a look of mute appeal to Simon, as though begging him to either plead with the knight to show a little restraint, or perhaps to slip a dagger into the man and silence him that way.

But the knight continued. 'Simon, you remember that Hoppon's house was the very nearest to the attack itself, eh? What would be easier than for the fellow to hop on over there and knock down an unsuspectin' guard, hoick up the lucre and hobble off again, eh? Or perhaps it was the monk killed the guard, not this Osbert, and Hoppon helped him to take the chest away?'

Simon recalled the log pile outside Hoppon's house. It was hard to imagine that he could have been involved – Simon had liked the fellow. He was as suspicious, tetchy and truculent as Simon's old servant Hugh. But it couldn't be denied that the man had the strength to pull large logs into his house for his fire. A man who could do that could as easily haul a money chest away.

Baldwin glanced over at him. 'What do you think, Simon? He was nearest the site of the attack, if Sir Richard is right. If Osbert had to have an ally, perhaps Hoppon was the man?'

'I find it hard to believe,' Simon said after a few moments of consideration. 'But you are right. We ought to ask him more about that night and see if he could have been involved in any way.'

He looked over his shoulder at the group of men and women behind them. Agnes and Edith appeared to have formed an alliance over the night, and even now were close together a matter of a few feet behind him. Edgar formed their rearguard, from where he could keep an eye on the women as well as Roger, whom he distrusted.

It made Simon think of another cavalcade, two weeks and a few days before, and an old man in his hovel, sitting near his fire of tree trunks, his little dog at his side, glowering at the embers as he listened to the sounds of horses and carts quietly rolling past. Simon could believe that the man would have sat there and listened – but to go from that to the picture of Hoppon leaping into the clearing and murdering a man, then carrying off a great treasure: that was too fanciful for him.

'You say you think he could have been involved in the robbery. I doubt it. He does not seem the sort of man who would do something like that.'

'You would trust to your belly in this?' Baldwin asked.

'My intuition about people has rarely been wrong,' Simon said shortly.

Baldwin said nothing, but he gave his old friend a look of great sadness, almost mourning. Both felt that their friendship had never been so sorely tested, and Baldwin felt it all the more, for he could not even hope that Simon would ever understand his action yesterday. It was clear that for Simon, his daughter's life was all, and his faith in Baldwin had been rocked to its foundations.

Jacobstowe

It was a pleasant little home, Edith thought as she crossed over the threshold with Agnes. Edgar was with them, and he stood outside with that little smile on his face that seemed to indicate ironic amusement about the scene around him, especially as he watched Mark limping slightly as he made his way to the church. The brother's pony had been given to Roger for him to follow Baldwin, Simon and Sir Richard at their pace, rather than having to slow them to his own, while they rode to Hoppon's house to question him.

Agnes had already been to fetch her little boy, a fellow christened Antony, but who had invariably been known as Ant. 'It was my husband used to call him that,' Agnes said sadly.

'He always gave everyone a nickname.'

'My husband sometimes does, too,' Edith said. 'He can be so childish like that.'

'Hush, dear,' Agnes said as Edith began to sob. She fetched a little ale in a cup and passed it to her. 'Drink this.'

Edith took it, and wiped at her eyes. 'I am sorry, but the thought of him lying in the gaol at Exeter fills me with horror. They were talking about putting him into court to stand for treason, and you know what that would mean. No one ever escapes from a charge like that.'

'Perhaps he is freed already,' Agnes said. She was at a loss for words as to how to soothe this woman.

'I only pray that he is,' Edith said. She snivelled a little. 'I am sorry – I fear the loss of my man, but you are already widowed.'

'At least I already know the worst,' Agnes said flatly. She looked at the child in her arms. 'But I keep waking in the middle watches of the night and wondering where he has gone. There is nothing worse than that loneliness, when you realise that he's gone for ever.'

'You may find another man,' Edith said tentatively.

'The vill may decide to impose one on me,' Agnes said without self-pity. 'At least it would mean food in our bellies, I suppose.'

Edith said nothing. They both knew the reality of widowhood. It was hard for a woman to survive when her man died. All too often the community would suggest alternatives, no matter how unsuitable the woman might think them. 'It is hard when you are unfree,' she said.

'It is harder when you were born free,' Agnes said. 'But my son, he was the son of a serf, so he is a serf too. And I was married to one, so I relinquished my freedom willingly for him.'

Edith nodded. Then a vision of her husband's face came before her eyes again, and she dissolved in tears. Agnes went to her, and the two women sobbed together for their men, one in misery at her loss, the other terrified that she would soon experience the same; both in fear for their futures.

Chapter Thirty-Three

Hoppon's house

He could hear them long before they arrived. That was one of the benefits of a little area like this. Sound travelled.

The noise of squeaking harnesses and jingling chains came to him clearly over the creaking of the trees and the soughing of the wind in the dried leaves. 'Easy, Tab,' he said, snapping his fingers as the dog rose on his haunches and started a low rumbling deep in his throat.

Hoppon walked from his door to the open space before it, and rested his backside on a log that lay handy. He had used this as a chopping board for so many other logs that it was scarred and notched with a thousand axe blows, but it was also in just the right position for him when he was tired from gardening or when he had returned from his daily walk down to the river to fetch water. The aches and pains of old age were inevitable, as he knew, but the gradual deterioration was depressing. There had been a time when he wouldn't have needed so many little resting places. Before the damned fire, he would have been able to stride about his place without a problem. But now every step was that little bit painful. Not outright, harsh, ferocious agony, but debilitating, slow, steady, nearly not hurting, just a constant ache that flared whenever the weather was about to change.

'God, why didn't you just let me die in the fire?' he muttered. Not that he had to ask. He knew that answer already:

God wanted to test him, just as the priest once told him.

'Hoppon, God give you a good day,' the first rider said as he sat on his horse, gazing about the place with his dark eyes.

'God speed you, sire.'

'You remember me?' Simon asked, taking his horse forward until he was level with Baldwin. 'This is the Keeper of the King's Peace, Hoppon. We want to ask you some questions.'

'Oh?'

'About the night the travellers were slain,' Baldwin said.

Hoppon grunted and rose to his feet. 'You want to know what about the night? It was dark.'

'We think that there was a man with the travellers who was a spy and was there only to destroy all those innocents,' Baldwin said. 'He was with Sir Robert's men. A one-eyed fellow called Osbert.'

'Wouldn't surprise me.'

'You knew him?'

'Few about here didn't. He wouldn't hurt me, mind. Always respectful to me, he was. But that didn't mean he'd be the same with others. And he was always keen for profit.'

'Do you know more about him and the robbery?' Simon asked.

'No.'

'You see,' Baldwin said, 'we were trying to think whether this man Osbert could have had an ally near here. He would need someone who would be easy to call to his aid. A man who would be within a certain distance. Someone of strength, and determination.'

'So you thought of me, naturally,' Hoppon said. He jerked his chin to the south-west. 'But I wouldn't have seen a thing. The trees between here and there are too thick.'

'In the dark, fires light the sky,' Baldwin mused. 'And in still air a scream will travel further than an arrow.'

'I was asleep when it happened, then, for I saw no fires or lights, nor heard any cries for help.'

'So you want us to believe that all those fellows passed by you, and you did nothing to see where they went?'

'They were too quiet at first. The second lot made more noise, but they were later.'

'How much later?'

'Well, a goodly while. Perhaps as long as an hour of the night?* It was long enough for some twigs an inch and a half thick to burn right through.'

Simon was frowning. 'So this first group, this was Sir Robert's men on the way there, and then the second was his men riding away again? Or do you mean that there was another group of men?'

Suddenly Hoppon was keen to be away. 'I don't know. I was indoors. That's what I told the reeve when he came asking, and it's what I told you too. I was inside. I can't rightly tell who was here, who passed and when. It was none of my business then, and it still isn't now.'

'You are wrong, Hoppon,' Baldwin said. 'It is your business, because it is all of ours now. We think that a few men stole the money before Sir Robert even reached the camp. Probably the man Osbert helped a monk to take it somewhere to be hidden. Perhaps they were helped by a man who was apparently crippled many years ago, but who is still enormously strong.'

'You think I could carry a chest full of money?' Hoppon smiled. 'All the way from there to here? Or do you think I

---

*Night was separated into equal 'hours', as was daylight. There were twelve hours of daylight, and thus summer hours were longer than those of winter.

carried it further? Up to his house? Do you think this leg is a fiction just to test the gullible?'

Baldwin set his head to one side. 'I think you may be able to walk farther than you say, friend. I think you may well be able to stroll to the woods over there and back, even with a chest on your back. Especially if you have a man like Osbert to help you.'

'You think I'd help him and his sort?' Hoppon spat.

'You say that no one would help him,' Simon said. 'Why? Were Sir Robert and his men well known about here? Nobody seemed to know of his men particularly when I was asking. Was that simply because all feared him?'

'Not Sir Robert, no. I dare say he was a moderate lord in his own way,' Hoppon conceded. 'But Osbert is a different animal. No one liked him.'

'He was well known here?' Simon asked.

Sir Richard grunted. 'The man is keen to place the blame on any other fellow, eh?'

'I tend to agree,' Baldwin said. 'Hoppon, you were near the assault; you could easily have walked there and back. I say you may have joined Osbert in the attack and that you have the coin here. What do you say?'

'I say, *ballocks* to you! You think I've hidden money about the place, you go and fetch it. Now! I've never robbed any man in my life, and if I was going to, I wouldn't rob the bleeding king! You think I'm mad?'

Simon stepped in front of the bristling man. 'Hoppon. I don't think you had anything to do with it. But you say Osbert was known around here. Why should he be known? Nymet Traci is a fair distance away.'

'But he came from just over the hill,' Hoppon pointed out.

'What? Where?' Baldwin snapped.

'Osbert is John Pasmere's son, from over there. Didn't you know?'

Pasmere's house

Osbert chewed the dry bread and sipped his ale through it, trying to moisten it in his mouth. 'You eat this all the time, old man? Christ's cods, it's a miracle you've any teeth left!'

'Shut your noise, boy. It's better than most eat about here. There's not much in the way of food since your precious master returned to the castle.'

'Aye, the churl was keen to rob all about,' Osbert said with a low chuckle.

'So were his men. I heard about the murder of Jack.'

'Eh?'

John Pasmere sneered. '*Eh? Eh?* Jack Begbeer. A good man, he was. Not some miserable lying churl who deserved to die with a knife in his gut.'

'In his throat, old man. I'm not so useless with a knife that I could miss a target like that.'

'You killed him yourself?'

'The others were all cowering from him,' Osbert said. He took a slurp of ale from the cup at his side, chewing slowly. 'I couldn't let them see a peasant get one over me.'

'My own son turned murderer, eh? Wonderful. So now we'll both hang.'

'Only if we're caught. And I don't mean to be.'

'I never thought this would end with friends being killed, Os.'

'Then you were a fool. Innocents always die. Don't go all soft on me.'

'You used to play with old Jack, though. What'd he ever done to you?'

Osbert looked at him. 'What does that matter? He had

provisions we wanted. And we had more weapons and I had more men. He should have let us take them.'

'Was he raised to surrender to any cutpurse at the side of the road?'

'Perhaps not. If he was, he'd be alive now.'

'You shouldn't have killed him, boy.'

'What'll you do now with the money?' Osbert asked, bored with the recriminations about his actions.

John Pasmere stared into his little fire. He listlessly collected up fallen twigs and flung them into the flames. 'Me? What would I do with a hundred pounds in silver? Or a third of it?'

'A half, old man.'

'You keep your half, and let the monk have his. There's too much blood on this money. I want no part of it.'

Osbert was tempted to tell him then, but it was pointless. 'You sure of that? If you are, I'll just go.'

'Yes. Go. I don't have a son. Not any more. You are dead to me, Os. Take the money and flee. I only pray that one day you will go and beg forgiveness at the altar where Jack used to pray.'

'P'haps. One day.'

'Do it, Os!' his father hissed, staring at him.

Osbert looked pathetic. 'What is this? You were happy enough to win the money with me. What makes you so cross about it now?'

'When we won it, those people would have died anyway. I didn't have any part in killing them. Nor did you, truly. They would all have been killed by Sir Robert. But Jack, that's different. He was a good man. He didn't deserve to have his life shortened. Can't you see that, boy?'

Osbert fingered his nose, then pointed at his empty socket. 'See this, old man? I won this fighting for the likes of the king and Sir Robert. What did it get me? Two shillings, one from each. And later Sir Robert realised I was still alive, and he gave me board and lodging. In exchange for some peace and meals, he let me run about the county stealing for him. What's the difference between him and any outlaw? But since I took the money he wanted, I've got a life of my own again. You ask me why I killed Jack. Because I could. Because I saw no reason *not* to kill him. Ach, you can't understand. You haven't been marked like me. But now all is different again. Sir Robert's dead, and soon his son will be too, if I'm any judge. There's nothing for me here now.'

'Then stay and farm with me!'

'Do I look like I'd make a good farmer?' Osbert said with a measure of contempt. 'It's not the life for a man who's used to commanding others and taking what he needs.'

John Pasmere looked back into the fire. He appeared to shrivel into himself, misery etching his features. 'Then go. And we won't see each other again. I have no son.'

Osbert said no more, but drained his cup and finished his stale bread. He left soon afterwards, while Pasmere remained silent, his eyes glittering with the flames of the fire. Osbert took his father's old barrow, and followed the track up north that led into the little coppice, and then out beyond to the thicker woods where the trails were harder to find.

The chest lay in the hollow under an old dead oak, and he went straight to it, pulling the heavy coffer out and staring at it with that odd tightness in his breast that he felt only when he had something like this, a valuable prize to enjoy. There was a lustfulness to his pleasure when he took a good one, and just now he felt the sensation like a fire burning in his belly.

He would have to make good his escape. And he knew exactly how to do that. He bent his legs, put his hands on either side of the chest, and then swiftly heaved it up, allowing it to drop into the barrow. It settled a little, and nearly fell sideways, but he managed to catch it in time, and propped it up with a branch. He had other work to do.

It was a good thing he hadn't told his father about the monk, he thought, as he pulled the robes from a rotten, hollow tree. There was a bulge in the soil nearby. In the last few days leaves had piled up over the body, he saw. Soon the wild animals would have eaten all that remained of the fool. How any man could think that his life would be worth a bean after helping Os to take such a prize was beyond him, but the fool had, and now he'd paid the price in full for his stupidity. When they'd reached this place, Os had had Anselm help to thrust the chest into the hole, and while the monk was bending down, he'd taken a large branch and smashed it over his skull. Anselm had fallen like an axed steer, collapsing instantly. He didn't even shiver or rattle his feet; he was alive one moment, and dead the next. Which was good, because Os had a use for his robes now. He pulled the habit over his own clothing, and bound it at his waist with the rope Anselm had used. His father should be proud: ballocks to praying at Jack's church – he was as good as any priest now, he thought.

The idea made him chuckle as he pulled the hood over his head and took up the handles of the barrow. He pushed it hard, and before long he had reached the old, unused track. Still chuckling, he set off westwards.

The place was the same as Simon recalled it from the day before – was it really only yesterday that he and Sir Richard had come here trying to learn where the men had gone? It felt as though it was an age ago. A lifetime ago . . . a friendship ago.

He couldn't look at Baldwin. The memory of his friend's hesitance, or rather his refusal to let his weapon fall when the life of Simon's daughter was at stake, was enough to make Simon feel sickly. It was foul, as though he had looked for a well-known and respected companion, only to find a stranger. The shock of that discovery made him question the entire basis of his friendship. It was as though a chasm had opened between them, undermining the relationship they had developed over almost a decade.

Simon and Baldwin were almost together, while Sir Richard rode behind them, throwing the occasional surly, suspicious glare at Roger, who jogged along beside him. As they reached Pasmere's lands, Roger dropped from his pony and walked about the yard. After some while staring at the ground, he began a circuit around the house, while Sir Richard watched him from beneath his thick brows. At last, irritable at the lack of welcome, the coroner took a deep breath.

'Pasmere!' he shouted from the roadway. 'Are you in there?'

There was a muttered oath from inside, and then Pasmere's face appeared. He glanced at the faces before him, before scratching at his beard. 'What?'

Simon could see that something had changed about the man. His face was paler, and for a moment Simon thought that the old man was struck down with a disease. There were stories of men and women who had succumbed, and not all had died of the famine that hurt so many in the last years, but then he saw the reddened eyes and realised that this was only a man who had been weeping.

'Friend Pasmere, are you well?' he enquired.

'I'm fine. What's the matter? You get lost yesterday or something?'

Sir Richard moved forward on his mount. 'You should remember to be civil to officers of the king's law.'

'Why? A civil man can be killed as easily as a rude one,'

Pasmere snapped. 'I am only a feeble old peasant, yet two knights, you, Bailiff, and these others can feel free to come and demand answers of me. Why should I answer if I don't wish to?'

'Friend, I only asked if you were well,' Simon said soothingly. 'Something has happened to you. Can we help?'

'No. It's nothing.'

For some reason Simon felt sympathy for the man. Perhaps it was the aura of general despair about him, or the feeling Simon had that he too was all alone now, having lost his friend in the last day, but he felt that there was a connection between his own misery and that of this old man. He said nothing, but dismounted and walked over to John Pasmere.

'Pasmere, I cannot swear to be able to help you, but you are grieving. Let me help you if I may.'

'You cannot help me.'

'Tell him to speak about his son,' Sir Richard said. 'In God's name, we have to find that murderous puppy!'

'I have no son,' Pasmere said. 'He is dead to me.'

'Why is that?' Baldwin demanded from his horse.

Simon said nothing at first, but he held Pasmere's gaze, and gradually he saw the anger pass from the older man's face. 'Master, I am sorry. There is nothing more painful than to lose a son.'

'You have?'

'My boy was younger. There is no day I don't miss him.'

'I will miss mine too,' Pasmere said, and sighed. 'He was a good boy when he was young, you know? Always loyal and keen. Clever, too, with his hands. He could fashion anything out of wood, if you gave him a good knife to work with. Aye, he had the brain of a man apprenticed as a craftsman, he did. But then all went sour.'

'Why was that?' Simon asked.

'He went up to fight for the king at Bannockburn, twelve years ago. He got that wound and lost his eye up there in the Scots' lands, and never trusted his lords again. The king was there, and his own master, but they fled when they saw the battle turn against them. All those men wallowing in the brooks and mud, and those who ordered them to go left them to die. It was a miracle that Os didn't. Perhaps it would have been better if he had,' he added musingly.

'What happened?'

'Oh, he was fortunate. Some Scot took him in and nursed him back to life, but from that moment he was bitter about people – especially the king and those who made wars and then ran away when it grew warm. The king did pay him a shilling for his service, and Sir Robert paid him the same, and he was welcomed back to Sir Robert's household when he was healthy enough. And then the fool made enemies in the king's court, and all were forced to turn outlaw. My boy stayed with his master in all that time, and when Sir Robert returned to Nymet Traci, he brought Os with him.'

'We have to find him, you know that?' Simon said. 'We will find him and catch him if we may, but if he refuses to surrender to us, we'll have to take him any way we can.'

'He is not my son any more,' Pasmere said.

'Where did he go?' Simon asked.

Pasmere remained staring at him. He could not speak at first. Then, 'If you had a son as old as mine, would you be able to betray him? Ever?'

Simon shook his head. He gave Pasmere his hand.

It was then that Roger returned from behind the house. 'Sir Baldwin? I think I have found his tracks.'

Chapter Thirty-Four

Hoppon's house

Tab was as alert as ever, Hoppon saw.

At first he thought it might be the men returning from Pasmere's place, but then he heard the squeaking of an axle, and realised that it was not coming from the road they had taken, but instead from the ancient road further to the north of him.

It was enough to make him frown. There were all kinds of stories about that old road: how in years past some army had swept down and through this part of the country, leaving behind roads and forts. But they were daft old legends so far as Hoppon was concerned. The idea that some race of giants had lived here was more likely true. Still, the road was real enough. He had dug around up there once when he was younger, and a short way down under the grasses he had found a solid, paved roadway. When he looked east, it stretched for miles, probably as far as Crediton. Now that would have been a magnificent task, building a road all the way up there. Not that anyone used it any more. They all stuck to the muddier routes because they were more gentle in the way that they flowed around hills rather than taking a direct line straight up and over them. It was easier for people with heavy carts or packhorses.

But there were some few who knew the old roadways and used them. Sometimes, when he had been younger, Hoppon himself had been known to make use of them. They were appallingly overgrown in places, it was true, but they were still the best for those who knew of them, when there was wheeled transport to consider. Especially when the wheeled transport was something best kept from public view. And a man who was trying to evade the king's officers would be well advised to make use of such a secret route.

Hoppon listened as the noise grew closer. Tab began to rumble deep in his throat, and he put his hand gently over the dog's muzzle. 'Be still, boy! No need for that. Let him be.'

He listened, and the noise slowed slightly. That would be where the incline rose towards the top of the hill towards Jacobstowe. If he was right, and this was Osbert, why was the man heading in this direction? It would surely have made more sense for him to go east, towards Crediton and Exeter, rather than here, towards the scene of his crime.

Hoppon listened wonderingly, as the sounds began to dim again, but then he pulled a bitter face and grimaced as he pulled himself upwards once more. 'Ach, come on, Tab. Can't let him just run like that. What'll happen if he escapes? He'll only find some other poor bugger to kill and rob, and then where'd we be? Guilty as hell, that's where, for allowing him to run and kill again. He might be a neighbour, but he's still an evil bastard. Can't have him escaping.'

Roman Road

Simon was remounted almost before Roger had finished speaking. He slapped the rein ends against his beast's rump and was already moving even as Pasmere called, 'Don't hurt my boy! Please, don't hurt him!'

It was a plaintive call that Simon would remember in his dreams for many months to come.

Roger was running to keep up. He took them to the back of the house where the barrow had been stored, and pointed out where the line in the dirt and grass showed the wheels' passage. There was nothing to discuss. The last desperate plea from Pasmere was proof enough that Osbert had come this way, and the four men began to make their cautious way forward.

Simon hated entering thick woods like these when there was a risk of ambush. He had not been overly concerned back at Abbeyford after that attack, for the inquest itself had already been conducted, and none of the perpetrators was likely to have been there still. Whereas here there was the distinct possibility that Osbert was still close by. The only thing that was assured was that if he was pushing an old barrow, he would likely be too tired to think about pursuit. He was probably content to think that the attack on the castle was an end to the matter from his point of view. Simon knew that all too often criminals displayed astonishing foolishness after an initial success. It was as though their early achievements led them to believe that they were safe from all further dangers.

But this man had displayed great cunning and skill so far. And he was no invalid, for all that his wound must almost have killed him when it was inflicted. Not many would survive such a blow, Simon knew.

The woods here for the most part were oak and beech with the occasional great elm towering over all else. There was no sign of Osbert, and increasingly they found there was no sign of the barrow tracks either. Here, in the freshly fallen leaves, there was little to show where it could have gone. And that meant that a resolute man could easily have placed himself up in a tree nearby after doubling back, and if he had a bow . . .

There was no point worrying about such matters. No. Better to ride on, and hope that the man would find it hard to pick a target. They continued, Simon aware at all times of the sound of his own breathing, the rasping quality in the cool air. It made him feel like an old man. Never before had he experienced this kind of strange harshness in his lungs. It was almost as though they had turned to stone, and it made him light headed. 'Where is he going?' he muttered to himself.

Baldwin overheard his words, and although he was not certain Simon wanted to hear from him, he thought it could do no harm to respond. 'Up ahead is the road from Jacobstowe to Bow. I suppose he may be heading for that.'

'Why, though?' Simon wondered. 'The faster route, and the safer one, would have been the road to Bow from his father's home.'

'That would have taken him back to Nymet Traci, and I doubt he'd have wanted that,' Baldwin pointed out.

'And if he passed by there, he'd be going nearer to Bow,' Roger grunted, ducking to avoid a heavy branch. 'He wouldn't want that either.'

Simon nodded, but he was unconvinced, and when they reached a clearing, he knew he had been right to question the man's direction. 'He's collected something from here,' he said. 'The tracks are much easier to see now. They cut into the leaves and mud. The barrow is a lot heavier.'

'The money,' Baldwin guessed.

'So I would think,' Simon agreed. He was about to ride on when he caught a smell. 'What is that?'

'It's dead, whatever it may be,' Sir Richard said cheerily.

Simon saw the hillock in the leaves and pointed silently. It was Baldwin who let himself down from his horse and pushed the leaves apart. 'A man, undressed, and somewhat the worse for his neighbours in the soil,' he said.

The sight was repellent, and Simon was forced to turn away as his stomach rebelled. 'He has a tonsure?'

'Yes. This must be the errant monk – Brother Anselm,' Baldwin said.

Simon nodded. Looking ahead, it was hard to see precisely where the tracks led, but he kicked his mount forward and they all moved on, Baldwin on foot now, his eyes scanning the ground about them. 'Look! He turned west here.'

It was a strange place, this. As Simon's horse reached the point where the track turned off, the sound of his horse's hoofs grew markedly louder. It was not the trees, for they all looked much the same as before. And it was not some echo, but a louder, ringing sound. It made Simon think that the ground beneath was more substantial than the soft forest floor. There was another thing, too: the trees that grew here were sparser up ahead, as though there was a distinct line of soil that was harsher for plants. And then he found an old trunk of a tree that had pushed its way up through the soil. It had been constricted, the bole more bulbous above the ground than below, and all at once Simon saw why. As it reached up, the tree had dislodged some obstructions: dressed stone.

'This is an ancient road,' he breathed. Looking ahead, it was easier to see now. The road was so old that plants of all sorts had colonised it, but for all that the arrow-straight route was clear. It was a softer, yellower green than ordinary grass, and although the brambles had smothered it in places, there were yet more areas that were moderately clear.

They could move a little faster now. Although the branches and fallen trees hampered their movement, at least their path was better delineated, and they could see ahead for some way.

For Simon's part, the idea that they should ride on at speed was taking hold. Although this man was not responsible for the capture of his daughter, nor for the threat of rape or death in the castle when Simon and Baldwin were trying to rescue her, yet he was aware of an overwhelming sense of hatred. Perhaps it was merely that Osbert was the last of the appalling group that had done so much to hurt the people of this area;

perhaps it was the realisation that this man had killed and would do so again. It was not any desire to serve the Cardinal de Fargis, of that he was certain. No matter what the reason, he was determined to capture the man if possible. Osbert had participated in so many deaths, not only Anselm's, and had tried to profit himself at the expense of all those he had seen murdered. It was enough to satisfy Simon.

And then he had another thought. This direction was leading back towards Jacobstowe.

'What is he doing, going back to where he committed the crime?' he wondered aloud.

'It's the only direction people won't be looking for him,' Roger said grimly. 'And from there it's not a long journey to Bude or some other coastal port, is it? He's going to try to leave the country.'

Roman Road near Jacobstowe

Hoppon was forced to hobble at speed to try to keep up with the man.

Since leaving the house, he had gone as fast as he could, his old dagger clattering at his side as he went. He had grabbed it at the last minute, hoping that he would not be forced to resort to it, but reluctant to go after Osbert without it.

If it *was* Osbert, of course. There was nothing he had seen so far that indicated that it was the man. It could as easily be some tinker or tranter who had happened across the old road and had decided to take the straight route. Except that now it was not an entirely straight route. A man trying that old path must negotiate the trees and roots that had churned the surface, as well as avoiding the great holes where men had dug up the dressed stones for their own use. And not many tranters would think of going by such a hidden route. Hidden routes meant hidden dangers. Men were happier to stay on the main roads.

He caught a glimpse, just a fleeting one, through the trees, and the sight made him set his jaw and hurry onward. Tab seemed to catch his mood, and stopped gambolling about his legs, instead moving with more purpose, as though he could see sheep to be rounded up and was keen not to fluster them.

The squeaking was loud now, and it was no surprise that Osbert couldn't hear his approach. The noise was sharp and painful; then there was a loud crunch, and a curse.

'The old git, he couldn't even look after his barrow,' Osbert said, and crouched low.

Hoppon could see that the wheel had dipped into a large hole, which had been concealed by the grass, and now, from the sound, part of the barrow was broken. It was enough to hold Osbert up. Hoppon moved forward cautiously, but even as he did so, Tab realised that his master felt that this was his enemy.

With a low snarl, the dog hurtled forward, determined to protect his master at all costs. He didn't see Hoppon's desperate signals. For his part, Hoppon saw only a monk in his robes, and urgently whistled and shouted to his dog. And then he realised that the monk had no tonsure.

Osbert heard the snarl and was up and facing the danger in an instant. It took him just a moment to see that there was only one dog, not, as he had feared, a whole pack of hounds on his trail. But one was enough. He drew his sword even as Tab launched himself at his leg. The dog's teeth managed to grip his hosen, the canines ripping into his thigh, and then he brought the sword down, the point stabbing. It entered the dog's back behind the shoulder blade and slipped down into his lungs, tearing through the ribs.

Tab gave a whimper and tried to pull away, but the terrible pain of the blade transfixed him. Try as he might, he couldn't escape, and although he snapped up at the blade in a frenzy, it was to no avail. With the blood spraying from his nostrils as he desperately tried to get away, Tab began to shiver, and at last slumped, while Osbert set his boot on the dog's back and tugged his sword free.

'You old cretin. Did you think you could stop me?' he snarled as he approached Hoppon.

Near Jacobstowe

Simon and Baldwin were both feeling the excitement mounting now. Simon instinctively drew a little nearer to Baldwin as they rode, their pace increasing as they found areas of brighter light, where the trees were thinner. All he could hear was the snap and crackle of his cloak in the rushing air.

The path was dangerous, he could see. There were stones dug up every now and again. No doubt it was the locals taking them in order to build houses and sheds. Dressed stone was not so easy to come by that a Devon farmer would turn his nose up at it. But it did mean that there were the twin risks of both potholes and loose rocks above the ground, either of which could break a horse's leg. But for now, Simon did not consider the risks. He was concentrating on the capture of this last member of the castle's team.

'Simon! Hold!'

Baldwin's urgent cry made him turn, and then he saw the two figures at the side of the road. He reined in, his horse digging long ruts where his hooves skidded on the soft grass, and was aware of Sir Richard and Roger pulling up to avoid him, then he was off his horse and running to the man.

Hoppon was breathing stertorously, his hands fixed over his belly as though trying to hold his blood in his body and let none escape. From the stains on his shirt and the gore that soaked the grasses at his side, he had not long to live, Simon thought. The man's face was already grey and pasty from the cold as death took his warmth from him.

'It's Osbert. I heard him on the path. Thought to stop him. Speak with him. Tab wouldn't wait; went for him. I tried. Tried to get him, but he was too quick.'

Simon saw the little dog's twisted, bloody body and felt a wave of revulsion. This pair were no threat to anyone. There was surely no need to kill them. As he watched, Roger walked to the dog, and to Simon's surprise crouched at the dead animal's side, stroking Tab's soft ears and the rounded head, while tears ran down his cheeks. There was no sobbing, no overt anger, but Simon could feel the man's emotion. It was a slow, building rage.

'Where did he go?' Simon said quietly.

'To the town. Jacobstowe. He's clad in monk's robes. Anselm's robes.'

'You will be avenged, Hoppon,' Simon swore. 'We'll send a man to look to you.'

'No. I'm . . . dead. Catch him. All I ask. Jacobstowe.'

Simon nodded and stood, but then he was struck with a wonderful terror. Edith was in Jacobstowe. She was in danger!

He ran to the horse, leapt into the saddle, snatched up his reins, and was off.

Jacobstowe

Osbert was sweating as he shoved the cursed barrow up the road. It had been hard work to make it so far, and now the swyving wheel was buggered, it was hard to keep the damned thing in a straight line. It wanted to waver off to the right all the time. At the first opportunity he would have to get rid of it and find another, one that was working. Or he could get this one mended, perhaps. It wasn't as though he needed to worry about money, after all.

This roadway was rutted and muddy, which didn't help. It was as though the land itself was trying to hamper his escape. At least Hoppon had been so incompetent in the way that he'd tried to slow Osbert's progress that his impact had been minuscule. Hopefully no one else knew that he might come this way. With luck, he could rent a cart at Jacobstowe, for it would be impossible to carry the box any distance. It was far too heavy, and the square sides made it a difficult object to transport on the shoulders. Perhaps, he wondered, he could sling it from a pole, if he could find some rope. Set a pole like a yoke about his neck? No, the damn thing was simply too heavy. He needed a cart of some sort.

Blessed relief! At last he could see the buildings of Jacobstowe. He would see if he could find some means of transport there, and hopefully soon be on his way in more comfort. Even if there was nothing to be had, surely there would be a smith or wheelwright who could mend the barrow.

He shoved with renewed vigour at the handles, and slowly made his way up into the vill itself, where he cast about him with eager wariness, trying to make sure that he was safe and that no one had made any apparent gestures, pointing at him, or hurrying away at the sight of him. There was nothing. Nothing at all. As he pushed his ungainly barrow down the road into the vill, he felt the anxiety sloughing away like dried mud from a waxed cloak, and he began to walk more upright, like a man who was at ease in the company of others. He even nodded to a man who made the sign of the cross at him.

This was easy. He ought to have got hold of such garb before, if this was how people looked at a monk. It was much easier than any other form of concealment. He would have to keep this by, just in case he might have a need of it in the future. It was good and thick, too. Be useful in the cold weather. Not that he would have to worry about the weather. It wasn't as if he was going to be stuck in the misery of mud and soggy leaves again, like when he was living rough with Sir Robert.

Shame Sir Robert was dead. In his own way he had been a good man. Still, the bastard had never compensated him for the ruin done to his face. One shilling. Twelve lousy pennies. That was all his dedication had been worth.

As he entered the main street, he reflected that it was all for the good anyway. The bastard would have been a problem before long. As soon as people started saying that the money had definitely been there, Sir Robert would have started thinking. There'd never been anything wrong with his brain, after all. No, and the man would have soon begun to wonder whether even his oldest companion might be worth questioning in more detail. Osbert would have. He wouldn't have waited so long, neither. He would have had a man like himself stretched over a table and beaten until he admitted where the money had been hidden, and the man would have been very fortunate if that was all that had happened to him.

The road opened out here in the vill. There was a broad area in the midst of the houses, which had been churned into mud by the passage of carts and horses. To the north end of the vill there was a marvellous sound, a ringing noise, like bells. A smith, he told himself, and threw himself forward.

But as he moved, he heard the noises he had been dreading for all the last miles. A roar, a bellowed shout, and the blast of a horn.

Chapter Thirty-Five

Jacobstowe

It was Sir Richard who saw him first. 'There! There, in the monk's sacking! That's the bastard!'

Simon had been staring at the ground, wondering whether they had been led astray by some malevolent spirit who had persuaded them to follow a will-o'-the-wisp trail rather than the murderer's, and he glanced up with shock to hear the coroner's bellow. 'It's him!' he cried, seeing the man thrust at his barrow with more urgency, and grabbed his horn, giving the three blasts that warned others of felons being pursued. Then he was spurring his mount to greater efforts, leaning down, willing the beast to be first in this race. He wanted the man's blood on his sword.

Faster and faster along the road they flew. Mud and dirt sprayed up on all sides, and Simon was liberally splashed when Baldwin's mount went through a broad puddle, and then they were up the last little rise and entered the vill at the canter.

There was no sign of the man at first, but Simon could see the marks in the filth of the road, turning to the right, heading east of north. He shouted and pointed, pulling his horse round in a tight turn. The poor creature slipped, his hoofs throwing up huge clods of mud and foulness, and Simon thought he was about to lose his seat and tumble to the ground, but then the horse gave a convulsive push with both hind legs, and Simon felt the surge of power at his backside, then they were hurtling dangerously along a narrow little lane. There was a turning, and this time he wasn't so lucky. He felt the horse start to slide, and had only just time to kick both feet from the stirrups as the world seemed to swerve around him. For a heart-stopping moment he appeared to be suspended in mid-air, with all the time in the world to notice Osbert further down the road staring back over his shoulder, to see Baldwin reaching out in a futile attempt to save him before Simon could hit the ground; and then the sudden acceleration of the mud and grasses as they rushed upwards to meet him.

The landing was not so much painful as simply numbing. It was as though his entire body was jarred, with each and every bone dislocating and resetting itself. All he could do for a moment was remain still, wondering when the pain would begin to affect him. It was not easy to tell. There was such a sensation of shock that such a thing could have happened, that he was sure there would be an overwhelming agony in all parts of his body at any moment.

'Simon, are you all right, my friend?'

Gradually easing himself up, Simon took stock. 'Yes,' he said with some surprise. 'I think I am.'

'Then mount, man! We'll lose him else!'

Simon shook his head. He felt as though he had been woolgathering for an hour or more, and when he looked about him, the others were all with him still, each of them looking more concerned about his welfare than they were at the thought that the felon could escape. 'Get after him, then!' he shouted.

His horse, God be praised, had survived the fall. There was a slight lameness in the front right leg, but nothing serious, he thought, gently handling it. Perhaps it was a strain. If so, a ride might help it to heal.

He climbed into his saddle again and followed after the others as they trotted along the road. But soon it became obvious that they had made an error. The track continued for some few yards and then stopped. There they found a barrow. But it was empty, and there was no sign of Osbert.

He had thrown them! They had thought he was stupid enough to just run out into the open country, but he wasn't so dull witted. He wasn't some gull ready to swallow any garbage slipped to him. He'd deliberately let the barrow run on and left it under a hedge, before grabbing his money and clutching its massive weight to his chest.

Crouched over, his back complaining at the unnatural gait, he ran as fast as he could, through a hole in a hedge, and from there back the way he had come.

The chest was a terrible weight. The mass of coins inside the box meant that it was all he could do to manage a restricted hobble. It was like clutching a man's weight concentrated into metal and wood of only some two feet by one and one. But although a pound in money weighed less than a pound of silver, the thing was unbearably massive. He would have to throw it aside soon, if he couldn't . . .

He managed to keep on going until he reached a gate. Sobbing with the effort, he yanked it wide, and stumbled into the street. There before him was the huge tower of the church. He threw a fearful glance all about him – in the last resort he could claim sanctuary inside that, but he didn't want to. Better by far to find a horse or some hiding place. Panting, his eye turned this way and that, desperate for a decision, but he could see nothing. It was then that he heard a scream.

Edith almost fell to the floor when she recognised him. She had seen the monk hurrying through the vill, and then the clear notes of the horn had shivered on the air and she had rushed back indoors with Ant and Agnes, hiding as the sound of hoofs came and passed by. If there was a felon in the vill, it was no time for her or the others to be out on the street. Too many people were knocked down by fools galloping their beasts in the middle of towns. And she had no desire to be killed by a felon trying to escape the law.

'It's quiet now,' Agnes had said after they had been hiding inside for a while. She had been quite still as they waited, as though utterly petrified, holding the Ant close to her, his head at her throat, her hand over the fragile skull as though to protect it against any harm. It made Edith realise just how much she would suffer were she to lose her own husband. She couldn't – to lose Peter would be to lose herself, she knew. It would remove the first structural plank on which her life depended. Especially now that she had the beginnings of new life in her womb. The idea that she should – that she *could* – lose her husband before he had even seen their child was so devastating that she had felt the room to grow stuffy, hot, unbearable. She rose and pulled a shawl over her shoulders, walking outside cautiously.

The sound of riders had faded to nothing now, but still she peered about the open area carefully before stepping out into the cool air. It would be an irony of some poignancy, she thought, were she to be slain now in the road, when only the day before she had been saved from death by her father and Sir Baldwin.

She was standing and smiling to herself at the singular nature of fate when a figure appeared around a corner. It was the monk, but he must be in pain, for he was bent almost double, as though nursing a terrible wound in his belly, and for an instant, that was her sole thought: that a felon had stabbed him, or he had fallen prey to the horses of the hue and cry, and was soon to collapse.

That was why she began to move towards him, but then he looked up and saw her, and she recognised him instantly.

He realised who she was at the same moment, and he felt his face twist with rage. The bitch was here! There was no chance he'd escape the bastards now. She knew him, that much was clear. Her face crumpled, and there was a blanched horror in her eyes that he couldn't miss. But now there was the sound of men approaching.

Shit! *Shit!* All his plans were going awry as he stood here dithering. There was a need to get away, to be miles from here as quickly as he could, but he couldn't just run, not with this box. And now that bitch had seen him, he was sure to be followed. They would know exactly where he had gone. He had to kill her, if he wanted any possibility of escape.

'No!' she cried, and her face was contorted with fear. But he knew what he must do.

He accordingly took a pace forward, and set the chest on the ground, as though exhausted, before drawing his knife and approaching her.

There was a scream, and a baby began to cry, and he saw that there was another slut behind her, this one with a pup at her tit. Another one to remove. But then, when he looked back at the blonde, he saw that there was something else in her eyes: a wildness, such as a cornered cat might show. She was scared, yes, but she'd made a decision to sell her life as dearly as she could. Even as he stepped over the dirt and mud, she darted back, pushing the other maid before her, and then reappeared in the doorway with a long knife. And she held it like she knew what to do with it.

'Ach, shite,' he muttered to himself.

Because just then he heard the hoofs returning. They had learned his little trick and were coming back. If they saw him here, he would have no choice but to surrender. They were too close already. *Shite!* If they caught him here in the open, they'd cut him to pieces.

He turned and fled back to his chest. Hefting it, he felt his belly muscles start to tear, his shoulders begin to sing with the agony of strain and tension. There was only one place he could go. Ahead of him was the gate, and he hurled himself towards it, aware all the while of the sounds coming closer and closer, the hoofs, the horn blowing, the roars and bellows. With a convulsive effort, he hefted the box on to the gate, then with a heave that made him see spots before his eyes, he hoisted it up and over, to fall with a rattle and crash at the other side. The gate had a thong holding it. He lifted it, slipped inside and shut the gate. Then, with the last strength he could summon, he picked up the chest again, and covered the last twenty yards to the church door. There he shoved the door wide and made his way with faltering steps to the altar, where at last he could drop the chest and fall to the floor, gripping the altar cloth with trembling hands. He bent down over the cloth and kissed it.

'I claim sanctuary!'

Brother Mark was in the vestry, a small shed that would have collapsed under its own weight had the church's walls not been so close that it could lean like an old horse against a tree. The priest here was an accommodating fellow by the name of Father James, and he had made the monk most welcome, especially when he heard that he was sent by the cardinal to learn all he could about the murders at Abbeyford.

They had been chatting in a desultory fashion, as monks and priests were wont to do, neither trusting the other entirely, for the monk thought the priest a little too worldly, and the priest thought him an arrogant fool, but they had begun to notice some mutual interests, and after some little while their conversation had grown a great deal more amiable. By the time of the shouting from within the church, both had drunk a goodly portion of wine, and their friendship had been sealed.

'What on earth is that?' the priest demanded as the clamour began.

'My heavens, I think I recognise that voice,' Mark declared as he heard the coroner's bellow. No one could have missed his shout.

The two rose hurriedly, James spilling his wine, and both hurried out into the cold air, running about the church to the door at the north and rushing in.

'What is the meaning of this?' Father James demanded as he saw the men ranged about the altar, *his* altar. His rage was entirely unfeigned. He was unused to seeing people brawling in his church, and he would be answerable before God if he was going to permit it now. 'You, sir – yes, you! Leave hold of that fellow at once!'

Sir Richard glanced up guiltily. 'Ah, I know that this looks bad, Father, and I apologise . . . Oh, that you there, Brother? Could you explain about this fellow?'

Mark shook his head. 'That disreputable-looking figure is actually the coroner for Lifton or somewhere. The man he has grabbed is one of Sir Robert de Traci's retinue, and responsible for much of the trouble about here. He was the fellow who led all those travellers to Abbeyford and saw them slain.'

'And what is he doing here?' Father James asked of Osbert, ignoring Sir Richard's expostulations at his description.

'I claim sanctuary, Father. I demand it. If these men take me, they'll see me dead. I must be protected.'

'Release him,' Father James said.

'This man has killed, Father,' Baldwin said. 'He led those travellers to their doom, he oversaw the torture of a monk, brother to your friend Mark there, and killed that man, Pietro de Torrino, and also Brother Anselm from Tavistock. We found the brother's body earlier, I'm afraid, Mark. He has killed another man today, a fellow called Hoppon, and he has robbed the king of a hundred pounds. It's in the casket beside him. Do you mean to tell me that a known, unrepentant felon like this can demand sanctuary?'

'Yes. He has reached the safety of the altar. You will not take him from here, not for the requisite forty days. He is as safe and inviolable as a new-born innocent babe. Let him free!'

'Father, he is a murderer,' Sir Richard repeated.

It was Roger who shook his head and muttered, 'We have no rights in here, Sir Richard. Master Simon, we should leave this place. The law as you know it has no effect once you enter the doors.'

Sir Baldwin was cool as he took Sir Richard's arm. 'Come, Sir Richard. There is no more for us to do in here. You are a coroner, though, and you can enforce the laws as they apply.'

The coroner nodded. He reluctantly allowed his grip on Osbert to relax. 'Do you have a weapon about you? Answer quickly!'

Osbert licked his lips. He had wanted to keep at least one knife about him, but it was correct that if he wished to remain safe, he must adhere to the law. He pulled his knife from within his robe and gave it to the coroner.

'Right, you dishonourable and dishonest felon, you have the right to remain here for forty days and nights. After that time, I can come in to fetch you. You will either have to leave of your own free will, which means surrendering to the full weight of the law, or you will have to agree to abjure the realm. You understand? Either hang, or run to exile. There's nothing else for you.'

Osbert nodded grimly. But in forty days, even the most

observant guards could fail in their duties. It was likely that he would be able to escape in ten days or so. The coroner and his friends would not remain here all that time.

'In the meantime,' Baldwin said, and bent down, 'you will not be permitted to profit by your theft.'

'No!' Osbert shouted, but he dared not relinquish his grip on the altar cloth, and could only look on in horror as Baldwin pulled the casket away from him.

'All those murdered people, and all for a few pennies that you cannot even hold on to,' he said. 'I hope you feel it was worthwhile.'

Chapter Thirty-Six

Jacobstowe

Mark watched them go, Father James walking with them, and felt a strange bubbling resentment deep in his breast.

This man was safe now, secure and protected with the full strength of the Church behind him. No man might touch him, unless he was captured outside the church, and then, if he was molested, his attacker would be guilty of a serious offence, just as a man who tried to drag him from the church would be. A man who committed such a desecration of the church could expect to be hanged.

'Bring me water, monk. I'm thirsty.'

Mark allowed a fleeting frown to pass over his face. 'Perhaps you should fetch it yourself.'

'I am your guest here,' Osbert said.

'No. You are the guest of Father James. He is gone to ensure that the money you stole is safe.'

The dig struck home. A cloud settled on Osbert's features. 'After all that effort and trouble, to lose it all here is enough to make a man turn to the Church. What do you think? Is there a church I could go to for a job? Perhaps a lay brother's position in Tavistock, eh? That'd be good. You and me, we could sit and chat. Talk about the fun we've had in the last week or so, eh? You looking for me, and me hiding from you. Oh, so you're back?'

Mark turned to find that Roger had returned inside. 'I am here to make sure you don't try to run.'

'You think you could stop me?' Osbert sneered.

Mark pressed him. 'Why did you kill Anselm? He was never a threat to you, was he?'

'Him? He was a fool. Jesus! You'd have thought the cretin would have realised that bringing a puppy might just make for problems in the future, wouldn't you? How would he think to look after it?'

'And that was why you killed him? Not so you could take his share?'

'Look, he wanted to join me. It was Basil's idea in the first place, to get one of the monks on our side, and Anselm was the easiest man to pick. He was bored stupid with his companions in any case. Did you know that? He was perfectly happy to sell them to us. That was before he knew he was going with the money, of course. It was easy to persuade him, letting him come and help me take the money.'

Mark was revolted. 'So he wanted to share the money? That was all?'

'Yes. For so much coin, most men will forget their morals. He was happy to see all those folk die in exchange for his share. I killed the only guard, and he helped me to carry the money out of the camp. Then . . .' He paused. 'Then I helped him take it away and hide it, and I went back to see that there was no alarm. Easy.'

'And the dogs?' Roger had been silent for so long, Osbert seemed surprised to hear him.

'What of the dogs? I didn't want them raising the alarm.'

'It seemed unnecessary to kill them. Just like the murder of the children.'

Osbert looked at him blankly. 'They were only dogs.'

Roger nodded. 'Brother, you remain if you must, but I cannot share the same room as this dunghill rat. He makes me want to puke.'

Mark wanted to speak, but found he couldn't. His mouth was too dry. There was no mistaking the revulsion in Roger's eyes as he turned and left the church, and Mark felt much the same. Anselm had very likely done as Osbert had said. The poor fellow had entered the Church when he was young, and it would be no surprise that a man, even a monk, would be willing to commit a crime for such wealth. Split two ways, his share of a hundred pounds would be two years' income for even a well-paid man. It was a staggering sum for one used to no possessions whatever.

'There is one thing, of course,' Osbert said in a sly tone. 'Now I've nothing. But the man who'd help me escape from here could share in the money with me. A full fifty pounds, maybe more, would be his share. Just think of that.'

Mark did think, but not of the money. Instead he was remembering Anselm, the cheerful, joking, ironic monk who had lightened the atmosphere of the abbey so often. It was hard to believe that he was actually dead. Somehow Mark had hoped that he had survived the attack when his body hadn't been found with Pietro's. That this man had killed him, after he had perverted him from his brothers, was repugnant.

'Fifty pounds.'

Osbert looked up. 'It's a lot of money. It was enough to tempt your brother.'

'My brother? But you killed Anselm, didn't you?'

'He wanted to run away from me. He was dangerous to me as well as to himself. All I did was hasten his end by a very little while. And he didn't suffer. I killed him quickly.'

'So you might do that to me, too.'

'I'll swear here and now, as I believe in Jesus and in God, that I will not kill you or hurt you if you help me escape.'

Mark thought hard, and his gaze went from Osbert to the

door open behind him. The money was vast. A man could live like a lord on fifty pounds.

In his scrip was the little enamelled green crucifix that Pietro had worn. He drew it out now, and studied it. It was so pretty, he thought it should never have been worn by a monk. Clearly the brothers in foreign abbeys took their vows of poverty less seriously than did the English.

'Where did you get that?' Osbert said sharply.

'I found it under a bush near the glade where you killed all the travellers.'

'It was taken by Anselm. I threw it away. I didn't want him stealing from the others.'

Mark frowned. 'He took it? But you said that he was gone with the money when you returned.'

'Aye. And then I went back to—'

'So how did he take this from Pietro? If Pietro was asleep, having a man take his crucifix would waken him.'

'Perhaps he knocked him on the head to take it? I don't know. But he had the crucifix later and I took it from him.'

'No. He wouldn't have stolen from Pietro. He would have been fearful in case he woke the man. It would only have been taken when Pietro was dead.'

'So?'

'If you had taken it, you wouldn't have thrown this away. It's gold and enamel. Surely it's worth a lot of money. You killed Pietro and then stole this for yourself, didn't you? And Anselm saw you and took it away.'

'He snatched it from me! I didn't know the fool would come back. I'd made him go so that he'd be safe. I was trying to look after him, but he came back. Some sort of guilt or something. He wanted to see what he had caused to happen. And he saw me there with the others. I saw him too, the prick! All I was going to do was tell him to go back to where he was safe, but the fool wouldn't. He told me I was cursed if I tried to take the crucifix from a dead monk. Damn his soul for a fool! I hit him when he threw it away, though.'

'He was right,' Mark said quietly. 'Perhaps the crucifix itself is cursed.'

'You think a lump of metal can be cursed, Brother? Then throw it away yourself. Come, though, you didn't answer me. Will you help me? Half the money will be yours if you do.'

'How would you get it?'

'If you will help me, we can get it easily. Those fools won't think to guard it well. They'll take it back to Tavistock, I expect. In the middle of the night, you help me out of here, and we'll find them, and then it's just a little tap on their heads and we'll have the chest without needing to kill anyone. It'll make no difference to anyone, Brother. If you help me, you'll have half and I'll escape earlier, that's all.'

'You won't escape from here.'

'You think so? I'll be out in a few days. This little vill won't want to spend time holding me here for no money or purpose. No, I'll soon be out, and when I am, the money would be useful. What do you say?'

'I will leave this crucifix. I have no more use for it, I think,' Mark said softly. He stepped forward and very carefully placed it on the altar cloth not far from Osbert. 'It can stay here.'

Baldwin was bitter, but there was no point in growing angry. The law was the law, and while inside a church a man was answerable to the ecclesiastical courts, not the king's. It would be dangerous to try to prise Osbert from the sanctuary cloth where he sat now.

'I will not have him dragged away, and that is final,' the priest was saying, wagging a finger under Sir Richard's nose.

The coroner appeared to swell with anger, and if Simon and Baldwin had not been there to prevent him, he might have pushed past the priest to haul Osbert out.

Mark stood at Father James's side. 'The good father is quite right, Sir Richard. There is nothing to be done for some days, as you know. Unless this man commits some new crime in the church, he must be allowed to remain here, safe and well.'

'What sort of crime?' Sir Richard asked hopefully.

'Stealing the cross or some plate,' Father James said acerbically. 'And only a fool would do such a thing.'

Mark nodded. He was feeling shaky, but he looked at Sir Baldwin, hoping he would understand. Mark had grown to respect the knight. 'Oh! I left Brother Anselm's crucifix on the altar. Father, would you go and fetch it for me? I feel unwell.'

'Yes, my son. Of course.'

Baldwin was watching him closely as the priest strode off into the church again. 'Brother? Are you well? You look quite pale.'

'I am well, I think. But I hope—'

There came a cry from inside the church. 'Brother? Are you sure you placed it here? I can see no sign of it.'

Baldwin's expression hardened. 'Simon, I think that the sanctuary-seeker may have stolen a small crucifix. Sir Richard? If he has stolen something from the Church, that means he is not eligible for the Church's protection, does it not?'

'I will fetch him out!' Simon said, and was about to move when a hand took his arm.

'No, Father, please. Don't.' Edith had been at the gate, and had heard much of the conversation. Now she hurried across the grass and gripped his elbow.

'Edith?' Simon put a hand out to her and smiled. 'Are you all right now?'

She gave a weak smile in return, but the anxiety was still in her eyes. 'That man, I saw him, Father. He was one from the castle, wasn't he? I remember him.'

'You'll never have to worry about him again,' Simon rasped, and was about to return to the church, but her hand caught him and held him back.

'*No*! Please, Father, as you love me, don't do it!'

'What? After what he and his friends were going to do to you?'

'They did nothing to me, though. Not yet. But if you go in there and kill him, they'll have changed you, Father. I couldn't bear that. Please, don't go in.'

Simon was about to draw away, but Baldwin was still at his side, and the knight sighed. 'Simon, I know that this may seem foolish, but I agree with her. There are good reasons for avenging your child, I know, and you will probably think me the worst of advisers, but the fact is, it will not help you to kill this man. Nor will it make the experience any better for your daughter.'

'Father, if you kill him, it will make me feel responsible for his death, and I don't want that. I saw you fight once before, you remember? Against Wattere. And yet if he had not tried to rescue me, I might not be here now.'

'He tried to rescue you?' Simon said.

'He came to my room and gave me a knife, and then he created the fire to distract the others so that I could try to get free. It was the merest bad luck that Osbert came to find me and all but cut poor Wattere in half when he found him there.'

'This is avenging others too, Edith,' Simon said.

'No, Father. It isn't. And I wouldn't have his blood on my conscience. Not now, of all times.'

She rested a hand on her belly as she spoke, and as he glanced at her uncomprehendingly, she gave him a weak smile.

'Dear God, child! My little girl . . . You mean you're . . .'

'With child, yes.'

Simon grinned, then gaped, and then in swift succession a frown, a slightly gormless smile, and a pale, fretful expression passed over his features. 'You must need to sit, Edith. Please, come with me, and we'll find a chamber that is comfortable. You must tell me all about it.'

'Really, Father? I would have thought you knew enough, with two children.'

'I didn't . . . Dear Mother of God, this is marvellous! Wait until we see your mother,' Simon said as he led her across the grounds towards Agnes's house.

Sir Richard grunted to himself. 'So, what of this fellow, then?'

'Leave him a while,' Baldwin said. 'There is no hurry.'

Mark heard something, and shot a look inside the church. The priest was hurrying out. 'Preposterous! He says you gave him the crucifix, Brother Mark. Did you say that he could have it?'

'Of course not! I merely left it there.' Mark could not add the words 'by accident'.

Sir Richard squared his shoulders. 'In that case, Father James, I think he has broken the terms of his sanctuary. I have the right to bring him out immediately.'

'I would beg that you leave him,' Father James insisted. 'I will not have blood spilled in my church. It is unnecessary.'

'You mean you don't want to have the church reconsecrated?' Sir Richard chuckled. 'We'll bring him outside, never you fear, Father.'

'That was not my meaning, as well you must know,' the priest said angrily. 'In Christ's name, I merely seek to save a soul.'

'You wish to save him, you tell him to come out here and

agree to abjure the realm,' Mark said quickly. 'There is no need to kill him. Let him abjure.'

Reluctantly the coroner agreed to the compromise, and Osbert came out with a shuffling gait, as though appreciating that this truly was his last opportunity.

Sir Richard stared at him. 'I don't suppose that this will have the slightest impact on your conduct, man, but you have agreed to exile. You will abjure the realm, taking the route I give you, carrying a cross to demonstrate your penitence, wearing only the meanest of hair shirt and simple robes, and you will go by the fastest route to the nearest port, which is . . .' He hesitated and stared at Baldwin.

It was Roger who answered. 'Send him to Plymouth or Dartmouth, Coroner. They'll serve.'

'Right, then. Dartmouth it is. You will go there across Dartmoor, from Oakhampton, straight down to the port, and when you get there you will do all in your power to find a ship to take you away from the king's lands. All you own and possess is forfeit to the crown for your crimes. Do you accept these terms?'

'Yes. All right,' Osbert said.

'Good. Because if you fail in any particular, you will be declared outlaw and can be hunted to death by any man. If you fail to do your utmost to obey my commands, I will set the wolf's head upon you, man, and you will die. Personally I hope you do turn outlaw, so that I can hunt you down myself. You will not be permitted to abjure a second time.'

Chapter Thirty-Seven

*Second Saturday before the Feast of St Martin in Winter**

Near Crockern Tor

In the mistiness, Osbert winced as the rain sheeted into his face. In this weather, his thin shirt and coat appeared no more substantial than a single thickness of linen in the face of the onslaught that was being hurled at him. Without his hat, the rain was like fine gravel thrown in his face. The weight of the cross on his shoulder, the proof of his penitence and the protection of his body from any who might choose to attack, for it signified that he was defended by the Church, was a dull and constant ache. The edge stuck into his shoulder, rubbing it raw beneath his shirt and setting up a savage anguish that would not cease. He had never seen so massive a cross for an abjurer, and he felt sure that it was evidence of the coroner's loathing of him. Sir Richard must have ordered it to be made so. If he could, Osbert would enjoy visiting some of this on Sir Richard in return. He hated to leave a debt unpaid.

For all the pain at his face and shoulders, it was his feet that hurt the most. They were shredded by stepping on rocks and furze. But there was no help for it. Abjurers were fortunate to be allowed to keep shirts and coats – but none could keep

---

*2 November 1325

boots or hats. These essentials were taken away for the king. He must, Osbert reckoned, have an insatiable appetite for such clothing, since he took all from every abjurer.

He was near a vast lump of rock that stood resting on three others to form a roofed shelter, in which two ponies stood. They could attempt to dispute his right to take some rest there, but if they were to do so, they would learn quickly that a man in desperate need was not to be trifled with. And he had a large baulk of timber on his shoulder that could easily act as a weapon.

It was a good enough place, he felt, to sleep the night. There was nowhere to seek companionship on the moors here. The lands to the south where he must travel to find his way to the port would all be as open and foully rainswept as this, and another resting place would be hard to find.

He hunkered down, chewing a little of the dry bread that the vill had provided him. It was stale and full of cinders and burned grains, much like the peasant breads he had eaten as a child, and the crunchiness and the taste of charcoal were like a reminder of his youth. It was quite good to experience them. But when he got to France – damn the souls of the men here who'd sent him away – he would only eat white bread. And there, so it was said, the weather was always summer. It would be warmer than here in the miserable wastes of Dartmoor, anyway. But anywhere would be, he told himself, glancing about the landscape with a curl to his lips.

It was then that he saw a figure, or so he thought. It was a hunched form, that of a man who was bent under an intolerable load, it seemed, and then a wash of rain pelted across and the man was hidden from view.

A man. Clearly a man, Osbert told himself. After all, the old tales were nothing more than that: myths invented to upset children, stories designed to petrify the recalcitrant, used deliberately to make children fear disobedience and keep them in check. They were not likely to make a man fear.

No, the idea of the devil wandering about the moors to pick up unwary travellers, that was invention. As was Crockern, the spirit of the moors, vengeful, resentful, cruel. Just as the idea of pixies leading travellers astray into bogs and mires to leave them drowning slowly was clearly untrue. There was nothing to any of them. And yet . . .

Where was he? Osbert peered closely, but there was no sign of the indistinct shape he had seen. It had disappeared into the murk before him as efficiently as a wraith dissolving in a mist. And it made him shiver suddenly, as though there was a ghost out there right now, watching him.

No! There was nothing there. It was just the way the swirling mist was moving. He squatted again, telling his heart not to be so fearful. It was in truth nothing to worry about. And yet he found that his eyes kept returning to that place, as though he half expected to see someone appear again.

It was unsettling. Very unsettling. He moved back into the safety of the chamber, leaning up against the rock, and tried to rest. The cold was ferocious, and he could feel his feet starting to stab with pain now. When he looked at them, he had to wince. The furze and stones he'd passed over had slashed at them, and now the soles were mingled blood and filth, and the little of the skin he could see was blue with cold.

There was a rattle and a thud outside. His head snapped up, and his eyes moved quickly all over the landscape in front of him, his heart suddenly pounding. No one there. No one and nothing. The swirls of mist moved about and the rain fell in a constant curtain, obscuring all beyond a few feet from him, but his heart told him that there was something out there. Something that wanted his death.

He hadn't regrets. He had enjoyed most of his life. What

was unreasonable was that for the first time in his life he had tried to make something happen for himself. All the other projects he had worked on, he had been trying to help his master. This was the first situation in which he had been attempting his own profit – and it was the first and most ruinous failure he had suffered.

A clattering made him jerk awake. For a moment there he had started to slip into drowsiness and his head had begun to nod, but now he was fully alert and staring about him.

There was no animal that could have made that noise. That was a stone being tossed, or he was a Scotsman. Outside was a man, and someone who meant him ill. Well, Osbert was no coward, and he would not be easy prey. He slowly eased himself upright again, clutching the heavy cross in his hands, and edged to the front of his shelter. No one would say that he hid cowering in the back of a cave while someone was pursuing him.

There was a snick as a small stone hit the roof, but he wasn't stupid enough to look up. The man was out there, hidden in the gloom, trying to tempt him to look around so that he could be hit from behind. He wasn't going to fall for that, he thought.

An appalling, smashing explosion of pain over his ear, and Osbert was thrown sidelong into the rock beside him. His first coherent thought was to wonder why he was lying on the ground, and then he was trying to rise, but as soon as he did, there was a slam at his head again, and he was on the ground once more aware of the trickle of blood running down the line of his jaw and pooling below his Adam's apple. Slowly he began to get up again, and this time the blow was over the back of his head, driving his face into the dirt and rock of the moor. He felt his nose crunch, he felt the water and mud in his nose, the tang of blood in his mouth as the teeth snapped, and his empty eye socket was filled with icy water. He tried to roll away to see who had attacked him, but it was impossible to even move that much.

And then there was one last crashing blow to his head, and he knew no more.

Crediton

The road back home was quiet.

Edith was aware of a faint unease in her belly as they rode, but she wasn't going to tell her father that. There was enough on his mind already.

Sir Richard and Simon had ridden to Tavistock to speak with Cardinal de Fargis already, and had told him all that they had learned, as well as returning to him the chest with the king's silver. The cardinal had been glad to receive it, Simon was sure, but it was not enough to compensate him for the death of two good monks.

'Pietro was an old friend. And Anselm, so sad to see a man tortured by his desires. That he should have allowed them to rule his heart in so marked a manner – that is terrible. The poor man.'

'He was willing to plot to have all those travelling with him murdered,' Simon pointed out.

'Was he? Or was that a matter over which he had little or no control? I do not pretend to see into a man's heart, Master Puttock. That is God's task. For me it is enough that I see so much sadness. So much greed and jealousy.'

'You mean the selection of the new abbot?'

'Which of the two men would you choose?'

Simon looked away. This was not something he could do. Any answer he gave must be hazardous, for whomsoever he chose would be sure to hear of it, and then the other would learn that Simon had not supported him. And either of the two monks was a bad enemy to have. Busse was known to have dabbled in magic to try to win his post, while de Courtenay was a perfect menace, and with his powerful connections could make life intolerably hard for a man like Simon. 'I . . . er . . .'

'Yes. I too have a similar problem,' Cardinal de Fargis said with a wintry little smile.

'It isn't the kind of decision I'd be qualified to make,' Simon said.

'Either will prove to be a dangerous influence if the other is made abbot.' The cardinal continued as though Simon had not spoken. 'So perhaps it would be better if neither was to have it. And neither was to remain here.'

He looked up suddenly, and appeared to notice Simon for the first time. A faintly bemused expression wandered over his face. 'Ah. And you heard about the king's messenger?'

'Yes. A great pity,' Simon said, remembering the man with whom he had travelled.

'He had a great number of messages still in his pouch, my friend,' the cardinal said thoughtfully. 'There were several from men around here who were writing to my lord Despenser. I think you should be very careful in his presence. He is a most dangerous adversary.'

It was those words that echoed in Simon's mind now as he rode home, but Edith had no idea of the cause of his grim face and apparent ill humour. For her part, she was filled only with a determination to get back home to her husband as soon as possible.

'You will come to see your mother?' Simon asked.

'Only for the night, Father. I have to get home and see my husband.'

'Of course,' Simon said, and there was a stilted pause.

'I think I should return home,' Baldwin said after a few moments.

'I would be sad to see you leave and not come to visit, Baldwin,' Simon said. 'Margaret will be disappointed.'

Edith looked from one to the other, and then back at Edgar, who wore a most untypical expression of seriousness. She was suddenly struck with a sense of how these two men, both of whom she adored, had been driven apart. There was a gulf between them, where before there had been only comradeship. She would have thought that nothing could have caused them to become so distant from each other, and the fact that it had been caused by the threat to which she had been exposed served only to make her feel guilty. Looking back at Edgar again, she felt a quick resolve.

'Nonsense,' she said. 'Sir Baldwin, you must certainly come and rest at Father's house. You have risked your life to help us, and I would not hear of you continuing tonight.'

'Edith, if he says that he should carry on to his wife, you are in no position to prevent him,' Simon said.

'Father, I owe perhaps my life to Sir Baldwin. If it were not for his swift response in riding after me to rescue me from Sir Robert of Traci, you would not have learned of my predicament and I might well still be there now – raped and injured. Yet you would see him leave to continue his journey at night in the cold? For shame!'

Simon's jaw clenched, and he threw her a look of such pain that she wanted to apologise, but then with relief she heard him repeat his invitation to Sir Baldwin to stay the night.

'Please do, Sir Baldwin,' she said. 'And then perhaps tomorrow you can ride with me to Exeter to protect me? I should be most grateful for your company.'

'Of course,' Sir Baldwin said with a gracious little bow. 'I

would be honoured to ride with you, if your father has no objection.'

'How could I object?' Simon responded, but he looked at neither of them. Instead his eyes remained fixed resolutely on the road ahead.

Tavistock Abbey

Brother Mark stepped into the chapter house and crossed the floor to the stone seat at the further wall. He sat, his eyes downcast, as he contemplated his decision.

It was some little while later that the other brothers filed in.

In the past, all the monks would have been chattering and laughing as they walked in, but not today. Not for the last few days. There had been a curious air of nervous expectation ever since the body of the messenger had been found and rumours had begun of the messages from Brother John found in his shirt. Although there had been attempts to keep news of the messages secret, it was impossible to prevent so many monks from enjoying the potential of such juicy gossip. It had flown about the abbey in a matter of hours.

It was the cardinal who entered last, and he walked to the middle of the chamber and looked about him with the cold, measuring eye of an executioner considering his next victim.

'I am aware of the stories that are circulating about the two brothers who are in contention for the abbacy. They are both here now. I require them to step forward.'

Mark watched as the two monks approached the cardinal and stood, one at either side, their hands clasped, heads down like penitents.

'These two have acknowledged their faults, and will now show their repentance by exchanging the kiss of peace,' the cardinal said.

Of the two, Mark reckoned that Robert Busse was the less reluctant. With a show of distaste, he stepped forward and waited. Brother John wore a glower of loathing on his face as he contemplated his enemy. But then, he had plotted the murder of Robert. If the rumours were all true, he was guilty of terrible ambition and pride. Brother Robert himself was little better, though, if the stories of his thefts of gold and silver from the treasury were correct.

Brother John gave a gesture of disgust and went to meet Robert, and both gave a quick glance to the cardinal. He made no movement, and the two suddenly came together and exchanged a swift peck. As they stepped apart, Mark was sure that both would have wiped away that kiss if they were not being watched.

This was shameful. It was the sort of situation that Mark would expect from knights. He could remember now his animosity to Sir Richard de Welles, and felt shame. Sir Richard was a deeply honourable man in comparison to these two. It was appalling. It left Mark feeling tainted by their presence and their awful shame. Perhaps his own offence was less significant than he had realised. It was possible, after all, that God had given these two as a proof that his crime was of little import by comparison.

The chapter meeting continued with the business of the day being conducted swiftly enough, and then the cardinal made to leave.

'Cardinal, I have to confess . . .'

'Then you must walk with me,' the cardinal said.

Brother Mark was perplexed, for the brothers were supposed to confess their sins in full chapter, so that all would know their guilt. It was a most effective means of persuading monks to consider carefully before committing an offence against their order. But if the cardinal said that Mark must

walk with him, walk he must. He scurried out after him, and found him taking the air in the cloister.

The heavy rain of the last couple of days had ceased now, but it was still very damp all about, and Mark was aware of the splashing as he stepped through the puddles on the pavemented cloister area. 'Cardinal, I have to confess to a crime. A serious crime.'

'You helped tempt a man so that he could be extracted from a sanctuary.'

'I . . . yes.'

'The man was already guilty of participating in murders, in the murder of two monks, I think?'

'But no matter what the crime, he was in the church, under the protection of the Church.'

'True. And he had killed two of the Church's most devoted servants.'

'But surely I still committed a crime?'

Cardinal de Fargis stopped and looked at him. 'What do you wish me to tell you, Brother Mark? That you were wrong to leave temptation in his path? If you had not, would he have abjured the realm? Yes, in all likelihood. So you hastened justice. And you did not force him to take the crucifix, did you? It was he who guided his own hand to take it. Not you.'

'I just thought that my—'

'Brother Mark. I understand that the item taken by the man was the crucifix worn by poor Pietro. Yes? Then I think we can look on the matter as being one of divine judgement. You were the willing tool of God. He chose you to bring justice to the man Osbert. And for what he did to poor Pietro, he deserved no sanctuary.'

Bow

The priest brought another bowl of water to him as he lay sweating, complaining about the cold, whining and moaning in his agony. It was enough to make the priest weep gently to himself, sad at the sight of so much misery and despair.

William atte Wattere had no idea where he was. The room was a darkened chamber that could have been a gaol, but with his burning anguish there was no need for bars and locks. He could not have stood had he wished to.

He had been here in the bed since the evening he had been brought here. The father had seen to all his needs as best he could, but it was clear by the end of the first day that all he could hope to do was alleviate some of the man's dying pains. There was clearly no aid for him while his soul remained in his body. All a man could hope and pray for was that his suffering would at least end when he was dead. And it was for his life after death that the priest was praying now. As he mopped Wattere's brow with a rag dipped in cool water mixed with vinegar, his lips mumbled the prayers he hoped would be most efficacious.

'You've seen him?' Wattere spoke suddenly, his good hand snapping up and grasping the priest's wrist.

'My son, calm yourself. Who? Who do you ask if I've seen?'

'The man . . . He's there! Don't let him take me!'

The ravings of a madman. But with this enormous wound, it was a miracle he wasn't dead already. The sword had cloven through his shoulder, through his collar bone, and wedged in his shoulder blade, so they said. It had taken his assailant some while to lever it free. And that sort of wound was only rarely survived. The fever had broken the next day, and no one expected him to live. With his whole body shrieking, it was hardly surprising that he would see nonexistent people.

Still, the old priest glanced over his shoulder to make sure. 'My son, there's no one there.'

Wattere's face had paled. Now he too looked up over the priest's shoulder, and his eyes were wide. 'You can't take me! I won't go, Osbert. You did for me with that murderous puppy your master . . . You say I betrayed you? You betrayed all!'

The priest mumbled calmingly as Wattere spat and shouted, but there was no soothing him. He was like a man having his arm removed, twisting and wrenching, screaming as his wound opened and gaped again, shrieking abuse at the man he supposed was before him.

'Go! Won't anyone take this man away? Leave me alone!'

The father had to lean down to hold him in the cot, he flailed so hard, and in the end he had to accept defeat, and bellowed for help. A boy had been outside, and he came in at a run when he heard the priest call, sitting on the wounded man's knees while the priest tried to hold Wattere's upper torso down, trying to avoid pressing on the wound but attempting to keep him still.

It was not to last long. With a last curse at the spectre whom no one else could see, there was an end. Later the priest would wonder whether the noise he heard was authentic, or whether his mind had imagined it, but he thought he heard a sound like a small cord being broken as the man's spirit left him. The body, empty now, sagged like a sack of old beans, and there was a slight gasp, then a rattle from his throat, and the priest made the sign of the cross over his staring eyes, beginning to recite the Pater Noster.

He would have thought nothing more about it, had not the news come to him later that the man who was the sergeant of the evil devil at Nymet Traci had been called Osbert. And that he had disappeared.

Chapter Thirty-Eight

*Sunday before the Feast of St Martin in Winter**

Exeter

Edith was glad to be home. As she entered her house once more, and saw her maid busying herself at the fire, it felt as though she had dreamed the last few days. The arrest of her husband, her capture by the hideous Wattere, her suffering and terror of rape by the son of Sir Robert de Traci, all faded as soon as she crossed her own threshold again.

'Father, Sir Baldwin, please, be seated,' she said and went to fetch wine for them. She would have to throw them out soon. It was good to have them escort her home, while Baldwin had sent Edgar back to his own house to tell Jeanne what had been happening, but at the gates they had heard that her husband had been released and was back at his parents' home to recover from his ordeal.

The wine was served, Simon heating his dagger's blade in the fire and then stirring the wine with it to warm it, and she watched with appreciation as the two men began to chat. It had been a very hard evening the previous day, and much of the journey today had been quiet, but she felt sure that the pair were recovering their friendship. She had worked hard to try to ensure it. At her parents' home, she had managed to draw

---

*3 November 1325

her mother to one side and explain what had happened, but Meg had been too shocked by the story to take it all in. And then, of course, the news that her daughter was soon to be a mother in her turn was enough to drive all other thoughts from her mind.

Soon the wine was drunk and the two men exchanged a look.

'You should fetch your husband home,' Baldwin said.

'Are you sure that I cannot get you anything more?' Edith said.

'Seeing you here, happy and safe, is all I could wish for,' he answered.

'We can escort you to Peter, anyway,' Simon said. 'We will ride on from there.'

And so it was quickly agreed. The two men led their horses, and they walked with her along the narrow ways until they came to the house where her parents-in-law lived. There, at the doorway, Baldwin took his leave. 'Simon, old friend. I hope to see you again soon.'

Simon grasped his hand, and nodded his head. 'I am sorry for my foul temper, Baldwin,' he said, still a little stiffly.

'Simon, I can understand. I only hope you realise that I acted in what I thought was the best interests of all of us.'

Simon took a deep breath. 'Yes. I know you did. And I am truly sorry that I doubted you at the time – but what would you do or say? My daughter was there . . .'

'There is no need to say anything,' Baldwin said gently. And he meant it. He could only imagine how Simon must have felt at the sight of his daughter being threatened with rape and humiliation. It was a scene he would remember for the rest of his life.

Edith took her leave of them both and knocked on the door. It was soon opened, and she was led through to the hall.